The Short of It

The Short of It

Sometimes it Takes the Tragedy of One to Rescue Another

Matt Brown

AuthorHouse™
1663 Liberty Drive
Bloomington, IN 47403
www.authorhouse.com
Phone: 1-800-839-8640

Published by AuthorHouse 06/19/2012

ISBN: 978-1-4772-1380-3 (sc)
ISBN: 978-1-4772-1381-0 (e)

This book is printed on acid-free paper.

This novel is dedicated to my wife and son, as without their love and inspiration I'm sure it would've only resulted in yet another unfinished project. Thank you and love to you both. You are the stars that shine in my sky.

I would like to thank my parents for their dedication in spending endless hours going through the various drafts ensuring it was right. I am truly grateful.

CHAPTER ONE

"I like this shirt . . . . but it looks like a fucking tea towel!" This random, but not uncommon, perception and self analysis entered Carter's mind as he caught a glimpse of his reflection in the bus window. He was travelling home from work on his usual bus route in the manic Friday rush hour traffic. The weekend had arrived again, and the sun was out in full force as it had been for most of the day. It gleamed down on busy London streets teasing people, stuck in their sticky oppressive offices, with the belief that it would remain for the weekend for them to fully enjoy. It had been one of the hottest days recorded so far that summer, creating that familiar uncomfortable humidity that was always seemingly enhanced to travellers on public transport. People polluted the homeward bound journey as usual, and of course the same annoying busy rush hour rat race came with it. Carter knew that all he had to do was remain calm and put up with the nightmare journey for the thirty minute ride back to Islington.

He co-rented a small but accommodating two bed flat which was on the second floor of a three floor development. It was a perky place that he always kept untidy, and which was never in the slightest inviting on the eye. Carter had rented the flat for the last three years with his best and closest friend, Will Harrison, who was actually his only friend in fact. The two had met at college when studying Media and Performing Arts and struck up a friendship from day one. Will, in truth had been much more successful since college and was working as a senior technician in a TV facility in Soho.

Carter on the other hand had been less fortunate and was still working in mobile phone sales and insurance in Holborn. He had always stayed in contact with Will in the years that had passed since finishing college, and frequently met up in bars in the City after work, too often in fact.

Carter Jakeman was approaching his late thirties, thirty-eight to be precise. He was nothing out of the ordinary appearance wise; short black hair, medium build, very rarely dressing to impress and near enough always sporting stubble. His job required a uniform so he wasn't really ever seen out in public wearing anything else. He wasn't too displeased with the design of his work clothes as they were very simple and did not draw attention. The uniform comprised of a black polo shirt with a small company logo in yellow on the left side, black trousers and black shoes. Carter usually opted for black trainers as opposed to shoes as they were far gentler providing more cushion to the feet.

Carter had moved in with Will after the room became vacant, which was roughly and somewhat conveniently at the same time that Carter was on the verge of moving out of his childhood home, the home that he eventually shared with just his father, Max. Max Jakeman had passed away from natural causes which had promptly urged Carter to move on to somewhere else and cope, somehow. There was no way he was prepared to stay in the place alone with nothing but memories as company. Max had spent most of his years working as a plumber, and had always enjoyed his work. It was only in the last couple of years before he retired that he became a postman, just keeping himself busy whilst bringing in some extra cash. Carter's only other immediate family were his mother Gwendolyn, who had passed away from lung cancer some years before, and his younger brother Marcus who worked as an editor for a magazine called Press and journalise UK.

Marcus had lived in and around the UK for the past five years, but was based between two main sites in Scotland in Glasgow and Edinburgh. He was married to Claire, after the two met at Stirling University whilst studying Journalism. They had two daughters, Eve and Starlet, aged four and eight respectively. Carter mainly only saw his nieces via Skype, and had sadly only ever met Starlet in person once. He had always regretted not being able to meet them in person more often. Carter just didn't have the money to be able to travel up and visit them, and sadly his low self esteem and lack of confidence had always played its role in preventing him from doing so. He would conjure up the right excuses at the appropriate times to avoid any interaction with people wherever possible. He saw himself as a failure, a person who was just naturally not strong enough emotionally or physically, or attractive enough, to be happy in his life. However, he did not want to burden anyone with this, and always tried his hardest to keep his feelings guarded and hidden. This had been a weight on his shoulders for as long as he could remember, and had even driven him to explore a variety of anti-depressant medications in an attempt to get some relief, but they had never worked. He had been diagnosed with bipolar disorder in his early twenties, and was a year after his mother had passed away, causing him dramatic changes in moods and emotional states from day to day. Some days he would be very high and enthusiastic and the next almost drinking himself into a coma. There was never a balance. Following Max's death, Carter felt unbearably alone in their house, refusing to come to terms that this episode of his life had gone forever. Gwendolyn was a very beautiful and outgoing woman who had always worked hard, mainly in office support roles, in order to provide an extra source of income for her boys. She had always been caring and equally supportive to both of her sons.

Carter originally had regular contact with Marcus, managing to speak at least once a month, but in recent years they had drifted apart, probably only speaking on a couple of occasions, once at Christmas time and once on Eve's second birthday. Marcus's job had become increasingly busy and he had travelled abroad quite a lot on business representing the company. He was a very successful and focused individual, had quickly moved up through the ranks of the company, steaming through a variety of promotions, undoubtedly due to his impetuous tenacity and a roaring enthusiasm to succeed. In most ways Marcus and Carter were complete opposites. They were both raised lovingly by their doting parents, had always bonded well and enjoyed each others company. Even when Gwendolyn passed, they were present and strong for their father, and vice versa. Unfortunately, Carter happened to be the weaker of the two. He was very smart but his frustration and disappointment at not being able to achieve his dreams due to his depression evidently worsened and damaged him over time. Perhaps his brother had more luck, was better looking, and was always in the right place at the right time, as they say. Who knows? Carter's less attractive occupation was working in phone sales. He would cold call prospective customers offering them phone insurance. The pay was not great but it had the added bonus of working on commission, allowing Carter to be just about financially secure. However, in the economic crisis, how seriously secure could one be? After all, the recession was at its worst. Will would always support Carter no matter what and would help him out financially when and where he could.

* * * *

People were bundling onto the bus at every stop, swallowing up the most diminutive of remaining space, rather then patiently waiting for the next one to come along. "A matter of minutes!" Carter thought.

Never having been successful in attaining a seat on public transport, he was once again left standing pushed up in the corner by the door, where if pressed any harder, he was sure that one day his head would be squashed so much that it would explode. The usual disgruntled, discontented expression stuck on his face like a drawing, not even the slightest glimpse of any movement a possibility. An office worker stood immediately behind him and whose elbow had in fact been engaged with Carter's lower spine for almost half of the journey so far. The man was smartly dressed, a clean cut guy wearing an overdosed amount of expensive aftershave, and who was, of course, the perfect stereotype of the classy city type. A Ralph Lauren suit no less and D&G sunglasses. The aftershave was most likely one or the other as well, although it may as well of smelt of socks in Carter's view. "What a total prat!" he thought. The man's mobile phone rang, letting off a distinct annoying sound of some downloaded Rap song. Carter immediately sounded his disapproval by letting off an obvious and exaggerated sigh. The mobile phone was in the guy's inside pocket, leaving Carter knowing that even though there wasn't anymore space in which to manoeuvre, the man would have to answer his precious little call no matter what. Then, right on cue, the elbow that was at first awkwardly prodding against Carter's spine had now begun drilling in, as the guy started to shift position, delving into his inside jacket pocket for his phone. Sweat ran down Carter's face, a face which had started to turn an increasingly infused beetroot type colour. His patience was running very thin at the utter arrogance of this person! Not even saying, excuse me or Sir, or do you mind? Carter felt his lower back muscle twinge and he duly cracked, blurting out the first words that came to mind, "Oh for the love of shit."

The faces of other passengers turned in unison towards the direction of the outburst, the back of Carter's head. The guy knew that the outburst was directed at him and quickly responded: in a confrontational manner "What's your problem? Hey!" Carter just ignored him knowing that in only seconds the guy would have to answer his call before it rang off. He could now do nothing but listen to this crass man's phone conversation, which strangely enough seemed to revolve around his forever blossoming lifestyle and overwhelming success. "How sickeningly typical," Carter thought. The man's voice was so unnecessarily loud, and he was so obviously into himself, enjoying the sound of his own voice whilst declaring his busy schedule for his fun filled weekend. This of course involved parties, lots of girls, and driving his Ferrari. "Ferrari?" thought Carter, while grinning slightly. "A Ferrari and he is taking the bus in rush hour, well he is either a fake or cheap bastard, actually, probably both!" Carter sought some comfort in thinking that the man's voice sounded more like a constipated cat with an uncontrollable craving for heroin, while at the same time being repeatedly poked by a cactus wielding mouse. Carter's imagination was as weird as they came, but comical all the same. Before he knew it, he saw his bus stop approaching and was relieved to say the least. He could get away from the highflying business boy at last! The bus pulled into the stop, the driver using his usual 'slam on brakes for no reason' technique, throwing everyone forward, with Carter almost falling out onto the pavement as the doors were opened mid flight.

Carter had no intention of rising the next morning. His plan was to sleep until he was bored of sleeping. Maybe the usual one-over dosage of Cipralex, mixed with a good helping of the Shiraz Cabernet Rose he acquired earlier in the day would help him relax and mellow into a very much wanted comatose state. Hopefully this would last him well through into the following day. Will was not due home for at least another hour so Carter thought he would pop to the shop and get some supplies, some extra cans and another couple of bottles of wine. There was no way that the one bottle of Rose was going to last them, or even just him, all night. He knew that they had pizzas in the freezer so were all good on the food front. He was toying with the notion of getting in some cigars, but wasn't too sure. A cigar, although utterly pleasurable would make Carter very tired, and tonight especially he wanted to watch the new movie rentals that Will was picking up on the way home from work. They were planning to watch the movies back to back whilst consuming copious amounts of alcohol, and the odd pizza slice, a usual Friday night for them both it had to be said.

Carter walked into his local off-licence on the corner, which stood conveniently next to his local pub and to the kebab shop which happened to be the next door along. Carter had always appreciated his luck in that all three of these luxuries were stacked almost on top of each other, and only a two minute walk from his place.

"Not you again. When are you gonna go out and find yourself a woman? Just kidding, how are you doing Carter?" said the shop keeper, Mohammed Khan, jokingly.

"Not too bad Mo, but now you have pointed that out, fucking terrible. No I can't complain. I'm alive, right. Saying that I'm not sure how alive I'll feel come this time tomorrow but hey, it's the weekend right!" he replied whilst placing his small plastic shopping basket of drinks onto the counter.

"Well you have a good night, and tell Will that he owes me money for that bet. He hasn't been in here since", Mo said giving Carter his change. Carter, turning to leave the shop replied "You got it. I'll remind him when he gets back. See ya later."

Carter walked into his flat, and purposely ignored the mess as per usual. He went to the fridge and loaded the beers, pushing them right to the back to make way for the wine. He put two cans in the freezer, eager to chill them quickly. He pulled off his rucksack and dropped it down by the sofa and threw his keys on the kitchen worktop. He noticed the voice message light flashing on the phone but chose to ignore it as he knew it would most likely be for Will. No-one ever called wanting to speak to him anyway. Carter pulled off his shirt and threw it through the bedroom doorway onto his bed, kicking off his shoes as he entered the room. He fell down on to the bed trying to cool off, laid his head back and closed his eyes . . . .

* * * *

"Carter wake up, Carter, CARTER!" He opened his eyes and saw Will standing over him.

"Sorry mate must have drifted off." said Carter, sitting up and rubbing his face trying to bring himself round. There was no reply from Will. Carter looked up at him and noticed a look of despair on his face, immediately realising something was wrong.

"Will? Are you ok? What is it?" Carter enquired eagerly.

Will took a second, seemingly to steady himself, drew in a deep breath before saying "There is a message on the phone . . . . It is from Claire . . . . Oh man I'm sorry . . . . it's Marcus . . . . there was a car accident . . . . he's gone Carter, he's gone."

Will broke down into tears as he delivered the tragic news. He retreated back into the living room, unable to look at his friend's face. Carter looked down and momentarily went in to shock, which was quickly followed by an overwhelming sense of confusion. He had no need to question Will further as the message was loud and clear. A million thoughts ran through Carter's mind, mixed feelings of emotion, disbelief, dread, anguish, loneliness . . . . He stood up and noticed that his hands were trembling, he felt physically sick and his heart was racing. He tried to compose himself and slowly put on his shirt and walked into the living room. Will, who had now managed to pull himself together, turned and faced Carter, again reiterating how sorry he was. Carter, with a somewhat automatic and distanced response said,

"It's ok Will, I . . . . I need to call Claire . . . . Oh my god, the girls . . . . My brother . . . . Oh God!"

Carter broke and fell down to his knees, as the reality and magnitude of the news hit him full on, reducing him to an uncontrollable bout of tears. Will ran over and knelt down beside him trying to console him the best he could.

* * * *

Carter took a long swig out of his can of lager, and lifted the handset. He knew he had to call Claire. He punched in the number and took another gulp before hearing the voice answer at the other end of the line.

"Hello." said an obviously broken hearted voice.

"Claire, its Carter,"

"Oh Carter," Claire replied, the sound of sorrow swamping her voice.

Knowing how fragile he was as an individual, she attempted speaking with a sense of comfort and reassurance, amidst the stifled tears. However, Carter heard Claire begin to cry and realised that she passed the phone on to someone else to talk to him. It was Shannon

Miller, a close friend of Claire's. She was obviously there to comfort her, care for the girls, and be on hand to take and make calls when needed.

"Sorry Carter, this is Shannon. Claire cannot speak at the moment. She is . . . . well this is just . . . . I am so sorry that . . . ."

Carter interrupted and asked "Shannon, what the hell happened?"

"It was earlier this afternoon, and Marcus had left work early to come home . . . . and . . . . it was on a main road where he lost control . . . . he went instantly."

"My God, and the girls, have they been told?" asked Carter.

"Yes, they know Daddy will be away for a while, but that he will still come and visit them in their dreams."

A tear ran down Carter's face. There was a brief pause in conversation before Shannon said: "I'll let you know the details of the funeral over the next few days, once things are sorted out on that side of things. I'm sorry Carter."

"OK Shannon, and hey, thanks for being there for Claire and the girls."

Carter slowly lowered the receiver and stood still, frozen, for a few seconds. He tried to process what was going on, before Will, returning from the bathroom, broke the silence.

"Carter? How is Claire holding up?"

"She's not! That was Shannon, a friend of Claire's, and she will let me know the funeral arrangements over the next few days . . . . He lost control of his car apparently and . . . . it was instant . . . . no pain."

Carter took one last mouthful of his can before throwing it in to the bin. He wiped away the remaining tears from his eyes and went to the fridge and grabbed two more beers, chucking one to Will.

* * * *

The pair decided to get ready and go out to the pub instead of staying in for the rest of the evening. Neither of them was in any mood to have a quiet night in after receiving the devastating news. They went to a pub located down a side road off the Holloway Road. It was a quiet, quaint little place, a bar where you would find characters such as writers, teachers, choir singers and generally peaceful types. It had a juke box so there was music, but Carter and Will both just wanted to be surrounded by some kind of activity, thus creating a distraction from the news. They arrived in the bar at around 8pm and sat outside where there was a row of wooden benches. The benches were enclosed by a black railing that secluded the area for pub frequenters only. It was cosy, and the summer evening brought with it a feeling of comfort and much welcomed warmth. They sat and talked for an hour, drinking a fair share of pints, before slowly becoming a touch more relaxed. Carter was beginning to psychologically firm up to the news. His shock was subsiding, and he knew he could rely on the drink to help with that. Every now and again the conversation would return to his brother and the accident, but they would quickly change the subject and move on. That is what Carter wanted and Will respected that. It was just past 9.45pm when Carter wanted to start on scotch rather than continue with the onslaught of beer. He felt very bloated and wanted to rid himself of that uncomfortable feeling that was building in his stomach. Will was only too happy to start on the spirits, and upon arriving at the bar, chose to opt for a vodka and Coke as his tipple. The pub began to increase in numbers, and the noise levels rose, which encouraged an already intoxicated pair to also become louder and relax down even more. They became slightly less tense and joked around a bit more. It was around 10.35pm when Carter and Will contemplated whether to leave the pub and to go back to the flat. There were three very good reasons for this. One, because they had alcohol sitting in the fridge waiting for them, two, they had movies sitting there waiting to entertain them, and three, they had both run out of cash!

They arrived back in the flat just before 11pm, and were very merry at that point to say the least. The death of Marcus had been well and truly locked away by Carter's brain for the time being, a barricade that the alcohol had assisted in building. Will rushed straight over to the freezer and took out the pizzas, as they had not eaten anything so far that evening, not even a bag of crisps, or any of the complimentary peanuts at the bar. Will slung the pizzas in and fired up the oven, switched on the timer and removed two cold cans of beer from the fridge. Carter meanwhile had turned on the TV and removed the two movies from Will's satchel. One was a horror and one an action movie. He turned to Will asking which one first, and Will replied, "Action first, no doubt."

The pair had always shared a great love for movies, and always tried to go to the cinema when financially viable. But usually they would get back to the flat, crack open some beers and watch movies indoors. Will, specifically had a love for action and horrors, whereas Carter's preference was much more varied, having a huge fondness for films from all eras and genres. He did have some favourite actors and directors who stood out to him, and whose work he adored. Oliver Reed was one, who not only did he perceive as one of the greatest screen actors of all time, but was also an entertaining character outside of the film world. One of Carter's favourite movies was the Charles Dickens adaptation of Oliver!, which of course starred Oliver Reed as the infamous character Bill Sykes. Carter had loved movies for as long as he could remember, right back from watching all the classics from the eighties when he was younger, movies such as The Goonies, The Karate Kid, The Lost Boys, and plus a whole barrel load more. Marcus too had a love for movies and the brothers had shared many happy occasions in the past, sitting in front of the TV with their parents. Carter had always hoped, and in fact believed, that his future was destined to be in the film industry, and that he would one day be in a position where he was directing his own film. Sadly, along with Carter's confidence issues this dream seemed to have withered and fizzled out over the years, which resulted in a Carter that became so depressed and hollow over time, that he began to believe that even if he did try to get into the industry, the industry would reject him.

Carter proceeded in taking the action movie from its case and slipped the DVD into the player. The pair dropped down onto the sofa and cracked open the beers, and Will pressed play on the remote. As the previews started to play Will looked at Carter and said "You OK mate. How are you shaping up?"

Carter said nothing in return but just shook his head slowly, indicating to Will that he wasn't prepared to talk about it, and in no way wanted to be reminded of it. Will understood and looked back at the screen. As the film began to play Carter began to drift and started to visualise some memories from his past. The death of his brother was now coming to the forefront of his mind once again, and this time he did not attempt to shut it out. He started to think back to when it was the four of them in their family home all those years ago, happy and content, and how now, as if in just a few seconds, everything had suddenly changed, and he was alone. He started to get snapshots in his mind of random thoughts and memories, one of his father with a big smile on his face when arm wrestling Marcus at the dining table, another of his mother playing piano to them both on Christmas Day, and them all singing together, and of Marcus waving at him from the porch before riding away on his bike. He also remembered when they played cards late at night in their room, when they should have been in bed asleep, and one of Marcus standing up for Carter at school when being confronted by bullies trying to take his lunch money. Carter had not remembered a lot of these things until now, but memories were becoming apparent to him naturally and in abundance, and for once he relished it. He felt a feeling of warmth come over him, just for a second, as he let his mind release, illuminating these visions of his past. He embraced them.

* * * *

The alarm from the oven sounded and Carter jumped, almost off of his seat. Will laughed at him, before pressing the pause button on the remote to go and grab the pizzas from the oven. Carter sat back in his chair and was shocked that twenty-five minutes had passed, when it seemed more like five. He had not taken in any of the movie so far, and was not at all bothered. The pizzas were sliced and presented by Will. Carter took a slice, before Will plonked the plates down on the coffee table and pressed play to continue the movie. Carter found himself once again, almost immediately drifting away and reminiscing, not only of family memories now but also of himself, his life, and how depressed he was. Why had it happened to him? Why bipolar disorder? These thoughts were flooding him, and even though he wasn't even searching for answers, he was being bombarded with these thought provoking flashbacks. Carter continued to drink throughout the remainder of the movie, and the second movie in fact, before collapsing in a heap on the floor. Will had already fallen asleep during the second movie, at which time Carter had relocated to the floor, enabling Will to stretch out.

* * * *

Saturday morning TV was playing away as it usually did in the flat, with Will making sure he watched Saturday Morning Kitchen. It was if it was the end of the world if Will could not watch his beloved cooking programme, followed by Football Focus of course. The toaster ejected two golden brown and perfectly executed pieces of toast, and Will pulled himself off the sofa to get them. Carter was awoken by both the smell of the bread and by the annoying popping sound of the toaster. He lifted his head off of the living room floor and briefly massaged his neck before letting off an almighty yawn. Will, realising Carter had surfaced, offered the toast to him and he accepted. Carter pulled himself up onto the sofa and stretched out, making the most of the comfy cushions, before having to sit up again once Will returned. The nightmare reality of the previous evening wandered back into Carter's mind, almost immediately after waking. He knew that he would have to talk to his boss first thing Monday morning and make him aware that he would be away to attend the funeral once the date was confirmed.

"Will, I'm thinking about taking a week or two off around the time of the funeral. I think I just need to take some time out for a change. I've accrued some hours so think I'll use them now as well," offered Carter, as Will returned to the sofa.

"Sounds like a great idea, you haven't been off for well . . . . well for too long! Take some time out. Maybe do a little explore of the Highlands while you're up there?"

"Yeah maybe, I'll see."

The pair tucked into their morning tea and toast, while slouching back on the sofa. Morning turned into afternoon and the only movement that either of them had managed to muster in this time had been breathing. The laziest of Saturday mornings had been played out right there in North London. Carter challenged Will to a game on the PS3, but Will had to decline as he had a date that evening and wanted to get ready. Will Harrison was quite the opposite of Carter in appearance, but they shared almost exactly the same interests and sense of humour. Will was thirty-seven and quite tall, had light brown hair, and dressed smart casual most of the time. He was also a bit of a Casanova, very handsome, and had a regular stream of girlfriends. However, he never allowed himself to become too attached to any of them for any length of time. He was far more interested in just having a good time for a while without any pressures of commitment. On occasion, Will had tried to set up blind dates for Carter, but sadly they always ended up in Carter being drunk and depressed and usually embarrassing himself. Will quickly realised that Carter's nerves would not go, and no matter how hard he tried to get him to feel comfortable and confident around a woman, it was like trying to get a politician to tell the truth.

Will's date this particular evening was Sophia Carr from work, who was employed there as a PA. The pair had been out a few times before, and both really enjoyed each other's company. Neither was interested in anything long term or anything serious, so this relationship suited them both. That evening, Will had to travel into the city and meet Sophia at Leicester Square at 7pm sharp. They would usually go for a couple of drinks, some dinner, and then onto a club until late. Carter would usually be awoken when the pair crashed into the flat in the early hours and into Will's bedroom. He would then have to put up with the noises that would follow, and would usually bury his head under the pillows to block out the sound. Even though Will was very much the lady's man, Carter was never at any point in any way jealous of his best friend, in fact he applauded him. He was happy that his friend was happy. Will was always surprised at this, but was at the same time in many ways grateful to Carter for feeling this way.

Will returned from the shower, towel wrapped around him at the waist, and spraying himself with his usual Lacoste aftershave. Carter, playing the PS3 glanced up at him and grinned,

"Oh here he is; God's gift to the world of women. There is no stopping him, the modern day answer to Elvis himself. And how the hell do you keep your stomach so toned as well, given all the beer you shovel into you?"

Will, responded by smiling and acknowledging the sarcasm, whilst checking himself out in the mirror. He started to comb his hair before saying,

"Oh yeah, you better watch out, make way on the dance floor, I'm coming to town. Oh, and I go to the gym by the way!"

They both laughed before Will dashed off to his bedroom to get dressed. Carter paused the game and glanced over to the phone. He thought that maybe he should call Claire when Will went out for the evening. He decided not, as she needed time to be alone and grieve. Carter leant forward and turned off the PS3, starting to think once again about Marcus being gone. He knew that at some point he was going to have to deal with it, and that playing PS3 games to try and distract himself from the issue was neither really appropriate or healthy for his grieving process. He stood up and walked over to the mirror and stood very close to it, holding there for a moment. He looked deep into his eyes in the reflection, as if attempting to search for an inner strength of some kind, a comfort of some sought, an answer . . . . help! Nothing came. He looked down and turned away. Will re-entered the room and looked very smart, as he always did when hitting the town. He realised that Carter was thinking about Marcus, and felt a slight guilt that he was going out to meet Sophia rather than stay in and keep him company. But he knew that by cancelling and staying in would upset Carter even more, and presumed that he wanted some time alone.

"OK mate, you gonna be ok?" said Will, just about to leave.

"Sure, I'll be . . . . well you know . . . . I'll be fine. Go and have a good time, and no doubt will hear you later!"

Will laughed and walked to the door to leave, before turning to Carter and saying: "Anything, just call me alright?"

"You got it." replied Carter appreciatively.

Will closed the door behind him and left. Carter, as soon as he heard the sound of the door close, suddenly felt emptiness inside and realised just how much at that point he relied on Will's company. He was now alone in the flat; everything seemed very quiet, almost imposing, as the walls seemed to be drawing in on him. He tried to think of some ideas to keep him occupied that evening. He wasn't in the mood for playing the PS3, and he didn't fancy watching the TV. He thought about going to the cinema but nothing that he wanted to see was showing. Where could he go just to kill some time and not be alone? The pub!

CHAPTER TWO

The door of the apartment swung open with a startling force, as Carter once again almost entered his flat by falling into it. It was a rarity for him to be able to just walk in through the door in a normal, relatively straightforward fashion, with no additional theatre performance-like drama. If by chance the flat was being burgled at the time of Carter's entrance, the criminal would have most likely thought it was the police charging in, or a madman, and most likely jumped out of the window to escape!

It was midnight, and Carter was very drunk, overspending that evening in order to get completely wasted. And he had succeeded. He stayed in his local pub all evening, perched up at the bar knocking back a host full of Jack Daniels and Coke. Now back in his flat and very bubbly he decided that he wanted to continue his private party, and immediately made haste for his record collection. He was very proud of his records, a collection that boasted a variety of artists such as Led Zeppelin,

The Smiths, Pink Floyd, Dire Straits, Johnny Cash, and Buddy Holly, to name but a few. He pulled out a random batch and went into the living room, getting a cold beer from the fridge en route. His first artist of choice was to be Led Zeppelin and he took the record gently from the sleeve and steadied himself, just enough time to place the record on the turntable and the needle on the record without scratching it. In truth, it seemed that no matter how wasted Carter was, there was absolutely no chance whatsoever that he would damage any of his records, or his DVD collection also for that matter. They were far too precious to him, as antiques are to a collector, a race hound to its owner. He had always preferred to listen to the old Vinyl records, as opposed to CDs, as he thought the music sounded so much more pure and raw. He felt that CDs were sounding so much more overproduced as time went by, and that the magic was sadly slowly being eroded. The crackling sound of the needle added an extra quality to the sound of the tracks. The first track kicked in and Carter cranked up the volume, opened his can of beer, and started to sing along with the music, paying no consideration to neighbouring flats either above, below or adjacent. If they had banged on the wall to disapprove or knocked on the door to complain, he would not have heard them anyway. He let himself go. One song flowed into another, one record replaced by another, as he danced around the flat drinking more and more, swaying more and more. Then, one song started to play that drew his total concentration, Comfortably Numb by Pink Floyd. As the words drifted in he began to float away into a kind of trance, alcohol assisted of course, as the song started tugging at his emotions. He swayed backwards and forwards, gazing into nothingness, his mind absorbing the music and the lyrics. The room had already started to spin due to his long drinking session and he found it hard to stand in one place, recklessly becoming more and more unbalanced. He tried to sit back on the sofa to listen more intently, attempting to stay grounded to one spot, but this proved unsuccessful. He slipped and fell to the floor, hitting the side of his head on the corner of the coffee table. He lay still, stunned as his vision began to blur. He could just about make out the time as being 4am on his digital clock, before he saw blackness.

* * * *

Will and Sophia returned to the flat and could already hear the loud music playing from way down the corridor. They realised that something didn't seem right. Will knew that Carter would not be playing music that loud at that time in the morning, as neither of them would have ever intentionally disrespected their neighbours in any way. Will fumbled around for his keys and opened the door. They saw Carter lying on the floor and blood was clearly visible on the carpet where his head lay. The final part of Comfortably Numb was bellowing from the speakers. Sophia let out a scream, obviously fearing the worst as Will rushed to his side.

"Carter, Carter!" Will repeated in terror.

"Sophia turn the music off, Sophia turn off the music and call an ambulance for Christ's sake."

Sophia rushed over to the phone and dialled the emergency services. She pulled the plug out of the socket in a panic to stop the music, before hearing a voice coming from the phone.

"Hello, emergency services. Which service do you require?"

*   *   *   *

The ambulance raced along the high street at speed, lights flashing, in order to get Carter to A&E at The Whittington Hospital in Archway. There was next to no traffic on the road as it had just hit 4.30am, and rush hour traffic would not appear for another couple of hours. Carter began to regain consciousness but his eyes remained closed and body still, as he heard the sirens and two voices speaking. One was a member of the ambulance crew, and the other, to Carter's relief was the familiar voice of Will.

"Looks like you got home at just the right time, the wound is quite deep. It needs to be addressed ASAP." said the crew member.

Carter noticed a sudden pause before Will responded with a nervous and slightly panicky voice.

"He just found out only last night, well Friday night that his brother died in a car crash. I wish I had stayed with him, I should have stayed at the flat with him."

Carter blacked out again, with the two oblivious that he had even come around at all. The ambulance pulled into the entrance, the crew wasting not a second in offloading the stretcher from the vehicle and aiming for A&E. Will and Sophia rushed along behind. The reception area was filled with the busy maniacal mayhem that occurred pretty much most Sundays in the early hours, with the victims of a heavy Saturday night, who had either partied too hard or fought too fiercely.

There was only one receptionist on the front desk looking stressed and was obviously struggling. The queue was long; people were becoming abusive, raising their voices, venting their anger at the delay in services. The odd night nurse would appear and call someone else in from the waiting area, which in turn caused more uproar. It seemed that the more impatient people became the less important other people in need of treatment became to them. The system of being seen was determined on the seriousness of the injury sustained, and that would justify who was prioritised and who wasn't. Many of the patients who were given low priority would become quite stressed, and were usually the most troublesome.

* * * *

The view of the reception area came and went in a flash for Will and Sophia as they followed the ambulance crew straight past and down the corridor. Carter's injury had assured him of definite priority. A head injury would be prioritised anyway, but one that resulted in a person losing consciousness meant that it was of paramount importance that they were treated without delay. The paramedics had done their best onboard the ambulance to temporarily dress the wound, but it was now for a doctor to thoroughly assess it. They approached the treatment room, the door was opened and the stretcher carrying Carter wheeled in. The room looked more like a small ward. There were beds lined up along each wall, some of which were hidden by curtains pulled around to retain privacy. There were a number of nurses buzzing around and a doctor who was scurrying backwards and forwards between patients. The room was extremely active and was obviously enduring another busy morning. There was a circular shaped reception desk situated right in the middle of the area from which a senior nurse appeared and approached the crew.

"OK guys, what has happened here, do we have a name?" asked Senior Nurse Nicola Crossman, who spoke with confidence, a confidence that is usually found amongst professionals who are in no doubt as to their own high levels of skills and capabilities.

"We have a Carter Jakeman, late thirties. He has sustained a deep gash to his head. He fell earlier this morning and was found unconscious by his flatmate who called 999. We brought him round briefly at his home, and he could say his name and correct date of birth. He fell unconscious again when we got him in to the ambulance, he was slurring his words, but that could also be because he was intoxicated. We have given it a temporary dressing but the cut looks quite deep."

"OK thanks. Just bring him over here please," said Nurse Crossman while signalling to an area of space that could accommodate the stretcher. She then called for two male nurses to go and transfer the body on to a bed.

"I take it you are this gentleman's flatmate?" said a voice that came from the side of where Will and Sophia were standing. Will looked and saw a health care assistant to his right.

"Yes I am. My name is Will Harrison."

"OK Mr Harrison, could you please accompany me to the reception desk so that we can register your flatmate as a patient?"

"Yes of course, certainly." replied Will.

Sophia told Will that she would go and search for a vending machine to buy some coffees and that she would be outside smoking a cigarette if he needed her. Will followed the assistant to the reception desk, manoeuvring around the various obstacles that rushed out in front of him, some as if they had appeared from nowhere. His mind was confused but he himself had completely sobered up by this point due to the shock. Adrenaline had taken over and his only concern was that Carter would be OK. Will gave over Carter's details so his demographics could be registered onto the system. He didn't even notice that the paramedics had gone; he would have liked to have thanked them. The curtain around the bed to where Carter had been relocated was pulled around, resulting in Will having to remain patient for the time being while Carter was being treated. The assistant told Will that he could wait in the waiting area outside and when there were any updates he would be notified. Will thanked him and left—he didn't want to be in the way and become a nuisance.

Will spotted Sophia walking towards the automatic exit doors holding two coffees. He quickly followed her knowing that she was on her way to have a smoke, and he himself was contemplating having one as well. They sat together on a wall just outside the A&E entrance. A clutter of fag ends littered the floor, indicating to smokers that this was the area in which to gather. A night porter and a tired weary old looking cleaner were the only other two people there getting their early morning fix before returning to their duties. The old cleaner looked and sounded like he had just smoked about three in a row.

Will thanked Sophia for his coffee and held it in both hands to warm them. She asked if she had missed anything, which he quickly confirmed as nothing yet. It was a waiting game, as it often was when waiting on news within the hospital environment. She drew a cigarette from her packet and lit it.

"Would you mind if I have one Soph?" Will asked, adding "I am fucking shaking here, shook me right up that has."

"No worries." responded Sophia whilst handing him the packet.

After lighting his cigarette he picked up his coffee, holding one in one hand and one in the other. He turned to Sophia and said,

"Well I'm sorry you've had to go through this tonight. You can have the keys to the flat if you like and go back and get some sleep?"

"No, I'd rather stay. I mean, I know I don't know Carter very well, but I would like to stay. And to keep you company as well. I know how close you guys are."

"Thanks Soph."

Will's expression then changed from a warm smile to a more serious and troubled look,

"I'm worried about him. He drinks all the time, and now with the news of his brother. Anything could happen. I mean. I know him well enough, or I think I do, to know that he wouldn't do anything intentionally to harm himself, or worse, but I am very concerned about him. I know I drink a lot, but shit!"

Sophia put her coffee onto the wall next to her, and placed one hand on Will's shoulder. The two of them shared a comforting smile before being interrupted by a voice. It was the health care assistant from the treatment room.

"Mr Harrison . . . . Thought I would check out here, the nurse would like to have a quick word."

Will flicked his cigarette to the floor, having hardly even smoked any of it, and headed straight back inside. Sophia took a couple of quick drags from hers before disposing of it. She picked up the two coffees and followed, quickening her pace to catch up with Will. They re-entered the treatment room and was greeted by a dark haired woman with a comforting smile.

"Hi, my name is Nicola Crossman and I am the senior nurse on duty this morning. I understand that you are Mr Jakeman's flatmate and you found him unconsciousness."

"Yes I did, we called the ambulance immediately. Is there an update?"

"Well, the wound is quite deep and he had lost some blood. He is being treated at the moment. We need to give him a scan just to be sure, and then he will be seen by a doctor again later today. We'll keep him here for at least the rest of the day, and we are going to transfer him to the ward a bit later. We will have a bed available from about 9am. Now it is up to you, but I would recommend that you go home and get some sleep. Visiting hours later today will be from 1pm to 3pm and you can find out which ward he is on from the admission's office just to the right of the main entrance to the hospital."

Will agreed that it made sense to go back to the flat. He thanked her for her help and walked out into the foyer. Sophia took her phone from her handbag and called for a cab.

* * * *

The cab driver took quite a detour in search of a more efficient route as traffic had built up on the main road. It was light outside by the time they arrived back at the flat. They were both shattered and didn't want to do anything other than to crash and sleep for a while. However, Will looked at where they had found Carter and knew that he would have to clean the dry blood from the floor first. He told Sophia to get some rest and that he would go to bed after clearing up. He sat down on the sofa for a moment.

"Oh Carter." he said in a quiet reflective voice.

Gathering the necessary cleaning products from the kitchen cupboard, he cleaned the blood away and threw the empty beer cans into the bin. He went to the bathroom, flushing the stained tissues down the toilet, before washing his hands thoroughly in the sink.

By the time he made it to the bedroom he saw that Sophia had already gone to sleep, and despite her best efforts in trying to pull the curtains across enough in an attempt to block out the seeping sunlight, she had made it worse by accidently breaking two of the brackets on the left side of the curtain rail. Now even more light encroached into the room, and more importantly it was shining directly onto the side of the bed where Will was going to sleep. It was very humid in the flat, so Will grabbed his little desk fan from the table and returned to the living room to sleep on the sofa. He set up the fan on the floor and had it blowing full blast over him. In a matter of seconds he drifted off.

* * * *

Will woke to the sight of Sophia standing in front of him holding a cup of coffee.

"Oh I was just about to wake you up . . . here I made you a coffee."

"Thanks. What time is it?" responded a very weary Will.

"Nearly midday." replied a fresh faced Sophia.

She had been up for about an hour and had attempted to make the flat look a touch more respectable and tidy. However that did seem to be a never ending task. Will picked up his mobile phone from the floor and checked for any messages, more to the point any messages from Carter, but there were none. Sophia had to leave as she had plans for Sunday afternoon that she could not change, the usual traditional Sunday roast at her parents' house. Will thanked her for being there and said he would text her later with any updates from the hospital. Sophia kissed him goodbye and left the flat.

Will got up and went to the bathroom to splash his face with cold water. He still felt very tired but knew the strong coffee would soon kick in, if not, he was going to make another one. As he walked towards his bedroom he stopped as he noticed something out of the corner of his eye. It was Carter's mobile phone. Will crossed to the table and picked it up. He scrolled through the contacts list until he came to the name Simon Jones. This was Carter's boss and Will thought he would send him a text to notify him that Carter was not going to be at work tomorrow. He tried to make it sound as innocent as possible, trying to avoid drawing Simon Jones to the assumption of it being a drink infused accident. His text read:

"Hi Simon, this is Carter Jakeman's flatmate, Will Harrison. Just a quick message to say that he will not be able to come into work tomorrow as he has had a fall at the weekend while trying to fix some curtains! He will call you at some point tomorrow to explain further."

Will put the phone back on the kitchen worktop and headed for the shower, as he wanted to fully freshen up and make sure he got back to the hospital for the start of visiting hours. He set the shower dial to a mild lukewarm temperature, as it was another very hot day.

* * * *

It was almost silent. The dull droning sound of a small TV located at the end of the ward was the only source of disturbance. Pre-visiting hours were like the calm before the storm for nursing staff. They had already finished their morning rounds and had distributed medication and injections accordingly, providing to the needs of every patient's individual requirements. It was now 12.45pm, and all but for two staff covering the small ward reception desk, it was as if deserted. The beds were full of course, the ward comprising of five beds on either side, most patients were either lying down or sleeping. Except one! In fact the only person who was not in bed was the patient right down at the end of the ward, and who was watching the small TV, the same small TV that as of 9am that very morning was in its original and more convenient spot centred at the end of the ward, enabling all patients to see and hear it equally. However, the patient had obviously selfishly relocated it for himself so he could have total control over what was showing. He had already been warned by the ward sister earlier that morning to leave it alone, but he had since chosen the right moment to stealthily nab it undetected. He was an elderly gentleman, very rude and set in his ways. He was very slim, almost gaunt looking, had slight stubble and very short grey hair. He had recently had an operation on his left leg and was due to be discharged home at some point over that coming week. The staff were only too keen to see the back of him, as he had been nothing but problematic since being admitted. Whenever he needed anything he would purposely shout out aggressively, upsetting the fellow patients and staff. It would be random sarcastic remarks such as,

"When are one of you sweethearts gonna give me a bath? You can get in with me if you like."

Another, when being served food he would always have something to say, like

"Oi. I ain't eating this. Can I have some real food instead please! Yeah I've never really been fond of eating shit!"

He was constantly warned by his consultant about his attitude, but to no avail. Realistically they knew that it was only a matter of time before they would be rid of him. The old man continued with his obnoxious jibes,

"Jesus! There is nothing on this bloody telly. Haven't you got Sky so I can put one of those dirty channels on? Might get the matron in the mood!"

It was during this elderly man's latest outburst that Carter's eyes opened and he awoke. His bed was on the opposite side to the annoying elderly man, and at the other end of the room, to Carter's relief. He had already spoken to the doctor on duty earlier about his head injury, and that the wound would now need time to heal. They had carried out a scan and had put stitches in not long after Will and Sophia had left the hospital that morning. Carter had been resting since. He had been informed that Will and a young lady had accompanied him into hospital at about 4.40am, and he had arrived both unconscious and intoxicated. He was aware that he would most likely be seeing Will soon, as visiting hours were only moments away, and he was looking forward to that. He felt embarrassed about what had happened, and he prepared himself mentally just in case a lecture was about to come from Will.

In his earlier conversation with the doctor, he had been warned about his current lifestyle, and the effects this could have on him long term. The doctor had told him that next time he may not be so lucky, and that if he kept drinking excessive amounts of alcohol it could only result in illness or death. Carter sat up and shifted into a more comfortable position. He looked to his left and down the room toward the elderly man who had awoken him with his shouting. The man was moaning and mumbling to himself about anything and everything on the TV, and at regular intervals would look around as if he was about to unleash the next string of obscenities and abuse into the air. Carter smiled to himself, finding something funny about the man's taunts, and he did think they were quite comical, even if offensive. Then sounded a voice that distracted Carter.

"There you are! Mr, I'm going to scare the life out of my best friend, Jakeman!"

Carter turned to see Will standing on the other side of the bed, and was pleased to see him to say the least.

"Will, I am so sorry. I must have just tripped or . . ."

Will interrupted Carter's apology and explanation and said there was nothing to forgive. He pulled a bag up from his side, containing some grapes, a banana, a bottle of orange juice, and a newspaper. He placed the items onto the side table, while enquiring into Carter's current state.

"So how are you feeling? Have they been round to see you yet? When can you get out of here?"

"Well, my head hurts like a bitch, but they said that I am fine and should hopefully be home later this afternoon. Thanks for the goodies by the way."

"No worries, it would have been more but I had to pay Mo back for that bet I lost, and had no other cash on me." replied Will as he pulled up a plastic visitor chair for himself.

"No this is fine, I'm sure the high quality fine dining hospital a la carte option is due to arrive at any time soon." said Carter.

They both shared a laugh, not only at the a la carte comment but also at the whole event, and the predicament that Carter was now in.

"Bollocks on toast!" yelled the elderly man from down the corridor causing Will to jump, almost leaving his chair.

"That's what I want for lunch." repeated the man.

"What the f. . . . ?" Will said in amazement, beginning to laugh.

"Don't ask. I've had this entertainment all morning." replied Carter.

Right on cue a trolley carrying the first batch of lunches rolled into the ward, pushed by a big sturdy nurse who had just started her shift. The patients in the other beds started to rise slowly upon smelling the aromas of promising food through the air, but who equally knew that that promise would be short lived once they had started eating it. Other family members and friends started to arrive, gathering chairs where they could to visit their loved ones and sit with them at their bedsides.

The heat was almost unbearable on the ward that day. Carter had never understood why visiting hours and meal serving hours were the same, and why they kept it so hot in there! "Illogical and annoying." he thought to himself. The big nurse, who seemed to have a huge unnatural set of muscles for a woman, muscles that were probably bigger than those of both Will and Carter's put together, started to hand out the meals. Carter and Will sat in silence, equally anticipating the meeting of the mighty nurse and the elderly uncouth man at the end. She approached him. Carter and Will's eyes were glued to the scene.

"Here you go Jimmy." said the nurse plonking the plate and water down behind him on his bed table.

"That's Mr Rafferty to you . . . ."

He turned around to look at the nurse, and upon seeing her, blurted out

"Bloody hell, what are you one of those trannies?" assuming from her burlesque physique that she was in fact a man dressed up as a woman. He continued,

"Where did they find you? The Army?"

The nurse's face turned bright red with embarrassment but she held her cool.

"Now don't be rude Mr Rafferty, or I'll be the one taking you for your bath later!"

"Well no, on second thoughts I'll do my bath on my own thanks. If you get in there with me the water will get out! Forget it."

He turned back to face the TV screen and tried his best to avoid any further interaction. The nurse coolly added one more thing before continuing her route.

"Oh no you won't Mr Rafferty, you and I together. I'll be back soon!"

The nurse turned and continued to deliver the remaining lunches to the rest of the patients, a slight smile on her face, while Carter and Will giggled at what they had just witnessed. The elderly man now sat in total silence and it was obvious that he had been put in his place, intimidated at the idea of having any kind of wash from that point on.

Carter's bed was the last delivery for the nurse and she placed the tray down on the bed table.

"Is it safe?" said Will. "Sorry I mean the food, not . . . ."

Will realised that this could have sounded like a reference to her encounter with the old man, rather than a light joke regarding to the general consensus on standards of hospital food. Carter interjected by saying,

"Thank you very much nurse and good job with the TV man down there. He has been rude all day!"

The nurse smiled and agreed with Carter, and once she had taken a discerning look at Will for his un-thought out comment, she turned and waddled back out into the main corridor to continue her meal distribution to the next ward along. Will and Carter looked at each other with a sigh of relief, as she was scary and intimidating.

"We need to have a talk Carter, a serious talk." said Will becoming more sincere in tone.

"Why? Are you breaking up with me?" said Carter jokingly, but at the same time knowing that the conversation and probable lecture was unavoidable.

Will smiled—but this quickly disappeared.

"No come on mate, I'm not joking around here. I'm worried about you. You are my best friend, and yes we have a good drink at the weekends and so on. But there is not a night that goes by where I haven't seen you having a drink. You need to start thinking about you're lifestyle. You are not in your twenties anymore. I kind of feel bad bringing this up at this time, but . . . ."

"I know Will. OK, I know! I understand that you are worried but this was just an accident."

"And what about next time?" interrupted Will abruptly.

Carter's facial expression shed a thousand words of sadness and depression as he looked down in defeat, putting the cutlery back down onto the plate. He slid the plate slightly away from him, as Will continued,

"I'm saying this for your own good. OK if you don't want to do it for me, do it for Marcus."

Carter became very angry and the mere suggestion of using his brother as a weapon of guilt against him was inappropriate and ill-timed. Will had actually thought this as he said it, but it was too late.

"Don't you dare bring my brother into this Will." shouted Carter, his temper frayed, which caused anxiety in the ward.

Will tried to quieten and calm him down, but by now old man Rafferty himself had been set off by Carter's angry outburst,

"Don't you shout at me." he yelled, just using any excuse to be rude and confrontational.

Carter composed himself and everyone realised it was just a one off outburst. Carter apologised to the people within immediate vicinity. Jimmy Rafferty returned to watching his TV and did not carry on with his own meaningless shouting.

Will pulled Carter's mobile from his inside pocket and handed it back to him before saying,

"Sorry, Carter, I shouldn't have said that. I just want you to be happy and all right. That's all. Look, I have let Simon know you won't be in tomorrow and that you'll call him to explain in more detail. I didn't mention the bad news though. He texted back just before I left saying that he will speak to you tomorrow."

"Ok thanks." Carter replied.

There was no real conversation between them following that. Will sat and read through the paper and Carter laid down on his side facing away from Will, pretending he was asleep. It was an awkward moment but deep down Carter knew that Will was right and was only looking out for him, like he had done so many times before. Will had been such a good friend over the years. Someone you could rely on, trust and confide in.

* * * *

Carter had moved into digs, a large old house close to the college, with some other college students. It was his attempt at being more independent now that he was an adult. Carter loved his family very much and the move had in no way been forced upon him. In fact his Father had supported him in his decision both financially and with encouragement. His Father had also said that if it didn't work out and he wanted to come home his room would always be there.

Each student in the house had their own bedroom with all other facilities being shared. It was here that he became firm friends with Will. They also attended many of the same classes. Another student at the house was a brash loud guy called Danny Roper who tended to hang out with Will and Carter when they went out of an evening. Carter didn't really like Roper as he was far too pushy and tried to control everything. Will who was a strong character in his own right resisted Roper and the pair would often argue. Carter on the other hand was less strong-willed and would often have to mediate between the other two to keep the peace. Will admired Carter's diplomacy and negotiating skills while Roper tended to look on him as a wimp and someone he could control. Will knew this and was always on hand to protect Carter from Roper's influence.

It was about this time in Carter's life that his bouts of depression began to get worse. He and Will partied hard, resulting in Carter especially finding it hard to meet assignment deadlines. He often had to study late into the night just to keep up with the course work which meant that he was constantly tired and worried.

Sometimes when he was really depressed he would lock himself away in his room for days on end and just sit in the dark in a state of despair. Will knew what he was going through and on occasion he would discuss it with him and try to cheer him up. Roper on the other hand would bait him mercilessly. Carter would be alone in his room lost in his misery, sometimes sobbing, when there would be a loud banging on his door followed by Roper shouting,

"Come on Carter snap out of it!" followed by an added comment as he moved off down the hallway usually something on the lines of, "You fucking cry baby."

This became a regular taunt whenever Carter was ill. Will was not always fully aware of what was going on. Then one day as he was going down the stairs, he overheard Roper tormenting Carter with such jibes. Will pulled him to one side and told him to leave Carter alone, to which the obnoxious Roper just laughed and walked away.

One Friday evening, when Carter wasn't feeling too down, Will suggested that they have a night out and chill out. It was after finishing one of their more demanding college assignments, so he suggested maybe a club somewhere to blow off steam. It just so happened that Roper was passing at that precise moment and added,

"Yeah sounds great, I'm in."

"Well actually I was thinking of just Carter and myself if you don't mind?" said Will whose annoyance didn't go unnoticed.

"What's your fucking problem, frightened I might take your little boyfriend away from you?" responded Roper, blowing a kiss in Carter's direction and sneering at the same time.

Will clenched his fists and moved towards Roper when Carter stepped between them and said: "It's OK Will he can come if he wants to. It'll be fine."

"OK as long as you're all right with it." said a slightly more relaxed Will.

"Right!" said Roper, "I know just where we're going. It's a club in the city. Plenty of booze, girls and anything else you might need."

Before Will could say anything Roper dashed off upstairs to get ready.

The club turned out to be a dark dirty cellar, very noisy with a lot of dodgy looking characters. As the night went on, and the drink flowed, the mood between the three relaxed and they began to chat about the usual young man's topics. Will had spotted a girl he fancied and told the others that he might be home late and moved off to get acquainted with her. Roper moved closer to Carter and joked,

"Will wants to be careful you know. One of these days his dick's going to fall off. Some of the women down here are not what you would call clean if you know what I mean."

Now that Will was otherwise engaged Carter's interest in the evening was waning. Roper's remarks about Will continued and Carter didn't want to upset him by telling him to shut up. He looked at his watch—it was 11.30 pm. He turned to Roper, who had his eyes shut and dancing to himself, and shouted over the music,

"Danny it's getting late I think I'm going to go."

Roper opened his eyes which were wild and glassy and stared at Carter.

"Are you fucking kidding? The night's just getting going? Have another drink."

"No really Danny, I think I've had enough."

"OK Carter not a drink. How about something else? What about some ecstasy or some coke? They do some really good shit here. There's a guy over there selling. I had some snow earlier and believe me . . . . very good shit."

"Not for me Danny!" said Carter putting his empty glass on the bar preparing to leave.

Roper leaned in towards Carter just inches from his face with his breath reeking of beer,

"You fucking lightweight. Your boyfriend's gone off and found himself a girl, leaving you all alone hasn't he? So now you're going to run off home to your little room and cry yourself to sleep. Why don't you grow up and stop moping about. Snap out of it!"

Carter left the club with those final four words spoken by Roper ringing around in his head. Roper always used those four words, knowing that Carter despised them. What he hoped would be a good night had ended badly.

The next morning Carter got up early, laundry and breakfast being the first things on the agenda. He was sitting at the kitchen table sipping his strong black coffee when Roper staggered in looking much the worse for wear. Carter felt his body tense up instantly, his heart sink and his hand holding the coffee cup began to tremble. Roper had obviously been out all night, and looked like he had. He paid absolutely no attention to Carter, as if he didn't exist, but as he left the kitchen, he couldn't resist but mutter the words,

"Fucking lightweight!"

Carter smiled to himself and was relieved that Roper had left the kitchen. Moments later Will walked in.

"Morning Carter, bet you're surprised to see me up at this ungodly hour?" said Will grabbing a cup from the drainer.

"I am actually, yes. What happened? No luck last night?" responded Carter teasingly.

Will looked up at Carter and smiled. He said nothing but waited for Carter to restart the conversation.

"OK, why are you up this early?" Carter was intrigued.

"I haven't been to sleep yet!" replied a proud faced Will.

"What?" said a shocked Carter.

"She's still upstairs. I just came down to make a coffee. She has only just fallen asleep. Man she is wild!"

"I'm surprised you stopped even when she fell asleep to be honest with you!" said Carter joking and making fun of Will.

"Ha ha ha, very funny." responded Will.

"I have my moments!"

"So how about you're night. Did you have a good time?" asked Will, filling his cup with a spoonful of coffee.

"Not that good! Roper pissed me off. I said I wanted to go and call it a night and he started to have a go. You know the usual. Maybe he's got a point. Maybe it is me being selfish. I know I put a massive strain on the house when I'm down and . . . ."

Will looked Carter in the eye and said earnestly,

"Don't worry about Roper, he's a prick."

Carter smiled back at Will and replied,

"Thanks you're a good friend."

"So are you." said Will.

"The thing is Will I'm thinking of moving back home. I don't think I can take any more of Roper. I tried to talk to him about it once and he told me to fuck off."

Will looked surprised at Carter's decision to move out and was not aware that the taunting had carried on so seriously. He assumed that after he told Roper to stop before, he had.

"How bad is it Carter? Does he do it often?" asked Will looking concerned.

"Every time. I can't stand it any more, and I'm sure it only adds to my problems." replied Carter, refraining from becoming upset.

Will felt beside himself and the anger rose within him.

"I'm sorry mate I had no idea it was that bad. I wish you would've told me."

Carter stared into his cup "It's OK, it's not your problem".

As he uttered the words 'It's not your problem' Roper walked back into the kitchen.

"What's this 'it's not your problem' crap you were saying as I came in?" he said, looking directly at Carter.

Before Carter could answer Will walked around the table towards Roper.

"I thought I told you to leave Carter alone. The last thing he needs when he's not well is a prick like you making things worse. So I'm telling you for the last time cut it out!"

He started to laugh and leaned towards Will.

"Listen, you don't tell me what to do OK. As the cry baby said, it's not your problem so fuck off and mind your own business. If I want to say something, I will."

Before he had finished the last word, Will's fist hit him smack on the nose, exploding in a spray of blood. Roper fell back shocked at what had happened. He looked down at the blood dripping onto the kitchen floor, then back up at Will as the second punch caught him in the right eye. Danny slumped back against the worktop putting his arms in front of his face to protect himself. Will stood his ground but made no attempt to hit him again. Roper, the fear showing in his eyes, made no attempt at retaliation. Instead he walked out of the kitchen and up to his room. Will, still shaking with rage, stared out of the kitchen door. Carter looked at him said,

"Wow."

"Yeah fucking right, 'wow'", said Will, his voice trembling as his body was pumped full of adrenaline.

Within minutes Roper appeared at the kitchen door, his suitcase in his hand and a handkerchief held against his bleeding nose. His right eye had started to puff and discolour.

"I'm getting out of here. You're both fucking mad."

"Yeah, and you're still a prick." Will confirmed.

Roper turned away, saying only a few more words before leaving,

"I'll come back for my other stuff later."

Carter stood and watched him go. He looked up at Will, not saying a word, but his expression showed just how grateful he was of what Will had just done. Luckily in the weeks that followed the now vacant room was occupied by the extreme opposite of Danny Roper. In moved a girl, Jennifer Shier, who was soon to become great friends with both Carter and Will.

* * * *

Just before visiting time was over a doctor appeared with good news. Carter could be discharged. Without hesitation he got ready to go, and the two made their way to the entrance where Will called for a cab. The words that Will had said on the ward were still playing out in Carter's mind, but he slowly put them to one side and was just so pleased to be going back to the flat.

"Are we OK?" asked Will while they stood waiting at the main entrance.

"Of course we are, Will. And I appreciate it all you know? Thanks." Carter said with an added sincerity.

They smiled and quickly changed the subject. Will was relieved that Carter took it OK and he also felt better now that he had said his piece. It had to be said, by friends as well as doctors.

Carter stretched out his arms and took in the fresh summer's day air as the cab pulled up in front of them.

"Harrison?" the cabbie shouted from the window.

"You got it." replied Will, and they both jumped in.

The car pulled away and out of the hospital exit, turning right to head back down towards Holloway.

"Christ it's hot!" said Will. "So, when we get back to the flat just take it easy. Anything you want, from the shop, whatever, you just ask me OK?"

"Thanks, although I'm not sure I just want to stay indoors all day."

"Well what did you have in mind?" Will asked, expecting a serious answer.

"Pub?" said Carter with an exaggerated smile on his face. He was obviously joking, making light heartedness of Will's earlier motherly advice moment.

Will looked at him bluntly and didn't humour him at all, simply saying "That's not even funny."

CHAPTER THREE

"Hi Simon, its Carter."

"Hey, Carter . . . . Just give me one sec! OK, how are you feeling? Your flatmate told me that you sustained a curtain related injury?"

Carter froze briefly, and realised that Will had not given any real detail as to what had actually happened and avoided the awkward assumption that the accident was drink related.

"Carter?"

"Yeah, sorry . . . . Well I managed to slip and hit my head on the table. Ended up in A&E."

"Oh no, how are feeling now? I assume you are home now?"

"Yeah I got discharged yesterday afternoon. I needed stitches. But not sure I'll be ready to come back for a few days yet. Look I need to talk to you about something Simon, I had a call from my sister-in-law on Friday evening, and . . . . well . . . . my brother Marcus has been killed in a car accident."

"Oh my God Carter I am so sorry."

"It's . . . . well it just means that . . . . well I would like to take some leave. I mean, I know I am off sick now, but I'm expecting a phone call with funeral details at any moment. And I think I would like to take some time out, if that's possible, in addition to compassionate leave?"

"Look Carter. You have worked here for quite a while now, and in that time you have been nothing but hardworking and an asset to our team here. I also know that you have hours owing you as well as leave. How long were you thinking of taking?"

"Maybe two weeks."

"No problem, you got it. I tell you what, let me know the funeral date when you get the call, and you've got your two weeks. Sound OK?"

"Fine, sounds just fine."

"Cool, and Carter I am so sorry about your news. I've got to go OK. Speak to you soon."

"Ok, thanks Simon, see ya!"

Carter replaced the handset. He gently positioned his baseball cap on his head, careful not to knock into his stitches and decided to go for a walk to get some fresh air. The flat was stuffy and humid making him feel nauseous. It was a beautiful Monday morning, and the weather was in no way showing any signs of changing. It was as hot as the day before, and the whole sky cloudless. Days like these were to be made the most of, especially in the UK. Most people were at work so it made it more comfortable and easier to do things such as going to the shops, as opposed to the weekends when everything was just far too crowded. Carter never enjoyed shopping at the weekend.

He stepped out into the street and into the sun, immediately embracing the sensation of warmth and freshness in the air. He turned left, heading towards Islington. There were quite a few cool shops down on Upper Street that he liked so he headed for there, but didn't want to be out for very long as he knew that Claire or Shannon would be calling. As he walked down he noticed that there were police officers in a cordoned off area outside the tube station. There were two police vans and he caught the sight of one police officer directing a person into the back of one of them, his hands cuffed. Carter knew that the area could be quite rough at times, and he assumed that there had been some sort of mugging or fight. There were quite a few people congregating, trying to see if they could make out what had happened, but the officers were keeping them back and away from the incident. It looked as though it took place just inside the tube station, preventing the public from getting any real distinct view of anything at the scene. There were quite a few university students hanging around, as the university was opposite the station and slightly to the right. Carter carried on walking, keeping his head facing forward, not the slightest bit interested in what had happened. He would rather steer clear of anything like that and hoped that no-one was seriously injured. He believed that the public were becoming dangerously more and more desensitised to crime. It was rife and seemed as though it was always the daily newspaper headlines. Carter was disgusted with the crime rate and concerned about the future, almost giving up hope on the possibility that at some point there would be a reduction in crime. The incident now firmly behind him, he strolled further along the road, his hands pushed tightly into his pockets, his gaze fixed to the ground. He sometimes felt vulnerable when out and about on the street, even in daylight he did not feel totally safe, especially after what he had just witnessed. He remembered back to when he was mugged some years before and held at knife point.

He was on his way back from college when it happened, and was alone. He had been looking in a shoe shop when he realised that two guys were watching him. He assumed that they just thought he was a loser and looked weird, or both, so did not initially pay a huge amount of attention to them. He left the shop and started to head for home, when he looked around and noticed that the two guys were following him. His heart started to pulsate faster, but for some reason he didn't quicken his pace or run. In no time at all they had caught up with him and stopped him, first by asking for the time. He knew that they would want something, and they followed by saying,

"What have you got for us? Come on cough up."

He was in no way prepared to object, so he quickly plunged his hands into his pockets and scrambled for anything he could find. He pulled out his hands, dropping some pennies onto ground.

"Calm down you little prick and give us the money. What's in your bag?"

Their questions were relentless, giving him no chance to answer. They kept repeating the same thing over and over, crowding him so there was no other place to turn or run. One of them kept adding the odd "I'll cut ya!" here and there to scare him further.

Carter opened out his hands to show the two muggers what he had, and to both their and his disappointment, it was about thirty-eight pence made up of 2p and 1p coins. He knew that this wouldn't cut it, and neither would his college book on the greatest movies ever made, which had already been snatched out of his rucksack mid mugging.

"I'm sorry, but that is all I have." he said.

One of the muggers became more agitated and immediately pulled a knife from the inside of his jacket holding it against Carter's stomach, as the other grabbed his arm to prevent any attempt of escape.

"You better have something, because I ain't leaving you with nothing. Either I get something, or I'll give you something. Ain't you got anything?"

"No." Carter answered, aware of the panic and tremor in his voice.

Then completely overtaken by fear he started to shout for help, regardless of the consequences. It was by a pure stroke of luck and perfect timing that a van pulled up just across the street. Two men got out and ran to Carter's aid. The muggers released him immediately and were gone in a flash. Luckily he escaped unharmed.

* * * *

As he approached Upper Street he turned left toward Highbury Fields and took a gentle stroll around the area. It was away from the road and was quieter. He noticed that he was getting a headache so wanted to get away from the sounds of car horns and raised voices for some peace. There were a few people playing football in the fields, student types who were most likely between lectures. Mothers were pushing their prams around in abundance, and cyclists raced past every couple of minutes adding some more movement to the otherwise fairly serene surroundings.

Carter sat down on a wooden bench and was pretty much in line with the half way line of the football field, giving him an almost perfect view. He drew a deep breath and gently rubbed his fingers along his temples trying to alleviate some of the pain. It was slowly working. He concentrated on the players and relaxed. Some were very good in fact; skilful and fast which started to fascinate him. He sometimes enjoyed watching football and always appreciated a decent footballer when he saw one. He himself had never been the sporty type, only ever managing to play cricket for his secondary school team a couple of times. He was run out on both occasions when in bat, he did not bowl, and was a dreadful fielder. Carter was more of a strategist when it came to sport, or games in general, usually flourishing in ones that allowed him to fully utilise his brain with minimal physical coordination. Chess was one of his favourites and used to play quite a lot with his family when younger. He enjoyed playing snooker as it allowed him to use his brain to judge, plan and memorise a run of shots ahead. He could determine mathematically, as he could in darts, what he needed to score in order to win. He enjoyed the placement, pace and the cue skill required to maximise his game. Will was quite a good snooker player as well, and he and Carter went on occasion and played against each other. When Carter first moved into the flat they would join in snooker competitions in the local snooker hall, but it never really lasted. Neither was able to reproduce any kind of good form when they were either being watched or when money depended upon it. The pressure was just too much.

Carter looked up to notice the football rolling towards where he was sitting, quickly followed by a voice yelling,

"Excuse me mate! Over here!"

One of the players was waving and hoped that Carter would kick the ball back over so they could continue with their game. Carter stood up, picked up the ball and with one mighty kick he miss hit it, slicing it, making it go wayward. It travelled to the right and over the tennis court fence, landing sadly on the back of a very unfortunate and unsuspecting tennis player's head.

"Oh for fuck sake . . . . !" said Carter as he pulled his hand up and covered his mouth in shock, disbelieving his luck.

"Good shot mate, ten points for that one! You could play for England with shooting like that." shouted the football player as he jogged over to the tennis court to retrieve the ball himself.

"Was that you? Watch what you're doing?" said the tennis player.

"It wasn't me, it was him over there!" said the footballer, refraining from laughing.

Carter waved indicating that he was sorry, and fully embarrassed, he began to walk away in the opposite direction, attempting to get away from the incident as quick as possible. He could hear the voices and whistles of the other players, taunting him but also applauding him for what had happened. He didn't look up, just kept his head down and feet moving, and quickly.

As Carter reached the main road once again he noticed his headache had gone. He crossed over and headed down on to Upper Street. Even though it was a work day, the street was still very busy, and Carter did briefly contemplate whether or not to continue, when something caught his eye. It was a poster advertising a charity that was very dear to him. It was called SANE and the poster heading was The Black Dog Campaign. The charity was in place to try and improve the quality of life for individuals who suffered from mental illness. They did a variety of things to try and combat the stigma that was attached to mental conditions, some of which were things such as trying to identify the causes, researching certain medications and measure what impact the illness had upon a person. This was also aiming to achieve a change in attitude of the general public by raising awareness and providing emotional support to the people affected. They had been around since the mid eighties, but had recently become more prominent in the public eye. This was helped by the constant campaigning, some of which Carter had voluntarily been involved with on a small scale; celebrities who were sufferers were being more vocal and promoting the charity, and due to these things, amongst others, it had become more and more well known.

The poster advertised a picture of a black dog statue and stated that a number of the statues were soon to be dispersed and placed all over the city. These dogs were to have a collar of hope and wear coats that had been designed by celebrities, artists and members of the public. Carter was a member of the SANE community online where he himself had a blog set up. He had shared a story before which reflected on his own battles with depression, and how a variety of antidepressant medications had been unsuccessful in the past. He shared his opinions on certain issues which allowed him to express his feelings and try to confront his own demons, writing how he believed that the degree of depression was dependent on every person's natural individual makeup and that people had different levels of weakness. This in turn created a divide between those who could be helped and those that couldn't be. Carter's actual blog:

"I do believe that some people are just born stronger than others and their own individuality and makeup is what determines us all and our ability to live. I have no idea as to why some are stronger than others, or some more skilled than others. Me, I don't have an answer, and God I've tried to find one. To be honest I have kind of accepted that I am just naturally weaker than many others. That's the way it is. My body prevents my soul from flourishing."

Carter had found some solace in the Charity and well respected it, although he hadn't been in touch or on the website for some time. They had helped so many people and his heart went out to all of them. The team were so committed to people like Carter, and did their utmost to provide solutions, help and support. Even though medication had not been the answer to his own condition, it had helped him get through some tough times. Being able to read other stories on the website, as well as share his own with people was rewarding to him. There was a time when he would sit and read all of them, over and over again, just for the reassurance that he wasn't alone.

* * * *

The aisles of the shop were filled with a whole catalogue of different movies, a sight which was like a glistening cascade of little gems in Carter's eyes. He was standing near to the middle of one of the rows, browsing through alphabetically until his attention feasted upon a movie that he had wanted to buy for some time. He had only seen it once before but thought it was a work of genius, a movie that combined a unique balance between that of comedy and of being quite dramatic. It was sophisticated; satirical; funny but sad; cool but un-cool in a way; and was coated with all the necessary ingredients of entertainment that enabled certain movies to have that nice settle down movie feel, a movie where you could just chill out and relax with a nice bottle of wine and enjoy. And that is what Carter needed.

As he picked up the DVD he noticed that someone was close behind him peering over his shoulder. He stepped to the side and looked around but did not recognise the person. It was just another customer, a man in his late twenties looking at the range of DVDs, but was one of those people who would get too close and pester. Carter hated those people, as he thought it was not only rude and inpatient, but a blatant invasion of personal space. He noted also that with this person, as in other similar circumstances, that as soon as he had moved aside, the person would step forward into the space where he had been standing without even a thank you. Whether it was in a supermarket, or on a bus, or anywhere in fact, they just couldn't wait a moment, or just say excuse me at the very least. As he stood in line to pay for the movie, the same person, as if God intended, stood behind him. Carter looked down at the DVD the man had in his hand, and it was When Harry Met Sally. "W?" Carter thought annoyed. "But that letter was not even in the same row as me!"

* * * *

The headache started to rear its ugly head once again as Carter looked across the street at the bus stop. He wanted to get back to the flat, and as his stroll had ended up lasting a few hours, he was feeling tired and his head was sore. A bus was approaching so he had to run to catch it, which made his head throb a little. He stood by the stairwell as there were no seats available, which did not surprise him in the slightest. He removed his cap and held it down by his side as he was feeling hot. The journey was smooth and quick which was a relief, meaning he could get to some painkillers sooner rather than later. He crossed the street, carrying his cap in one hand and his DVD in the other, his shirt quite visibly wet with sweat. He started to feel sick and a bit unsteady on his feet, so he just wanted to get inside.

Upon entering the flat he knocked back three Paracetamol tablets, located Will's fan and turned it on. He pulled off his shirt and threw it through the open doorway into his bedroom, which, just like the football, missed its intended location of the bed and landed on the floor, joining a variety of other items of clothing. He started to feel a bit steadier on his feet and relatively normal again, maybe it was because it had been so hot outside and he had become dehydrated. His head was still banging at that point, and gave no signs of relenting. The voicemail indicator light was flashing on the phone, and as he found himself in the rare situation of actually awaiting a call, he quickly walked over and pressed the play button.

"You have one new message, sent today at twelve, fifty-five."

"Hey Carter, this is Shannon. I spoke to you on Friday. I am calling you as a date has been arranged for Marcus's funeral. It will be this coming Thursday morning. As one of Marcus's closest friends up here was a local priest, we were not only able to get a date arranged quickly, but he made himself available to take the Service himself, which is what Claire wanted. Claire has sent all of the details to your personal email address. She said you are more than welcome to stay with her at the house, but thought you would probably prefer a hotel. But she would like it if you come over for dinner when you get here. Claire did try calling you earlier but got no answer so I said . . . ."

The voice message time allocation cut out, stopping Shannon from finishing her sentence. He chose not to turn on his laptop and look at the details at that point, opting for a hot bath instead. He knew that he could not run from the fact that his brother was gone forever, but he could prolong the inevitable of having to deal with it full on for a few moments longer. As he tried to relax in the bath, he could feel his muscles start to lower as if sinking, becoming more flexible. With every breath he could feel the hot soothing water swarming around his skin. He placed a sponge on his head so the water could gently run out and over his wound. He closed his eyes. He was not prepared to move until the water temperature dropped to the point that it was no longer enjoyable or bearable. Even though the flat was very humid and warm, he didn't fancy a shower. He just wanted to have a bath and fester for a while. Time passed and both his mind and body were relaxed, his headache had gone and he just soaked up that rare feeling of total bliss. His mind wandered and moved from one thought to the next quite quickly, rapidly skipping between thoughts and not allowing to remain focused on anything in particular for any sufficient length of time. He kept himself amused by replaying dialogue from some of his favourite movies. There were in fact certain movies where he knew the whole script off by heart.

He eventually became aware that the bath water was no longer warm or even lukewarm. It had become quite cool. He had a thought, a moment of genius he believed. He thought he had found the newest most innovative solution to bathing. As he stepped out of the bath, he pursued this line of thought. "Maybe there should be a bath that had a built in remote control, a control that could be set up to suit everybody's exact requirements. So, for example, Will could come home and think, Oh, I know what I need, a nice hot bath. He would walk in, press a button and the bath would say. (Hi Will, welcome home. Your bath will be ready for you in exactly fifteen minutes. Would you like bubbles this evening?). And hey presto, not only would the bath be ready on time, but it would be regulated to Will's exact specifications on temperature and bubbles. Wow, this is amazing. And as everyone knows, the worse thing about being in the bath is when it starts to get cold. Well there could be another button that allows the temperature to be resumed to the correct heat, result! Entrepreneurs here I come, I should go on Dragons Den with that, could make a bundle."

As he dried himself off and walked back into the living room the excitement of his bright idea subsided somewhat as he opened up his laptop and powered it up. He put the towel to his head to dry his hair, and accidently brushed past the stitches. He felt a sudden sting and dragged the towel off his head. He touched the area carefully with his hand and found no sign of blood, so it was just the unwelcome dose of sharp pain that he sadly had to endure. He continued to dry his hair, but this time with extra caution. The laptop was up and running and the screen was on. Carter was instantly confronted by his desktop wallpaper, a photo of him standing with Marcus on his tenth birthday whilst on a beach on holiday in Cornwall. They and their father had built a giant sandcastle that day, one so big that it was as if it was visible for miles around. They had dug it deep so they could kneel down in a hole, which then positioned them behind the high walls of sand, as if they were inside a castle. As the tide came in and the waves came crashing with it, it was their job to make sure that the castle walls didn't breach. They had to constantly rebuild it with sand for as long and as quickly as possible before the next wave did any further damage. The game would last for as long as the walls remained strong and securely in place.

"That was a good day." said Carter, as he continued to click on the Internet icon to check out his email inbox. There he found the email from Claire, "Funeral details attached." typed in the subject field. He clicked on the message to open it. Message read:

> "Dear Carter
>
> First of all I am sorry that I haven't been able to speak with you more over the phone, but with everything that the girls and I are going through here I know you understand. I tried calling you earlier this morning but no answer. Thankfully Shannon has been on hand to pick up the pieces. The girls are OK and know that he is gone. I look forward to

> seeing you, just hoped it was under different circumstances.
>
> Please find attached the details you will need for Thursday. By the way you are more than welcome to stay with us here, as long as the sofa is OK. Let me know, the offer is there if you want it.
>
> Take care and stay strong.
>
> Claire x"

Carter sat back in his chair for a moment to take in the message, and partly to control his feelings. He then sent a quick reply to Claire thanking her for the details and for her offer to stay. He humbly declined, instead opting for a hotel stay where he knew he would not be in the way and could sleep in a bed. If he had stayed there he would have felt very awkward, imposing and self conscious, and wouldn't have been able to muster up the confidence to be able to pull that off for any length of time convincingly.

Carter sent the response to Claire and navigated away from his inbox to bring up a search engine. He began to look up hotels in Edinburgh, ones that were within a close radius to the location where the funeral was to be held. Most of the room prices were showing as quite expensive, and given the time of year that was not a surprise, and availability was looking difficult. Carter had some money saved and accepted that he would have to pay a bit more for a room than usual, but didn't care this time. In this case he would make an exception as not only was this a long overdue period of annual leave, more importantly the circumstances for him being there in the first place justified it, so money was not at all an issue. He browsed through the options available and finally settled on one. The Herald Hotel was quite a reasonable price in comparison to some of the others. Not only did it meet his immediate requirements of being in close proximity to the chapel, but also benefited from being in a central location, within a reasonable distance to all the shops, sights and cultural hotspots. It was pretty much in the heart of the city and not at all far from Edinburgh Castle. At a short notice deal of £28.50pp, he snapped it up and booked the room online. He chose a single room that came with an en-suite and the usual basic necessities. The picture of the hotel displayed an old stone walled front which also pleased him, and pushed him to choose this one, as he did have a fascination of old style buildings. Then he had to book the train. He went onto the East Coast Trains website and began to fill in the travel destinations. He would have to go from London Euston, stop off for an hour in Carlisle for the connecting train to Edinburgh. He booked the cheapest fare he could which happened to be the 9.10am the following Wednesday morning, and had a journey time of around five hours. He would have to collect the tickets from the ticket office at Euston Station before departure. He returned to his email inbox and retrieved his confirmations from both, and was happy and relieved that he had sorted out his transport and accommodation. He printed off the reference numbers and confirmation details for both and powered down the laptop.

"Hey man, what's up? How are you feeling today?" Will said as he walked into the flat.

"Hey . . . . Well I had a bad headache earlier, which thankfully has worn off now. I think it started when I was put on the spot by Simon when asked about my curtain related incident! What the hell was that all about?"

"Oh I know, I forgot to tell you. Sorry. I didn't want him to get the wrong impression and assume that you had fallen over when drunk, so thought the curtain one would cut it."

Carter began to laugh, "Yeah thanks for looking out for me on that one, and I did manage to avoid going into it in any real detail. He has agreed for me to have two weeks off commencing from the funeral date . . . . which I now know, it's this coming Thursday, so I'd better call Simon and tell him. I have booked the train and the hotel so all sweet on that front. Claire has emailed me the details so all set, so just packing to do!"

"That's quick! OK, about me not coming along. I mean I know we haven't talked about it, but I mean I only met Marcus a few times, and really the main reason I would be going is to support you. It's just work at the moment is . . . ."

"It's OK. I thought that was the case. I appreciate it and I'll call you and let you know how everything went. I'll be fine."

Will smiled and continued to ask Carter about what he had planned for the two weeks following the funeral. Carter was going to try and visit as many of the local attractions as possible and maybe hire a car to have a drive out and see the Highlands. He was not exactly sure but was going to take each day as it came. Even though he had been up there before he had never made time to actually go and see the sights. He grabbed his mobile and called his boss to give him the details, and Simon granted leave from that point. Carter thanked him and they agreed on a return to work date.

* * * *

The plan for that evening was to go and pick up some Chinese food from across the street, just chill out and put on his newly purchased DVD and mellow in the flat. Will was definitely up for watching the movie, as he hadn't seen it before but had read reviews. Also, he would always trust Carter's judgement of whether a movie was worthy or not.

Will walked back into the flat holding a bag full of Chinese. The aromas floated around the room, like a homing beacon for Chinese cuisine enthusiasts. Carter was most definitely one of them. His favourite dish was beef chow-mein with no bean-shoots and a curry sauce, a pancake roll on the side. Will usually went for a simple dish such as chicken curry and egg fried rice. Having smelt the food wafting through the flat Carter came in from his bedroom, and immediately headed for the bag. He was quite hungry as he had hardly eaten all day. Maybe due to him recovering after his accident he had lost his appetite. But that appetite was definitely back in time for the Chinese food. Will pulled two plates from the cupboard and placed them down on the kitchen top, then two forks and two spoons from the drawer while Carter opened the containers and scooped the contents onto the plates.

"Fancy a beer?" Carter asked.

"Go on then I'll have one with dinner. And so will you!"

"I know. I'll only have one, or maybe two. After all I am now officially on leave."

The pair tucked into their Chinese while the movie started to play. The food was amazing, as it always was.

They had been using that particular Chinese restaurant for a long time, as the food had always been faultless. The owner would throw a few prawn crackers in as well and the odd portion of chips for them every now and then as they were loyal customers and had come to know them quite well over the last few years.

* * * *

Tuesday morning and Carter was up early. He set himself down in front of the TV with his breakfast which consisted of toast and a black coffee, which he had while watching the morning news. Will had already left much earlier for work. The news was as morbid as usual, surprising Carter not in the least. As he watched, and without paying any reasonable amount of attention to it, he started to plan his day. He would have to pop to the chemist and get some bits and pieces, toothpaste, shower gel, shampoo, travel tissues etc. He would have to pack that afternoon as well, so thought that maybe it was time for sorting through his clothes and whether he had enough stuff that was clean to take with him. He doubted it.

Carter finished his breakfast and put the empty dishes in the sink and walked into his bedroom. He gathered his clothes from the floor and heaped them all into a pile on his bed. There was probably enough for a couple of washes in the washing machine.

"That is poor. I really need to start taking my washing more seriously" he said with a mixed expression of shock and a cheeky grin on his face.

He knew that it wouldn't be likely that household chores were going to become the priority of his life. He set the first wash in motion and returned to his room. As he looked in his wardrobe he scaled it from left to right, examining each shirt, both short sleeved and long, each jumper, deciding which selection he was going to take with him. On the far right of the rack he came across his one and only black suit. It was still covered with the protective sleeve from the drycleaners, which would have been the last time that he had worn it. That was the day of his father's funeral. He gently removed it from the wardrobe and placed it down on to the bed. He sat down next to it, and rested his hand down upon the sleeve feeling the fabric. He started to become emotional and quickly distracted himself by standing up and going to the bathroom, trying to concentrate on which items to pack rather that let the depression take hold. It was too late. As he walked into the bathroom he fell to the floor and onto his knees, and cried and cried. He felt a flood of dark emotions pass around his body; he could not control himself. His vision became blurred and he felt numb as he started to suffer a panic attack. He let himself fall back so he was sitting on the floor with his back leaning against the closed bathroom door. He covered his face with his hands and just sat there shaking with nerves and sweating profusely. Two hours passed and the bathroom door opened.

Carter walked in, his nerves now in check, and carried with him a razor, some shaving foam, a hair brush and some deodorant. He also had his bottle of Cipralex which was still half full. Even though Cipralex would not relieve his depression on its own, when he mixed it with alcohol it would have an effect that would take the edge off and calm him slightly. Even though he knew this concoction could be potentially dangerous to his health, it was all he had. He used this only when he got desperately low; when he was sick to the stomach with depression; when he felt that he could just burst into tears for no apparent reason; and on rare occasions in the past where he had self-harmed. He walked back into his bedroom and over to the wardrobe. He stood up on to his tip-toes and stretched upwards, reached on top and to the back of the wardrobe and pulled down an old dusty suitcase. He got a mouthful of dust as it dropped down, which forced him to quickly run to the kitchen and wash his mouth out. He started to gather clothes and some personal items and cluster them together on the bed, separating them into individual groups. This would make it easier for him to pack later that afternoon as he could judge exactly how much stuff he had, and how much he needed to take.

He took the first wash out of the machine and sorted through it, putting things that he actually wanted to take with him into the airing cupboard next to the boiler. This would ensure that they were dry enough to be packed last minute before he needed to leave the following morning. The other stuff he hung over an unsteady, half broken clothes horse which had been propped up by a cook book so it could still just about hold clothes without unbalancing and falling over. He turned and grabbed the rest of the dirty washing and threw it into the washing machine and set another cycle going. He then had time to pop out and get the remaining necessities for his trip, so he grabbed his cap and keys. He locked the flat door and started walking downstairs to the street when he heard someone call his name. He stopped and looked back up the stairs behind him. He could see no-one. He walked back up to the top of the steps and looked down the corridor.

"Hello?" he shouted. There was no answer, so he decided to turn and get on with his day when he heard his neighbour, Rufus Watson, shout,

"Hey Carter can I have a quick word?"

"Yes sure, hey Rufus. I could have sworn I heard a woman's voice calling my name?"

"Very funny!"

"You OK Rufus, how are things?"

"Look Carter, I feel a bit awkward bringing this up but the music the other night, man that was loud. I mean I don't mind, I like a good party, but my son was trying to sleep."

"I know and I am sorry. It was totally my fault and inappropriate. I had some bad news and I had more than a few to many. It won't happen again."

"Bad news, is everything OK now?"

"It's fine. Look I gotta run. I'll see ya Rufus, and sorry again." Carter did not really want to discuss the bad news in detail, so he graciously turned, waved goodbye and quickly descended the stairs.

* * * *

As Will made his way home from work he called Carter's mobile to ask if he would like him to get anything on his way back. Carter said no as he had already packed everything that he needed earlier. Carter had also attempted some writing earlier that afternoon and had planned to add some more dialogue to his screenplay, but that had somehow ended up with him playing the PS3 instead. Carter had been writing the screenplay on and off for what seemed like a lifetime, and had never really dedicated any regular amount of time on it to get into a rhythm. It was based on the story of a man who lived at home with his sick mother and who cared for her on a full time basis. He had to deal with her ever fading health and deterioration, and she had always refused to go into a care home. Dementia had set in during her later years and the man had to make a choice. Now that his own mother no longer recognised him as her son, was he to go against her will and put her into a care home so he could have some kind of existence himself, or would he carry on and struggle at home until the end. He chose the latter and stayed at home, the days becoming harder and harder, his patience and his own sanity brought into question. It then became unbearable and he ended up contemplating whether or not he should end her life and her pain himself.

Carter had so many ideas in his head for his screenplay, but could never decide upon any kind of outcome. Therefore he would leave it a couple of weeks and go back to it, then weeks would become months, and so on. There were a few screenplays that he had in motion, more scraps though than anything definitive.

Will said "Well now your packing is done, do you fancy meeting me for a couple in the pub? I'll be there in about twenty minutes. Just on the bus now. Have a couple tonight, as I'm not going to see you for a couple of weeks!"

"Yeah sure, I'll see you in there." replied Carter.

* * * *

"So what are you going to do without me then Will? Let me guess! Have a lot of the fairer sex stay over as company no doubt?"

"Well you know how it is. I can't sit in the flat on my own for too long, get too bored and restless."

Will raised his glass and Carter responded by raising his.

"Good luck mate. Hope everything goes well, you know what I mean, as well as these things can. To Marcus."

"To Marcus." Carter replied as they clinked their glasses and took a swig of their drinks.

Carter had a moment of anxiety as the reality and extent of the situation was to become so much more real in the coming days. The two stayed there for another few drinks, and mainly spoke about Will's job and how he knew that he would soon have to work a string of weekends, which he was not particularly happy about.

The bar was quiet that evening and that made it much more pleasant and fitting for them both. It wasn't that hot either, as the temperature had noticeably dropped during the day. There was a nice breeze that drifted into the bar on occasion, making it more relaxing. They sat at a table toward the back of the bar and next to the jukebox, although neither of them were interested in playing DJ that evening. Will had to be at work for 7am the following morning so they decided to call it a night at about 9pm, as Carter himself also had to be up early to catch his train. They strolled back to the flat, stopping off for a bag of chips on the way in.

"We need to start cooking food at the flat, and no, pizzas don't count!" said Will as they walked in.

"OK deal. As soon as I am back you can welcome me home with a nice Beef Wellington, with potato fondant and asparagus, served with a nice red wine reduction."

"Hmm." responded Will.

Carter laughed at Will's lacklustre response but did at the same time agree that they should change their diet, not only to eat more healthily but from a financial perspective as well. They had spoken of this a few times before but it had never come to fruition. It wasn't much longer and Will went to bed, but not before once again wishing Carter all the best and to keep in touch. Carter stayed up for one last check of his travel itinerary and made sure that he had packed everything. He had already put his confirmation details in the inside pocket of his coat and he would pack the shirts from the airing cupboard just before he left. Confident he had thought of everything he locked the front door, turned off the lights and went to bed. He lay awake for a while and thought about the days ahead. He thought of Starlet and Eve and how they would now live the rest of their lives without their father. He started to become concerned as to how the loss would affect them. He prayed that they would be OK. He thought of Marcus and how different it could have been if he didn't leave work early on that day. "Was it fate, was it just his time?" Carter thought. Either way, he had been taken from the world too soon. He had been snatched from a family who depended on him, who loved him, who would now, in almost a blink of an eye, never have the chance speak to him again.

CHAPTER FOUR

The underground platform of Holloway Road station was extremely crowded, with people cylindered together like upright sardines. The only sign of relief was the distant sound of a train rattling at high speed through the tube tunnel towards them.

"Stand behind the yellow line!" said the voice from the tannoy speaker.

The commuters were hustled together so tightly that no-one was even able to see the yellow safety line, let alone stand behind it. As the train raced into the platform and pulled to a halt, a sudden surge occurred and people nudged and edged forward, each of them hustling for a better position to enhance their chances of boarding even though the doors to the train had not yet opened. Carter was amongst this madness, but knew he would not make that particular train as he was towards the back of the queue. The train was already crowded, which indicated that probably only a few from the platform masses would be successful in finding an inch of space. It seemed that as quickly as the doors opened they rammed shut again, only allowing time for a quick shift in position from those off and those on, one of the latter being a poor tall middle aged man whose head happened to get caught between the doors upon closing, prompting a loud outburst of the word "Bollocks!" back into the direction of the platform. The train slowly pulled away with the faces of those just boarded pushed up against the window sharing the same angry expression. It was that mixed expression of hatred with an added edge of psychosis, which happened to be quite common in the faces of London commuters. Two more trains came and went before Carter was able to get on, his rucksack was heavy and he had no chance to manoeuvre and no space in which to remove it, giving no relief to his shoulders. He was holding his suit, and made every attempt for it not to be squashed between fellow passengers. The train plunged into the tunnel and headed for the next stop, he was hot and sweating as were most of the other passengers, but he could find solace in that he knew he only had to endure this for two more stops.

The train eased into King's Cross St Pancras and Carter disembarked. People buzzed around in all directions with exuberance, quickly moving from here to there. He headed for the way out as he had to walk a short distance up to Euston Station to catch his next train. He noticed the clock above the destination timetable; it was 8.22am. He had time. He approached the exit, and placed one of his hands between his left shoulder and the strap of the rucksack, creating a cushion and softening his discomfort. The day was slightly bleak compared to the days before and was very humid and oppressive. He walked along Euston Road constantly navigating his way around oncoming city folk. Most of them were using their mobile phones and not paying any real attention to where they were walking, totally oblivious to other people or obstacles in their path. The odd person here and there would bounce off of a lamppost or trip over an uneven paving stone, or suddenly realise that they were walking in the wrong direction therefore having to double back. This provided some morning entertainment for Carter as he strolled along.

The traffic on the main road was very busy with buses and taxis being the most common sight. He knew a short cut and chose to take it to get away from the main road madness. He turned right down one street, diagonally crossing over and turning left down the next. Euston Station was then in his sights so he gained pace, not because he was worried about the time, but he just wanted to be there. As he walked in through the main entrance he looked up at the departure screen and noticed that his train was displayed there, London Euston—Carlisle: 9.10—Platform 6. He headed straight to the ticket office and provided them with his booking reference details, after which his ticket was given to him. He was all set to go. He found it hard to believe that there was no queue at the ticket office, as in rush hour he assumed it would have been quite manic. He was quite impressed that his journey so far had been hazard free, but did not at any moment believe he would have the same luck for the rest of his journey. As he hadn't had time for breakfast he decided to quickly grab something before he boarded the train. He knew that there would be a buffet car on board but he couldn't wait, and was paranoid that his seat would be miles away from the buffet car anyway, so he didn't want to chance it. The nearest place he could see was a little coffee stand situated conveniently over by some cash machines. He headed over, again having to zigzag through the barrage of people. He drew some cash from the machine, enough to cover him for the next few days at least.

"Yes Sir, what can I get for you?" said the coffee making attendant, a pleasant man of around fifty.

"Could I have a small black Americano and a cinnamon swirl please?" replied Carter as he took some change out from his back pocket.

"That's £2.85 please, sir."

"There you go thanks!"

Carter only had to wait a few seconds before the man handed him his coffee and bun. He still had fifteen minutes before the train was due to leave, so he paid a visit to a bookshop to pass a few minutes.

Upon boarding the train he noticed that it was in fact quite nice compared to some other over-ground trains he had been on in the past, and the seats looked quite comfortable. There were now power points available for travellers to use laptops, or to charge their phones etc. As he walked down the aisle to locate his allocated seat number, he saw a man toward the back of the carriage who was placing his bag on the luggage rack. The man was huge and did not look like the sort of character who you would want to be on the wrong side of. He wore a white basketball vest, a pair of blue shorts and an angry face. It was an expression that looked as if he was about to unleash some anger and inflict pain on someone, or eat them. The man flopped down into a seat, and Carter was at that point only a few steps away from him. Approaching the end of the carriage he could see numbers 15d, 15c, and 15b, and then there was his seat number, 15a, and was right next to the big angry faced man who occupied 15b. He double checked his ticket and hesitated awkwardly, trying not to give off any sign to the man that his seat was next to his. The man had the aisle seat, leaving 15a in between him and the window. His right leg was already covering a quarter of seat 15a as it was.

"Is this your seat?" said the man in a deep unwelcoming voice.

"Err no, I think I am actually in the wrong carriage." replied Carter unconvincingly.

"What carriage are you looking for?"

"Err . . . ."

"It will say it on your ticket. Here show me I'll have a look." The man reached forward so he could see Carter's ticket details.

"No its OK thank you, I'll be fine." Carter replied quickly but was too late.

"This is the right carriage pal! And seat 15a is right here, next to me!"

"Really, I thought I . . . ."

"Wait a minute! Is it because I'm sitting here? What's wrong? Don't you want to sit next to me? Is that it?"

"No, sorry I didn't realise that . . . . So it is my seat, OK thanks."

The man stepped out and allowed Carter to squeeze into his seat and after putting his suit and his bag on the rack above he sat down. Then came the moment that Carter dreaded, the moment when the man turned to sit back down into his seat. It was as bad as Carter knew it would be. The man's body immediately pushed up against him. It was invading his space. There was an instant feeling of sweaty warmth rubbing up on that side of him, and with that unsociable odour that accompanied it. Maybe the man was exaggerating slightly by purposely making Carter feel even more uncomfortable as he realised that he did not want to sit next to him. The smell of sweat and the body heat this man was giving off did absolutely no favours to Carter's appetite, and the cinnamon swirl stayed securely away in its packet. He started to predict where it was most likely that this man was going to get off, hoping it would be soon. The man's accent was not a Scottish accent, neither was it a northern accent, it was not clear at all where this particular accent was from, so Carter could not guess as to where he was headed. The train began to pull away from the station and Carter started to plan a strategy on how to get away from the annoying lummox. He had to bide his time for a while as otherwise it would be far too obvious. What could he do to get away from the guy, a toilet break? He could make that last twenty minutes, or a trip to the buffet car. Another twenty minutes? That wasn't going to be good enough and he needed to get away from him for good. Maybe he would've departed by the time Carter decided to make a move, but maybe not.

Fifteen minutes into the journey and Carter noticed that he had gone to sleep. This was the last thing he wanted to encounter, other than if the man had started trying to spark up a conversation with him. That would have been far more horrendous. The man was encased in sweat, some of which had seeped into Carter's clothes where the two were pushed up at the side of each other. He was also snoring loudly and dribble was noticeably running down his chin. Carter began to feel sick with hunger, and needed to eat something. He had to get out. Maybe, if he managed to get out without waking the man up, then when the man actually did wake up he would just assume that Carter had got off at an earlier stop. That was plan A, to try and get out without waking the man. "How was that possible?" he thought. The two of them were touching and any movement from Carter could wake the man up. He paused and started to build up some much needed courage, as this experience was now fast becoming unbearable. Other passengers were looking at them making him feel even more uncomfortable and embarrassed. Enough was enough he thought so he stood up, looked behind him and checked if there was an empty seat for an escape, but to his disappointment the seats behind were taken by an elderly couple. There was no way out that way. He could not ask them to move. Also, there was no way that he could climb over to the one in front as it just wasn't the right angle to do so. He sat back down and briefly laughed at his predicament, as if in defeat, but then the train slowed and stopped at a station. Maybe this was this guy's stop Carter thought, and was sleeping through it. This was Carter's chance, to wake the man just in case that it was his stop, thus creating an opportunity for him to make his move. Carter started to tap the man again and again but to no avail. He started to say "Excuse me!", but the man did not stir.

"Hey!" shouted Carter as a last ditch attempt.

"What?" said the man, startled from his deep festering slumber.

"Wasn't sure if this was your stop, just thought I would check with you so you didn't miss it."

"Oh, no not mine. I'm all the way to Carlisle!"

The doors closed along with the man's eyes as he planned to return to sleep. Carter had to strike now.

"Excuse me I need to use the toilet. Can I get past?"

The man stood up, reluctantly, and allowed Carter just enough space to squeeze out. He walked through to the next carriage and stopped by the doorway, took a deep breath and composed himself. He looked down at the left side of his shirt and it was soaked with sweat, so he went to the toilet and leant up against the hand dryer, enabling the hot air to effectively dry out his shirt.

"I can't believe this is f . . . happening . . . . to . . . . me. Stay calm Carter. Let's just stay calm." he said to himself while standing waiting for his sleeve to dry.

He was so relieved to be free from the man. His next task was to find an empty seat in another carriage where he could relocate and relax. It didn't take long before he found one. Actually there were quite a few empty seats scattered here and there. Above each row of seats there was a little screen that displayed details of upcoming stations and when each seat was going to be unavailable from. The seat Carter found was going to be available until York, so he knew he had a bit of time. He decided to leave it a few minutes to give enough time for the man to go back to sleep, so he could then sneak back and get his bag and suit, hopefully undetected. Carter took his long overdue swirl from its bag and took a bite, and instantly felt revitalised and a touch more human once the little sugar rush crept in. Each bite was better than the last, and the train had now reached the countryside. The windows were displaying the continuous landscape of the beautiful English countryside. Little cottages lined with old stone walls, quaint windmills and farmhouses cast vigour and character across the land.

He walked back into his original carriage to retrieve his bag and suit and upon entering could see his nemesis shifting around in his seat, so was obviously awake. This was going to be tricky. How could he get his belongings without the man seeing him? It seemed impossible. A distraction was needed, but nothing came to mind. He slowly walked up behind the man and reached up to the rack above, trying to remain as quiet and discreet as possible, making every effort not to be seen. He managed to get to the strap and pull his bag off, the sound of the train providing camouflage for the shuffling movement. However, the suit proved to be a touch more difficult. As he moved in closer, the man turned and saw him. This was followed by a very awkward moment for them both. The man stared at him in disgust, as he knew Carter was trying to make an escape. Then plan B came into Carter's mind. Plan B was to pretend to get off the train. Carter having realised the next stop was only a minute away, as coolly as anything just said "I'm getting off at the next stop."

The man nodded but only half believed him, and Carter knew that he would not be convinced until he had seen Carter actually get off the train. He walked and stood by the door, and could not believe how he managed to always get caught up in the most the ludicrous situations.

"This is another experience to add to the Carter Jakeman shit list." he thought.

The sliding doors opened and Carter smiled at the man as he stepped off the train. He walked along the platform with them both maintaining eye contact throughout, and when he was fully out of sight he ran to the next carriage and got back on.

Carter found an empty seat and plonked himself down.

"Oh shit, maybe that guy had seen that my destination was Carlisle when checking out my ticket earlier?" Carter thought as he tried to eliminate all remaining possibilities that he may still have known that he was on the same train.

"Going to have to be quite stealth like when I get off at Carlisle as well. Oh well I'll just say I have a twin."

He sat back and stretched out in his seat, tilting his head to the side so he could look out of the window. Rolling hills of green countryside layered the land outside. The sun had burst through spraying shimmering rays of colour down, fracturing the landscape with shards of golden luminosity. He became transfixed by its beauty and his eyes started to become very heavy. He was only too happy to get some sleep before he had to move seats again at York.

* * * *

The minutes passed by as Carter fell deeper and deeper into a heavy sleep. He dreamt of when he was young, when the family would take similar train journeys every couple of years. They had devised a family travel game that became a kind of family tradition, where they could play together when on their travels. It was called I saw it first. The game revolved around a list of sights that you would possibly see while on your train journey. Each sight would have a score, higher or lower depending on the likeliness of a sight being seen, meaning that whichever player managed to see the sight first would get that corresponding score. For example a lighthouse could be on the list and could be worth ten points, a red convertible car could be fifteen points, and a castle could be twenty points and so on. The player with the highest amount of points at the end of the journey was the winner.

* * * *

"Ladies and gentleman we will shortly be arriving at York station. Please ensure that you have all of your belongings with you before departing the train."

Carter prepared himself to move seats as this was where his particular seat had been reserved from. People boarded the train and each one quickly looked for their allocated seats, but none came to claim the seat where Carter was. The doors closed and the train was once again on the move. Carter could not believe his luck, and assumed that the person was either too late or had cancelled for some reason. He now had a nice comfortable seat for the remainder of the journey. Maybe his luck was changing for the better, he thought. He relaxed back down into his chair and took out his mobile phone. He spent some time playing on some of the games he had stored on there to pass the time. One was a movie quiz, which he would usually play for hours on end, and always achieved the highest score. He would usually occupy himself by playing his games during his lunch breaks in work. Rarely would he go out for lunch with anyone from work, and even if he did the conversation would be lacking after a short while. He could never relax with his work colleagues and always felt uncomfortable as if he was expected to strike up conversation with people he barely knew. Again this was the lack of confidence that Carter had been battling with for most of his life. In truth he did not despise people at all, but was in fact in many ways envious of them. People that were able to just fluently speak with confidence, naturally bond in conversation with a stranger, or faultlessly establish a connection with someone and conduct themselves accordingly, impressed him. Carter could never understand why it was that as soon as he was in a position where he had to project himself he would freeze up, his heart would beat faster and his voice would flutter with nerves.

He would become sick to the stomach, he could not think properly which would result in him pausing mid sentence to catch a breath. He did know that a major contribution to this was his own lack of confidence in the way he looked. He had never felt comfortable with his appearance, but also could not understand however how his body of emotions would just turn on and off like they did. One day it would be bearable, and another day the floodgates would open and he would not cope at all, being left deflated and in an embarrassing mess. This would then have the usual snowball effect which led to him feeling depressed and hurt, which then led to heavy drinking to try and block out and hide from his demons, which then led to angry outbursts of sadness and taking pills, which then could lead to other dangerous incidents, such as slipping and bouncing your head off of a coffee table and ending up in A&E for example!

Carlisle station approached to Carter's delight, as he looked forward to getting off and having a stretch and some fresh air. It wasn't long before he had to get his connecting train so had some time to have a wander and buy a newspaper or something for the onward journey. As he prepared to step from the train he remembered the man from earlier, so he hesitated and decided to hang back for a moment, allowing other passengers to get off first. He peeked around the door and looked up the platform but there was no sign of him. He waited a few more seconds for the platform to clear, and stepped down. He was virtually in line with a little station shop that sold teas, coffees, travel sweets and those sorts of things, so he made his way over to there. He remained conscious that he could be spotted at any moment if the man was still there somewhere. The little shop was not that busy with people so he chose to hang in there for a few minutes and check out some of the books they had on offer. He picked up a small travel crossword book and a packet of sweets and paid. He began to smell chips coming from somewhere outside, further down the platform, which played havoc with his appetite. There was no way that he could not go and get some. He was drawn to the smell like a bee to honey, the smell of those delicious chips coated in salt and vinegar was only a stone's throw away. His rumbling stomach would only have to wait a matter of minutes before it was treated to the magnificence of those chips. He reached the doorway, where people were already congregated. The door opened and there he was! The lummox was standing at the counter waiting for his order. Carter retreated back and walked up the platform. As he had not been seen at this point he thought he'd wait for the man to come out and then he could sneak in and get some for himself. To bide some time he walked upstairs onto the causeway to find the departure screen. His next train would be leaving from the same platform that he came in on and was due in exactly ten minutes. He looked through the window and could see the doorway into the little chip shop and saw the man outside wandering away up the platform. Carter quickly descended the steps to return to the shop, gathering pace the closer he got to the doorway. He stepped in and approached the counter to order.

"Could I have a bag of chips please?" said Carter to the young lady at the counter.

"How long for the chips, Perry?" shouted the lady towards an enclosed area at the back of the shop where the kitchen was.

"About ten minutes, we run out so just got more on now." said a voice from somewhere out the back and out of view, and who also unhelpfully sounded as unenthusiastic as humanly possible.

"About ten minutes!" confirmed the lady to Carter, as if he hadn't just heard the droning voice shout out from the back.

"My train is due in here in ten minutes. I'll wait. It will only be ten minutes though won't it?"

"Well yes he just said ten minutes." said the girl while annoyingly chewing gum.

"OK, cool I'll wait."

Carter took out his phone to check for messages. There was one from Will asking him if he had meant to leave his black shoes behind.

"Shit" said Carter, realising he had forgotten them.

He texted Will back and thanked him. Once he had checked into his hotel he would have to go out and find a shoe shop straight away. He set a reminder on his mobile to go off again later in the afternoon. The minutes seemed as though they were passing very slowly, the wait for chips had never before seemed so gruelling and tedious. Catching his eye to the left was the train pulling into the platform.

"OK excuse me, that's my train. Are the chips ready yet?"

"Perry?" shouted the lady, but with no real urgency. "Perry?" slightly louder.

"Yeah?" replied the out of view mystery that was Perry.

"Are the chips ready yet?"

"Yeah." confirmed Perry.

"Yeah they are ready?" confirmed the lady to Carter.

"Well? Are they ready for consumption yet?" Carter said sarcastically.

"Sorry?" said the lady not really understanding what the word consumption actually meant.

"If they are ready, can I have a bag then please? That is my train and I need to get on it!"

Carter began to panic and feared that the train was going to close its doors and leave at any moment. He knew that he should forgo the chips and get on the train.

"Perry?" said the lady in an equally droning voice with still no sense of urgency.

"Oh fuck off Perry, you couldn't cook a bloody omelette if you had a week!" shouted a frustrated Carter as he gave up and turned to leave the shop. He pushed through the door in utter frustration and ran and leapt onto the train.

"Phew, that was close." he said to a gentleman standing opposite.

"Not really Sir, it isn't leaving for another ten minutes!"

"Great!"

Carter turned and faced the shop. He returned and approached the counter quite sheepishly, and calmly said "Could I have my bag of chips please?" The lady was obviously used to the odd obscenity thrown here and there and after giving Carter a quick look of disgust went to prepare his order. She returned with a nice big bag of steaming chips which he duly covered with salt, vinegar and ketchup.

"And err . . . . tell Perry I'm sorry will ya?"

Carter returned to the train to search for his allocated seat. He put his rucksack and his suit on the luggage rack by the sliding doors, kept a hold of his bag which contained the crossword and sweets, and with his bag of chips he walked further up the carriage to his seat, which happened to be a table seat. He placed his bag of chips on the table and sat down, looked up and could not believe his eyes. It was the same man he had been avoiding earlier, the lummox, who was now sitting in the seat diagonally opposite and facing him. As he could no longer be bothered to think up another excuse to escape and was also now thoroughly pissed off, he simply said, "Oh shit!"

*   *   *   *

A line of taxis were parked outside Edinburgh Waverley railway station, and was the first thing that Carter saw when exiting. He joined the back of the queue and placed his rucksack down on the floor between his feet. The plan was to get to the hotel and have a much needed shower, then on to Princes Street which was the premier shopping street in the city where he would find a pair of black shoes for the funeral. As the queue quickly decreased Carter took a look around him and noticed just how interesting the surroundings actually were. The station was located in a narrow and steep valley, and located between the new town and the medieval old town. The valley itself was bridged by the three-span iron and steel 1897 North Bridge which passed alongside the station's eastern section. Carter loved fabulous pieces of engineering and was amazed by its grandeur and historic prowess. Carter knew bits and pieces of the city's history, partly due to his college studies of the paranormal when he had once written an essay on haunted cities of the UK. He loved researching and studying the paranormal, as it had not been proven either for or against and was still very much a mystery, a mystery with the possibility of discovery. The battle between the sciences and the unknown was truly captivating for Carter and always had been. On occasions he would attend ghost nights and ghost tours in London, where he could meet other enthusiasts and believers and share stories. He originally wanted to go on and study Parapsychology at a higher level of education after college, but the only University that offered it as a course in its own right was based in Coventry, and it was just not possible for him to commit to that on a full time basis at that time in his life. Living with and caring for Max was crucial and did not want to leave him on his own. He also knew that the valley was originally filled with a freshwater loch that had been drained in the early part of the nineteenth century. It was called the Nor Loch.

Carter was next in line for a taxi and it pulled forward in front of him.

"Where to?" asked the driver, in a broad Scottish accent.

"The Herald Hotel please."

*   *   *   *

The hotel room was spacious and was decorated in a style that appealed to Carter. Fine panelling and latticed windows with curved timbers supporting the ceiling were among some of the features that drew his attention. The windows afforded a unique view of the cobbled street outside. The accommodation as a whole was a step back in time and was exactly what Carter was hoping for, oozing tradition and charm, meeting the requirements of the discerning modern guest. The lounge bar downstairs boasted a large open log fireplace and had caught his eye upon arrival, and a large a vast beam that spanned the whole width and was supported on stone piers. Carter was pleasantly surprised to have got this room at such a decent price, probably due in some part to him booking it at such short notice. He walked around the room and checked out the other amenities. There was an en-suite shower, tea and coffee making facilities, a fair sized TV, a safe and a telephone. He hung his suit in the wardrobe and started to empty his clothes and toiletries from his rucksack onto the bed. He took enough casual clothes to last him for a few days but planned to buy some more in the city to last him for the rest of the week. He packed away his clothes tidily, which was very out of character for Carter, but in a way he did not want to spoil the look of the room. He felt that he would be disrespecting its splendour if he left it in his own usual messy style. He looked in the mirror and turned his head slightly to check out his wound; it looked surprisingly better and seemed to be healing nicely.

Princes Street was only ten minutes from the hotel so he decided to walk, and as he had been sitting down all day he welcomed some exercise. It was quite windy but still very warm and he was hopeful that the sun would shine the following day for the funeral. He was always brought up with the belief that if the sun was shining on the day of a funeral then it meant the deceased was happy and at peace. He pulled his mobile from his pocket, scanned the contacts list for Claire, and pressed the button to call her.

"Hello?" answered a quiet, fragile sounding voice.

"Hey Claire its Carter, I'm here. I got here about an hour ago. How are you?"

"Hi Carter, yes not too bad thanks. Just getting things prepared here, girls are OK."

"OK, is there anything I can do to help out?"

"No its fine thanks. What you can do is come round and see the girls if you like?"

"Yes sure, I'd love too. I'm just on my way to Princes Street to get some bits and pieces and once I'm done I'll be there."

"OK, thank you Carter we are all looking forward to seeing you, especially Eve!"

"Same here, she does look very beautiful from the pictures that Marcus . . . . sent me before." said Carter, pausing awkwardly mid-sentence at the mention of his brother's name.

"I know . . . . she is." replied Claire, too pausing and her voice trembling.

"I'll see you in a bit."

Carter felt slightly upset with himself that he had dropped Marcus's name into the conversation the way he had, in the past tense, but was sure that Claire would understand. He continued along the high street which was busy with tourists, tourists who were mainly in big groups and who had travelled to the city maybe only for a day trip, attempting to squeeze in as many of the city's attractions as possible before being coached off somewhere else. Princes Street stretched for about a mile so there were plenty of options available for him to buy a smart pair of shoes. Many UK high street brands were situated along the street and it wasn't long before he was in one of them. He found the shoe section and browsed the selection. His eyes feasted upon one pair in particular which cost fifty-five pounds. They were a pair of linea stitch black leather shoes with laces. Carter asked for assistance to try one on in his size and they fitted perfectly. They were very smart and very simple which he thought was exactly appropriate for the following day.

He arrived back at the hotel to have a quick shower and drop off his shoes before going to visit Claire and the girls. As he sat on the bed draped in his towel, he had a quick look at one of the hotel and city guides that was on the dresser, and found a small section on the history of Princes Street. He would have a quick read before going to Claire's, as he hoped that it would distract him from the sudden urge of nerves that had struck him in the past few minutes. He knew that seeing Claire and the children, combined with his naturally delicate emotional position, this was inevitable. As he read through the paragraph his mind started to fixate a bit more on the content of the brochure rather than the worry of his visit. The section that he was reading was mainly about the south side of Princes Street, the gardens in fact, and the floral clock and the war memorial that were there. He also discovered a bit more about the street upon reading the next page, which stated that it was maybe one of the few streets in Britain to have an order of Parliament placed upon it. This was done to prevent any further development for building on the south side which would preserve its open vista. Carter closed the guide and placed it on his bedside table, stood up and started to get ready to leave. His hands were shaking with nerves as he dressed and his breathing became increasingly irregular and shaky, but was in no means uncontrollable. He walked down to the front reception desk and ordered a taxi, before going out to the street to await its arrival. He realised at that point that he hadn't got anything for Claire or the girls. No flowers, no gifts, no nothing. "Was this a time for flowers and gifts?" he thought. "Should I get the taxi to stop off somewhere so I can quickly buy something? No I'll get something after the funeral, something before I leave."

* * * *

The taxi pulled into the driveway and up to the house, the house as of only a week ago was a happy family home. Carter wiped his forehead with a tissue, wiping away some sweat as his nerves were now in full swing. He heard the sound of the taxi wheels spin on the pebble stones of the drive and back out on to the main road behind him. He stood at the door, motionless, finding it difficult to knock. His arms suddenly became heavy and rigid, his hands were still shaking and even though it was warm out he felt chilled to the bones. He turned around and faced away from the house but knew there was no way he could just walk away from this moment. He lifted his arm and tapped on the door. He heard the faint patter of feet on the wooden floored hallway inside and realised that it would be either Starlet or Eve who would open it. It was in fact Eve, the youngest girl who Carter had only ever seen via pictures. She looked up at him and had the sweetest little face; Carter immediately welled up with sadness.

"Are you Uncle Carter?" she asked in the softest voice.

"Yes I am. And you must be Eve?" Carter replied as he knelt down to her level trying to prevent him-self from crying. Claire approached the door.

"Hey. Come on sweetheart show Uncle Carter in. Come in, come in." said Claire as Carter rose to his feet. She noticed him wipe away a few tears from his eyes as she ushered Eve back into the house.

"Wow she is beautiful. Hey Claire." said Carter with a reassuring warm smile.

Claire reached forward and took Carter tightly in her arms and he reciprocated with equal warmth and comfort. It was a moment where they both knew how strong they had to be for each other, a moment where they could share their sorrow. Carter felt slightly better after their embrace and followed her into the lounge. Starlet was sitting in the corner watching a dancing programme on TV, but was quiet. Eve was sitting on the floor playing with some dolls.

"Starlet, look who it is. It's your Uncle." said Claire.

Starlet looked around but did not smile, it was obvious that she had taken it much worse than Eve, maybe being older and having a bit more understanding as to what had actually happened.

"Hey Starlet." said Carter, hopeful of any kind of response.

"Hello." was all she said before turning back to watch the TV.

Carter looked back at Claire, who indicated to him to follow her out of the room. They walked out into the kitchen and left the girls in the lounge.

"No Shannon?" asked Carter.

"Yes I told her to get some sleep before tomorrow. She is upstairs. She has been so great to have around, don't know what I would have done without her . . . . I went to see his body today Carter. He looked so peaceful. I asked him why he had gone."

Carter, anticipating that Claire was about to burst into tears moved forward and placed his hand on her shoulder.

"Hey. Look, he is still here. He is living through those two beautiful children in there." Claire composed herself and nodded at Carter in agreement. She turned and filled the kettle with water before placing it down and turning it on to boil.

"A drink?" she said.

"Yes please, a coffee would be perfect, thanks."

"You can have something stronger if you like."

"No it's fine. That's how I got this.", said Carter as he pointed to his head.

"Oh my God, what happened? Did someone attack you?"

"No, I had a bit too much to drink and I slipped and hit my head on a table."

"Does it still hurt?"

"No not really, just shook me up a bit I suppose."

Claire took two large mugs out of the kitchen cupboard and placed them down on the table. Carter pulled out a chair and sat down, pulling out another readying it for Claire.

"Are you hungry? I could fix you something to eat. Or would you like to stay for dinner with us?"

"Err, thanks to both offers but I am . . . . well I actually . . . . I,"

"It's OK Carter I understand. It's fine."

"Thank you."

Claire, already knowing of Carter's issues, picked up straight away that he became quite uncomfortable upon being invited for dinner, so she eased the tension. Carter respected her for being so understanding.

"Maybe later in the week would be cool, as I'm staying up here for a while. I took some annual leave from work. I think I just need some time to clear my head."

"Oh that's good Carter. It would be nice for the girls as well to see a bit more of you before you go back."

Claire sat down and placed their coffees on the table. There was a brief but not awkward silence before Carter asked "So I'm assuming that Starlet isn't coping that well?"

"No. She didn't seem too bad at first, but that was probably more due to the shock than anything else. But in the last few days especially she has lost her appetite, had nightmares, has hardly spoken to Shannon or me . . . . and when I ask her she tells me it's fine and that she is fine. Not sure what more I can do. Maybe when the funeral is out of the way, and we return to a routine of some kind we can try and get on with our lives. I think she just needs some time."

"You're probably right, and people, children especially do react to news like this in many different ways."

Claire and Carter continued talking for a while, mainly on stories revolving around the girls. Claire told him about their interests, their likes and dislikes and some funny family stories. It was just past 7pm when Carter decided to make a move and return to the hotel. After all the next day was going to be a huge and emotional day for all and he wanted to try and get a decent amount of sleep beforehand. He said goodbye to Eve and Starlet, Eve having already fallen asleep on one of the sofas. Starlet said nothing and just stayed glued to the television. Shannon was still fast asleep upstairs so he would have to thank her for all of her help when he saw her at the funeral. As Carter stepped out of the house Claire reached out and took his hands in hers. No words were spoken or had to be spoken, but they just shared a look. It was a look of reassurance and that even though the horizon brought with it nothing but anguish they would get through it together, as a family.

* * * *

By the time he had arrived back at the hotel he felt quite deflated and upset. Seeing Eve's sweet face for the first time in person and how vulnerable she looked stuck in his mind and he could not help but keep being reminded that her father was gone. He questioned the future of the family, and how they would grow past this traumatic stage of their lives. Would Eve even remember Marcus when she got older? Would this tragedy have a long term effect on Starlet's life? He walked into his hotel room and sat on the bed and did nothing but just think things through, replaying the 'whys' and 'what ifs' around his brain for the next fifteen minutes. He decided to go to dinner downstairs in the hotel, as he was too tired, grouchy and sad to have eaten out.

He was shown to a two seated small rectangular shaped table toward the back of the restaurant, which was conveniently placed next to the open fireplace. The fire was not burning as the evening was already warm enough, but he just liked looking at it. He took his mobile from his pocket and checked for any messages. There were none. He put the phone down on the table in front of him and looked around the room, noticing that the restaurant was in fact considerably quiet that evening with only two other middle aged couples and himself dining there.

He saw the waiter approaching from the background. He was extremely tall, very skinny and quite gaunt looking. He was clean shaven and had black slick back hair. He asked Carter if he would like a drink and Carter requested to see the wine list. The menu was already placed on the table so he started to look. Carter was a two course guy and would almost never order a dessert, partly because he was always far too full once finishing a main. As he surfed through the starters his mind was made up as soon as he spotted the Calamari. The main course was a bit more difficult. However he knew that it was going to be a meat based dish. He spotted Haggis and was tempted momentarily, as he had eaten it many moons ago and really enjoyed it. Instead he chose to have the Rib-eye Steak which came with a peppercorn sauce, mashed potato and seasonal vegetables. He closed the menu, indicating that he was finished reading and ready to order, and back came the waiter.

"The Wine list" said the gaunt waiter as he handed it over to Carter.

He noticed that the waiter's accent was not Scottish, and thought it sounded more like a Danish accent, but he could not be too sure. It was definitely European. The waiter asked if he needed more time or was he ready to order, upon which Carter gave him his two choices. The wine list was quite small to Carter's surprise, but nevertheless he saw that there was a French Pinot Noir on offer and decided on that instantly. He only ordered a half bottle, just to try and settle him for the evening, as he had become quite stressed out earlier, before and after visiting Claire's. He was also worried about the children, and having been in the house he saw in the flesh the extent of the effect that everything was having upon the family. He felt gutted and infuriated, not only at losing his younger brother but at the sadness that he witnessed behind the eyes of his family, particularly Starlet. The waiter placed his carafe containing his half bottle of chosen red on the table and poured a small amount into a glass to taste.

"Very nice, can I have some more please?" said Carter jokingly, but the waiter failed to get the joke and just topped up his glass and walked away.

Carter took another slurp and looked back at his phone, which was still void of any messages. He started to think about the following day. He was glad that he hadn't had the chance to see Marcus at the funeral directors as he preferred to remember him as he was, a vibrant, intelligent and friendly man, an honest man. It was when Carter began thinking of these qualities that he realised just how much of a brother he had lost, and regretted that he hadn't had the chance or really made an effort to spend more time with him. Carter began to feel angry at himself and vented his frustration by taking a large gulp of wine. He grabbed the carafe and topped up his glass again and placed it back on to the table as a plate appeared in front of him. It wasn't even a plate, it was a bowl. And it wasn't what he had ordered. Instead of seeing Calamari, he was confronted with what looked like a carrot and coriander soup, and a lumpy one at that. He looked up and called the waiter back.

"Excuse me I didn't order the soup!"

"Why?" replied the waiter.

"I'm sorry, did you say why? How the hell does . . . . ?" replied Carter, bemused at the lack of sense the waiter's response made.

"Well why did they ask me to bring the soup to table four? This is table four."

"I couldn't give a flying f . . . ." said a now very agitated Carter, before being interrupted mid rant by a second waiter.

"Excuse me Sir, I am sorry it was my mistake. The soup is for table seven. Your order will be here shortly. Sorry."

"OK." said Carter as he watched the two waiters walk away obviously pointing blame at each other.

Carter was usually understanding and calm in these situations. But recently he had found that he had less patience and became angrier at things. He was not surprised at his bluntness, however, as he believed it was down to the loss of his brother.

It wasn't long and the Calamari rings topped with parsley and a slice of lemon was a welcomed sight on his table and he thoroughly enjoyed them. By the time he had finished his starter he noticed that he only had a half a glass of wine left and this would not last him through his main course. He debated whether to have some sparkling water with the main or order another half a bottle. When he saw his steak arrive he opted for the latter. The meat was tender, juicy and perfectly cooked, medium-rare which was what he had specified. The mash was creamy and smooth and exquisitely cooked, vegetables too were cooked to perfection. He was very impressed, especially by the dainty and precise presentation of the dish and upon finishing his meal he chose to remain there for a while longer to soak up the ambience, and to polish off his wine in the peaceful and cosy setting of the restaurant. It was dark outside which made the restaurant even more atmospheric and inviting.

Carter charged his meal to the room, thanked the waiter for the service and walked towards the stairs which lead up to his room on the first floor. He paused for a moment and realised he was no longer that tired, and he debated as to whether he should go up to his room or go out for an evening walk instead. He convinced himself to go out and walk off his supper. It was a pleasant evening and he was just a little jolly after his bottle of red wine, so he thought why not. However, this sadly was another example of how Carter would create excuses to cover up the real reasons as to why he was doing certain things. In this case he was trying to prolong the funeral of his brother for as long as he could. He wasn't in the mood to be alone in his room if he was that awake as he would just end up tormenting himself with thoughts and not be able to sleep. It would just enhance his feelings of unhappiness. He walked for about two hours and to nowhere in particular. He was barely concentrating on the direction, but just enough to know how to find his way back to the hotel. Carter recognised that the dark streets could seem quite eerie and imposing in some places of the old town. The main street was still quite busy and Carter only became aware of the time when people starting to flood out of the bars and restaurants on to the main street. That was time for him to start heading back to the Herald he decided. It started to feel quite chilly as the night grew later and he wished that he had brought his jacket with him. It wasn't long before he was back at his hotel and in his room. He got undressed, turned on the TV for company and got into bed. He flicked through the channels but found nothing on that was that interesting or exciting. He turned the volume down but left the screen on and he laid his head back down on to the pillow. He preferred it if the TV was still on as it added some company to the room, rather than him being just encompassed in darkness. He hated that as it meant the only company that he had was himself, and he didn't enjoy being in that company. He placed his hands behind his head and shifted to get more comfortable. He could hear some faint noises from outside which he decided to focus on. He could hear cars driving past, the odd voice shouting and hollering from a few streets away, and the odd laugh every now and again, harmoniously coming from groups of pub turnouts. As his eyes started to become heavier and he was close to falling asleep he clicked the power button on the remote and turned off the screen, and only a matter of seconds after that, he drifted off.

CHAPTER FIVE

Dawn rose gently and threw a beautiful crimson glow through Carter's window. The ember like tinted burn struck the walls and cascaded a variety of patterns across the wooden floor, slowly illuminating the bed itself. Carter was in fact already awake, fully dressed and sitting upright on his bed, his eyes too dry to cry after a long night of reflection, accompanied by the resurfacing of memories of times spent with his brother. He stared into the corner of the room and kept perfectly silent and still, perhaps not even noticing the morning sun's arrival. He had been awake since 3am, choosing to dress at that point, partly as he did not want to lie in bed thinking and reminiscing. Instead he chose to occupy himself in an attempt to distract his mind from the ever looming morning, a morning that brought with it nothing but an assurance of misery and pain. Carter began to remember another time from his past, a time of particular significance. It was the funeral of their Grandfather

Harold, back when Marcus and he were both children. It was the morning of October 28th 1983, and the date of the funeral brought with it an even more sombre tone as it was the same date as their Grandfather's birthday. He would have been eighty years of age. Sadly, pneumonia had taken hold of him and he was drained of all energy and life very swiftly, a sad and unexpected end to a once strong and powerful man, who had served bravely for his country during World War II.

* * * *

"Wake up boys, it's time!" shouted their father up the stairs. Neither Carter nor Marcus had any time in which to respond before the voice repeated "Boys I said it's time, get up and get ready."

The second time the voice was vented with a more unsettling, escalated anger, with accompanying undertones of growing impatience. Marcus quickly responded.

"We are up and we will be there in a minute. He sounds very upset."

"Dad and Grandpa was very close Marcus, and we must be strong for him. He may get angry with us but we must remember that it is only because he is upset and misses him so much."

"So do I." Marcus replied, now out of bed and rapidly getting dressed.

Carter sat up organising himself mentally for what he knew was going to be a very long and emotionally challenging day ahead. Carter added encouragingly and with an equally supportive smile "I know Marcus, it will all be OK."

Marcus and Carter arrived downstairs to the sight of their mother standing in the hallway, seemingly hesitant and standing a few footsteps back from the kitchen door. She turned to the boys and gently put each of her index fingers over their lips, ensuring they understood that this was a fragile moment and a time to remain quiet. Their father was sitting at the kitchen table, head in his hands, clearly needing a moment alone. Carter could make out through the crack in the door that his father's body was trembling, and knew he was witnessing the sight of a broken man who was at that moment inconsolable. Carter had never seen his father that way before and was not really sure how to react. Should he go into the kitchen and sit with his father? Should he leave him on his own? What was the right thing to do? Carter at that moment felt completely helpless and a strong sense of fear shot through his body like a bullet, a vulnerable depressive wave of emotion that he found hard to control, and he began to weep. Even though Carter tried in earnest to prevent Marcus from hearing or seeing him cry, Marcus did hear and glanced to his left and saw the tears fall down Carter's cheek. Marcus placed his hand on Carter's arm for comfort, and Carter looked to his brother and simply said "Sorry."

Marcus, almost in a whisper, leant in toward him and said "It will all be OK, our strength as a family will get us through this. Be strong. Father will heal in time."

Carter realised then the extent of Marcus's growing strength and that his younger brother was fast becoming a man.

* * * *

The mobile phone alarm on the bedside table let out its usual annoying and deafening morning scream, and immediately transported Carter back from his memories to the day he now had to face. He did not need to leave until 8am but wanted an hour to get prepared, drink some strong coffee and avoid any unwanted panic of being late. He rocked himself forward and up into a standing position, catching his reflection in the mirror as he stood up straight. He halted for a second and took a look at himself, paying particular attention to the bags under his eyes and how down and gloomy he looked. He attempted to reassure himself by saying “be strong,” but his words faded half way and lacked conviction, knowing those words would make no difference to his inevitable weakness nor would they help make him positive. His general lack of confidence had prevented him from being able to alter his emotional state. Carter walked over to the complimentary tea and coffee table, checked the kettle for water and turned it on. He turned and leant against the wall, putting his hands in his trouser pockets as he waited for the water to boil. He looked at how neatly placed items were in the hotel room and how much better a room looked when clean and uncluttered, in stark contrast to his flat back in London. The only part of his London pad that he ever kept meticulous was his pride and joy—his DVD collection. As though preserved, they were neatly shelved and in alphabetical order and split by genre. His only two other prized possessions that seemed to stand out as being cleaned at least once in the previous few months were the plasma TV screen and the PS3 games console. The rest of the floor at the flat was covered by a random accumulation of items, ranging from dirty washing, a beanbag that had a tear in it and inevitably discharged polystyrene balls out all over the floor whenever any pressure was put on it, three month old issues of magazines, empty wine bottles, and the odd half written screenplay that he hadn't bothered to finish. Some pages had been hidden under the ever swarming growth of polystyrene balls in some fairness. He mainly kept the curtains closed at the flat, not only because of his general hatred of the imposing outside world, but so that the lack of cleanliness of the glass, could go conveniently unnoticed. Will was nearly as bad in that respect, but did give more of an effort toward household chores.

Carter sat down on the bed. He grasped his cup of coffee between his hands and embraced the warmth that the hot beverage brought with it. He closed his eyes and tried his best to relax, but after only a few minutes had passed he stood and walked around the room, almost pacing, desperately trying to keep his mind off the day. He took some sips of his coffee, which was probably strong enough to bring an elephant out of a coma. Carter put the remainder of his coffee on the table and grabbed his jacket. He took one last look in the mirror as he picked up the room key to leave, double checking one final time that his appearance was appropriate.

As he walked out onto the cobblestone street he was greeted by the beautiful sunny morning that he had hoped for. The sky was a deep rich blue which was an added bonus and brought a smile to his face. He had already been given directions to the cemetery by the hotel receptionist when he had arrived the previous day, and was already aware that it wasn't too far away. In fact it was only about a twenty minute walk from The Herald Hotel and as it wasn't overly hot that morning he decided to walk there. He turned left and started walking, taking the second left on to Morrison Street and then the first right on to Shandwick Place. He crossed over at the traffic lights taking the next two lefts followed by the next two rights until he reached York Place. It was a very dainty old building where the funeral was to take place and was very peaceful as it was away from the main streets. It was set back from the road and had a long single path that led up to it. Cars were parked at the back of the building and he could see some people outside waiting but he couldn't make out who they were. As he walked down the path he was flanked on each side by gravestones, some of which he noticed were dated back to the early 1800s. He could see further over that there were more modern gravestones, some with a shiny black marble effect and huge golden letters. Some graves had different things added to them to display a point of significance and importance to the person that lay there. One had a dart board engraved on it, and another a chess board. It displayed the passion of what that person had enjoyed when alive. As he got closer to the building he realised that the people standing there were for another service altogether, a service that was already playing out. They started to follow the funeral car toward an empty grave to the right of the building and he could make out what looked like a sheath in the shape of an anchor on top of the car, with flowers arranged spelling out the word "Grandad," on the side. It showed that the deceased was probably a naval man who had served his country. "So many stories and so many memories all accumulated into one place at one time." Carter thought as he reached the doorway to the chapel. There were a few people who were already standing to the side and chatting away to each other, although Carter didn't recognise them. He assumed that they were in fact there for Marcus, maybe some friends from work. No-one else had arrived yet, but Carter was early. Claire had already asked him the previous day if he would like to travel with her and the girls in the car along with the procession to the cemetery, but he thought it more fitting and more supportive for the girls if Shannon was there with them, someone they were more familiar with and undoubtedly more comfortable with. Carter took a peek inside the chapel and thought it was very beautiful indeed. It was the perfect setting for an occasion that was full of emotion and sadness. It was simple but cosy, welcoming and in no way at all daunting; spacious yet appropriately confined and private. It was perfectly balanced. The large crucifix hung from the wall at the back of the chapel, next to a long draped red curtain alongside it, its purpose was to be pulled around coffins that were for cremations.

As he stepped back outside and turned to look at the driveway he could see some cars pulling up, and a few people were already walking along the path towards the chapel. Then the funeral car came into view and turned left into the grounds, followed by the car carrying the immediate family. They both slowly approached the chapel forecourt. Carter's heart sank and he felt overwhelmed with a feeling of sickness to the stomach. The sheath of choice simply read "Daddy," which added extra sorrow and regret to the way he was feeling. As the cars pulled to a halt he could see Claire, Shannon and the girls through the window. Claire, although not crying, was looking wilted and grey faced, and Starlet especially was looking shattered and broken. He looked to the right and saw the coffin. He just stared at it and the full reality of things came instantly into place. Claire, the girls, Shannon, followed by others entered the chapel, choosing to spend no time whatsoever outside. Carter was relieved that the flowers he had ordered online back in London were placed neatly on the car in front of him, and his personal message printed on the tag. The pallbearers opened the double backed doors of the vehicle and prepared to take out the coffin, when Carter had a sudden urge to do something. He walked over to the car and asked the pallbearers if he could possibly join them in carrying his brother through into the chapel. They understood and said it was no problem at all. They sized him up according to his height alongside the other bearers so they were as level as possible. This enabled the coffin to be carried evenly. They pulled it out and raised it up and onto their shoulders. One bearer offered Carter some helpful advice on how to walk and hold the coffin, and how the coffin would be placed when inside. The head bearer walked to the front and led them through the door and into the chapel itself. Carter was situated to the back right side of the coffin, and the first sight he got was the right hand side of the room, where he was met by the faces of everyone in each row on that side. He could see tears and sadness on some and a proud look on others. Slow orchestral music was being played in the background. Carter concentrated on walking and doing his bit to keep the coffin steady. He was mainly focused on how proud he was of his brother and that if nothing else his brother would have liked the fact that he had joined the bearers to carry him in. As they approached the front, Carter caught sight of the vicar for the first time and he too looked very glum and saddened. His cheeks were quite rosy and his stature was of a bold proportion. This vicar had a presence about him, an authoritative quality. He looked to be in his mid to late fifties and had a handlebar shaped grey moustache and wore the usual long black gown. As they neared the front of the chapel and to the position where the coffin was to be placed, Carter looked to his right and his eyes met with Claire's. Although she was filled with heartbreak, she gave him a little smile of acknowledgment, showing how pleased she was that he had offered to carry Marcus in. They placed the coffin down and Carter stepped to the side and found a seat. Everyone sat down at that point as the vicar took his position behind the small podium centred behind the coffin.

"We are all gathered here today not only to share in our love for dear Marcus, but to celebrate his life and his eternal journey forthwith. It is a sad day for all, a day of loss that brings with it many worrying and upsetting emotions. The feeling of abandonment, of loneliness, of hurt, and some of you will feel anger. But I implore you please think of what Marcus would want at this time. He would want you all to be joyous and to show fortitude, to remember him with fondness and love. The Lord has now taken Marcus into his arms in Heaven and will guide him onwards and protect him for eternity. I know that we can no longer see or speak to Marcus, but he is here with us in spirit, is in our hearts and living on through his beautiful children sitting here before me, Starlet and young Eve."

The sounds of weeping were now evident and Carter could hear tears being shed all around him. He started to well up himself and had to do his best to hold himself together.

"No!" shouted a voice that was seeped in anguish. Some people jumped in their seats as they were clearly startled by the scream, and members of the congregation turned to the direction from where it had come.

Carter sat up in his seat and looked around to get a better view and saw Starlet running down the aisle and out of the chapel, inconsolable and frantic. Running behind her was Shannon trying to catch her outside to calm her down and console her. Claire sat head down, one hand holding a handkerchief over her eyes to try and hide her tears, and her other arm tightly wrapped around Eve. She sat motionless and in shock as she witnessed her whole world shattering into a thousand pieces around her. The vicar continued calmly and tried to divert everyone's attention back to him.

"Marcus was a man considered as a friend by all, a man who is actually supporting me too in this moment and assisting me at this awkward time, as he was a close friend of mine too. But I am comforted by knowing that he will be, in no doubt, flourishing in the sacred realms of spirit. The man who I consider a true friend is holding out his hand, offering belief and light, casting a vision of peace and sanctuary into our hearts. What at this moment seems like only a faint glow of hope will in time take on a more defined and prominent shine, an embrace that will protect us and provide us with comfort. Everybody please stand and join me in prayer. Our Lord who art in Heaven . . . ."

As the prayer was being spoken and repeated by all Carter started to feel sick and dizzy. He also felt an anger sweep over him and began to feel anxious and on edge. He tried to distract himself by thinking of something completely different to try and take his mind off it. He started to think of some words he had written in poems and screenplays in his past, and one in particular came to the forefront of his mind. It was a poem that he remembered writing one night a long time ago, not long after his mother had passed, a night when he was very drunk and fuelled with rage. The poem was about an old man who had lost his daughter to illness and was standing in church confronting the cross and questioning death and the afterlife, crying out for answers, cursing and daring a response or the slightest sign that God existed. On failing this, the old man turned to the Devil instead and offered his soul. The one sentence Carter could remember from this poem and which happened to be the last line spoken by the old man at the height of despair and just before he took his own life. "Steam rose from the inner depths of my being, tolerance levels fathomed at the hilt, and the darker moments have never been so sinister and unveiling as they are now."

Carter began to self analyse and came to the conclusion that at that precise moment it was himself and his own feelings that were playing out inside the old man in the poem, questioning death and why, if there was a God, how could He justify the amount of pain and anguish that had to be suffered. He found that he was yet again asking the same questions, the same questions that he asked at his mother's funeral and the same that he asked at his father's, and his grandfather's. Carter thought it was due to his current emotions that enabled these words to resurface in his mind. Not too long after, the feelings did start to subside and he regained some sense of normality. The vicar continued with the service, providing more comforting and reassuring words and delivered them well with warmth and sincerity. As Marcus's favourite song was played out Carter spotted the pallbearer give him a nod, signalling that it was time to take the coffin back outside to the car, where it would then be driven to the plot where his body would be finally laid to rest.

* * * *

As people walked back from the graveside, Carter happened to be walking closest to the vicar and decided to speak to him.

"Excuse me vicar? I just wanted to say how good the service was, thank you."

"You're very welcome, did you know Marcus well?"

"He is . . . . was my brother?"

"Carter?" asked the vicar.

"Yes, how did you know my name? And what is yours by the way?"

"My name is Reverend Melvin Norris and I know more about you than just your name."

"Really? From Claire?"

"From your brother."

"Oh?" said an intrigued Carter.

"Yes as you heard in the service I knew him well, I baptised Eve. I hadn't seen him much that recently I have to say, but I do remember him speaking to me about his brother, Carter in London. He thought the world of you, although he was concerned that you may not have been fully aware of that. I'm so sorry for your loss."

Carter stopped and Reverend Norris continued on back towards the chapel. He didn't expect to hear those words, but was happy that he did hear them, and he too thought the world of his brother. He looked beyond Reverend Norris and could see that Starlet was back with Claire and in her arms. It looked like she had shed a mountain of tears, which were probably needed in order for her to be able to start to heal in her own way. He began to walk towards them and saw that Shannon was approaching him from the opposite direction.

"Hey Shannon." said Carter as he leant in to greet her with a kiss on the cheek.

"Carter, so nice to see you,"

"Look, I just want to say how grateful I am for all the support you have given Claire and the girls. I am truly thankful."

"It was nothing, my pleasure. I was only too happy to help."

"Well you have been a rock. I . . . . err think the service was, went well. Reverend Norris is a nice guy huh?"

"Yes he is and from what I saw of the service it was as good as these things can be I suppose!"

"How is Starlet now? Thanks for jumping to the rescue."

"Well I sort of predicted that she would crack in there, so was kind of prepared to jump in when necessary. Are you coming back to the house for some drinks with the rest?"

"Of course, yes definitely."

"Do you want to ride in the main car with Claire?" offered Shannon kindly.

"No it's fine, you go ahead. I'll make my own way back there."

"Are you sure, I can get one of the others to give you a lift back there if you like?"

"No I'm sure, but thanks anyway. I'll see you there in a bit." said Carter with a smile.

Shannon smiled and returned to the waiting car, as the rest started to disappear back to their cars and out of sight. Carter held back for a minute, put his hands in his pockets and turned back to where the gravesite was. He walked back over to the grave so he could have a moment alone. He knelt down, looking into where the mahogany casket containing his brother was placed.

"Hey. I am so sorry that I have not been the brother that spent more time with you and the family, and that I have not been the strong brother that you deserved. Trust me it wasn't out of not wanting to be. Thank you for my childhood and the memories that we shared together, I'll cherish those moments forever. I hope the words the vicar spoke in there are true, so we can once again be a family together in the future. I love you and I am sorry that I didn't know how much I meant to you until now . . . . rest well and God bless."

Carter's head dropped and he released a lot of overdue tears at that moment, the tears that had been held back and locked away for some time were now free.

As the last of the cars disappeared from sight Carter walked back out onto the main street and headed back toward his hotel, where he planned to call for a taxi to take him to Claire's for the reception. He needed a bit of time to clear his head and take in all the emotion from the funeral. He spotted a bar just down on the right hand side and decided to leave going back to the hotel after all and instead go in for a quick drink to pull himself together. He could get a taxi to pick him up from there. Upon entering he could see that there were already a few punters in there, most likely the usual faces that could be found in that particular pub most days. Many of them were old men, obviously long retired and in constant search for company and cheer. Carter ordered a double brandy and sat down on a stool at the bar. As he put his change back into his pocket his hand stumbled across his bottle of Cipralex. He took one out from the bottle and knocked it back with a gulp of brandy.

"Excuse me. Is there any chance of ordering a taxi?" said Carter to the landlord.

"Yes no problem Sir. Would you like it straight away?"

"Yes please, thanks."

"OK, where are you heading?"

Carter told the landlord Claire's address and proceeded in finishing off the brandy. It tasted so delicious and brought instant warmth to his body. He looked around the bar at the different characters sitting there, some were very jolly and quite loud, especially for that time of day, and others were quite miserable and reserved and looked deep in thought, no doubt thinking of times gone by perhaps. Five minutes later and the taxi had arrived and it was parked outside on the street corner. Carter thanked the landlord and left. He could see a man waving at him from the opposite side of the street and he made his way over to get in.

CHAPTER SIX

Friends and family gathered at the house in abundance for the reception. Some people who were not able to make it to the funeral had however managed to get to the house to show their last respects. The murmuring tones of voices from inside the house, could be heard almost in a whisper, and were at times as soft as the breeze outside. Every now and then there would be a sudden increase in volume and an injection of noise as if someone upon noticing a drop in sound tried to help improve the atmosphere. Claire was rushed off her feet, keeping busy not only to try and sidetrack herself from the event, but also to try and speak to everyone who was in attendance. She looked drawn and exhausted and was running on adrenaline. Shannon was taking care of Starlet, and Eve was kept busy playing outside in the garden with some other children of a similar age. The spread of food was a variety of different styled finger foods, ranging from samosas to burritos. Marcus was a keen lover of international cuisine and would've thoroughly appreciated the effort that all of the girls had made in preparing it. People were enjoying the delicious food as well as the drinks in the bar in the dining room which had been stocked up and readied for the occasion.

Reverend Melvin Norris stood close to the bar, like a magnet to its immediate vicinity and frequently topped up his glass with either wine or brandy. It seemed as though he alternated between the two and found it hard to settle on one. He had a few men gathered in close quarters, the usual types you would find at times like these, who were there to gently mock him while at the same time question him as to why he had chosen a life that needed such dedicated devotion to the Church. It was more bantering than any form of malice.

Carter wandered between rooms, not really in the mood to engage with anyone in particular, doing his best to avoid eye contact. He clasped a glass of rosé and just mingled around in the background, mainly listening in on conversations that people were sharing about Marcus. He was hearing stories of a man who was so adventurous and generous, outgoing and caring to all he knew. People were also sharing personal experiences of times spent with Marcus as well. An elderly lady spoke of how he had always made the effort to help carry her shopping in for her and that it was an absolute pleasure to have him as a neighbour. Another man told of how Marcus had helped raise money to donate to the local primary school to help prevent it from closing due to financial constraints. The stories flowed and Carter was engrossed and comforted to hear that his brother was so well received in life. He only wished that the clocks could turn back so he could have had more time with him. Carter started to feel that it was the wrong brother that had been taken, but did not wallow in self pity, but just accepted the fact that Marcus had more to offer than he ever could, or would ever be able to give. At that point he realised just how alone he was, and how equally insignificant. He circulated further, and chose to stand within earshot of the Reverend and the accompanying gentlemen, but without actually being in a position where it was likely for him to be invited to participate. He heard one man ask the Reverend if he ever regretted making such a devotion and dedication. And Carter could do nothing but smile at his answer.

"Do I regret devoting my life to something I firmly believe in? The answer is no. Do I regret devoting my life to something that has not yet been proven? The answer is no. Do I regret devoting myself to something that will not provide any fathomable truth to explain all of the bad things that happen around the world? The answer is no. Do I regret devoting my life to religion and not to science? The answer is definitely no. Do I regret that my faith has been put in questionable doubt on more than a few occasions? Then the answer is yes. I feel that the question you should be asking gentlemen is to yourselves. Do you regret the lives that you have chosen?"

The Reverend, as cool as could be, sipped at his brandy, and expected that he would only be confronted with expressions of immediate reflection and defeat, rather than any further questions. The faces of the men held nothing but blank expressions, as the question posed seemed to only provide them all with only one answer, yes.

Carter chuckled to himself and turned his head away where a picture caught his eye. It was a photograph of Marcus on his own standing by a lake, holding a fishing rod in one hand and a decent sized catch in the other. It was such a great picture and had been edited to black and white and enhanced using another editing tool that gave it a sphere-like effect. Carter had not been aware that Marcus had done any fishing. He wondered if he had ever had any other big catches, and also where that particular photo had been taken. He could make out some hills in the background and what looked like some boats further out in the distance on the water. He looked back at his brother's face which wore a huge smile.

"He was such a great guy." said a soft voice with an American accent which came from the side of where Carter was standing.

Carter turned to see who it was and was amazed at what he saw. It was no-one he recognised but, however, it was a recognisable beauty that was standing beside him.

"Yes he was." replied Carter, awkwardly pausing between the words and looking somewhat dumbstruck.

The lady was a vision and posed a striking figure. She had blonde hair and wore a long black gown. Her hair seemed to glow as if topped with a halo and her hazel coloured eyes dazzled; with a voice as soft as an angel. Carter was momentarily defenceless and tried his best to gather himself and act normal.

"Hi, my name is Mary Lee." she said while offering her hand out to shake his.

"Carter Jakeman." said Carter with confidence. "Nice to meet you Mary, did you know Marcus well?"

"I worked with him for a while about a year ago. How about you?"

"I am his brother."

"Oh my, I am sorry for your loss. You must be devastated."

"Well . . . . yes. Still finding it hard to come to terms with it, denial I suppose."

"I understand. I am so thankful to have known him at all. He helped me a lot when I first started at the company."

"Oh so you worked with Marcus?"

"Yes only for a while. He was so generous and helpful, filled me with confidence from the start. I had not long arrived from the US and was quite apprehensive about living and working in a new country, but Marcus made it much easier for me and made me feel so welcome."

"Would you like a drink?" asked Carter, noticing that her wine glass was near empty.

"I would love one, thank you."

"I'll be back in a second. I take it that is the Chardonnay right?"

Mary nodded as Carter walked away to refill her glass, he briefly glanced back to have another look at Mary. He reconfirmed to himself just how stunning she was. He could not believe that he had offered her a drink and that she had actually approached him. He was surprised that he did not opt for his usual unorthodox method of withering away from the conversation and making haste for the nearest exit. He was captivated and interested, and felt a rush of sudden confidence. He thought his new found interest and spurt of self belief was due to his emotions being distracted by the occasion and solely fixated on other things. Perhaps he was caught by surprise and did not really have time to react and get nervous. Maybe his emotions were confused and unsure how to react. He refilled the glasses and eagerly returned to the lounge with a spring in his step but noticed as he approached the doorway that he could feel another headache coming on.

He walked back into the lounge but could not see Mary amongst the crowd of people there. He looked more carefully around the room, trying to look between people to see if she had moved and was speaking to someone else toward the back of the room, but no luck. He walked out into the hallway and looked out to the garden but could not see her there either. He turned back into the lounge and felt slightly downhearted, but at the same time it did not surprise him. After all, past experiences taught him if something was too good to be true regarding him and the fairer sex, then it most definitely was. It wasn't the first time that a girl had done a runner from him, and he was sure it wouldn't be the last. "Why on earth would she want to speak with me anyway?" he thought.

He sat down on a chair that had been placed next to the sofa and took a sip from his own glass. The room was now quite loud and crowded with guests, but to his relief he noticed that his approaching headache had subsided. To his right he could see some family photographs on the mantelpiece, snapshots of happy family faces and beautiful memories. He could see one photo of the family, which had been taken in New York, standing in front of Radio City Music Hall, and another which he assumed to be Athens, where they were photographed standing in front of what looked like the ruins of the Acropolis. Carter wore a proud grin and was happy that Claire and the girls at least had managed to have some wonderful times spent with Marcus that they could cherish. He started to reflect on what it would've been like in his own life if he had met the girl of his dreams and if he was not bipolar. Would he now have children of his own and be off travelling to all these wonderful places around the world? Would he have a successful and fulfilling job? He quickly diverted his attention back to the room, and back to pictures of his brother. As he moved to place Mary's glass onto the side table she suddenly reappeared, and was standing right in front of him.

"Hey, thought you lost interest in me already?" Carter said with a cheeky but relieved smile, as he handed her wine glass to her.

"No way, I was just freshening up. Thank you for the refill." Mary smiled.

"No problem at all."

"So Carter, were you and Marcus close? Do you live here in Edinburgh?"

"No, I live in London, and sadly to be honest we have barely spoken in the last couple of years. Not due to any ill feeling or bad blood or anything like that, just life sort of got in the way."

"Oh I'm sorry to hear that." said Mary comfortingly.

Carter took on a more serious expression and his eyes momentarily left Mary's, as though his mind had wandered off to access a more deeper and heartfelt area of reflection.

"You know it's strange, even though Marcus is my younger brother, it is not until now that I realise just how much it has been the other way around all of these years. He was always there for me, even though in the last few years we have not seen each other that often, he was always there . . . . a phone call away. And now that he has gone, I have no way of thanking him for that. That's hard to take."

Carter began to choke up slightly with emotion but managed to compose himself by drawing a deep breath. A reassuring smile from Mary also helped.

Mary started to ask Carter about his life, and what he did occupationally, attempting to change the subject and prevent them from an obvious awkward silence.

"So what do you do for a job?" enquired Mary, utilising her tone of voice to instil a more upbeat tempo to the conversation. Carter replied equally as positive and with an added comical tone, "Well trust me Mary, talking about my job isn't gonna lighten the mood!" They both laughed.

"Try me." follows up Mary.

Carter humbly explained, "I sell mobile phone insurance. It's commission based work so although I do have a fixed baseline salary, in effect I have no fixed income as it can fluctuate, but I am responsible for quite a large catchment area so in theory I should always be OK financially."

Mary replied with a witty response "You're right, it hasn't lightened the mood!"

They laughed again, realising they shared a similar sense of humour and were already enjoying each other's company.

"OK what about outside the office?" quizzed Mary.

Carter replied in a much more confident manner, with the delivery of lines that a half decent stand-up comedian would be proud of, "Who said I worked in an office? It's more like a shack with stacked up stationery boxes for desks."

Carter was in the zone, cleverly mixing humour with seriousness, but managing also not to sound in anyway immature or out of his depth. He added,

"OK, not very much on the social side I'm afraid. I don't have many friends outside of work, or in work actually for that matter, one in fact, Will, who I share a flat with. I read quite a bit, autobiographical literature mainly, have attempted screenplay writing, and absolutely love movies. I'm a big movie fan. Go to the movies quite a lot actually. Bit of a loner really."

There was a pause as they both shared another smile, but it was in no way an awkward pause. At that moment Carter realised that he was actually making conversation, not just to anyone, but to a very attractive woman, and for once it did not seem like the most challenging thing in the world. He wasn't stressed about what he would say when she finished her next sentence or what he would say next in order to keep her interested and stay talking to him. For once he had backup conversation and humour swirling around his mind, as if he had artillery at the ready, and was remembering all sorts of facts and trivia from where he did not know. He felt confidence oozing through his veins. And if only short lived, he would cling to this rarity and clasp onto it with both hands, embracing it for what it was. Mary and Carter talked for another hour, mainly focusing on conversation around movies and music, of which Mary too conveniently had a love for both. Wine was flowing and it was evident that there was a connection their between them, a chemistry brewing.

*   *   *   *

Mary Lee was thirty-two years of age and had come to work with Marcus in Edinburgh a few years before. She was initially employed as a proof reader at the company, but had more recently worked her way up to editor for another magazine having moved onto another company within the city. She was very sophisticated, intelligent and had a great sense of humour. She moved to Edinburgh from San Francisco after securing a work placement, and due to a burning desire for journalism and travel it seemed like the right move to make at the time. As she told Carter all about herself, Carter could not believe his luck. She ticked all of his boxes. She was perfect.

* * * *

Carter's mobile rang but by the time he had fumbled around in his pocket it had rung off. It was a missed call from Will, no doubt wanting to know how the funeral went. He noticed that Will had left a voicemail and Carter decided to listen to it a bit later. He slipped the phone coolly back into his pocket and carried on the conversation.

"Are you sure you don't want to take that?" enquired Mary in case she was keeping him from an important call.

"No it's fine. It's my flatmate in London. I'll call him back a bit later."

"Are you sure, you can if you like. I may go and see if Claire needs a hand with anything in the kitchen. I'll catch up with you a bit later if you like?" said Mary.

"Yes sure, absolutely, great idea." said Carter with all the enthusiasm and excitement of a kid in a candy store.

Mary walked out of the lounge and Carter stayed put as he had at that moment noticed a seat become available on the sofa. He slumped back into the comfy cushions and felt his back muscles relax as he took another sip of his wine. Mary was all he could think about. He started to recall their conversation and could not find any moment during it when there was an awkward moment, or any embarrassing moments at all. He felt his phone vibrate so he reached into his pocket to retrieve it. As the room was still quite loud he decided to go out to the garden so that he could hear Will's voicemail. As he walked out into the air, two of the children playing darted in front of him which gave him a start, as they had unexpectedly come from the side of the house. He nearly dropped his wine glass but managed to juggle it enough to just about keep hold of it. Noticing that the kitchen window was next along he had a look to see if anyone from inside had just seen him wiggling around in a frantic state trying to save his glass. Mary was there, giving him a wave through the window. She had a smirk on her face which immediately alerted Carter that she had witnessed his little crazy dance.

"Brilliant, now she probably thinks I'm a right maniac!" Carter muttered under his breath as he returned a wave and a smile.

He pressed the voicemail button on his mobile and turned away from the house, walking towards the back of the garden. The children were loud so he had to strain to hear the full message.

"Hey bud, it's Will. Hope it all went well today. I'll raise a glass to both you and Marcus tonight if I don't hear from you before. Nothing much going on here, just the usual. Everything is OK at the flat, except for last night when a mouse ran across the floor in front of me while I was coming out of the bathroom. Don't worry though. I'll catch it before you get back. Speak to you later mate and take care."

Carter was about to return Will's call but realised he needed the toilet, and desperately, so he headed straight back into the house. He passed Claire on the stairs and she still looked busy, as if in some way trying to rush the day to its end rather than participate in any of its remainder.

"Hey Claire, did Mary find you? She was looking for you to see if you needed help with anything in the kitchen?"

"No? Who was it?" shouted Claire back up the stairs just as Carter vanished out of sight and into the bathroom. Claire returned to the kitchen to see if anyone had been looking for her.

As a well relieved Carter exited the bathroom he caught a glimpse through a slightly ajar doorway a little further down the corridor. He could make out what looked like to be the corner of a desk, and he assumed that it was the study. He could not help himself but take a look. He approached the door tentatively, feeling as if he was about to spy on someone, or uninvitingly go through someone's private possessions. He slowly pushed the door open and entered the room. It was a small room which served as a cosy study. The desk was flush to the wall to the right and carried only a laptop, a desk fan and a second house phone on top of it. It was neat and tidy, as was his brother about such things, everything in its place. On the left side of the box room were shelves. The middle shelf held more photographs of Claire, Marcus and the girls. The bottom shelf had some plain paper stacked there, some gloss paper, and some pens. It was the top shelf that really captured Carter's attention. On it was a photograph of him and Marcus as children. It was placed within a photo frame that had a little box attached to the back where you could place accompanying things of significance. He paused for a moment but then decided to open it up. Inside there was a gold ring with a small black plated front, a ring that as of that moment Carter had completely forgotten about. The ring belonged to their Grandfather who had worn it most of his life. He had given the ring to Carter not long before he passed away. Carter, knowing how much Marcus liked the ring decided to give it to him. Marcus had become quite ill when he was young, an illness that initially started with the flu, making him lose quite a lot of weight. Carter thought the ring would make him feel better and because he believed that their Grandfather would channel strength through the ring to Marcus and make him well again. Carter felt so touched and privileged that his brother had kept it all those years, keeping it in such a safe place alongside a photograph of them together. He heard the door creak slightly behind him and he realised that someone had discovered him in there. It was Claire.

"Claire I'm sorry, I didn't mean to be nosy or anything but I . . . ."

"Hey Carter its OK, I'm glad you found it. I was going to give it to you before you left. That ring meant the world to Marcus. I know the story and I think you did a very lovely and generous thing to a brother who was sick. He would want you now to have it back."

"Thanks Claire. I just wish I would have told him how much he meant to me."

"He knew Carter. Trust me, he always knew."

Claire stepped in and gave him a hug which gave him a much needed sense of relief. Carter placed the ring back into the picture frame box and placed it into his inside jacket pocket whilst wiping away a few tears.

As he and Claire arrived back downstairs they noticed that a few people were readying to leave. Claire walked on ahead to go and thank them for coming and to say goodbye. Carter decided to head for the kitchen to get another glass of wine before returning to the lounge. He hoped that Mary hadn't left yet. Although his confidence had slightly dwindled and he doubted if he would be able to muster up the courage to re-spark a conversation with her, he still hoped that he could see her one last time. Even if it was just to say goodbye. He sat down in the lounge and started to contemplate an appropriate time for him to call a taxi. After all he did not want to linger, as he knew how hard the day had been for the family and knew that Claire would want some alone time with the girls. Just at that moment he saw her walk past the door towards the kitchen so he decided to call after her.

"Yes Carter?"

"Can I help you with anything Claire? Clearing up or washing up? Anything?"

"Thanks, Carter, but people have already offered."

"Sure?"

"Absolutely, it's fine, thanks all the same."

"OK, well I may head off in a bit. I'll say goodbye to the girls and probably call a taxi."

"Thanks for coming Carter. It would have meant everything to Marcus that you were here. Before you go back to London I'd love it if you could come over for dinner one evening. So the girls get to spend some time with you as well. Sound good?"

"Yes, would love too. I'll call you tomorrow to arrange something. Thanks Claire. Try and get some rest tonight OK."

"Will try!"

Claire kissed him on the cheek and Carter went to find to find Starlet and Eve so he could say goodbye. He could see that Eve was still in the garden so he made his way out there first. "Uncle Carter." she called as she saw him walk out onto the lawn.

"Hey little one." replied Carter as he picked her up for a hug.

"Are you going now?" said Eve sounding disappointed.

"Yes, but I will be coming back to have dinner with you all in a few days."

"You promise?"

"Promise." confirmed Carter.

Eve smiled as Carter lowered her back down to ground level. She ran back and resumed playing with her friends. As Carter searched for Starlet, he kept an eye out for Mary, although he didn't hold much hope of seeing her again and had assumed that she had already left. Starlet was nowhere to be found downstairs, so he decided not to go up and look for her, in case she wanted to be left alone with her thoughts. He grabbed his mobile from his pocket and looked through to find the local taxi service number he had stored previously. He lifted the phone up to his ear to wait for an answer, but as he looked up he saw Mary in the garden. She must have been in the lounge when he was out there, and the two had somehow missed each other.

"Hello!" said a voice coming from the mobile phone. "Hello taxi service." repeated the voice.

"Yes, sorry wrong number." said Carter as he ended the call and slipped his phone back into his pocket. His eyes were firmly fixed on Mary and he walked forward towards the garden. His mind was in question as to whether to even go and talk to her again or just to leave it as it was. He even thought she might be avoiding him. Before he knew it she was standing before him.

"Hey Carter, I thought you had left?" Mary said looking happy that he hadn't.

"No, well . . . . I've just been mingling you know. Talking to little Eve out here . . . . I thought that you had left."

"No I was just about to. I have just helped with some of the clearing up, and I have noticed that some people have left already."

Carter felt a tug on the bottom of his jacket so he looked down puzzlingly.

"Uncle Carter, you're still here. I thought you were leaving?"

"Hi Eve, yes I am going now. You have a good time with your friends OK?"

"I will." replied Eve as she ran off to rejoin the remaining children.

Carter looked up and noticed that Mary was getting her coat from inside so he made his way back in. He followed her into the lounge to collect her handbag.

"Look . . . . Mary. If you haven't got anything planned would you like to have coffee with me? Or go for a walk maybe? That is of course if you are not already spoken for, as that would be . . . . well . . . . not . . . . wise." Carter's nerves began to get the better of him and he was close to losing his cool, before Mary interjected.

"I would love to. And no I am not seeing anyone at the moment."

"That's great!" said Carter looking pleased with himself. "Shall we?"

"Sure." replied Mary.

They were about to leave the lounge and head for the front door when Carter felt a hand on his shoulder.

He stopped and turned around to find it was Reverend Norris.

"Just thought I would bid you a safe journey, and wish you all the best." said a warm and obviously very merry Reverend. Carter could make out a host of different aromas coming from him as he spoke, a mass concoction of spirits and wine varieties. The Reverend had made the most of the bar. Carter quickly turned his head to introduce Mary but she had already left the room.

"Thank you Reverend." said Carter as he shook his hand. "And thanks for the kind words that you told me afterwards. I'm very happy that you told me."

"It was my pleasure. Look, I knew your brother better than most here, and if I know anything at all, I know that he is OK. He lives on in those who love and cherish him the most, his wife and his daughters, but also within you Carter."

"Thanks again Reverend, I appreciate it. Farewell." said Carter as he stepped back and walked away.

Reverend Norris, slightly swaying, turned and made his way back to the remaining few who stood over by the bar. As Carter walked outside he drew in a deep breath of fresh air, let his shoulders ease off and was relieved that one of the hardest days he ever had to face was nearly over. A few more people were getting into their cars which were parked on the driveway and Carter wondered what the atmosphere would be like in the house that night, as it would be the first night following the funeral. That would be when the reality of what had happened would really kick in. He just prayed that they would be strong and cope as best they could. He was disappointed that he didn't manage to say goodbye to Starlet, and was concerned about her following her reaction at the funeral.

He comforted himself by thinking of how people handle stressful times in different ways. He looked forward to going round and having dinner with them some time later that week, and hopefully would have the chance to catch up with Starlet then.

It was late afternoon but the sun still hung high in the sky. Carter slowly walked away from the door and onto the driveway, making space for another couple of people to leave the house. He looked around but could not see Mary. He assumed that she was still inside saying goodbye to Claire, so he happily waited outside. He looked up at the house and was very impressed by its appearance. It was a huge house and the front was designed in a Tudor style, comprising of dark beams and white walls. It also had a double garage and a spacious front driveway, which could easily accommodate between four to six cars. He was so proud of what Marcus had achieved. The house was truly beautiful.

"Hey you. Are you ready?" said the sweet and tender voice of Mary. Carter, wearing a smile, turned around and replied. "Most definitely."

They walked for a while, the conversation mainly revolving around Mary's upbringing in San Francisco. Her mother worked as an editor for a newspaper called The Gateway, and her father was a doctor in paediatrics at a children's hospital not far from the Golden Gate Bridge. Mary very much took after her mother and always knew that her career would be within something very similar. Her parents were still alive and well and still working. She kept in regular contact with them, mainly via Skype. Mary had no brothers or sisters and grew up in a spacious property within the San Francisco Bay area, on Oak Street. The property consisted of two buildings, a rear cottage and a multi unit front building. It was over three levels and also had an accessible rooftop where the family would often sit in the sun and soak up the illustrious city views. Although Mary's parents' jobs required them to work unsociable hours at times, they would always manage to spend quality time together as a family as much as possible. It was clear to Carter from Mary's description that she was very close to her parents, and found it hard sometimes being so far from home. They had always been supportive of her both creatively and financially, and were one hundred per cent behind her idea and passion to work abroad.

Half hour passed and they were strolling quite happily back towards the centre of the city, not really heading for anywhere in particular but just moving in that general direction. Their conversation was light-hearted and enjoyable, almost distracting them from their surroundings, direction, and sense of time in fact.

The sun had started to make its decent, and was partly blocked by buildings and trees. Dusk had arrived and it was fresh and beautiful outside, perfect for a walk, and the orange glow from the dipping sun was being distributed causing a variety of contrasts in reflections creating the perfect romantic setting. Carter, every now and again, glanced at Mary to see her face and her expressions, wondering how she could make every word sound so delicate and uniquely captivating. She spoke lucidly and with so much enthusiasm for life that Carter hoped that some may rub off on himself. The city streets were not bustling and were quite placid in comparison to his shoe shopping experience the previous day. Everything just seemed so tranquil. The conversation flowed between them almost non-stop for a while longer and they agreed that they would stop for a coffee at the nearest café, as they had been walking for some time and were ready for a refreshment of some kind. It wasn't long before Mary spotted a Costa Coffee shop and they walked over to it.

"Sure you wouldn't rather go to Starbucks?" said Carter jokingly, suggesting that the American outlet maybe preferable to an American citizen.

"Very funny, and no." replied Mary refraining from laughing at his somewhat nonsensical joke.

They entered the shop and joined the queue.

"What would you like?" said Carter indicating that he was buying.

"A Cappuccino please, thank you."

"Would you like anything to eat?"

"No I'm fine thanks, but by all means don't let that deter you from getting something."

"Actually, I'm pretty full from the buffet back at the house. Managed to walk some of it off now though!"

"That's true. Well shall I find a place to sit?"

"Sure, OK." replied Carter.

Carter caught a strong aroma of cinnamon drift by and was immediately sure that his order would have some thrown in.

"Can I help please sir?"

"Yes could I have a Cappuccino and a . . . . actually make that two Cappuccinos."

"Which size would you like those Sir?"

"Regular?" said Carter confused as to what the correct terminology was in this particular establishment.

"Two regular Cappuccinos coming up."

Carter moved to the side and waited for his order. Mary had found a table with two stools facing each other in the corner that Carter had actually spotted when they came in, and would have been his preferred seat of choice. He looked at Mary and was still so amazed that they seemed to have bonded so well and so quickly. She was sitting looking out of the window, occasionally looking around to see if Carter was approaching.

"Two regular Cappuccinos!" shouted a voice from behind the counter.

"Thanks." replied Carter as the man, within a second, had returned to his station and was already preparing more beverages for the queuing customers. Carter dusted a light layer of cinnamon onto his drink, grabbed some napkins and walked over and joined Mary.

"There you go. One Cappuccino."

"Ah thanks Carter."

"My pleasure" "So do you live close by to here?"

"Not far, I have a one bedroom apartment, sorry . . . . flat, which is nice with friendly neighbours, and I have a cat called Snowball."

"Snowball?"

"Yeah well it beats Fur-ball!"

"True." responded Carter, with a burst of laughter.

"I love my cat, and have had her for a while now. Always good company, apart from when she occasionally claws at the furniture."

"You know it's funny. My furniture back at my flat in London looks like it has been clawed at. But we don't have a cat!"

"Really, go figure. Two guys sharing a flat together. What's the worst that can happen right?"

"Correct! An inevitable decline of hygiene and cleanliness for starters, followed by a scattering of dirty clothes that never seem to find their way into the washing machine, topped off by a mountain of dirty dishes and a very strange rancid smell that can only come from one source . . . . socks!"

"Oh my God, thanks for the in depth description." Mary said while laughing at Carter's quick and witty observations on male cleanliness.

The pair spent the best part of an hour there chatting away, telling tales from their respective college days, and sharing opinions on current affairs and certain world crises. They did however manage to avoid political discussions and, more importantly, the topic of religion. People have such strong views on both, that in most cases they go from a friendly conversation; to an opinion; to a debate; to a heated debate; to an argument; and ending in silence. Both parties are then enraged and hate each others guts, which isn't healthy for anyone. This of course is usually more common when alcohol is present, as Carter could certainly vouch for from his own experiences.

It started to get dark outside and there was noticeably more traffic was on the roads as people were finishing work and driving home. This sprung an indicator to them both that maybe it was time to head off. They walked out of Costa's and stopped outside on the street.

"Well, I think I may go home now. I am very tired. But it has been lovely meeting you Carter."

"You too Mary. It has turned from a very daunting day into a more than bearable one. I have had such a wonderful time getting to know you, a true pleasure."

"You too, and thank you for the Cappuccino."

"Hey, you got it." said Carter as he tried to impersonate an American accent. It didn't sound as good as he hoped.

"OK, see ya!" said Mary slowly turning away.

Carter stood still as he watched her walk away. He didn't know what to do next. He wanted to see her again. This was a moment that put him well and truly on the spot. Should he call after her and ask her to meet him again? They had got on so well after all. Maybe her just walking away was a sign that she was not interested in anything further? Maybe she was waiting for him to ask her? He took a step forward, then stuttered, reached out as if to call her, then faltered. "Oh for God's sake!" he mumbled to himself midst dilemma.

"Hey, Mary?" he said nervously.

Mary turned quickly, a look of delight on her face. "Yes Carter?"

"Just wondering if you were free tomorrow, to meet up maybe. I understand if the answer is no, but . . . ."

"I would love to." she answered smiling.

"Really?" said Carter with a look of shock on his face.

"Sure, why not. I'm working tomorrow afternoon but more than happy to meet in the morning for coffee or something?"

"That's great."

"Where are you staying?"

"I'm at the Herald Hotel which is on . . . ."

"I know it. That works out well as it isn't too far from my office. I'll meet you there at about 10.30am?"

"OK, look forward to it."

Mary disappeared up the street and Carter walked the other way, briefly punching the air in complete joy at what had happened. "Yes!" he shouted, to which a passing teenager called out the word "Dickhead!"

Carter didn't care, his world seemed as though it had just been turned on its head, and even though he refused to let himself get carried away and become too excited too early, he still could not believe what he had just experienced. "Maybe she just feels sorry for me or something?" he started to wonder, finding it almost unbelievable and impossible that she would be genuinely interested in him as a person. He found it weird that they had so much in common, as he always thought that his particular likes, dislikes and sense of humour according to others would be found to be unusual. As he continued walking he pondered over whether or not he would feel less confident the next morning, and maybe would not be able to carry himself off in the same way as he had, thus destroying his initial impression. Self doubt would accompany him all the way back to The Herald, tormenting his self assurances and hopes.

* * * *

With a spring in his step he walked through the hotel door and quickly climbed the stairs to his room. He opened the door and went and sat down on the bed, as if this location was his own mark of completion for the day. He felt a sudden rush of guilt creep over him. "Should I be this happy on the day of my brother's funeral?" "Forgive me Marcus." He took off his jacket and loosened his tie and flicked on the power to the TV via the remote. He laid down on the bed, using his elbows as leverage so he was still at an angle where he could still see the screen, although he wasn't paying any real attention to it. This day had taken him to the heights and depths of his emotions and he felt a strange mixture of elation and solitude. He was also shattered which was partly contributing to his self analysis of conflicting morals. He stood up, removed his tie and unbuttoned his shirt. He needed to take a shower. He held his head under that shower head for a good few minutes, letting the water wash through his hair and down his face. He felt it ease his tension and it provided a kind of massaging effect to his head and neck muscles. After drying himself off he was in two minds as to what to do about dinner. Should he go and battle the waiters in the hotel restaurant again, or should he pop out and have something. The time was just before 8pm and he decided to go out. He remembered seeing a fish restaurant a few roads away and decided to go and get a traditional Scottish fish supper. He switched off the TV as he left the room.

*   *   *   *

The fish restaurant was quite busy as it was one of the most popular in that area of the city. Inside was quite a big seating area and there were a few tables still vacant, most people opting for a take-away rather than eating in. Carter decided he was going to eat his supper there as he wasn't far from the hotel so it wouldn't be too late before he got back there. Carter placed his order and went and sat down at a table. He could not stop thinking about Mary. She was becoming his every thought, and he felt a little vulnerable that his feelings had become so open to someone. He felt as if he wanted to tell everyone about her. "Will!" he thought, and decided that he could squeeze in a quick chat before his food arrived. He reached for his mobile to call him. The phone rang but there was no answer. Carter planned to call Will the next day and give him an update.

Moments later the fish supper was placed down on the table in front of him. He was immediately impressed and couldn't wait to get stuck in. After he squirted some ketchup on the side of his plate he tucked in. He thought the food was delicious. He could see why the place had such a good reputation and he had noticed the awarded certificates placed proudly above the counter. He glanced around at the other customers, mostly families and couples. He felt a bit like the odd one out, being on his own, but didn't really mind.

His mind was focused more on his date with Mary the following morning. He also thought about Starlet and whether or not she would be alright, but knew that both Claire and Shannon would be strong, and be there for her. He set an alarm on his phone at that point, as he did not trust in himself to remember to do it back at the hotel. He also made a note to call Claire to arrange dinner one evening. It wasn't too long before he had cleared his plate, not even a trace of ketchup remained. He felt quite bloated and headed back to the hotel.

He asked the receptionist at the hotel for a wakeup call at 8am, as he was paranoid that his alarm on his mobile would not go off for some reason. He went upstairs and got ready for bed. He lay there, again with the TV playing to itself in the background, and he started to feel slightly apprehensive about meeting Mary again. "I need a drink." he said to himself, as if a proven remedy to lessen his nerves. He found it difficult to go to sleep due to a mixture of excitement and over tiredness. He focused on the lights on the ceiling that were being projected from the screen, concentrating on every movement in attempt to heavy his eyes and invite sleep. It didn't work. He turned off the TV and turned onto his side, closed his eyes and started playing out different methods of how to go sleep, counting sheep being one of the more desperate attempts. He pressed a random key on his mobile to activate the display screen light and could not believe his eyes. It was 1.15am already! He was sure that he hadn't yet slept a wink. He felt a slight acidic irritation in the back of his throat and guessed it was the salt from his fish supper. He got out of bed and grabbed a glass of water from the bathroom and knocked it back in one. He felt so thirsty and felt his headache returning, so he swallowed two painkillers before getting back into bed. His head was throbbing, and he could do nothing more than just lay still and ride through the pain until the effect of the painkillers kicked in. The soreness had now moved more to the front of his head and had developed into a migraine. He hoped, although unlikely, that the pills would completely eliminate the headache so he could get some sleep. However, he knew that he had also now become stressed and this would only worsen his situation.

More time passed but he was then too reluctant to check what time it was. One, because he knew it would anger him at finding out just how little time he had remaining for sleep, and two, his head was so tender that even the slightest motion would act as a trigger for what felt like a needle being driven into his corneas. He decided to concentrate his thoughts on more relaxing things, memories with his family from the past. He remembered one time where the family had gone to visit their Grandparents one Christmas. It was Christmas Day and Marcus and Carter were both as excited as each other, as not only did they know that more presents would await them there, but they loved their Grandparents dearly and it was always such a good time being with them. Their Grandmother would make double chocolate chip cookies, mince pies, sausage rolls, and her infamous rum truffles, which Carter and Marcus were allowed to have as a treat. Little did anyone know but their Grandfather used to sneak in an extra couple of shots of rum to the mixture without anyone noticing. He did enjoy a drink, more than most, especially over the festive period.

* * * *

Carter did not even notice but these couple of minutes thinking of these memories had eased him slightly, and he was on the verge of going to sleep.

* * * *

He could remember that when they arrived at their Grandparents house they were greeted by their golden retriever, Sherry, who fast approached the car as it pulled up to the house; its tail wagging with excitement and its mouth panting with happiness. Marcus jumped out of the car and hugged the dog immediately. He loved that dog.

* * * *

Carter's recollections of those events quickly transformed and became dreams. His body and mind had finally drifted into sleep.

* * * *

The fairy lights on the Christmas tree were twinkling gently in the window as they walked up to the house. The smell of freshly baked mince pies wafted up as the front door opened, bringing that traditional Christmas welcoming feel to all of them. Grandfather was already carving the goose outside on the kitchen worktop, tasting the odd slice as he did it. Grandmother was checking the roast potatoes and vegetables, and the sage and onion stuffing. The stuffing was Carter's favourite part. Up until that particular Christmas they had always had turkey on Christmas day, but their Grandfather had always wanted to try goose, as goose was the original family festive day meat of choice. Carter remembered his father saying in the car all the way there that goose was far too greasy as a meat, and it would only be enjoyable if it was cooked correctly, so he was impatiently waiting to see if they had pulled it off. Christmas crackers were being pulled at the table and Marcus and Carter pulled both of their own with each other. Marcus got a plastic see through dice and Carter ended up with a corkscrew, a corkscrew that Max didn't waste much time in acquiring. All but their mother wore the Christmas crowns on their heads, as she always believed that they gave her migraines as a child. The first slice of goose meat was tested by Max as the others sat at the table and eagerly awaited the verdict.

"I think it tastes gorgeous." said Grandfather. Max finished chewing his slither and looked up at Grandmother Jakeman.

"What can I say? I agree with him, it is absolutely gorgeous. Brilliantly cooked Mum."

"Thanks love." replied a proud Grandmother.

"Hang on! I kept an eye on it while it was cooking! Don't I get any credit?" added Grandfather.

"Yeah OK, well done Dad." said Max.

The family thoroughly enjoyed their Christmas dinner before going on to open their presents which were neatly placed under the tree. That year Carter remembered Marcus getting a train set and some action figures, while he himself got some puzzles and a pair of roller skates.

* * * *

"Carter, Carter, come in here! Look at my train set, it's ready." shouted Marcus from the adjoining room.

Carter ran into see the progress that Marcus, with the help of Max, had made in finishing the set which indeed was then ready for action. They watched for hours as the steam train raced around the tracks, up and down over small hills, through a little model village which contained the station, and through a tunnel that Max had built earlier that day in his shed. It was tremendous. Max had also given a whistle to Marcus to blow when the train halted and was ready to move off again.

* * * *

"So are you all set? You've got everything?" asked Carter as Marcus was about to leave for University.

"Sure hope so. Well if I have forgotten anything now then that's that." replied Marcus as he threw his heavy rucksack over his shoulder.

Marcus would not be home again till the end of that semester, maybe more. Marcus hugged Carter goodbye at the front door and walked away, up the garden path and onto the street. Carter went into the house and immediately walked through to the living room and looked out though the window. He watched Marcus walking further and further away until he disappeared down a side road in the distance. Carter's heart sank. He felt alone and abandoned, and although he would want nothing more than Marcus to go off and live his dreams, he wished he hadn't gone. He spent the following few days pretending that Marcus was still living there, imagining that he was in the next room, or that he was upstairs doing something, just so he had that feeling of him being close by. He would sometimes talk as if Marcus was there sitting next to him on the sofa. Weeks passed and the phone calls from Marcus would become more and more infrequent, until finally it was rare that they spoke to each other.

* * * *

The coffin was being lowered into the ground as Carter stood looking down into the hole. The coffin was half open, allowing everyone to see Marcus' face. Except it wasn't Marcus lying in the coffin, it was him. He looked up from the coffin at the people standing at ground level above him. There were then only two people standing there, Will and Mary. He reached out his hand and tried to speak but he got no reaction from them and they turned and walked away. He felt trapped as dirt began to be shovelled down upon him, his face was being covered and he could not get out. No one could hear his screams, he was alone. He felt the soil fill his mouth and push down into his throat. He started to choke, he couldn't breath, was panicking, flailing but trapped, smothered . . . .

* * * *

Carter jumped up in bed with sweat pouring down his forehead, the pillow case equally drenched. He was still gasping, wildly drawing long deep breaths to try to compose himself. He realised that he had turned in his sleep and ended up face down on the pillow, which he associated with his dream. Remembering his dreams disturbed him to say the least. It had sort of played out his life so far, ranging from his earlier more happier memories, to when he had to deal with his emotions and sadness, his fear of being alone, to eventually dying alone. He associated the last sequence with not only his thoughts on whether or not it should have been him laying there in that coffin in place of his brother, but the fact he had met Mary, and was this a sign of hope for him to change his life, be happy, and not alone, or his greatest fear of dying alone.

He walked out into the bathroom and washed his face with cold water again and again to cool down. His headache had gone, thankfully, so he returned to bed, swapping his pillow for the one next to it and laid down to recover from his nightmare. He checked the time and it was 4.45am. He was still quite shaken and wondered whether it was wise to go back to sleep. He didn't want to end up back in the same nightmare. He began to think of Mary and visualised her eyes. They were dazzling in every sense of the word. If she did not speak through her mouth he could hear a thousand words through her eyes. They filled him with comfort and he felt paralysed by their beauty. They gave him courage and belief. He was amazed at how he felt, besotted by a lady that he had only met for a day.

* * * *

The alarm from his mobile phone activated at the same time the hotel room phone rang, causing Carter to wake with a start. He was still half asleep and quite confused as to which one to deal with first. He picked up the room phone,

"Yep?"

"Good morning Mr Jakeman, this is your wakeup call."

"Thank you. I am . . . . I am awake!"

Carter tried to replace the handset whilst at the same time deactivating his mobile phone alarm which ended in him dropping both, which annoyed him into becoming fully awake. He gathered them quickly and concentrated on shutting off the noise on his mobile, before gently returning the other receiver. He got out of bed and stretched while thinking of what he should wear for his date with Mary. He only brought a small collection of clothes but he thought that just a casual shirt and jeans would be fine. After all they were probably only going to meet for a coffee and a chat, maybe another walk. He freshened up and started to get dressed. He could see that his wound had changed in the last couple of days and looked to be healing quite nicely. He suddenly felt sick with nerves. It was 9.30am and he was meeting Mary at 10.30am. He tried to remain calm and not panic. Being alone in the room was not helping so he thought as breakfast was served until 10am, this could be the perfect distraction he was looking for.

He walked past the breakfast bar en route to obtaining a seat. It had the usual cereal choices, bread and croissants, jams and marmalades, with the standard assortment of juices consisting of orange, apple and pineapple. As he sat down he noticed a breakfast menu in front of him which gave people the option to go for a fuller breakfast rather than the buffet. He could smell bacon and saw a gentleman with his wife at the next table along chomping away at a full English breakfast. Carter was very tempted.

"Good morning Sir, are you going for menu or buffet this morning?"

"I'm going to go for . . . . the buffet thanks." Carter said, pleased with himself.

"Would you like tea or coffee with that Sir?"

"Yes black coffee please!"

The waiter walked away leaving the path clear for Carter to go and choose from the breakfast bar. He did feel a little peckish. As he approached the bar he picked up a piece of bread and filtered it through the toasting machine next to it. He also picked up a croissant, some butter, and a little pot of strawberry jam. He retrieved his now toasted bread from the contraption, and before returning to his table poured himself a glass of orange juice. As he sat back on his chair the waiter was there with his coffee. Carter spotted the clock on the wall to the side of where he was sitting and it was 10.05am. Twenty-five minutes more and he would get to once again see the girl of his dreams. By the time he had finished his breakfast his nerves had gone, but he knew they were still on high alert. His eyes drifted to the clock—it was now 10.20am. Carter left his table and walked out to use the toilet which was just off the main foyer area. He stood and looked at himself in the mirror, straightening his shirt and adjusting his jeans at the waist to try to make him look a touch more presentable. It was now a matter of minutes. Just before he left the toilet to go and wait Mary's arrival at the main entrance, he was overcome with nerves and he dashed into the nearest cubicle. He was sick. Sadly, his recently consumed breakfast had now been redistributed. He leant over the toilet for about a minute, gathering himself and pleading to himself not to be sick again, and panicking that Mary would be arriving at any second. Deep breath followed by deep breath. He began to feel normal again and less frantic. After quickly freshening up again he took one last look at himself in the mirror before exiting.

Carter stood by the main door to the hotel and was there by 10.30am on the dot. He leant up against the door frame, leaving enough space for people to come in and out. He looked left and then right to see if he could see Mary approaching, but nothing. The fresh air, however, was doing him some good and he could feel his body start to tremble less and less. He looked out for taxis, some slowing as they got close to the hotel, but never stopping. After about ten minutes he began to doubt if she was going to turn up. He felt that she may have only agreed to meet him the day before so as not to hurt his feelings. He walked back inside; his head bowed almost in defeat and sat down on the green Chesterfield sofa in the foyer. The sofa looked to be of high quality, an expensive fabric that had been sewn with extreme attention to detail, which often used time consuming hand executing techniques from only the best of seamstresses. Time passed, maybe another ten or fifteen minutes, before Carter made the prediction that Mary was not going to come. He was gutted and decided to make his way back to his room, and to make things worse he felt another headache coming on.

"What is it with these fucking headaches, Jesus? I'm gonna go back to my room and eat a fucking bundle of painkillers to stop this bollocks!" he muttered in an angry but quiet voice.

Carter was only exaggerating and not at all serious about the amount of painkillers he would take, but just vented it out of pure frustration. Looking deflated and torn he started to slowly climb the stairs.

"Hey Carter! Carter hey, sorry I'm so late." sounded an out of breath voice coming from the foyer. His eyes lit up and his grin was uncontrollable. He turned around, trying to disguise his relief by acting cool and collected.

"Hey Mary. How are you?"

"Fine, I just got caught up this morning. I had to go to the bank on the way over here, and the chaos in there. Wow!"

"A hold-up?" said Carter, dropping his first gag of the day.

"Very funny." replied Mary, acknowledging his joke and politely shedding a brief laugh at it.

"It's fine." added Carter. "I almost gave up hope on you coming, but I'm glad you did"

"So am I." she replied, as Carter took the last couple of steps to foyer level.

"So? Do you fancy going somewhere to have a coffee, or maybe some breakfast? I am starving!" said Mary.

"Yes sure sounds perfect. I could eat!" replied Carter as he did feel quite hollow at that point.

As they walked towards the main door a lady appeared at reception and called out after him. "Sir? Excuse me Sir?"

Carter stopped and turned back, "Yes?" he replied as he approached the desk.

"Could I just take your room number for your breakfast please? I didn't manage to get it on your way in earlier."

"Six." said Carter grudgingly as now Mary knew that he had eaten.

"Sorry, you have already eaten?" said Mary.

"Well, yes, but it's a long story."

"And you weren't going to tell me? I assume because you did not want to make me feel uncomfortable about wanting to get something. You were going to eat with me and not say anything. That's so sweet!"

"Or just a greedy pig!"

"Ha ha. I know that isn't true by your figure. That is unless you have an amazing metabolism. But no, people can't be that lucky, surely!"

Carter laughed and agreed with Mary humbly and ever so slightly embarrassed. He made note of the compliment she had paid him regarding his figure and was touched. The two walked out onto the street.

"Come on, I know this great little place not far from here." said Mary.

* * * *

They sat opposite each other and he tried his best not to stare, but she was just so pretty. She had taken him to a quaint coffee and sandwich bar not far from the church where the funeral had taken place. He had actually seen this shop when walking the previous day. They both ordered a toasted cheese and tomato sandwich and a coffee. Mary had a briefcase with her, and was dressed in office attire. She wore a black suit and a blouse that matched the colour of her eyes. Her hair, tied back, was as golden as the desert sand; her eyes as blue as the ocean; and her face was as perfectly sculpted as the finest pieces of art.

"So you have to work this afternoon." Carter remembered.

"Yes I know. And on a Friday as well."

"So is it on a rota basis your hours or . . . . ?"

"No, it's a deadline thing. I was initially booked off today, but we need to run a publication earlier than we thought, so I need to go in and get that sorted. I need to speak with a client of ours over the phone but he was unavailable until this afternoon, hence me having to go in now rather than my preferred choice of this morning."

"What time will you finish?"

"Who knows? When it is done."

They finished their late morning breakfast and decided to take a walk. They headed in the direction of where Mary worked, so at least she didn't have to worry about getting back on time. She didn't have to be there until 2pm, so it gave them a couple of hours together.

"So, Carter . . . . no girlfriend then?"

"No, afraid not." replied Carter opting to offer no further comment at that point.

"That surprises me."

"Really? Why is that?"

"Well you are such an interesting guy, and normal, and funny. These aspects are what women look for in a guy. And such men are usually spoken for!"

"Well thank you for the barrage of compliments. I really appreciate it. And the feeling is mutual."

"Thank you also kind Sir." replied Mary with a smile.

They stopped at a set of traffic lights before crossing over to the entrance of a park further up the street. This would give them a chance to just stroll around peacefully and without interruption. The sky had turned quite bleak and it looked as if a storm was brewing. Although it was not cold, there was a stiff breeze in the air. The day had, however, become quite humid. They walked around the maze of paths as they continued to enjoy hearing one another's stories and experiences. The flowers were out and in full bloom which added an array of colours to their surroundings. The smell of the freshly cut grass added an extra pleasant quality to their walk together, even if the sky was in fact nearly the same dark grey colour as the stone path in front of them. After a few minutes they came across a small duck pond which had a wooden bench just to the side of it. It was such a nice peaceful little area, a niche just enough distance away from the path to remain undisturbed, a secret place off the main path. It was a romantic setting and was an inviting place to sit and spend some time. They naturally gravitated to it and sat down. A variety of birds were darting in and around the bushes surrounding the pond. Carter could tell the robins from the blue tits, but that was about it. Some of the ducks from the pond had waddled up to them, expecting to be fed, but as they had nothing to offer them, the ducks soon admitted defeat and returned to the water. They both agreed that they would have to come back to feed the ducks another time, as they felt so terrible at having to witness their poor little faces quacking for a treat, especially the ducklings. Also it was the two of them suggesting that they would be happy to meet up with each other again as well, which was positive for them both. Before they knew it their conversation was back in full flow. Carter had no fear, and he was speaking freely about a variety of topics, although none of them ventured as far as his bipolar disorder at that stage. But his euphoric state was intoxicating and infectious. Mary was laughing away and intrigued by Carter's stories of his younger years spent with Marcus, and some of the funny things they used to get up to. She found him fascinating and smart, enthusiastic and kind. They talked about Mary's likes and dislikes, her habits and general things that sparked for an exciting conversation. Information was moving backwards and forwards so quickly that they were unlikely to remember exactly everything that had been discussed at the end of it. They didn't worry, as in that moment they both felt elated, electrified and free.

CHAPTER SEVEN

Fine droplets of rain started to fall distracting Mary and Carter from their deep conversation, and having such a good time, thought they had only been talking for about ten minutes at most. In fact a whole hour had passed. It was time for Mary to go to work. The rain fell slightly heavier and the sky became even darker than before and having been so engrossed in conversation they hadn't even noticed. It wasn't too much longer before the faint rumbling of thunder could be heard in the distance. Quickening their stride to the same pace as the ever increasing power of the rain, they walked away from the duck pond and headed for the park exit. Carter offered to walk Mary to her office, but she insisted that he go back to the hotel, rather than spend even more time out in the rain than was necessary. He agreed, as he could see she wasn't going to have it any other way, but as they had not yet officially planned to meet up again, they stopped briefly, finding a sheltered spot beneath an overhanging tree branch to talk.

"Mary, this morning has been great. You are such good company."

"So are you." she replied pulling her coat up and over her head for protection.

"Look I know you've got to run, but do you fancy meeting up with me again?"

"I'd love to," she replied, her eyes bright and full of life.

"That's great. Well tomorrow is Saturday? Are you free?"

"Sure. I'll meet you at your hotel again, same time?"

"OK perfect."

"Gotta run!"

"Ok take care Mary, should really exchange numbers?"

Mary never heard him as she was heading off down the street, anxious to get out of the rain. Carter headed back to his hotel but regretted that he hadn't asked her for her number earlier so they could have planned meeting up somewhere else rather than the Herald again. He didn't mind but was not exactly sure how convenient it was for her to come there to meet him. It was not very gentleman-like he thought. He looked back to see if he could still see her, but she had gone.

* * * *

Carter arrived back at the hotel looking like a drowned rat, clothes dripping wet and feeling uncomfortably sticky from the effects of the humidity. Smug looking faces passed him on the stairs and in the corridor, as guests held their umbrellas close, prepared for the downpour outside.

"That's my shower done for the morning!" he jokingly commented to one snooty looking woman who passed him.

His comment was not reciprocated and he wasn't in the least bit surprised. Once in his room he immediately started stripping off, placing his wallet and mobile on the side table, before dashing to the bathroom to grab a towel to wrap around him. To his shock and horror he found the cleaning lady in there finishing off, placing fresh towels on the towel rack.

"Aghhhh, shit, Christ!" screamed Carter, the first words to spring to mind after being hurtled into sheer embarrassment. The cleaner jumped back equally horrified by his manic entrance.

"My God!" said the woman, as she took a quick look up and down his naked body, her eyes bulging in shock. Carter scrambled around for something to cover himself, the nearest thing being a small hand towel! It was convenient enough for one area temporarily. The cleaner, using more sense, handed him one of the big towels from the rack, and they stood in silence for a second while he covered himself.

"I'm sorry Sir, but the sign was on the door. The "cleaning in progress" sign!" said the lady.

"I apologise too, I rushed in. I didn't see it. Honestly I didn't. I'm not . . . ."

"It's OK Sir, I'm finished now anyway so will get out of your way."

"Ok, sorry again for the scare." said Carter as he watched the woman swiftly head for the door.

“Hey you’ve left your air freshener here!” shouted Carter spotting the can still perched on the side of the sink.

The cleaner had already slammed the door in a frenzied rush to escape. Carter laughed to himself, half with embarrassment and half because he thought it was hilarious. It reminded him to call Will, as this was the sort of story that would be a great one to tell, and one that Will would no doubt appreciate. Returning to the bedroom he grabbed his phone from the bedside table to make the call. However, he noted the time on the phone and decided not to call Will at that precise moment as it was Friday afternoon. He knew Will would be busy trying to finish up for the weekend and didn’t want to disturb him. Instead he chose to call Claire.

“Hello!”

“Hi Claire, its Carter. Just thought I’d give you a quick call to see how you and the girls are doing.”

“Hey Carter. Not too bad, well as good as can be expected I suppose. Just very tired.”

“And Starlet?”

“Better thankfully. She ate breakfast with us at the table this morning so that seemed positive. That’s the first time since . . . .”

“She is going to find it difficult. She is at that age. I’m sure she’ll be ok. Just needs time.”

“I know, we all do.”

“Look, about dinner. I would love to come over one evening. When is it convenient for you?”

“How about Sunday, I’ll do a roast chicken or something. Does that sound OK?”

“Roast chicken sounds like the real deal. Thanks Claire. I look forward to seeing you all then.”

"And you too. What time, shall we say? 4pm?"

"4pm sounds great. See you then."

Carter cut the call and dropped his mobile down onto the bed. He felt relieved that Starlet seemed to be improving. He sat down on a chair by the bathroom door to rest for a moment. The ordeal at being seen stark naked had taken its toll on him a bit, so he needed to sit and recuperate for a second. His thoughts immediately turned to Mary. All he could think about was Mary, and how he was already so very desperate to see her again. He couldn't wait. He had noticed that he had felt light on his feet and energised since he first spoke to her. The effect that Mary was having on him felt like an addiction already, a drug, and he couldn't wait for another fix of her. The time was 2.45pm and he felt he should do something. Although the weather outside was horrendous he was not prepared to stay in his room staring at the walls for the remainder of the day. He thought about sitting downstairs in the hotel bar for a while, have a couple of drinks and wait to see if the rain eased off. If the weather did improve he would then to go out and have a wander around.

* * * *

The bar was not that busy and it seemed that people had not let the outside conditions deter them from venturing out onto the Edinburgh streets. Carter had grabbed some information and sightseeing leaflets from the lobby and thought it was the perfect way to kill some time. He casually approached the bar and lifted himself onto a stool. He placed the leaflets down on the bar along with his mobile phone, and took a moment to absorb the pleasant surroundings. Character and snugness emanated from the bar, its dim lights adding an alluring gloom to it. It was the perfect setting to just sit back, relax and have a drink.

"Good afternoon Sir, what's your poison today?" asked the burly barmen, in a broad Scottish accent, and whose knuckles were as big as Carter's fists.

"A pint of lager please." replied Carter.

The barman stepped to one side, plucked a glass from above, placed it under the tap and started to pull. Carter looked around to see who else was in the bar. It was quiet but there were a few fellow stragglers milling around. At the end of the bar to his left sat a man dressed mostly in tweed, attentively reading a book. Carter tried to work out which book and could just about make out the name Machiavelli on the spine. "Could it be 'The Prince'?" he thought, and only because this was the only work of Machiavelli that he knew. Sitting behind the man, at a table slightly to the left, were two middle-aged women sharing a bottle of Burgundy. They both looked very serious, as if discussing something of extraordinary importance. Carter assumed it must be about their respective husbands, as the occasional baring of teeth indicated so. He turned to his right and there was another man, alone, sitting at a table and looking like he had been there for a while. He was slumped in his chair, a newspaper placed in front of him, probably unread. His face was flushed and his eyes had the revealing quality that he had had his fair share already. "Please don't come and talk to me!" thought Carter, the sound of his pint glass landing on the bar turning his gaze away from the man. He took a sip and it felt heavenly. Relaxed and content he proceeded in looking through his leaflets. The first one he picked up was of the infamous Edinburgh Castle. The castle that floated majestically on top of the high black rock and which indeed looked magnificent from every angle. Reading the leaflet he saw that it was open from 9.30am to 6pm from early April through to the end of September, and the last entry of the day had to be 45 minutes before closing time. News to Carter, as he delved further through the leaflet, was the castle was actually built on an extinct volcano. More interesting facts appeared such as how archaeologists had found evidence of human occupation there dating back as far as 900 BC. "That was the late Bronze Age wasn't it? Whatever it was, it was ancient!" he pondered as he proceeded further down the paragraph.

Edinburgh Castle was firmly high on the list of his places to visit. He picked up the next leaflet which advertised the Outlook Tower on Castlehill. This was a camera obscura which was located at the top of the Royal Mile. He remembered seeing a TV programme on the Tower some time ago and had been interested in visiting it ever since. Also he wanted to visit the Edinburgh Vaults. This was top of his list. He had researched the history of the vaults back when he was reading tons upon tons of material on haunted locations of the UK. He had virtually become obsessed by stories of ghostly activity, developing a love and a connection to old buildings of significance. This could be castles, old inns, churches and such like. He would visit as many as his life would allow him to. The paranormal not only provided him with a hobby cloaked in mystery and atmosphere, with all the suspense of a Hitchcock classic, but also posed him with another fascinating conundrum. The afterlife! "Was there any truth in it?" "Could all ghost stories throughout history have been made up?" Could all evidence gathered really have either been tampered with or were they all just simply a trick of the mind? Carter was unsure. He did however have other reasons why he yearned for proof; why he researched parapsychology in depth; his utter desperation to know. He needed to know there was something after this life, something that could potentially provide him with another chance, or an opportunity to be happy. Maybe reincarnation did exist, where his soul could be born encased inside a stronger makeup, in other words a body that was fit for purpose, not the one that he had been given, a body within which he felt imprisoned. He also wanted an assurance of once again being reunited with loved ones long gone. He needed that, more than anything else.

There was one other place that he just had to go to while he was in Edinburgh, and that was the local whisky tour experience. This made him especially excited, as it involved not only a tour of alcohol, but a tour of Scotch whisky, in which he had indulged on more than one occasion! He flicked open the page of that particular leaflet with his left hand, while he took a slurp from his pint with his right. The first thing he saw was the picture of a small crystal tumbler which held inside it the deepest amber coloured malt you could imagine, a perfect single malt whisky glowing in all its glory, enticing all to taste, and inviting your palate and senses with the promise of the most breathtaking experience conceivable. Further down the page were more details of the tour and what else was included in the experience. It explained that visitors would be sent off through a replica of a distillery inside a moving barrel. The idea was that you would, on the journey, witness the full process of whisky making. "Sounds like a plan." thought Carter as he read further. This was a must for his trip and by the time he finished reading the rest of the leaflet he was eager to visit it immediately, and also, funnily enough, had a sudden urge for a wee dram. He decided to go for the latter as one glance at the window still being hammered with rain immediately brought an end to any chance of him going outside.

He swiftly got the barman's attention and ordered a single whisky, as well as another pint. "Maybe Mary would be interested in going to some of these places with me?" he thought. "On the other hand, she has probably been to all of the main attractions before." he concluded. Carter also wanted to try and spend some time in the countryside, perhaps the Trossachs. However it would be quite an exhaustive drive to do everything in one day, given that he would want to stop at other areas along the way. He planned to ask at reception at some point where he could hire a car. He knew the airport would have a cluster of companies to serve such a purpose but was hoping for something a little less expensive. He only wanted a small car, just something to get him around. He made a mental note to ask Claire on the Sunday as to where the picture of Marcus holding the fishing rod was taken. He would like to go there.

A couple of pints later and he began to feel merry. The combination of genuine excitement mixed with alcohol was something he hadn't felt for a very long time, and it felt good. He looked over the leaflets once again, taking joy in the fact that he was only a stone's throw away from these very special places.

By this time a couple of more characters had entered the bar, a lady in her late thirties who ordered a dry white wine before choosing to find a seat conveniently away from the suspicious looking man who had drunk to much, and a man in his later years who ordered a double rum and sat just along from Carter at the bar. The gentleman specifically caught Carter's eye. He had a great white beard, wore a tartan flat cap, held a pipe, and carried a walking stick with the handle carved and shaped to look like the head of a tiger. He wore a three-quarter length black coat and big black steel toe capped boots. He was a large, well proportioned man and his hands were like those of a bear. The man necked back his double rum in one, the barman already placing down another before him, so obviously he was a regular customer.

"You alright Jock?" asked the barman.

"Aye, though it is coming down hard out there!" replied the old man.

"I know. I'm off shift in about an hour as well, typical! Hope it has stopped by then."

"Aye hopefully, however I fear this is in for the night."

Carter listened to them talk for a while longer before the old man excused himself from the conversation to pay a visit to the gents. Carter had noticed in this time how knowledgeable the man was of the city of Edinburgh, and indeed of its history. He was obviously born and bred around there. The man seemed gentle and content, but it was clear that life had in no way been easy. Carter was given the impression that it had been somewhat cumbersome for him.

"A great fellow he is I can tell you." said the barman, noticing that Carter had been listening to them talking.

"I take it you are friends?" replied Carter.

"Yes sort of I suppose. We have a good chat whenever he comes in. He isn't staying at the hotel though. He lives locally."

"How comes he chooses to drink in a hotel bar, and not a local pub?"

The barman looked at Carter with eyes that were obviously keeping a secret. He hesitated from disclosing the information, concerned that he would be abusing the old man's trust by telling a total stranger. He chose to tell Carter anyway.

"That old man there is Jocky Ragg. He and his wife used to come in here for dinner every now and again, celebrating birthdays or anniversaries and so on. But sadly, a year ago she died, and since then he comes in here probably three or four times a month. He stays here for a good few hours and then staggers home. It is sad, but I suppose it helps him deal with it better. And as they shared so many special evenings here together, I guess this is the place where he feels like he can still have a sense that she is with him. Beats sitting at home alone."

"No children?" Carter said quickly, conscious that the man would be back at any moment.

"Yes, one, but he died young in a bike accident. Dreadful."

"Oh my God!"

"I know. Can't imagine what that must have been like for them. Can I get you another drink?"

"Oh yes thank you, just a pint please." said Carter, realising that the old man had returned into the bar behind him. The man managed with a little difficulty to lift himself back on to his stool which was only a few feet or so away from Carter. The barman pulled another lager for Carter, before serving another guest to his left. The old man, Jocky Ragg, looked deep in memory, reflecting on times gone by, life all but sucked out of him but for the sheer strength and determination to just keep going.

The man was not seeing an empty hotel room bar in front of him. He was seeing his past memories playing out in front of him, like on a reel of film, opening up his heart to them, reliving the feelings, the love, the words spoken, the years of joy and happiness, and utilised those feelings to make him feel as if she was indeed still there by his side. This comforted him, and he used this method as a kind of therapy to deal with loss. The man was drinking his rum now with more steadiness, his hands as steady as a flat calm ocean. You could tell that with every sip, Jocky embraced the warmth that it provided. The flavour teleported his senses, smells and memories back to all different places of the past, each gulp would evoke a different time and place. Suddenly he looked to his left and saw that Carter was watching him intently. Carter quickly shifted on his stool trying to innocently look away.

"Are you up here on your travels my friend?" asked Jocky as he noticed Carter's leaflets on the bar. Carter slowly glanced around slightly embarrassed that Jocky would think him nosey, which he was.

"Yes, well kind of. No actually. Well a bit of both." Carter stuttered still feeling like a guilty little boy who had been caught doing something he shouldn't be.

"A bit of both?" questioned Jocky whilst looking a touch confused.

"Yes sorry. I am here in Edinburgh for my brother's funeral, and while I am up here I am going to visit some of the sites. So I am effectively on my travels in a roundabout sort of way."

"Oh, I'm sorry to hear about your brother." said Jocky with an added kindness to his voice.

Carter picked up his glass and took a drop, as did Jocky with his own after raising it slightly in the air. They toasted to Marcus' memory. As the subject of loss was common ground for both of them they decided to join in each other's company, although their conversation did mainly revolve around Edinburgh and its intriguing history of which Jocky was very proud and Carter as equally interested. Jocky held out his hand to formally introduce himself. "Jocky Ragg's the name, but most know me as Old Man Ragg. Nice to meet to you lad."

Carter shook his hand and after the usual introductions, Jocky edged his stool a little closer as if about to engage in a mammoth discussion on life, common conversation and stories that would be found in most bars.

Carter felt he would be fascinated by Jocky's life, and was more than happy to be talking with a local, a man who could give him all the insight into the city that he needed, and all of his life experiences that came along with it. Carter sat and listened as Jocky recollected all sorts of interesting facts and stories from the old days, with Carter every now and again signalling to the barman to refill their glasses.

Jocky Ragg was born locally, in the old town itself in fact. Back in the early 1940s, when he was just a little boy, he remembered how during the war, he would often frequent the bomb shelter in Princess Street Gardens. His father was a lecturer in the Department of Therapeutics at Edinburgh University. Most of his time was spent in research, but Jocky remembered how his father would come home and talk endlessly on a range of topics, telling him a whole plethora of stories. Even though his main area was chemistry, he could have just as easily have been a lecturer in history. This is where Jocky's knowledge and passion for the city's past first started, from stories told by his father. He remembered that one of his father's proudest achievements in life was back in 1939 when he had been involved in setting up one of the first blood banks in Scotland, at the Royal Infirmary. His mother worked part-time at a local nursing home, tending to the old folk, and carrying out various house chores. Since the war, however, Jocky had witnessed the city being torn down and rebuilt at a frightening rate. To his relief though the buildings were reconstructed using considerate and traditional methods, resulting in the city being able to retain its reputation as one of the most prestigious and internationally recognised cities in the world. He paid particular importance to how popular the Edinburgh Festival had become over the years, as he had a soft spot for comedians, as did Carter, and could even remember the first ever Edinburgh Festival being held back in 1947. Even though proud, Jocky's one and only negative comment about Edinburgh was from the year 1970 when Edinburgh held the Commonwealth Games. He remembered that time as a negative one as it was during the time his mother had passed away.

At touching upon a point of sorrow it drew his attention back to his wife and son. It was at that moment he chose to tell Carter about the loss of his son, and how he had died in a motorcycle accident. The year it happened was 1999, and was the same year a Scottish Parliament opened in Edinburgh after a gap of two hundred and ninety-two years. His son's name was Malcolm and worked locally as a butcher. Jocky quickly diverted his stories back to the city. He told Carter of how only in the last ten years the city had been victim to a ferocious fire. It happened in Cowgate and South Bridge in the Old

Town. Due to the extensive fire damage some buildings had to be demolished after being deemed unsafe. There was a slight pause, as Old Man Ragg took another drop of rum, and Carter pounced upon the opportunity to push the conversation more toward the more gruesome and gruelling side of Edinburgh's history, rather than just the twentieth century. Jocky chuckled, as not only was this area of interest popular amongst most tourists, but it was something that he knew a hell of a lot about, and was only too happy to share those stories with Carter.

"Where do I begin young Carter?" said Jocky.

"Absolutely anywhere, I am interested in all of it."

Jocky smiled with appreciation and Carter informed him of his own personal interest in history, and how he had studied certain historical references before.

"Well Carter let me start with one for the movies! The story of William Burke and William Hare. What a couple of jokers these two were."

Old Man Ragg commenced his story, telling it like his father had told him all those years before, with total enthusiasm and added suspense and drama. Carter was instantly captivated. He explained to Carter how the two men were initially grave robbers back in the 1800s, but as the study of anatomy grew and more students were taken in, the need for more bodies to dissect was imperative to their learning, and also to further discovery. So Burke and Hare started murdering people, taking them to the anatomy school themselves and receiving payment for bringing another body.

"Ludicrous as it sounds now Carter, back then it was work of genius, a way to get rich quick."

"I know of these two. Always amazed me as to why it took so long for them to be caught?"

"Well some say that the school itself was in on it, but were willing to turn a blind eye, as they looked at it as a necessity for the welfare of future generations, and were willing to make the sacrifice of a few to benefit the masses."

"How many did they murder Jocky? Was a fair few wasn't it?"

"Anywhere up to thirty apparently. Only one of them was hanged for it as well, Burke, and for only one murder which was the last body found, an Irish lady called Mrs Docherty. The other one turned King's evidence against him. You know what is funny? Burke's body was donated to the medical school afterwards for what they called useful dissection, how ironic!"

"Really, that is funny. So the other one walked free? I wasn't aware of that."

"Aye, a free man! You know that Burke's skeleton is still on display at the University Medical School? Maybe add that to your itinerary for your trip?"

Carter laughed and excused himself to go to the gents.

"Would you like another, it's on me." asked Jocky as Carter walked away.

"No I'll get these." replied Carter almost out of respect for Jocky.

"No Carter I insist." said Jocky in a tone with which Carter could do nothing but agree.

Carter hurriedly walked off to the gents. He was enjoying Old Man Ragg's company and was eager to return to hear more. Finding someone who not only had that vast amount of local knowledge, but who was also only too willing to share it, was a Godsend in Carter's eyes.

It was nearly dark outside and the rain was still falling, but it was more settled than earlier in the day. People were returning to the hotel after their long sightseeing day, with their feet tired and their stomachs crying out for nourishment. Most people were walking straight into the restaurant, their tables already reserved for the evening. Some made a quick dash for their room to change out of their wet clothes.

The hotel became slightly busier; the bar was filling quite quickly with guests, who were either hoping to settle down in there for the rest of the evening, or just having a quick tipple before sitting down to supper. Carter crossed the lobby and headed back towards the bar. He was conscious that Mary would be at the hotel at 10.30 the next morning, so did not want to get completely hammered, but also did not want to cut short his evening talking to Old Man Ragg short either. He reassured himself that he would be fine, as he often did once he had consumed a certain amount. As Carter approached the bar he noticed that Jocky had kept his stool empty for him. The bar was much busier now with customers and left Carter just enough space to sit back onto his stool.

"Bit busier now isn't it Jocky?"

"Aye, Friday evenings, at this time of year."

"That's another place I want to go to while I'm here—Arthur's Seat. You must get a cracking view from up there right?"

"Oh definitely. I haven't been up there for some time now I admit, due to the withering legs, but I used to go up there quite a lot in my younger days lad. The best views are looking west, where you can see the castle, and both the old town and the new."

"How long is the walk?"

"Anywhere up to two hours depending on how far you are willing to walk."

"Sounds nice. I'm meeting a lady tomorrow so I may suggest it as an idea."

"I'm sure the wee lass will find it very enjoyable." replied Jocky.

Carter realised at that point that it was more than likely that Jocky and his wife had probably had walks up there before, so he decided to stray from talking anymore about Mary, just out of respect.

"So what about the vaults Jocky? Full of mystery, I'm looking forward to going there."

"Oh yes. Actually there used to be a bar down there many, many years ago. They would serve oysters in there to the locals, but they were never fresh oysters. So what they used to do immediately after swallowing the oyster was to take a big swig of gin, strong gin I mean, which would then kill off the bacteria from the oysters in their stomachs, preventing them from getting sick."

"Clever, but at the same time rancid!"

"You said it lad. But remember in those times money was hard to come by, and people would go to near enough any lengths to acquire whatever they could."

They both momentarily pondered on those last words, and how things had changed so dramatically in time. The bar was now near enough at capacity, with almost every seat taken. Carter could not believe that the drunken man was still slouched in the chair with the newspaper in front of him and began to wonder if he was actually still alive.

They continued in conversation for a while longer, but were getting to the point where they were both repeating things as the alcohol was taking effect. And then it happened. They started to speak of their losses. Carter preferred to listen to Jocky talk about his wife and son than he having to talk more about Marcus. Jocky's wife's name was Mavis. She meant the world to him and had always been there for him, through all the challenging times, making him into the man he was. Following another shot of rum, he opened up even more. He said that early on in their marriage, when times were particularly hard, he knew that she had had an affair, and with whom. But he said nothing. He was so scared of losing the love of his life altogether he decided to remain quiet, and instead try to improve himself and their circumstances in the hope that he would fully win her back. He also unveiled that he once considered going and confronting the man, and even thought out the different ways in which he would make the man disappear. He found out a few months later however, to his relief, that the man had moved abroad and was now out of the picture. But he did always wonder if Mavis had been asked to run away with him, and if she had decided against it because she realised that she loved Jocky too much. Or maybe the man just left, not even saying goodbye. Either way, he would comfort himself by believing that the first assumption, that Mavis had stayed with Jocky as she knew that he was the right man for her, the one that was true.

* * * *

Last orders were duly called at the bar along with the ringing of the bell. The two of them were quite drunk at this point but did decide to have one for the road. Carter thanked Jocky for his company and for all the interesting stories that he shared with him. He wished him well as they finished off their final drink. Jocky had enjoyed the evening too and was pleased to have met Carter and have a good chat, for it made a change for him to speak with anyone at all now.

"Maybe I'll bump into you again at some point before I return to London."

"Maybe you will my friend." said Jocky as he turned and left the bar.

Carter drank the last drop of what he had left in his glass, which surprisingly by that point had also become rum. In one swift movement he turned too fast, and fell off the stool. Luckily he just about remained on his feet, but a few people had noticed and sniggered. He saw that the drunken man at the table with the newspaper was being nudged awake by the barman. Carter tried to look upright and sober, but it didn't work. He swayed and staggered to the stairs to endure the tedious climb up to his room. As he rested his left arm on the banister for support and leverage to manoeuvre his first step, he could see Jocky standing in the small alcove at the front door. It looked as though he was talking to himself, so Carter decided to wander over to see if he was OK. As he got near he could hear the words that were coming from Jocky's mouth, they sounded like a prayer or a poem. Carter stood out of sight and leant up against the wall by the doorway and listened.

"My love I now bid you goodnight. But don't worry I will be back again soon for another special evening. But I must go now. And you must understand my love that I cannot take you home with me. It is too hard for me to believe that I cannot have you at home, so I'll leave you here at our special place, and that way it will seem that you are just out for a while, and I'll know that if I need to see you I only have to come here and here you will be. I love you my darling wife, I'll see you again soon."

Jocky stepped out from the alcove and walked away. Carter was moved by the words he had just heard, and it reminded him of how similar it was to how he had dealt with Marcus moving away to University all those years ago, by pretending that the person was still with you rather than letting them go. He knew that this was an unhealthy tactic to take with regards to the grieving process, but sometimes it was just so hard to take. Listening to those words from Jocky had a slightly sobering effect on Carter, and he walked back towards the stairs and climbed on up to his floor. Entering his room he felt mixed emotions. Jocky was such a genuinely nice old man and for Carter to see him suffering like he did was upsetting. He was thankful that he got to spend some time talking to him, and felt touched that Old Man Ragg had opened up to him in the way he did. "Maybe that had helped him to some extent." Carter thought, people often say you may say to a stranger something you would not say to your close family and friends.

* * * *

Carter awoke to the sound of shouting coming from the street outside. He was still clothed and realised he must of just slumped onto the bed the previous night and gone straight to sleep. He looked at his phone which showed three missed calls from Will.

"Shit!" he said disappointed in himself for not remembering to call him. The time was just after 3am.

He approached the window and peered through the netting. There were up to four men outside having a very heated argument. One was accusing the other of something but he could not quite make it out. It was only a matter of seconds and the police arrived, just in time as well as a fight was brewing. One officer waved two of the men away and chose to speak to the remaining two only. Apparently these two particular men were known to the authorities as trouble makers. They were soon escorted to the police car and driven away. Peace once again reigned over The Herald Hotel.

After that brief flurry of entertainment Carter felt quite awake. He did however feel sick and had another bad headache, but he admitted that he only had himself to blame. He took a glass from the bedside table and filled it with water from the tap in the bathroom. He searched through his bag for painkillers but there were none left. All he had were a few Cipralex pills left which were in the side pocket of his rucksack. Against his better judgement he decided to take one, presuming that it may do some good to help him, relax his neck muscles, and thus helping alleviate his headache. He knocked back the pill and got back into bed. The TV was on standby, but he did not feel in the mood to use this as a way to make him go back to sleep and so didn't turn it on.

* * * *

He felt his temples morphing, as if moving rhythmically with the sharp stabbing sensations of the pain. It felt so severe at times that he thought his head was about to split open. The pain, when as striking as that, would usually give him a feeling of weightlessness;

a feeling that, as at times in the past, had resulted in him blacking out and fainting. The sun rose quickly and the light struck through the bedroom window with vengeance and seemed to cover the room with the brightest, most unbearable shine. Carter winced and tried to cover his face with the bed sheet, but no good. It was far too bright, the light was penetrating his eyes like pins being dragged across his pupils, he desperately covered them with his hands to try and block out the effects. It was still not working and he began to panic. He needed to get out of the room. He quickly threw on some clothes and made haste for the door. He stepped out onto the landing and it was just as bright, so bright now that his eyes seemed blurred and his vision impaired. He held out his arm and searched for the hand rail. He knew by following that he would reach the stairs where he could make his way down, to where he did not know. In the back of his mind he was trying to determine a place where it would be dark enough for him to gather himself and get relief. He reached the stairs before it hit him that he could have just gone into the bathroom and closed the door, but it was too late. He was already heading downstairs. No-one else was around. He called out to reception but there was no reply. He went through a door and into the restaurant area where it was less bright and he found he could take his hands from his eyes. He took a few deep breaths in quick succession trying to steady himself but he was worried that something was wrong. His mind automatically tried to eliminate all possibilities.

"Was it just the effect of alcohol last night that has made the light more sensitive? Was it the Cipralex pill? Have I had a reaction to it? Is there something wrong with my eyes? My God am I dying?"

As that last possibility crossed his mind he stopped thinking. He sat down on a chair at the back of the room and gazed at the floor, and just focused on it for a moment. He could feel himself improving, though he was reluctant to return back to the light. The restaurant door opened and there, in the doorway, stood a motionless silhouette. Carter squinted and tried to make out the identity of the person, and just assumed that it was a member of staff.

"Hello?" he called out, prompting the figure to make him or herself known. The doorway closed and the person was now in the room. However due to the sudden burst of light into his eyes he was still at a loss at being able to see the person's face.

"Carter?" said a female voice. It was a voice that was familiar to him but for some strange reason he could not distinguish from whom it came.

"Who is it? I can't see you from here. The light it . . . it . . . ." His voice was now tense and frustrated.

"Carter? It's me, Mary. Are you OK?" she said worried and concerned at seeing him sitting in the dark.

"Mary?" he replied looking puzzled.

Mary was now in view and he could make out her face in front of him as she drew closer.

"Yes it's me. We arranged to meet here this morning at 10.30?"

"Oh of course, yes sorry just didn't realise it was that time already."

"As I approached the entrance I saw you walk in here. Carter, are you feeling alright? You look as bad as your dead brother?"

"Excuse me?" said Carter in absolute astonishment at her comment.

"I said if you don't sort yourself out you will be as dead as your fucking brother!"

*   *   *   *

It was morning and his eyes slowly opened.

"Please tell me that was a dream?" Carter shouted aloud, as it had felt so real.

He wiped the tears from his eyes and composed himself. He never let himself read too much into dreams as to what they may have represented in his life, but in this case he spent a few seconds deciphering it. The spiteful words that Mary had spoken could only have referred to Carter's drinking and depression, and if he did not take steps to improve his life, and cope somehow, he would die. He further thought that it was even more fitting that it was Mary who appeared in his dream to say it, as she had become somewhat of a glimmer of hope for him within the last few days. He still had mild signs of a headache from earlier in the night but at least it had become more bearable. The nightmare had Carter in complete shock, and it took a moment before he could fully come to terms with it, and accept that it was only just a dream. He decided that it was no good him trying to read too much into it, and that he should do his best to forget it and get on with his day. He glanced at the clock, it was 9.38am. He had nearly an hour before he was due to meet Mary. He had a quick shower before making himself a strong coffee and turning on the TV. Will suddenly crossed his mind and he remembered the missed calls on his mobile from the previous night. It was too early to call Will at that point though, as it was a Saturday, and if Will didn't have to work on a Saturday there was only one thing he would be doing at that time of the morning, and that was sleeping. Carter also knew that any disturbance to that would result in punishment, so he decided to call him later instead. He glanced at the clock again and it was 10.11am, so he decided to get ready to go and meet up with Mary. As he slipped on his navy blue polo shirt he thought about Old Man Ragg and how he had thoroughly enjoyed meeting him. He was also impressed at how much Jocky Ragg had drank. Carter, not paying attention to it the previous evening, began trying to calculate it in his mind. He worked out that Jocky must have had close to a bottle of rum that evening. Carter pulled up his jeans and grabbed his shoes from the corner of the room. 10.16am and he had one thing left to do, make sure he had his wallet and room key. He switched off the lights and decided to get down to the foyer a couple of minutes early, not only to make a good impression, but so Mary didn't have to stand around waiting for any period of time. He arrived in the foyer bang on 10.20am.

* * * *

Mary had arrived holding two coffees and a loaf of bread back at the hotel that morning, suggesting they return to the duck pond in the park. Carter found that to be such a sweet gesture, and was happy that Mary seemed to like it there too. It was such a romantic spot after all, and had seemed to become an instant hit with both of them, their own special place.

"So, why are you still working in mobile phone insurance if you hate it so much?"

"Well, it's not that I hate it, more that it suits me slightly better than most other occupations."

"Suits you? How do you mean?"

Carter had a moment of weakness where he knew that he was going to have to tell Mary about his condition. On the one hand he was reluctant in case it pushed her away, but on the other he cared for her so much that he wanted to start their friendship on the right footing, honesty and no secrets. His reason for doing this was inspired by Old Man Ragg, and how he confided in him the previous evening. How Jocky didn't hold back, and how he made the decision to talk about his loss and then that was it. It was out in the open, and no doubt felt better for it. Now it was Carter's turn to talk.

"Mary, I, I think I should tell you something about me now, as it shouldn't be something that I have to hide. I want to be honest with you."

"OK." said Mary looking a little bemused.

"I suffer from bipolar disorder and have done for some time. I have so many issues with self esteem, self confidence, fear of abandonment, the list goes on. This is something I have had to deal with for a long time. Depression. Now losing Marcus as well has been ever so much harder to take, or accept if you will."

Mary gently reached out, taking his hand in hers and held it tightly. A tear slowly emerged and ran down his face, as not only as he had taken one huge step in talking about it, but also the feeling of Mary's hand, and her sudden supportive and caring nature made him well up with a mixture of joy and sadness.

"It's OK to talk about this Carter. I am so genuinely pleased that you have told me. I understand how hard that was for you." said Mary as she expected him to cry further. He didn't, and instead looked back at Mary, and soaked up that moment for as long as he could.

"I can't believe that I have just said that. I never speak of it. The last time I did was to a shrink! Ha ha there is another thing you should know. I used to see a shrink. I bet this morning is getting better and better for you right?" said Carter with a huge comical smile on his face.

"You got that right! Anything else? You're not a serial killer or anything are you?" she said laughing, also pleased that he was joking about it as if a weight had been lifted from his shoulders.

"Well?" he said jokingly, as if tending towards yes being the answer.

"Don't you dare!" Mary replied as they both shared a laugh together.

They were back as normal, the awkward situation and possible rejection that Carter had anticipated didn't come, and they seamlessly returned to flowing conversation, laughing and joking. Carter felt as light as a feather and at times had to remind himself that he had done it. He had spoken of it to a girl who was absolutely stunning. He was amazed at Mary, and quite impressed at himself for once.

"So the answer to your previous question as to why I am working in a job I hate, is mostly contributed to the depression, as well as a touch of laziness at times. Seriously though, it seems that over the phone I can just talk and talk with ease, totally relaxed and with confidence. But in person it's a whole different story."

"Maybe you should have gone into radio?" said Mary with an edge of sarcasm.

"Yeah well I've definitely got the face for it!" Carter said instantaneously, intentionally pointing fun at himself.

Mary burst out laughing at the joke, but quickly made it clear she was not at all laughing at his appearance. Carter played on this awkwardness from Mary, and while trying to refrain from laughing himself, he said, "Well thanks a lot. Now my depression has just hit an all time low!"

"No, you cannot, you . . . ." said Mary unable to compose her laughter enough to be able to string a sentence together to defend herself.

"I'll make sure I buy a face mask before the next time we meet!" he said.

That comment did the trick, and Mary was then laughing even louder. Carter too at that point gave in and joined in her laughter, he had no choice as it was utterly infectious. Mary composed herself a few seconds later, and covered her hand in front of her mouth, as if using it as a tool to conquer her giggling fit. She took on a more serious expression and looked at Carter, "You want to meet me again?" she said with a happy and hopeful look on her face.

"Absolutely." he replied seriously.

"But with no face mask!"

"No face mask!" "Since meeting you Mary there is no need for me to hide behind anything any more."

Mary brought both hands up to her face, leaving only her eyes and above exposed, as if taken aback by what he had said and hiding her blushes.

"Carter that is so sweet. I cannot believe you just said that. That was so beautiful."

Mary began to shed a tear at the compliment, as Carter held her hand in comfort.

"Mary, you are the highlight of my day. I know we have only known each other for three days. But I think you are so great. And the fact that I opened up to you about myself also tells me that you are someone very special. I am so glad we met."

"Oh Carter, the feeling is mutual." said Mary before taking a tissue from her handbag and wiping away a few more tears.

They were both truly relieved that they had shared their feelings for each other and it was out in the open. They continued talking, both occasionally tearing off the odd piece of bread from the bag and throwing it to the ducks. The weather was back on track, the sun had returned and the sky was only dotted by a few clouds. He began to talk to her about the places that he wished to visit over the coming days and whether or not she would be interested in accompanying him. He would pay of course. She was very flattered but could not promise for sure as her job was very unpredictable. She said she would try her best.

"So why were you named Carter anyway? That doesn't sound like a British name?"

"Well it's kind of weird but one of my father's idols was from your neck of the woods. President Jimmy Carter. My father was a huge fan."

"Really?" "He must have been to name a child after him!"

"Yeah I know. I remember I asked him once, as I was getting quite a lot of stick about it back in school. God I wish I hadn't. I ended up having to sit there and endure the life story of President Carter, and how I should be honoured with the same name as such a man."

"That's kind of funny."

"Well sure now it is. Then I had to do my best not to fall asleep mid-lecture! I heard everything from his birth date right through to his favourite colour! He was only elected for one term right?"

"Yes he was, the 39th President I think."

"Wow that's impressive!" "I can remember bits and pieces from my dad about him. I know his wife was named Rosalynn. During his Presidency he was involved in things such as the Three Mile Island incident, and the Panama Canal Treaty. The Iran Hostage Crisis I think was another?"

"The Three Mile Island incident, was that the accident involving the radioactive gases?"

"Yes that's right." "Well there you have it. I was named after the 39th President of the United States. It could have been worse I suppose. Could have been the 13th!" Actually who was the 13th, do you know?"

"Oh my God, yes I do. It was Millard something . . . . Millard Filmore!"

"Millard!" "All of a sudden I am happy to have the name Carter. Hey, do you know every President by number or what?"

"No just some!"

"Actually I think I have heard the name Millard Filmore before somewhere. Could have well been in the same conversation I had with my father. Definitely jogs a memory."

It was 12.30pm and the ducks had consumed every last crumb from the bread bag. Mary suggested they go and find somewhere to have lunch themselves. She had nowhere particular in mind but thought they could just go for a walk and see what they find. Carter was happy just to be in Mary's company, so it did not really matter to him where they went. He did however feel quite hungry, as he had not managed to have breakfast, and the one slice of bread that he had from the loaf of bread earlier would not suffice for much longer. His hangover had worn off, partly helped by him being out in the fresh air for the whole morning. He felt OK.

CHAPTER EIGHT

Situated on a cobbled street off one of the main high streets was a quaint little Italian café. The front was very simply decorated but with a dash of elegance. The name of the café was called Carlotta's which translates as Charlotte's, and was designed in alternating colours of the Italian national flag. There were two small tables outside with a canopy for shade, but were already occupied by some lucky tourists.

Beautiful aromas circulated the room, filling the air with a variety of herbs and rich coffee smells. These fragrances were but a few that could be identified within seconds of their arrival. Their senses were immediately on alert, taste buds impatiently waiting to be tantalised. They approached the counter scanning the delicious looking pastries through the glass.

"Please take a seat and I'll come over to take your order." said a pleasant looking lady as she directed them to a vacant table. "Here are your menus. I'll be back in a few minutes for you. Can I get you any drinks?"

"Oh yes please, a coffee, black." replied Mary.

"And you, Sir?"

"A lemonade for me please, thank you."

They looked around and were very impressed and also pleased to have found this little gem of a place. It looked so unique and inviting, and had a lovely family feel about it. They sat at a small, square shaped table, which was covered by a chequered designed table cloth, of green and white coloured squares. The usual condiments of olive oil, balsamic vinegar, salt and pepper sat invitingly in the centre of the table.

"So what are you going for?" asked Carter as they both began to look through the vast selection that was on offer.

"My word, where do I start!"

The menu was full of exciting dishes, ranging from calzones through to a limitless array of different pasta and pizza dishes.

"I think I'll go for the broccoli and mushroom Rigatoni, something simple." said Mary.

"That sounds good. I may go for the same, although I am pretty tempted by the calzone."

"Would you mind ordering for me when she comes back to take our order? I'm just going the rest room."

"Yeah sure, no problem." said Carter as he took one last glance at the choices, before settling on the Rigatoni. It wasn't likely to be too filling or messy, or too stodgy, but just a nice bowl of vegetable pasta. He was always self conscious about eating messy food in front of anyone, as it could be so embarrassing ending up with different coloured sauces hanging from your face. The main culprit dish for him would have to be spaghetti, as he would always end up with splash marks all over his shirt and chin.

"OK Sir, have you decided yet?" asked the waitress, poised, smiling with her pad and pen at the ready.

"Yes I would like two broccoli and mushroom Rigatonis please."

"OK would you like anything else, any side orders?"

"No that's fine thank you, that's perfect."

"Thank you Sir."

* * * *

"You know what?" Mary offered. "I didn't even know this place was here. If I had, I would have come here every day for lunch. This pasta is amazing, such strong flavours from the sauce as well."

"Yeah I know. Great food. Delicious." replied Carter as he readied another piece onto his fork ready for consumption.

"So Carter, I don't mean to revisit what we were talking about earlier with your job and all, but are you planning to try to find something else?"

"You know what, I may do. But it is going to have to be something that I will really enjoy. Otherwise what's the point in leaving where I am at the moment, right?"

"That's true. I'm sure the perfect job is out there somewhere waiting for you Carter."

"Sure it is." replied Carter unconvinced, his voice lowered, almost as if he were talking to himself.

"It is worth a shot."

"Maybe?" said Carter, but with reluctance not to believe the possibility fully.

"You know otherwise it is like just going around and around in one big circle isn't it?" followed up Mary in an attempt to coax him a bit further out of his shell.

"It is yeah, one big circle of shit!" replied Carter, not meaning to speak out loud or to sound intentionally rude, but sounding slightly flustered.

They laughed and dismissed the awkwardness of how he answered and carried on talking. For the remainder of lunch Mary carefully averted topics to things other than those of Carter's personal issues. He noticed it, but did not mention it, as he was only too happy to change subjects and discuss other things. He would rather listen to things about her life, and was more than happy just to remain there transfixed by her beauty watching her speak, which was a treasure in itself. He was not yet nowhere near to being confident enough to delve further into his own personal torment. Even though discussing his issues briefly with Mary felt good, and was indeed a positive step, the notion of moving on from there so soon and getting to the stage of trying to analyse it, or justify it, was just too far off in the distance for him.

* * * *

The time had once again gone far too quickly for their liking; it was almost 3pm. There was a little row of shoe shops that Mary was interested in visiting, and Carter was of course only too happy to join her in looking. He was there to give her his honest opinion on her choices whenever she asked.

After the third shoe shop, however, his judgement became somewhat clouded, as his eagerness for her to buy a pair became more of an objective for him than anything else. “Gosh isn’t shoe shopping boring!” he thought, as he raised another half hearted smile. He didn’t want to mislead her into believing one pair was right over another if he didn’t firmly believe so, so he conjured up a plan which would enable him to get some fresh air, and escape the boredom of shoes! He told Mary that he needed to call Will as he hadn’t managed to talk to him since he left London, and Will was such a worrier at times. Mary of course understood and agreed to catch up with him outside.

* * * *

“Alright stranger? You OK?” said Will obviously pleased and relieved to finally have heard from his flatmate.

“Hello mate, yeah I’m sorry. Just been so caught up with things here. And I didn’t want to call you at work, or . . . .”

“Don’t be silly, it’s all right, as long as you are OK. How did the day go?”

“As well as could be expected you know. Had a brief moment where Starlet ran out of the chapel in tears, but she seems OK now.”

“And Claire and Eve, how are they coping?”

“OK I guess. I’m going there for a Sunday roast tomorrow.”

“Nice.”

“How are things in London, how have you been?”

“Not bad, just busy at work, again! Just chillaxing today though. Got Linda coming over later.”

“Linda? Wait, don’t answer! Linda, Linda? Linda from the launderette?”

"Yeah."

"She is crazy though!" said Carter with a sudden look of horror on his face.

"I know but I'm lonely here cooped up on my own. I need a distraction if you know what I mean."

"Of course I do. Just don't let her go into my room. Last time . . . . she . . . . rearranged things."

"Ha ha, all right you've got a deal."

"Cool. Look I gotta go, but I'll give you a call tomorrow or something. Got something else to tell you! Have a good night."

"Alright, well you too and good to hear from you . . . . finally! Talk to you tomorrow."

Carter saw Mary approaching the exit of the shop so as he said his goodbyes, he slipped his phone back into his pocket and gave Mary a smile, silently hoping that she had actually bought the shoes.

"Still no luck I'm afraid!" she said as if about to give up searching for the day. Carter was hopeful.

Mary heard her mobile phone bleep from inside her handbag. Her hand rummaged around the bag, searching for it among the chaos of make up utensils and other 'must haves'. This reminded Carter that he must take down her mobile phone number.

"Oh it's a text from a friend of mine, who I'm supposed to meet up with tonight. I had completely forgotten. We were due to go out."

Carter looked slightly suspicious. Was this a male or female friend? He probed, "Tonight, what are you and her, he, up to?"

"My friend has not long lost their job, and they have been quite unhappy, so we were going to go out for a bit of a morale booster, you know, couple of drinks. Hey why don't you come?"

"Thank you but no, I'll be fine. You go ahead. Not sure it would be exactly fair on your friend if a stranger turns up for the evening. Why don't we make plans to meet up, say tomorrow? Oh, wait . . . . I've been invited to dinner at Claire's at 4pm, but could do before or after? That is if you want to, I mean I don't want to sound as if I am pestering you into seeing me or anything!"

"Not at all, I would love to see you. Not sure tomorrow morning is so good, but why don't we meet up tomorrow night once you've finished at Claire's? Or will that be too late?"

"Not sure how long I'll be there for."

"OK, what about if you meet me after work on Monday night for a drink?"

"Sounds great. Shall we exchange numbers at last?"

"Oh yes, sorry, why haven't we done this already?"

The two exchanged numbers before he accompanied her to the bus stop. She had genuinely forgotten about meeting her friend, and realised that she would have to catch a bus to ensure that she wasn't late. As they reached the bus stop, and this wouldn't happen any other time, the bus arrived straight away. A disappointed Carter had hoped for at least another couple of minutes wait so that he could spend a bit more time in her company. But it was not to be. She jumped on the bus and he raised his hand to wave her off. Before the doors closed she turned and looked back at him, almost with an expression of regret at leaving him standing there, and said "It's just a friend by the way! And no it isn't a male friend either! Just in case you were wondering?"

"OK, well that's good." Carter replied but doing his best to conceal his obvious relief. "I'll be able to sleep tonight now. You know how paranoid manic depressives get, so thanks for letting me off the hook!"

"Ha ha, my pleasure. Just think of me and you'll be fine." said Mary with a wink and a cheeky smile.

The doors closed as Carter mumbled under his breath. "Oh don't worry—I will."

As the bus pulled away, and to his surprise, he saw the face of an elderly woman who was sitting at the back of the bus. She was staring straight at him. She shook her head as if in disapproval. He couldn't understand why, so he just poked his tongue out at her until she was out of sight.

He walked back to the hotel, and en route couldn't help but wonder if Old Man Ragg would show up again. He debated whether or not to go to the bar again, partly because he knew it was likely to lead to another hammering of his bank account, also because all that his room had to offer was a TV as a companion, and lastly because he feared that the drink could lead him to being haunted by another nightmare. After brief deliberation he concluded that maybe it would be better to have a night off from the booze. "But its Saturday night and I've found out to some extent today that Mary has feelings for me. Surely this is a night to celebrate. I could just have one or two drinks, won't hurt. Oh come on, Carter, you are on your holidays! Just be strong and don't go over the top!"

Carter made excuses and convinced himself, as he often did, that going out and drinking was in fact justifiable once again. Even though deep down he knew his initial feeling to have a night off would have been the right choice to make, the beast in him reared, ravaging any chance of logic prevailing, tugging at his weaknesses, and dragging him back to where he should not be.

* * * *

It was 10pm and no sign of Old Man Ragg so Carter decided to call it a night. In fairness he had only had a couple of drinks while he waited, keeping himself amused and passing the time by playing an app on his phone. He found that thinking about Mary passed quite lengthy periods of time quickly as well. The bar was very busy and he had been standing most of the evening. He could do with an early night after the previous night's hedonism, not mentioning the eerie nightmare he had. Leaving the bar he looked out to his left toward the main entrance and remembered what he had heard Old Man Ragg say the previous evening and he shed a little smile of acknowledgement before going on up to bed.

* * * *

Sunday morning came with all the relaxing qualities with which every Sunday morning should come. The sun was shining, the birds were in top form singing, there was a distinct freshness in the air and the general mood was relaxed and chilled out, as it should be. Carter walked into the breakfast room carrying his morning newspaper, a spring in his step after a wonderful full night's uninterrupted sleep. It was the first morning in fact that his eyes did not feel heavy and stinging. His head felt serene for once, rather than that usual annoying sensation and expectance that at any moment he would have one of his famous headaches. He was excited and looking forward to going to Claire's for dinner. He wondered what was most appropriate to take with him to give to Claire, flowers, a bottle of wine, both? He also wanted to take something for the girls as well, such as sweets or chocolates?

The waiter approached his table and placed a teapot and a tiny jug of milk down in front of him. Carter folded his newspaper and poured the tea. He had ordered a full English breakfast and had planned to go out for a walk after to burn some of it off. The traditional post-dinner walk now being classed as exercise! He planned to go out and have a look around town that morning. He wasn't going to head for anywhere in particular as he needed to have enough time to get back to get ready to make his way to Claire's.

* * * *

Carter, for once without his hands weighing heavily in his pockets, walked along Holyrood Road and embraced the fresh air on such a delightful morning. He wandered down one street and back up another, enjoying the historical presence that the old town provided. After a short while he saw the fabulous vision of a crown spire. It was that of St Giles Cathedral. He drew closer and decided to go inside. As he entered he was directed to an information desk where he was asked if he had a camcorder, and would he be taking any photographs. He said he would like to take some using his camera phone and was issued a photography permit at a cost of £2.00. He walked in and was amazed firstly by the huge stained glass windows. Then further on there were memorials and tombs of significant people throughout the ages, one which read Tomb of James Graham, 1st Marquess of Montrose.

Carter sat transfixed in front of a stained glass window, in awe of its flowing beauty. The variety of colours were blending into each other, and taking on different shades according to the intensity of the sunlight. He took another picture on his phone, but yet again failed to capture the same enthralling magnificence of that of the naked eye. He closed his eyes, the colours still distinguishable upon his eyelids, the natural coolness of the cathedral adding comfort, and the whispers from other members of the public were subtle and not disturbing in the slightest. The echo from the wooden doors every now and again added a soft eerie presence. He just sat, and listened.

He realised moments after that he had become completely surrounded by people filling the rows of the Cathedral. They had been so quiet in their approach he hadn't even noticed that he no longer sat alone. There was in fact going to be an eleven o'clock service held, so he decided that this was his cue to leave. As he made his way to the exit he caught the first verse of a hymn from the choir, and it sounded divine. He stepped back out into the street and turned right, straining to hear as much of the choir as he could before it faded out completely as he walked away.

* * * *

"Hi there." said Carter drawing the florist's attention. "I'm looking for a nice bunch of flowers for someone who has recently lost a loved one. What do you recommend? I don't know anything about flowers you see, but I do know enough that some represent certain things, and I just want to be sure I'm buying the appropriate ones, if you see what I mean?"

"Certainly Sir, I know what you mean. OK, well I would say a thrift as it represents sympathy, but I don't have any of those, so would instead recommend red carnations, which signifies admiration, and that your heart aches for the person you are giving them to. I could do you a lovely bouquet for a good price if you like?"

"Sounds great, after all you're the expert. Thanks."

Carter wanted to get a good bottle of wine for Claire as well as the flowers, as he believed that wine was always the best way to arrive at someone's house for dinner. Carrying his fresh bouquet of red carnations he proceeded in trying to locate a wine store or a respectable supermarket at least. Not too long after there it was. Old Town Wines. It was sophisticated in appearance and looked like the sort of place that took wine very seriously and well may house some quality varietals. He walked in and immediately a gentleman, looking as equally sophisticated as the interior décor, approached him with a moustache that even Hercule Poirot would have been proud of. He offered to place the bouquet down on the counter so Carter could scan the store unrestricted. Carter obliged of course, handing over the bouquet without a second thought, for his eyes had already begun inspecting certain vintages. Starting with Italy he could see that the lower priced wines were placed on shelves from about the waist down, making them easier to access as they would obviously have a higher purchase rate than those above. His looked up eagerly to the top shelf to see what was on offer at the higher end, and he was very impressed by the small gathering that was there. He knew little about wine, but had read some literature here and there on the fermenting process so was aware of certain classic wines. He remembered many years before when Max had made his own wine at home. He made tea wine and it did not taste the greatest unfortunately, in fact it was quite sickly, and Carter was certain that even the most forgiving of palates could not have withstood it. His Dad gave four bottles away to his grandfather and uncle one Easter, and the next time they saw him they too commented on how exquisitely horrible it was. Max asked if they had thrown the rest away, to which they replied "No we drank it!"

The shop owner appeared behind Carter and asked if he needed assistance, to which Carter replied "Yes definitely. Thanks. I am going to have dinner with my sister-in-law who has just lost her husband, my brother, and I want to get her something nice, no cheap plonk you know?"

"I am sorry Sir, for your loss and for hers." said the man, peering through his bifocals, noticing the mixed emotions in Carter's eyes.

"Thanks."

"Well Sir, do you have anything in mind so far, whether it is to be a white, a red or a Rosé etc?"

"Not sure—I was thinking a red to be honest."

"OK very deep and earthy oaky flavours from reds Sir, a good choice."

"Thanks." said Carter as he became aware of the gentleman's obvious sales technique at trying to flatter him in the attempt to lure him into paying more than he initially intended, but played along all the same.

"What about where the wine is from?" asked the owner, trying to narrow down the options.

"I was thinking either an Italian or French definitely."

"Another splendid choice I must say, Sir."

"And now the all important question, do you have a price range?"

"Anything up to about twenty pounds."

"Well I'm pretty sure we can find what you are looking for, Sir."

Carter felt slightly uncomfortable by the gentleman's antics, and it briefly crossed his mind whether to just go and find the local supermarket and buy something there instead. This thought was, however, quickly forgotten as the owner began talking about the wines on offer in more detail.

"OK, Sir. Here we have some Italian wines that I noticed have already caught your eye. Here you have the more popular classic Chianti at a price of £8.99. Working upwards we have a 2006 Barberesco which is a powerful red wine produced from Nebbiolo grapes and is priced at £15.99 per bottle. We have a 2009 Brunello di Montalcino which is created solely from Sangiovese grapes and that is £14.99. These come from a medieval town just outside of Siena, and the region is known to be the ideal conditions for the grapes to ripen to their fullest. This is due to the area being, sunny, warm, a hilly area which is important, and has few extremes in temperature which creates an ideal setting."

"Quite!" replied Carter giving off the impression that he totally understood the importance of the owner's comments. The owner continued, his voice becoming more and more grating with every word. Carter never did like monotone speech. "We have up on this shelf a 2008 Bardolino at £10.99 which is a light style, fruit filled wine made in the Veneto region. These are all good selections and would suit such an occasion as yours, Sir."

"OK can we have a quick look at the French selection please?" Carter said quickly, noticing some other customers waiting over by the counter for assistance.

"Certainly the French selection we have is just along here. I would recommend most of these. For example this Montagne St Emilion holds beautiful delicate flavours, an exquisite velvety texture, and is a firm favourite of mine. This is a 2009 and is £13.99 per bottle. Further up you are looking at a 2008 Pomerol at £12.50, also delicious."

The owner had noticed the other customers waiting patiently, so left Carter to decide while he walked over to tend to the others, walking briskly in an endeavour to stop them before they had a chance to consider leaving. Carter had decided and made his choices. He was going to get two. One to take to Claire's and one in case Mary invited him over to hers, he hoped. His two choices were the owner's personal favourite, the Montagne St Emilion, and the 2009 Brunello di Montalcino. He thought it right to get one each from Italy and France. The Italian was going to be the one for Mary, as he felt it held more romantic connotations. Carter approached the counter and waited for the owner to finish serving the other customers and noticed that the two of them were buying a selection of Rieslings, and looking at them, they seemed to be knowledgeable connoisseurs. A few minutes later, Carter placed his choices on the counter in front of the owner, who was pleasantly impressed by what he had chosen.

"So one became two then, Sir, and one from each country? Very diplomatic of you!" said the owner with a big smile on his face, stretching his curled moustache further around his cheeks. He was pleased with himself as not only did he believe that it was due to his sales techniques that had earned him a sale of two instead of one, but also that one was one of his own personal favourites that had done the trick.

"So what is one of the dearest then out of interest?" enquired Carter, watching the man wrap the wines as if they were delicate pieces of jewellery.

"Well the first one that comes to mind would be the Chateaux Petrus, which is a Bordeaux. And you would be looking to pay anywhere from a £1000 plus!"

"Per bottle?" said Carter in a state of disbelief.

"Yes, afraid so."

Carter bid his farewell and left the shop, flowers and wine in hand. The next stop was to be a sweet shop. He made his way back to the hotel and saw a small Co-op where he bought a box of chocolates each for Starlet and Eve. He also got himself a tuna and sweetcorn sandwich which would keep him through until dinner at Claire's. As he paid for them he hoped that Claire didn't have any reservations about the girls indulging in chocolate, as long as it wasn't before dinner anyway. He assured himself it would be fine. Carter arrived back at the hotel just before 1.30pm and despite being out walking around all morning he still felt surprisingly fresh and wide awake. He realised that he hadn't had a headache for a while and hoped and remained optimistic that he would not have one at Claire's.

In his room there was a vase by the window holding artificial flowers, so Carter filled it with water and placed Claire's flowers inside, leaving the artificial ones on the window ledge. He removed his trainers, switched on the kettle, opened up his sandwich and sat on the bed. He turned on the TV and there was a live Scottish cup football match being played between Dundee United and Hearts. He had a quick browse through the other available channels, but soon changed back to the game as it seemed quite intense and fast paced. This would keep his mind engaged yet relaxed for a while.

* * * *

It was a nice quiet drive that afternoon from the Herald Hotel over to Claire's. As the taxi travelled through the streets, Carter soaked up its amazing architecture. On the way he passed by the Edinburgh Law Courts and The Royal Museum of Scotland, the latter starting him thinking as to whether or not this should be added to his list of places to visit. As his taxi headed on further, the sun cast a stunning deep orange glow over the city, providing a panoramic view of the North Bridge and the north elevation of the Old Town.

"Quite beautiful, isn't it?" commented the taxi driver, as he caught Carter's expression on his rear view mirror.

"It is. Amazing." replied Carter somewhat lost for words.

* * * *

Claire was delighted that Carter had come over for dinner and she was only too happy to fill her time up with as much distraction as possible. She found it difficult to cope when alone. She needed distractions and company, anything to keep her mind drawn away from the fact that Marcus was gone. The girls were not home yet as they had gone to Shannon's, allowing Claire to go out with one of her other friends that morning for coffee. They sat down at the kitchen table and Claire poured Carter a cup of tea, strong and no sugar, just as he liked it.

"I feel so empty." said Claire, staring into a space somewhere between the tea and Carter.

"I know." said Carter, as his mind searched to find more comforting words.

"The thing is . . . . It's all sinking in now. Now that the funeral is done, the visits of friends are becoming less frequent, and we are getting back into some kind of normal routine, it really has started to affect me. The truth is he's not coming back to me Carter!"

Carter knew their emotions were the same on a number of levels and he immediately sprung from his chair and held Claire tightly in his arms. As he comforted her she let herself go and the tears flowed freely. She had held it all in for as long as she could, until, at this moment, the floodgates opened and she could not imprison her sadness anymore.

"It's OK to cry. Shhh, it's OK." Carter repeated.

"I'm sorry." said Claire as she began to try to gather herself.

"Hey, you have nothing to be sorry about. It's natural to cry . . . . and healthy for the grieving process."

"I just cannot let the girls see me like this. I need to be a rock for them. No weakness."

"I'm sure they would understand. Claire, they need you to be their mother; they are hurting too and together, as a family, sharing your good memories, and your grief, you will all become stronger."

Claire sat back in her chair and thanked Carter for his supportive and yet unexpected kind words. This was a side of Carter she didn't really know. She apologised yet again and felt embarrassed that she had started balling her eyes out, and only minutes after he had arrived. But at the same time, she realised he had been there for her. Claire asked him how his stay had been so far and what had been up to the last few days. He was reluctant to mention Mary. He decided not to mention her. It was insensitive, discussing a blossoming relationship in front of a broken hearted woman who had just seen her own relationship, her family, her future, destroyed. Time passed and he began to make Claire laugh as he described the wine shop owner and that every time the man got animated, when discussing a certain wine, he would bounce up onto his toes, his moustache twitching excitedly, like a dog would with its tail.

He spoke of St Giles Cathedral and how it had made him feel so relaxed. Claire understood as she had been in there many times before, and said that every time she went she had spent a considerable amount of time in there. The peace and quiet would start to make her feel somewhat lethargic, and she would have to leave. He could see how that was possible as he was sure that given a few more minutes he himself would have probably gone to sleep in there earlier that morning.

The doorbell suddenly rang and they both looked towards the door in anticipation.

"Here are the girls." said Claire as she rose to her feet and walked off down the hallway.

Carter could smell the roast potatoes and the meat cooking away merrily in the oven, and was looking forward to the tasty Sunday roast. The front door opened and he saw Starlet and Eve walk down the hallway towards him. He first noticed that Starlet was smiling and wore a beautiful smile too. He was relieved to say the least. They seemed positive, no doubt having had a good time at Shannon's. Shannon only dropped them off back at the house and left, so Carter didn't get the chance to say hello. They all sat at the kitchen table, the girls describing their morning and how they had helped Shannon to bake a cake. They were laughing at the amount of mess that was accumulated during the process, and that the floor seemed to have more flour and icing sugar on it than the contents of the actual cake. Carter was so happy to see them both so happy, especially for Claire's sake. He handed them the chocolates he bought earlier which were received with a huge smile. Eve attempted to unwrap one before the hawk eye type vision of her mother prevented it.

"Not until after dinner!" said Claire as she carefully and subtlety relocated the treats.

Claire started to serve up the roast dinner and Carter helped by slicing the meat and setting up the table. The food was placed in serving dishes allowing each of them to help themselves to their own required portions. As Carter sat down, after washing his hands, the girls had already begun serving themselves, and Claire was in the process of uncorking a bottle of wine. He noticed it was the one he brought with him.

"Oh Claire I got that for you to say thank you for dinner, you don't have to open that one now." he said suggesting that she should enjoy all of it, not him as well.

"No it's fine." she replied. "It's a very nice wine and it should be shared with a very nice guest. So there!"

Carter smiled and was thankful. She poured the wine and sat down. She told the girls to look above the kitchen sink by the window to where she had put the flowers that he had brought for her. He was glad to hear that the girls liked them and thought they looked very pretty.

The table chat mainly revolved around the girls' school and some funny teachers, and some nasty teachers.

Claire and Carter laughed away and he too contributed some of his own funny teacher stories, such as the teacher who would stumble into class drunk and fall asleep at his desk mid-lesson, before abruptly waking up forgetting where he was for a moment. This had them in fits of laughter by the time they had finished their roast dinner. Carter thought they probably didn't believe his true teacher story! Claire was a little stunned, surprised, that he seemed so relaxed for a change, and that he was so funny. She had never seen him so out of his shell before, or known that this side of him even existed. She didn't know what to think, and was a little confused, but at the same time just chose to go with the flow. Maybe the girls brought out the best in him she thought. It made her that much more relaxed and meant that she didn't have to struggle to make conversation. She was so pleased to see him that way.

Claire cleared the table, putting the dishes and cutlery straight into the dishwasher, before going to the freezer.

"Vanilla ice cream all round?" she shouted expecting the response to be as equally loud and enthusiastic. She was right. They, including Carter, shouted "yes," and watched as Claire scooped their portions into bowls. During dessert Carter decided to tell the family which sites he had planned to go and see while he was there, and even offered to take them along with him if they liked. Sadly, they were already due to go away for a week on their own.

"Some away time from the house." said Claire.

It was a holiday that had already been booked earlier in the year and was where the family had been going consecutively for the past three years. The mood in the room changed as the topic of discussion was drawn back to Marcus. Starlet's head dropped and she just sat quiet, as if in reflection of memories of the previous years' holidays.

"He would have wanted us still to go." said Claire.

She made her reasons clear to Carter, and why they had chosen to go back to such a special family place so soon. Even though it was a place that would hold constant reminders that Marcus was gone, it was also a place where they had all shared so many happy times together, and they needed to be there.

"Where is it?" he asked.

Claire explained that it was a place just outside of Stirling, a place where Marcus had always felt most happy and content. They would stay in a cabin by a lake, with views of the flowing green Menteith Hills as the backdrop. It was a place where they could all unwind in a peaceful setting that could only be compared to a personal paradise. There was a big house set on a small estate on the shore of the lake where the owners and their family lived. For guests, activities included a games room and a tennis court among other things. The family would often take a boat out in the evening as the sun went down. Osprey would fly there every year, migrating from Africa, and return to their usual spot, where Marcus would spend endless hours standing by the lake with his camera, desperate to capture that perfect shot of the Osprey as it plunged down into the lake, rising with a rainbow trout locked in its talons. Carter felt himself begin to well up slightly as he listened to Claire talk of this magical place, a place that obviously was their own paradise, their sanctuary. Claire continued to describe how Marcus would some mornings get up extra early and go out fly fishing on the lake, occasionally returning with a fish for supper. It was the freshest rainbow trout you would ever taste she said.

"Is that where that photo in the lounge was taken?" asked Carter.

"Yes, that was last year. He said he would replace that picture when he had caught a bigger one. That was going to be his mission this time round." replied Claire managing to control her emotions with greater strength at that point. Carter smiled, acknowledging her courage at being able to speak openly about the place.

"Can we go to the secret castle mummy?" asked Eve.

"The secret castle?" asked Carter with obvious interest.

"Yes it's a secret castle where a princess used to be locked up, before a prince came and rescued her."

"Wow!" said Carter looking over to Claire to await the full story.

"That's right Eve darling." "Well it's set out on an island, out on the lake. It is just a ruin now. But myth has it that once upon a time a beautiful princess was locked up there, and one day a brave prince went there and rescued the princess, and they fell in love and both lived happily ever after, eventually becoming king and queen."

Carter loved the story, even though he knew the myth was there for Eve's benefit, he loved how it made her eyes light up with expectation and fantasy. He asked about the cabins and Claire was only to happy to continue discussing it. Starlet was now looking up and seemed OK with the conversation, even if it did conjure up some sad feelings and memories. There was a strength growing within her, a strength not too dissimilar from that of her mother. Claire explained that there were a few different types of accommodations by the lake, ranging from A-Frame chalets, a small lodge, apartments, and the cedar cabins. There were ten cedar cabins and were simple and cosy, and oozed warmth and serenity. They were set back slightly from the waters edge. The family would always go for the same cabin though if they could, as they regarded it to be extra special with its central view. Cabin number five.

* * * *

Later in the evening Eve fell asleep on the sofa in the lounge, leaving the others still talking. Starlet felt tired and decided to call it a night and said her goodbyes to Carter.

"Goodnight Uncle C. Thanks for coming over. It has been fun talking to you. I hope it won't be too much longer before we see you again?"

"It has been great seeing you as well. You be strong OK. Have a good time at the cabin. Enjoy it."

"I'll try." said Starlet with a smile.

"I'll be back to visit more often I promise!" he said with conviction.

Starlet kissed Claire on the cheek and left the room and went off to bed. Claire gave him a look as though to say how happy she was that Starlet seemed to be healing. She had laughed so much that afternoon and was the first time Claire had seen her smile since before the tragedy.

"More wine?" asked Claire.

"Only if it is not keeping you up?" "Are you sure?"

"Yes, sure. Let me carry Eve up to bed and I'll open another bottle."

"Is it OK if I carry her up?" asked Carter.

"Yes sure."

Carter gently picked Eve up and held her in his arms, being as slow as possible so not to wake her. Claire watched and smiled, still kind of bewildered at Carter's transformation. He walked upstairs and Claire directed him into her room. The room had just enough light coming from the landing enabling him see enough to walk around the toys on the floor and over to her bed. Claire kissed her on her head and wished her pleasant dreams, and with extra care and concentration Carter gently lowered her down making every effort to ensure she wasn't disturbed. Claire stepped back and wondered if Carter would give her a peck on the cheek and whisper goodnight. However to her amazement he did one of the sweetest things she had seen and which brought a tear to her eye. She was witnessing a side to Carter that sadly no-one ever knew. He firstly kissed his own hand and touched her upon her forehead. He then kissed his own hand again and reached down to Eve's pyjama pocket, as if placing a second kiss into the pocket. He whispered in the softest voice he could muster and with all the love in his heart, "One for now and one for later."

* * * *

A couple of more hours went by and Claire and Carter were still sitting in the lounge still talking, although quietly as not to wake those above, and were still drinking wine. Claire had many bottles still left over from the funeral so wasn't running short of the stuff, which was surprising considering how much Reverend Norris had knocked back!

Darkness gradually crept in that night enabling them to fully open up to each other. For now they each had a shoulder to cry on; someone to talk to, and for Claire especially someone with whom she could share her burden. Carter was only too happy to be that person.

Claire, empowered by wine, slightly slurring her words, said "You know Carter. I wish Marcus could have seen you as you were today. You were so much fun and the girls adore you. Why haven't we seen that before?"

Carter hesitated in responding, debating as to whether to tell her about Mary.

"I don't know is my honest answer. I just feel so relaxed here. The girls are great and so much fun to be around. I suppose they just bring out the best in me."

"Well that's good to hear. You deserve better and so much more . . . ."

Carter interrupted before the direction of the discussion explored any further

"It's kind of late Claire. I think I may head off back to the hotel."

"Are you sure, you are welcome to stay over and sleep on the couch?"

"No it's OK I'll get back there. I'll just call a taxi."

Carter walked out to the kitchen and dialled a local number that he found pinned to a cork board behind the kitchen door. It was nearly midnight and he felt a mixture of drunkenness and overtiredness and could feel his hotel bed beckoning to him.

"How long did they say?" asked Claire as Carter returned to the lounge, grabbing his jacket from the banister en route.

"Ten minutes."

"Ah the usual response."

Carter slipped into his jacket and sat back down.

"Thanks Claire for a great dinner—I haven't had one like that for a long time. And have a great time at the cabin too. I know it will be mixed emotions for you, but as you say, you need to go."

"Thanks Carter. By the time we come back you'll be back in London. That is a shame, but at least the girls have got to see you. Please promise me we'll see more of you?"

"I promise Claire. I wish I didn't leave it this long. But that's a cross I'll just have to bear."

"Don't beat yourself up about it. Lives are busy and time goes so fast. Thank you Carter, for putting in such an effort for the girls, and . . . ."

There was a sudden silence as he realised she had fallen asleep. He covered her with a blanket that she had brought down earlier, just in case he had changed his mind and opted to sleep on the sofa.

"Goodbye Claire. I'll be in touch soon. I promise. And . . . . thanks."

He walked out and chose to wait for the taxi outside, instead of waiting for the sound of the driver's horn to make more noise than was absolutely necessary. He closed the front door behind him as quietly as possible, pulled up his jacket collar to protect his neck from the slight chill in the air and walked up to the entrance to the drive. Minutes later, headlights appeared in the distance and then slowed to a halt.

"Are you Carter?" Going to the Herald Hotel?"

"Yes."

Carter jumped in the back and pulled the door tightly shut. He was eager to lock out that nasty chill that had begun to seep into his bones. He rubbed his hands together trying to warm them, also blowing warm breath into them to quicken the desired affect.

“Turned quite cold tonight hasn’t it my friend?” said the driver.

“Not half. I’m shivering here.” Carter replied, while laughing at himself at how his voice was trembling with the cold.

“I love the city at night though don’t you?” “It has an extra sinister and chilling presence about it. Don’t you think?”

“That it does.” replied Carter as the taxi headed back towards the old town. “That it does.”

CHAPTER NINE

Monday morning rose and Edinburgh was bustling with people. The odd car horn would sound and echo through the city streets, as vehicles jostled for position impatiently to get to their destinations. The mixture of both workers and tourists alike made the place that more crowded. Customers flooded the local market stalls and newspaper stands as the Monday morning rush was in full swing with streets and pavements storming with activity.

One man who was totally oblivious to the outside commotion was Carter as he was tucked up like a baby in bed and in a deep sleep.

The previous evening, well early morning in fact by the time he got back to the hotel, was one of somewhat of an eventful one. The taxi never made it back to the hotel. As they were on their way back the driver managed to have a collision with a parked white van.

* * * *

Steam bolted from the crushed engine and the driver held his nose pinched closed to stop the blood gushing from it. Upon impact the driver's head had rebounded off the steering wheel. Had the driver been wearing his seatbelt he would have been OK. The car was a total write off. The front end was buckled, and the glass from the two front windows had shattered. Carter had not seen the van approaching as he had momentarily closed his eyes to rest them, and before he knew where he was he was jolted forward and back within a split second. His heart pounded with fright, startled and confused by what had gone wrong.

The driver had fallen asleep at the wheel. It was his last job of the day as well and he was due to clock off straight after the Herald run. Carter gathered himself wanting to do nothing more than get the hell out of the car. His passenger door was jammed and wouldn't budge so he had to shuffle over to the other side to get out. He knew he had to act quickly as he didn't know whether or not the engine would blow, so ran around to the driver's side and pulled him out, both staggering away to a safe distance. Police arrived within minutes so someone had obviously called the emergency services straight away. A passer by, a teenager of about eighteen, stopped to see if they were all right, by which time they could hear an ambulance on its way. As the police officers stepped out of their car the driver began to tremble and it was clear he was both in panic and in shock. He started pleading to Carter quietly, pulling him close so he could whisper in his ear, before the officers had a chance to make out what he was saying. He asked him not to tell them that he had fallen asleep at the wheel, and to make something up to divert the blame away from him. He went on to say that he had three children and needed this job to survive. He believed he would be fired if the taxi company found out that he was to blame.

"What happened here?" "Who is the driver of this vehicle please?"

The driver stepped forward to answer the officer. "I am officer."

"OK your nose is bleeding quite badly there, hold it tight the ambulance is nearly here." said the officer. "And who is the driver of the van?" "Is it you young man?" questioned the officer pointing his finger to the teenager standing by Carter's side.

"Me? No not me, I just came to see if they were OK." said the young man obviously wanting to clear his name as quickly as he could.

"He is right," said Carter choosing to step in to clarify the events as clearly as possible. "He came over after. I was a passenger in the taxi officer."

"Right, and who was driving the white van?"

There was total silence as neither the driver, who didn't want to say for obvious reasons, nor Carter, reluctant to speak as he didn't want to see a man lose his job. The ambulance pulled up and broke the silence. A paramedic quickly jumped from its open door and ran over to see how the driver was coping. By now the driver was sitting down on the pavement and the medic was kneeling beside him looking him over.

"You may have concussion." offered the young paramedic attempting to ask him basic questions as his name, date of birth and so on.

While the driver was being tended to by the medic, and the teenager had made his exit from the scene, the officer looked back at Carter.

“Do you feel alright?” No bumps or bruises?”

“No officer. I came out unscathed thankfully!”

“Need a quick statement from you if you don’t mind please, Sir?”

“All right, look there was no driver in the white van. It was stationary, just parked there, empty.”

“Are you telling me that he ran straight into a parked vehicle, at that speed, enduring that damage, and didn’t see it coming? Did he fall asleep at the wheel?” asked the officer angrily.

“No, he didn’t fall asleep at the wheel. I distracted him. I thought something ran out in front of the car and shouted from the back seat. He swerved and briefly lost control, resulting in the collision.”

“But there are no wheel marks on the road showing that he even tried to swerve to avoid whatever it was you thought you saw.”

“Well that is what happened. The driver was not to blame.”

“So if I go over to the driver now and ask him he is going to tell me the same story is he?”

“Yes he will.” said Carter confidently, hoping that the officer would believe him enough not to actually go over and ask the driver for confirmation. As the officer turned around to return to speak to the driver he had already been put in the ambulance.

“He may have concussion officer, so do you want to catch us up at the hospital, or do you have all you need?” shouted the medic, just about to close the swinging door of the ambulance.

“You go ahead. Get him to the hospital and sorted out. We’ll stay here and clear up this mess. I have his identity from his taxi ID anyway.”

The officer looked back at Carter, not entirely sure what else to ask or do with him. Maybe the incident was purely an accident.

"If you're feeling OK and you're not damaged in any way, you can go. But I will say this. Never again will you distract any driver the way you have tonight. Next time someone could seriously get hurt. You are lucky tonight, but just think if there was someone in that van, or a child! Go!"

"I understand. I am so sorry officer."

"Go!" said the officer as he had already looked down and was making notes in a little black notebook.

Carter sank his hands deep into his pockets, hung his head and walked away. He felt guilty and was conflicted that he had not told the truth, but at the same time did not want the man to lose his job. The crash had sobered him up completely and he felt cold and shaken by what had happened. He started to think how lucky he was to be wearing his seatbelt, because often he would forget to put one on.

As he walked further up the street he saw a flashing sign hanging out from a building not too far up ahead. He checked his watch and it was 00.45am. The closer he got he saw that the sign advertised a wine bar, a wine bar that was still bubbly and lively. He asked the bouncer at the door what time the bar was open until and was told 2am. Carter needed a stiff drink so he walked in.

The wine bar was mainly full of teenagers and university students in their early twenties. They were huddled together in individual groups mostly, only a few singletons sat at the bar, no doubt hopeful of finding a partner. There was a DJ at the back just behind the dance floor, which was crowded with people showing off their latest dance moves. Strobe lights darted around them, every now and again lighting up the odd individual just enough to be able to make out their face. It was quite dark inside and the lights were doing no favours to his headache that came on just after the crash. Carter approached the bar and ordered a double whisky. There was a group of Scottish guys standing next to him neither of whom were stereotypical of your usual tourists or university student types. They were locals all in their early twenties and had obviously been drinking for some time, either in this bar or others. They had heard his accent when ordering a drink.

"Hey pal? You! Are you lost or something?"

Carter chose to ignore the first question, but that only prompted the man to shout louder.

"Oi?, I'm talking to you!"

Carter looked around and straight at the man; he also had a quick count up of how many of them there were. "Yes?" said Carter.

"I said are you lost pal?"

Carter couldn't believe that he was being taunted and just after the ordeal he had been through, this was the last thing he wanted. He just wanted a quiet drink, so he tried to be polite and have a laugh hoping that they would see he was harmless and leave him be.

"Sorry mate, I didn't quite make out what you said at first. I've just been involved in a car crash and needed a quick drink."

"Yeah what car you got?" You look all right to me!" said the man as his friends started to join in and laugh.

"Please look, I just wanted a quick drink. I don't want any trouble."

"Who said anything about trouble? Why are you getting so animated? You wanna calm down pal, or you will have trouble! Do you hear me? Oi, don't turn away from me, answer me!"

Carter could feel a rush of anger come from the pit of his stomach. He was not usually the type to lower himself to that level and let someone get to him, but with everything else that was happening in his life he couldn't control himself. He knocked back his double whisky, turned and faced the man full on, and said "Actually I think it is you that is lost mate. Shouldn't you be in fucking Glasgow?"

The man lunged at him. His friends however stood in disbelief not expecting Carter to react as he did. Carter managed to dive to his left to avoid being tackled to the floor by the man. Suddenly he felt a tightening around his jacket collar as the hand of the bouncer started to drag him out towards the street.

"Get out troublemaker! Don't want your kind in here. You have only been in here five minutes and you've started a fight already. Now piss off."

"He attacked me!" said Carter, amazed that the bouncer was blaming him.

"You instigated it. I heard you swear at him from the door. Piss off!"

The man with whom he had the encounter was kept inside the wine bar, while Carter, smiling yet pensive, walked away and disappeared into the darkness. He would never go back to that wine bar that was for sure.

As he walked back to the hotel he was so surprised that he had managed to get involved in a bar fight, even though the fight did not actually have time to get going; it was so out of the ordinary for him. He always avoided confrontation, and never engaged in violence. It did, however, bring a smile to his face, proud that he did stand up for himself, which brought another touch of confidence, confidence which seemed to be growing day by day.

When he got back into the hotel the first thing he did was to splash his face with cold water, over and over again. He was exhausted and as he caught sight of his reflection in the bathroom mirror he noticed that he had blood on the front of his shirt. He realised it was from the driver which had rubbed off on him as he pulled him out of the taxi. He just wanted to sleep but couldn't before he had taken a shower. He undressed and slung the blood stained shirt on the floor by the bed. That would be the first job later that morning, to scrub every last stain from his clothes. Surprisingly the shower didn't make him feel any less tired; the bed beckoned and as he collapsed onto it, he was virtually asleep before his head even met with the surface of the pillow.

* * * *

There was a light knock at the door. Tap tap. It was just past midday and all was quiet, except for that tapping sound. What was it? Then, there came a distant voice, "Hello?"

Who was that? What was that noise?

The sound of a key turned in a lock, as a final tapping sound could be heard.

"Shit!" said Carter as he opened his eyes and realised what was about to happen.

He sprung bolt upright on the hotel bed facing the door. Before he could holler out in time not to come in it was too late. The door was fully open. There stood his cleaning lady, and with that same shocked look on her face, a look that was becoming all too familiar. Carter had slept commando that night as he was hot. During the night he had also kicked off his bed sheets which now lay in a crumpled heap beside him on the floor. So the first thing that the cleaning lady saw was Carter sitting fully naked, again, surrounded by blood stained clothes on the floor. To her credit though, she now considered him one of nature's harmless oddballs who had obviously just woken up, so she said calmly, "I'll come back later shall I?"

Carter, too embarrassed to reply, just shook his head in agreement.

As he finished washing out the stains from his clothes it was nearly 1pm. He pondered on the events of the previous night and he still couldn't believe his earlier ordeals. He was just thankful that neither incident ended more tragically. He noticed a missed call on his mobile and that a voice message had been left. He pressed the key enabling the message to play changing it to speaker setting so he could listen while he dressed.

"Hi Carter, it's Claire. I hope you got back all right last night? I just wanted to say thank you again for coming over and we all had a wonderful time. We hope you did too. Look we are going away to the cabin first thing tomorrow so won't see you before you go back to London. Just trying to get the bags packed this afternoon. So, anyway, I really just wanted to say have a safe journey back, good luck, and stay in touch. I'm serious, stay in touch. Thanks again!"

Carter felt deeply touched that she had called to say such kind words and had made himself a promise that he would call them as soon as he got back to London.

* * * *

Sitting outside a little café not too far from the hotel and one that provided him with a good view of the castle, Carter had a croissant and a cappuccino as he sat soaking up the afternoon sun. He wasn't sure when would be the best time to call Mary. As she was at work and he didn't want to come across as too clingy or desperate. He wondered if she would call him, maybe on her lunch break. It was now after 3pm. Nothing! So he decided to call her. The phone rang but nothing, no answer, just a voicemail. He assumed that she was busy, or in a meeting or something. He did not believe that she would intentionally avoid him, as he would have thought before their last visit. However their last visit did involve him opening up about his depression which may have given her second thoughts about meeting him. He could only pray that this wasn't the case. Another half an hour passed and his hand was hovering over his mobile, toying with the idea of whether to call her again. He ordered another Cappuccino. He had been sitting there for over an hour already and buying another Cappuccino made him feel better about the length of time he had been there. He looked at the castle and could make out the figures of people walking around the outer walls, and how small they were in comparison to the high walls.

He reached into his inside pocket and took out two pills. Unable to get a table in the shade, Carter sat exposed to the sun, which had been beaming down on his head for a while now. He had a feeling that it may trigger a headache and he was right. He had noticed one developing within those last few seconds. He took a sip of his drink which provided just enough liquid to ensure the pills went down smoothly. Two female backpackers at the table to his right, both of whom had been conveniently sitting in the shade, stood up to leave. He could hear their accent as they walked by, even though Carter hadn't travelled much, he felt they were perhaps from Germany or Austria. He picked up his drink and his paper and was just about to walk over and sit down on the now vacant shaded area, when two things happened. Firstly, two more backpackers seemed to appear from nowhere and beat him to it and sat down at the table. Then secondly, and more importantly, his mobile rang. He looked down at the display screen and it read Mary Lee calling. He felt a sudden rush of nerves and had butterflies in his stomach. He picked it up to answer it.

"Hello Mary Lee!"

"Carter! Hi. How are you? I just noticed that you tried calling me. I was held up in this stupid meeting and . . . . well you know. How are you today? Do you still want to meet up tonight?"

"Absolutely."

"Oh I have some other good news. I am off on Wednesday, all day. So if you wanted to do something then, or go out somewhere, we will have more time?"

"Sounds great, of course I would be delighted."

"Cool, look we can talk more about it tonight. Sound fine?"

"Perfectly."

"Great! Well about tonight! I know a nice little bar, beautiful little place and food is served there as well. It is just off of the Royal Mile down a cute little alley way called Jollie's Close. You can't miss it!"

"Brilliant! What time?"

"About eight?"

"Eight it is, see you there. Looking forward to it, take care."

"And you, bye!"

Carter slouched back in his chair, his shoulders dropped as he let his body relax down, and took another sip of his Cappuccino. The day ahead now looked that even more charming and wonderful.

* * * *

"Excuse me Sir, do you know of any car hire companies around here, other than those at the station?" said Carter to a man standing next to him at a street crossing.

"Oh yes I do. There is one on Murrayburn Road. Can't remember the name but there is definitely one there!"

"Thank you so much. And Murrayburn Road is . . . . ?"

The helpful man was only too happy to be of assistance, and gave Carter clear directions to the hire company.

It didn't take too long for him to get there, and as he turned into the road he could see the sign straight away, Budget.

Carter booked a car, just the smallest and cheapest economy car he could for that coming Wednesday, and was told to be there at 8am to collect it. It was a small 1.2 engine but was all he needed just for one day. He left the shop with his receipt and walked back to the hotel.

* * * *

It was nearly 5pm by the time he arrived back at the hotel and had built up quite an appetite from the walk. However, he didn't want anything too filling as he was going to have dinner with Mary in a few hours. He therefore decided to go and have a quick drink at the bar, and grab a quick snack to keep his hunger at bay until later. He sat over by the window, which gave him a view of the street. Half way through eating his crisps, he noticed a man on the other side of the road standing perfectly still, staring at the hotel. At first he thought nothing of it, but suddenly realised it was Jocky Ragg. He was standing quite close to the edge of the road, leaning slightly on his walking stick and gazing blankly at the place. Carter waved but there was no response. Maybe he couldn't see him. He thought about going outside and inviting him in for a quick drink, but at the same time knew that he himself would have to go and get ready to meet Mary shortly, so wouldn't have time. Old Man Ragg stood there for a few more minutes before slowly turning and walking away. It was as if he was he was just soaking up the place, the memories he held so dear, and perhaps relaying another message to his late wife. Carter smiled and was sad that Jocky had not seen him wave, but was quite sure, and hopeful, that their paths would soon cross again, and that they would meet up for one last drink before he returned back to London.

Carter finished off his drink and returned to his room to freshen up—he wanted to look his best for Mary. He rushed around the room, filled with a double impact of euphoria and nerves. An excitement filled the air, and the promise of the evening's date brought with it possibilities of further dates and maybe more. He wanted to look his best and regretted that he hadn't remembered to have a haircut earlier. He wanted to look cool but not come across as arrogant. Cool and casual is what he wanted, and kept repeating those words to himself as he got dressed and prepared himself in front of the mirror. He was ready, well as ready as he would ever be.

* * * *

Carter strolled down the Royal Mile, dressed in his best for his evening with Mary. Wearing his black jacket, a white shirt, jeans and black shoes, he really did feel his best and he felt a rare sense of confidence too. The slight evening breeze and the sun going down brought that serene setting to the forefront of the street, as though lighting the way ahead for Carter's footsteps to follow. It wasn't long and he had arrived at the quaint, welcoming but somewhat creepy looking alleyway of Jollie's Close. He was rather early, and intended to be. It was 7.30pm, but he wanted to get in there and make sure he got a table. Plus he wanted to call Will and say hello. It also gave him time to have a drink, a bit of Dutch courage before the dazzling Mary arrived.

The pub was just at the end of the alleyway and on the left hand side. He walked in, letting the old oak door swing shut behind him. "This place is awesome!" he thought as he stood there looking at the authentically old fashioned interior. "It is so 'olde worlde'!" He ordered a pint of ale from the bar and spotted a little table over by the far corner that was free, with a chair either side, so he went over and set himself down. The only source of light was a candle which neared its end, but offered a dim cosy glow as company. The delicate scent of burning wax engulfed the room and encroached into every nook and cranny, seeping into the dark oak fractured wood around him. The burgundy coloured walls and the dark stained finish of the furniture did little to change the room's appearance of being almost invading in manifestation. Carter loved this place at first sight. It had so much character and history to it. The fire was burning strong and the crackling of the logs brought a snug and convivial atmosphere to the contrasting sinister and questionable feel of the property. Carter thought it was perfect. His mobile phone rang in his pocket and he answered it straight away. It was Will.

"You beat me to it! I was just about to call you!" he said trying to convince Will.

"Of course you were!"

"Come on mate I was. How are you doing? How was Linda?"

"Crazy as usual."

"See! I told you. Don't have her around anymore."

"Also you wanna know what else happened?"

"Yes, what?"

"I woke up in the middle of the night and noticed she wasn't next to me. I got up and walked into the living room, and . . . ."

"And what?" said Carter becoming more stressed and concerned at what Will was about to say.

"Carter . . . . she was in your room again!"

"Fuck off!"

"No I'm serious, she was just standing there looking over your bed, and it sounded as though she was speaking some sort of voodoo shit."

"Will, come on, are you serious?"

"I think she cursed you man!"

"Will!"

"OK I'm joking. Had you going there though!"

"Come on mate, don't do that to me. Of course you had me going! She is crazy enough to pull that shit."

"Anyway, how are thing's going with you? You said yesterday that you had something to tell me?"

"Yes. OK, guess where I am?"

"Scotland!" replied Will sarcastically.

"Ha ha very funny. I'm on a date."

"Really? A date, what with a woman?" said Will hardly believing his ears.

"Yes with a woman. I met her at Marcus's funeral, and somehow we just hit it off. She is amazing."

"Mate, I am so fucking happy for you. What's her name?"

"Mary Lee. She is American."

"Cool. Is she hot?"

"Will, she is so stunning I wouldn't know where to start?"

"Start with her tits."

"Will! Please! Come on!"

"I'm only joking. I am genuinely happy for you mate. If you guys really hit it off though how is it gonna work out with you being in London?"

"I don't know. I haven't thought that far ahead. To be honest I am just trying to make the most of every moment with her right now. She should be here any minute."

"That's great Carter, it sounds like there is a real connection between you two already."

Carter confirmed to Will, as well as to himself, just how strong he felt that connection to be, “There is a bond there, a bond that wields like an axe.”

“Shit, that’s poetic! Don’t go saying things like that to her though; she might think you’re weird or something, or psychotic, even though what you said just then was pretty moving I have to admit.”

“What do you mean?”

“You know just don’t start coming out with silly things, keep it real and keep her keen. Trust me, I’m a pro!”

“OK!”

Carter noticed Mary enter the bar and realised he had to bring his conversation with Will to a close.

“Will, she has just walked in.”

“How she look?”

“Like a Goddess.”

“OK well you go get her, have a great night.”

Carter stood to his feet and caught Mary’s attention with a wave, before finally saying to Will, “Come what may my good man, for we are all just caterpillars waiting to fly”, to which Will quickly replied in panic “No! That’s what I mean! Don’t start saying any weird shit like that to her!”

Will noticed that Carter was no longer listening at the other end of the line, and had probably cut him off mid sentence, leaving Will shedding a smile and simply saying the word, “Twat!”

Mary was a true vision, encompassing every delight in appearance, glowing with elegance and floating towards the table like an angel. Her hair was down, flowing and shining, and she wore a red dress that highlighted every curve of her body, every motion of her walk. Carter was short of breath momentarily, almost paralysed. It was as if she had him in a trance like state, where she could control him whenever she wanted, switching him on and off like a tap. He managed to snap out of it as she got to the table and gave him a hug. He asked her what she would like to drink, to which she replied, a glass of red wine. He walked to the bar and ordered two glasses of wine, as he decided to join her in her choice. While the drinks were being poured he could not help but stare at Mary, watching her. She was sitting side on at the table and could not see him watching her. He couldn't help it. He could feel himself falling for her. He knew how dangerous the consequences of such feelings could be, but he could not control them, and did not want to. His love for Mary was flourishing by the second.

He returned to the table holding two large glasses of red wine, and sat down opposite her.

"Well, what do you think of this place? Isn't it cool?"

"Yeah, it's amazing and hidden away from the main street down a little alleyway as well. So perfectly placed and so much character."

"Exactly, I love it here. I have to admit I did stumble upon this place by accident. I got lost one day and ended up in here."

"Good place to get lost in?"

"Yes."

"Mary, can I just say that you look absolutely stunning this evening."

"Oh thanks Carter, you look very nice yourself."

"Thank you."

"So what do you think about me having Wednesday off work? Do you have anything in mind?"

"Well I actually have hired a car."

"Really?"

"Yeah, have to pick it up Wednesday morning 8am, and return it by 8am the following morning."

"That's great, perfect. Did you have anywhere in mind?"

They both started brainstorming ideas while occasionally sipping from their glasses. Mary edged her seat closer to his as they shared ideas and chatted about various things to do and places to visit. Carter explained to her that he would be very interested in visiting the Menteith Hills. He explained to her about the loch and how it had been a favoured place of the family. He told her that Claire and the girls were going to be there but did not want to interrupt them while on their break, so he would have to be careful not to bump into them if they did go. He started to describe to Mary the things that Claire had told him, about the lake; the cabins; the tranquillity; and how happy Marcus had been when staying there. Mary immediately understood how important it was for him to visit this place and agreed instantly. She told Carter that she would love to go to a place that held such meaning, and share that with him. He was close to leaning over to kiss Mary, but his nerves sprung into action and kicked him in the stomach, so he instead placed his hand on top of hers and thanked her. They ordered dinner and had a few more drinks, before their conversation was interrupted by the last orders bell. It was time to go.

* * * *

They arrived onto a little side street after walking from the pub in Jollie's close. This was the street where

Mary lived. As they stood outside the moment presented them with that time of the evening. The time of evening when it was time to say goodnight.

"Carter I have had such a lovely time tonight."

"As have I Mary."

"So Wednesday . . . ."

Carter, fuelled on red wine, love, and expectation leant in slowly to kiss Mary. She placed the palms of her hands on his chest, and took one step back.

"It is kind of late. I . . . . I just don't want to make the mistake of rushing into anything OK. I'm sorry, but I just want us to take things steady."

Carter was relieved on two accounts, one that is wasn't that she didn't find him attractive, in fact on the contrary, and two that she seemed like a decent girl, and wanted to genuinely take their relationship forward but without moving too fast. He admired that.

"Thank God!" he said out loud, to which she laughed. "I am totally fine with that, and absolutely respect that."

"Thanks Carter. I do like you a lot. I really do."

"Same Mary, I like me a lot too! I mean I like you a lot too."

Mary laughed, not entirely convinced if he had meant to say that as a joke or he had just messed his words up. She laughed anyway just in case.

"OK well goodnight Mary, and I'll call you . . . say tomorrow? We can organise meeting up Wednesday for our road trip?" Carter began to walk away.

"Yes sure, can't wait. And Carter?"

"Yes Mary?" he said turning around to face her.

"Thank you for understanding. That means a lot to me."

"Don't mention it. Until Wednesday!" said Carter as he raised one hand in the air waving goodnight as he strolled away.

It was quite a walk back to the hotel, about forty minutes, but he decided he wasn't ready to get back into a taxi again so soon, and after all, he could do with taking in some of the fresh night air. All the way back to the Herald he couldn't help but keep reliving the evening over and over again in his mind, the whole thing, the bar; the way she looked when she came in; the conversation; the compliments; discussing Wednesday's plans together; that she said she really liked him. He felt so happy. It was one of the best nights he had ever had; in fact, it was the best night of his life.

CHAPTER TEN

Banging, or thunder crashes, the sound of fire crackers had raised him with a start. Carter rushed to the window to see what had happened outside. There had been a loud banging sound, a sound similar to a fire cracker. He pulled back the curtain and looked down to the street below. He could see figures further down the road, running and fading out into the night. He looked at his watch and it was just after 2am. "Could it have been a gunshot?" he first thought. Then another sound, along with some lights which became visible further down the road, a variety of different coloured flickering lights. He assumed that it must have been some local teenagers playing around with fireworks. He held his hand over his heart relieved that it hadn't in fact been a gunshot that he heard. No-one had been hurt. Well not by a bullet at least, a firework maybe! He returned to bed and pulled the quilt high up covering his neck, defending his exposed skin from the chill in the air, slightly covering his ears. This would also muffle the sound at least. About another hour or so passed before Carter managed to get back to sleep. He could still hear the noise from outside, the odd bang here and there in the distance, echoing through the empty and desolate darkened streets. Why and how they had decided to go on a firework spree at this time of year was beyond him, and he couldn't even be bothered to think as to reasons why. He wasn't frustrated that he couldn't get straight back to sleep however, as he had the previous evening's events to occupy his thoughts and dance around his mind.

* * * *

After finishing reading his morning paper in the breakfast room, and drinking the last drop of his coffee, he decided he would go and do a spot of shopping around town. Before his big day out with Mary, he wanted to get a few things; some clothes for himself for the journey, but mainly gifts, gifts for Will, and more importantly for Mary. A haircut was also on the 'to do' list. He would start on the Royal Mile and see where he ended up, maybe finding somewhere quirky and charming to stop off for lunch.

He crossed Parliament Square and walked on towards The Canongate, stopping momentarily to admire the buildings around him. Everywhere he walked he found himself looking at something new, things that had somehow escaped him the previous days. There was so much there to see. He started window shopping, first judging each shop on the merit of their display, and what they would have that would be of interest to him. Before too long he couldn't help himself, and was entering all of them, a dangerous thing for him to do as he was known to overspend somewhat on occasion. He kept his focus firmly on Mary, and what he could buy for her, a gift which he hoped she would absolutely adore. He walked into The Old Town Weaving shop and perused the ladies kilted skirts' section. They were very expensive, far beyond his budget. He wasn't totally convinced that it would have been a good gift anyway, and quickly put the idea to bed.

"Excuse me Sir, if you are looking for gents kilts they can be found upstairs." said a posh voice coming from a very tall, crooked looking gentleman with an English accent behind him.

"Oh, no it is for someone else. Not for me!" replied Carter looking awkward and embarrassed.

"Forgive me Sir." said the man, and with a look of suspicion drawn upon his final gaze, he turned and walked away.

Carter made his exit a quick one, knowing that the gentleman in the shop probably did not believe him. Carter had a brief moan to himself as he walked on down the street, mumbling, "Why is there always someone poking their nose in. If I am looking at women's skirts then leave me to look. Don't assume just because I'm male that . . . . so unprofessional . . . . muppet!"

His moaning fit was quickly brought to its end as the next shop caught his full attention, The Royal Mile Whisky House. Before he even had time to consider anything, he found that his legs had already conveniently walked him inside. How proud he was of his legs! They always guided him to where his inner demons desired to go to the most. He knew however, deep down, that it was a bad thing and really not something to be proud of at all. All the same he did find it funny that sometimes it seemed that his body would act first before he had time to think. A while later and not surprisingly he exited the whisky house carrying a bag with a little something in it. He had bought a sixteen year old Benriach at £38.95, and was not pleased with himself at all. He tried to fool himself that Mary may like whisky and he could give it to her, but deep down he knew who really was going to sample the delicate and complex flavours of the single malt. He quickly buried that demon. Then three shops further down, another one tempted his desires and occasional inclinations. It was The Humidor, a cigar shop. He knew what the humidor was. It was an object that extended the quality of a cigar's life by keeping it moist within a contained wooden box. He had heard Will talk about them before and Carter knew that he wanted one. Carter wanted to buy something to take back to London with him for his friend, but not a humidor as he would never make full use of it. He never kept a cigar for any longer than one day before he smoked it. Carter walked in and the smell was intense and rich. He enjoyed the odd smoke of a cigar himself on occasion so pondered as to how many cigars to actually buy to make the return journey back to London with him. He decided to buy a total of four, two for Will and two for himself. He went for Will's favourite, the Montecristo number 4's. They were however £10.50 each, so Carter found himself nearly a hundred pounds down in total already and he hadn't got anything for Mary yet, no new clothes for himself, and not even his hair cut either! He walked out determined to fend off any further luxuries and be strong and keep his wallet firmly deep in his pocket. Next shop Fudge Kitchen.

"Don't take the piss!" he said, as if the shops were now conspiring against him by grouping all of his indulgences together in a bid to lure him in.

* * * *

There they were! Glistening and standing out from the rest, twinkling and shining, catching Carter's attention. Beautiful large freshwater pearl drops on sterling silver lever back earrings. Next to them in the display case was a message that denoted Beautiful romance and sparkle for very special people. He had to get them, they were exactly what he wished he would find, and thought they would suit Mary perfectly. He hoped. The earrings came with a gift box, sleek, black and elegant. It was right. Leaving the jewellery shop he was excited and relieved that he had found a gift that in his view would have the best chance of impressing Mary.

He was now nearing the end of the main street and was running out of shops to visit, but for the very last one, which was conveniently a clothes shop. He walked in and straight to the shirt section. He wanted to purchase one that was nothing too colourful, but quite plain and simple. He found two to his liking, one was navy blue and plain, and the other was chequered blue and white. They looked smart, and either of the two would be perfect for their drive out the following day. They were also in a 2 for £10 deal which he also found another fine reason to go for those particular shirts!

Impressed that he had managed to get all of his shopping done in such a short amount of time he thought about how to spend the rest of his day. He wanted something where he didn't have to spend any more money. That ruled out almost every attraction on his 'must see' list, apart from one, Arthur's Seat. He was due to be paid that coming Thursday so he would do the other sights, such as the castle, the whisky tour and so on, then. Arthur's Seat was the main peak among the rolling hills that formed a lot of Holyrood Park. It had been described by Scottish novelist, poet and travel writer, Robert Louis Stevenson, as "a hill for magnitude, a mountain in virtue of its bold design." Carter decided that he would do the Arthur's Seat walk later that afternoon. But first he needed to get a haircut before going back to the hotel to change. He remembered seeing a barber's shop a few days before, called Take a Short Cut, which was not far from the churchyard where Marcus had been buried, so he made his way there, stopping off only to buy a bottle of cold still water en route to rehydrate.

* * * *

Carter sat waiting, watching the broom sweeping backwards and forwards across the tiled floor. Masses of amounts of different shades of hair were being amalgamated into a corner where it would later be bagged up and put into a bin. He could see his reflection in the mirror and thought about what to ask to have done. He only really wanted a clean up, a tidy up of his messy, wayward hair. As he looked into the mirror he could see the reflection of the customer in the facing chair looking back at him, with an expression that had no need for words. The gentleman had a look of mind your own business stamped on his face. Carter looked away, and couldn't understand why people would become so self-conscious when sitting in a barber's chair. "Maybe it has something to do with Sweeney Todd, and everyone is on edge in case the barber loses it and just starts thrashing and cutting away." he thought, which quickly made up his mind as to whether he was going to ask for a shave or not! For midweek, the shop was quite busy, with two more customers entering and taking up the last two remaining seats near the door.

"OK Sir would you like to come over and take a seat?" said the barber whose workstation was at the very end and at the back of the shop.

"Yes. Could I leave my shopping here?" asked Carter, pointing to the floor down by the side of the cash till.

"Certainly, your things will be fine there."

Carter took to his seat, the chair wobbling as he sat down causing him to nearly fall out the other side. This was due to him not evenly distributing his weight on both arms of the chair simultaneously.

"Sorry, I always thought these things were locked down?" said a frustrated Carter, feeling a complete fool.

"Afraid not Sir!" said the barber, as he flung the black cloak cover around him, tying it off at the neck.

"OK Sir, what would you like today?"

"Well just a tidy up really. Could I have the sides and back blended, and just a bit off the top please?"

"How much off the top. An inch?"

"Sure yes, an inch off the top and a tidy up sides and back, thanks."

The barber got to work, starting with the left side of Carter's head, using the clippers to shave and blend in the length with that of the hair higher up. The teeth of the comb occasionally caught his ear, causing him to flinch. The scissors tugged at his hair as the barber pulled away too quickly, before allowing them to cut right through.

This was also adding irritation. Carter was getting pissed off and remembered why he had stopped going to the barbers, and let Will do it instead, or do it himself. Then came the razor, straightening up his sideburns and shaving away the hair from his neck, forming a squared off line at the bottom. A quick spray of water and the comb was back out, bringing his fringe to the front.

"OK close your eyes." said the barber.

Carter felt the pieces of hair fall from his fringe down onto his eye lashes, and further down onto his nose and lips, causing a tickle and uncomfortable itch. Carter, when prompted, opened his eyes and looked in the mirror at the perfectly straight fringe the barber had just cut.

"Christ I look like a monk!" thought Carter, before the pieces of hair were blown from his face by a hairdryer, turned on him without warning by the barber. The man proceeded to ruffle up his hair, as if trying to add some kind of artistic panache to it, before arming himself with the mirror. In true stage performance-like style the man glided to stand behind Carter to unveil the work of art he had created on the back of Carter's head.

"Well Sir?" "OK?" said the proud looking barber, to which Carter replied,

"It looks just as shit as the front, thanks."

* * * *

Carter was not too far from the little park where he and Mary had spent some of their special moments together, by the duck pond. He was at the foot of Arthur's Seat. The walk would start opposite the Palace of Holyroodhouse, climbing steeply to follow a path directly below the commanding Salisbury Crags. He would then have to head inland down a flat valley, and climb again to St. Anthony's Chapel, a ruin which sat high and above a loch. The route then turned back and would again climb again steeply, up to the top of Arthur's Seat. Edinburgh can be seen, as well as much of East Lothian, Midlothian and across the Firth of Forth to Fife, providing stunning views from the top. Carter had his rucksack, a bottle of water and a cheese sandwich that he would take with him on his trek. He planned to take it more as a stroll rather than a hike, meaning it would most likely take him about an hour and a half to reach the top. He had never been the hiking type, always opting for more comfortable transportation than actually applying any energy of his own. But on this occasion he wasn't going to miss out on the promise of the views from above. He placed his rucksack down onto the floor next to a fence post and began stretching, first his calf muscles, then his hamstrings. He stretched his back and rotated his arms in alternating circles to work out some knots and kinks. The weather carried with it a cool breeze which he hoped would be kind to him for his steep walk.

Carter took a moment, a short time in which to rest, as his feet was beginning to ache. He sat down on a bench and loosened his laces relieving some pressure around his ankles. He took a sip of his water and wiped the sweat from his forehead. He realised just how unfit he had become as he gasped for breath following the first part of the steep ascent. He had however, felt his lungs expanding during the first part, enabling him to take in longer and deeper quantities of oxygen. He stayed there for a few more minutes before pressing on. From then on and keeping his camera in a handy place in his rucksack, every now and again, he would stop for a quick breather and take a few photos. The views were already offering scenery of picture postcard type quality; the landscape opening itself up at every turn, and displaying so much detail and splendour.

Leaning forward with his hands on his knees, Carter stood at the top, resting. He looked out at the view in front of him and it was one of majestic beauty. The breeze brushed his face, cooling him down. He sat down on the grass and removed his sandwich from the rucksack. The sandwich looked inviting—and he was hungry. He only had a little amount of water left in his bottle and hadn't expected to have had to drink so much of it already. He couldn't resist but finish off the last bit there and then, thinking to himself that he would be able to last the return without liquid, as it was downhill and would be much easier. His cheese ploughman's sandwich tasted so good, every bite tasting better and better, as his body was nourished and thriving on adrenaline. He could have quite happily sat there for hours and wished that he had brought a couple of beers with him. A couple of beers and a sunset would have been ideal up there. He also wished Mary was with him. Having her up there would have been the pinnacle of romance. Carter stayed up there for an hour, mostly on his own, with only the odd traveller showing up here and there, hanging around for a while, admiring the view, and then leaving. Otherwise he was completely alone, undisturbed, in peace, and loving it.

He stood to his feet and threw his rucksack over his shoulder, pulling up the slack from the strap, making it tighter and easier to carry. Before he made the descent he thought what better place to call Mary, than right there at the top, a place with so much beauty. He was on top of the world. He took his mobile from his pocket.

"Hey Carter, how are you?" said Mary with a happy expression in her voice obviously pleased to hear from him.

"Good, you? I'm at the top of Arthur's Seat at the moment."

"Really, wow, look at you being all active. Enjoying the view I bet?"

"Absolutely, it is tremendous. Just about to make my way down actually, but thought I'd call you first. Is it a good time?"

"Yes sure, what time did you say you were picking the car up tomorrow?"

"8am."

"Well I can either come to pick up the car with you, or meet you at the hotel?"

"Why don't I just come and pick you up?" asked Carter as it seemed the obvious and most sensible option.

"OK then yeah, pick me up. I'm going to bring a picnic. How does that sound?"

"Sounds great." replied Carter with a smile.

"I'll be waiting outside at about 8.15am. Sound cool?"

"Absolutely, I'll be there. And looking forward to it."

"I'm looking forward to it too."

Carter ended the call and took one last look around him. There was so much to take in and look at, and he knew that the pictures he had taken would in no way do the view justice. It was one of those places you just had to go and visit in the flesh. He could see church spires sticking out at random points over the landscape spiking up into shot, places of particular significance could be identified scattered in every direction, vehicles darting back and forth and people who looked as small as ants.

* * * *

The route continued back along the tourist track to Dunsapie Loch, finally arriving down alongside the public road around the lower loch, ending back where he had started. The descent was pleasant and much easier on the legs for him. Reaching the bottom he was already seeking out the nearest pub, and he had already spotted three from varying elevated positions on his way down. He began to worry slightly that his feet and leg muscles were feeling a little tender, and hoped that it wouldn't get worse by the following morning.

Carter ordered two pints of ale and sat outside in the garden to the rear of the pub, the sun beating down on his shoulders, the faint breeze stroking the green leaves in the overhanging trees above him. The first pint vanished in a matter of minutes, quenching his thirst. The second however was to be enjoyed at a much slower pace. Other backpackers and travellers had thought along the same lines as Carter and had gone to the pub following their climb to Arthur's Seat. He remembered seeing some of them at different stages of his walk, some of whom he had passed on his way up, and some that had passed him on his way down. The pub had a nice friendly feel about it. Even though it was quite busy, it was calm, and there were no delays in getting a drink. The staff were obviously poised and used to the barrage of tourists returning from their steep ascents and in desperate need of a drink. The place proved to be in an ideal location for good business.

An hour passed and Carter was happy to stay there in the beer garden, hands behind his head, leaning back in his chair, feeling the warmth of the sun on his face. He had his eyes closed, only opening them to see where his glass was to have another drop of ale, and letting himself fully relax. He listened to fellow tourists talking about where they were planning to visit next, and tales of where they had been to so far. There were so many places being discussed, half of which Carter was unaware, and even if he did decide to visit them they would have to wait for another trip. Finishing off his third pint, and feeling merry, he decided to make his way back to the hotel, get cleaned up and go to dinner. He did not want to have dinner at the hotel as he wished to go and try somewhere close to, or preferably on the Royal Mile, to soak up the atmosphere and also to try somewhere new and different. He stood up and hoisted his rucksack over his shoulder. His leg muscles felt tight but not unmanageable, and he wandered out of the beer garden, stretching various areas of his body as he walked.

* * * *

Back at the hotel Carter had a shower and got dressed. He picked up a pamphlet that was on the table next to the TV, which listed some recommended local bars and restaurants. He fancied Italian. He found a couple which were not too far from his hotel, and both were reasonably priced. He read some of the customer reviews and they were very positive, rating the service and quality of food very highly indeed. La Casa Rosso looked especially appealing and that was his choice for dinner that evening. He was very hungry and being that the restaurant was close by, he didn't have far to return afterwards. He was determined to get a decent night's rest so that he could be at his freshest and brightest the following day. He felt that his exercise earlier would contribute and ensure that he had a good night's sleep.

* * * *

The effect of the three pints he had earlier had started to wear off, especially by the time he had finished his starter. He had ordered the bruschetta with tomato and basil and it went down a treat. He chose, against his better judgement as per usual, to have wine with his dinner. He ordered a half bottle of the house red and it tasted divine. He was still hungry and couldn't wait for the arrival of the main course. He had ordered the veal, served with a black pudding and shallot mash, wild mushrooms and a red wine sauce. Due to his earlier excursion and rare burst of exercise he was ravenous. He watched the other trays full of dishes being carried around to fellow diners and couldn't help but gawk and hunger after each and every one of them, hoping the next tray out from the kitchen was going to be his. It seemed like a lifetime before his main course was placed down in front of him. He already had his knife and fork at the ready when he identified his tray travelling from the kitchen through the air towards him.

Carter worked his way through the dish thinking about what the next day would bring. He was excited, but also apprehensive, as he hoped that Mary would thoroughly enjoy it and have a great time with him. However, at that moment, he started to feel a little pressure, a sudden attack of nerves, as if the day approaching was somewhat of a test. This pressure started to rapidly grow within him, and he feared his recent bout of self confidence was to be short lived, the pessimist in him was returning to the foreground, his defences weakening. He sat back in his chair, almost withdrawing himself from the returning wrath of his inner frailties, shying away from them, trying to hide from them. It was no good. They had taken hold of him, and he felt his body tremble; a deep sickness to his stomach, a cold sweat appeared on his brow. This was all so very familiar for Carter, and he felt a tear run down his cheek triggering his spiralling emotion further into a frenzied abyss of darkness. He placed his cutlery back onto the table and signalled to the waiter. Even though he would've liked to have a dessert he knew now he couldn't, he had to get out of there. He hadn't felt this low for some time, an attack of depression with such ferocious vigour, exacerbated by a strong sense of insecurity. His days since meeting Mary had given him confidence and joy, a self assurance. It was now time to feel the opposite end of the spectrum of emotions. There was never a balance. As he settled up with the waiter and pulled on his jacket he felt hollow once again, a cold shudder ran through his body, uneasiness, and an uncomfortable stream of emotion lay solitarily etched to the pit of his stomach.

He thought the night air would do him some good, so he decided not to go straight back to the hotel. Even though the evening was quite warm, he felt cold to the bone. He wanted to talk to Will but couldn't bring himself to call him. Every time he thought of Mary his nerves would rattle, and he could not control them. As he walked around the darkening streets he kept repeating words to himself to stay calm, but his mind and emotions were working overtime. He was now too cold and could go on no further. He would have to go back to the hotel, but not to his room. No way could he be in his room alone feeling this bad, it would be unbearable. He wanted nothing more at that point than a stiff drink and in somewhere warm in which to drink it.

* * * *

It was just after 9pm when Carter walked into the bar of his hotel, now looking half the man that had left the hotel earlier that evening. His face was pale, drained of all energy, and his appearance caught the eye of a few guests already sitting at the bar. Carter kept face front, intentionally not wanting to make eye contact with anyone, including the barman. He ordered his drink, a double brandy, and he turned and found the most isolated seat in the bar. It was the seat by the window where he had seen Jocky from before. His hand trembled from the weight of the glass as he lifted it up to his mouth to take a sip. He was distraught! Why he had felt so calm at dinner and then suddenly become the complete opposite? Was it a panic attack? What triggered it? Was it the impending day out with Mary? He debated whether or not he should continue with the relationship at that point. He continued to question himself. Did he deserve Mary? Should Mary have to suffer by being with someone whose moods and emotions could act so sporadically? Was it fair on such a wonderful woman, to put her in a position where she had that to deal with in her life? Carter brought his hand up to his face, closed his eyes and covered them for a moment. He felt the warmth from his palm on his eyes, trying to sooth yet another headache; a headache with stabbing sensations right behind his eyes. He had no pills with him. He brought the brandy glass back up to his mouth and sank another gulp. He focused on the pain, imagining that it was slowly rising from behind his eyes up and up until it had left his head, disappearing into the distance far from him. This would momentarily provide some relief.

"On the hard stuff I see!" spoke a recognisable voice coming from directly in front of him.

Carter looked up and was pleased to see who was standing before him, it was Old Man Ragg.

"Jocky. How are you? Nice to see you."

Carter, noticing Jocky had already bought himself a drink didn't bother offering. Jocky sat down opposite him.

"Are you OK Carter? You look a bit down."

"No, I'm all right. Just got a killer headache that's all. It's OK, it'll go soon."

They began talking and not before too long Carter hadn't even realised that his headache had gone. They were again engrossed in conversation, mainly talking about his earlier climb up to the top of Arthur's Seat. Jocky was impressed and happy that he seemed to be making the most out of his time in the city, especially as he had been brought there under difficult circumstances. Carter got them another drink each before they began discussing friendships, past and present, and in particular if he had a girlfriend back in London. He started to open up about his feelings for Mary. He had to. He trusted Jocky and he needed to talk. Carter, in the first instance touched upon his pitfalls, more to the point his depression and how it had held him back from succeeding in all sorts of situations, especially women. Jocky was understanding to say the least, and listened to him with such interest, concentrating on his every word. He continued to explain how his life and views on relationships and marriage was such a catch 22 situation for him, in the sense that on one hand he did want to find the right girl, fall in love and settle down with a family, but on the other hand his depression and confidence issues would always prevent this dream from being possible, acting as a personal barrier. He went on to say how incredibly surprised he was to now be in a position where he was seeing Mary, and how it was all moving so wonderfully. She was perfect in every sense of the word. He told Jocky that he had told her about his condition and she did not in the slightest seem fazed by it, or scared by it. However, he couldn't understand that when things started to seem like they were on a roll and too good to be true he was suddenly hit by such an attack at the restaurant, with such a flood of despair. Carter sat confused, still attempting to figure out why it had happened, but for Jocky on the other hand it was all as clear as day.

"There is the panic Carter! The worry! The fear that it all seems too good to be true! Your subconscious is just laying in wait, biding it's time, expecting everything to just fall apart. It is because you have spent a lifetime dreaming of it, but not chasing it, yearning for something, someone to come along, that you have to come to feel this possibility of being almost impossible. Even though your heart is screaming out for this lady, your mind is working overtime to keep you protected, protected from disappointment, from more regret and heartache!"

It all seemed so logical but nonetheless Carter's reply was not as confident. "Thanks Jocky. I appreciate it. And you are probably right. I just wish I could switch it off!"

"Well you have to make that choice. A choice that is a gamble I know. But you have to ask yourself. Do you want to give it a go now and see how things pan out? Or do you want to spend a lifetime alone thinking about it?"

"I don't want to be alone." replied Carter, his voice whimpering slightly.

"Well there is your answer pal, plain and simple. Trust me, I am alone now and know how hard it is. But what takes the sharp bittersweet taste from my mouth is that I have my memories which give me comfort; fond, grand memories that keep me proud, that keep me grounded. And I believe, no, I know, that at some point when the time is right I will see my darling wife again."

"You shall." replied Carter raising a glass expressing his admiration.

"Cheers." responded Jocky, raising his own glass to clink it with Carter's.

"It must have been hard at first though right? Like right after . . . . when you had the first realisation that you were going to be living alone. How did you hold it all together?" asked Carter as the two had now lowered all boundaries and were speaking freely and confiding in each other. Jocky sat forward in his chair and looked straight into Carter's eyes, smiled and said, "I failed miserably, but I tried valiantly. The world shook the day she died. The nights grew colder and the days seemed longer. My eyes wept constantly for longer than I care to remember. I had to come to terms with the fact that I was alone, and for the rest of my days it would remain that way. You see when you lose such a companion, a soul mate, you are not only tested by your strength as a man, but you are also questioned as a man whose sanity has become fragile. Some nights, alone in that house, I suddenly realise that my eyes are stinging . . . . burning, and to my surprise I realise just how much time has gone by without me having slept a wink. Sometimes I am sitting there, and before I know it, dawn comes up and the sun is shining in through the window. You see time no longer mattered. What kept me strong was that my wife would not wish for me to be left a broken man, and would want me to carry on, to live! That gave me strength; an energy that I never knew until that very moment was there."

"That is beautiful." Carter replied simply, overwhelmed and lost for words.

"So my advice to you would be to give it a shot. Try and keep focused on that dream, listen to your heart. It is easy to lose your sense of perspective otherwise, especially when you are tired of trying."

"That's just it! My condition doesn't result in me losing sense of perspective. It results in me being less tolerant and more susceptible to the emotional situations I find myself in."

"I know it is hard for ya pal." said Jocky as he stood to his feet and zipped up his jacket readying to leave "You are at a crossroads now Carter. You can turn left or you can turn right. Choose wisely lad!"

Carter held out his hand to shake Jocky's, and thanked him sincerely for being so helpful, and for being such great company once again. With that Jocky patted Carter on the shoulder and bid him goodnight, smiled and walked away. Carter still had a half glass left so chose to sit back and spend some final moments alone in the bar, soaking up everything Jocky had said. Jocky's words had helped Carter regain focus, and he felt his confidence had returned and been helpfully reinstated. For how long for he did not know.

Carter stood up and walked out of the bar, into the lobby and toward the stairs. He paused and looked at the front door,.half expecting, hoping, to see Jocky once again standing in the alcove, wishing his wife goodnight. He wasn't there. Carter carried on and went back to his room. He had managed not to get too drunk, ensuring that he had made his drinks last for longer periods in the bar. He had to drive the following morning and wanted to be fresh and bright for Mary, and the thought of taking her out while he was suffering from a hideous hangover, would have been totally disrespectful and unacceptable. He would never ever dream of being so rude. It was not in his nature.

* * * *

Carter and Mary pulled up alongside a great loch. It was heavenly. There was a mild mist resting gently over the water, and only the very faint break from the current caused the surface to add the gentlest distortion to the glass-like effect. Mary pulled out a picnic basket from the boot of the car, and before he knew it she had set everything up by the shore, ready for him to sit down by her side.

He could not see any fishing boats out on the loch; the mist was becoming thicker which made it even harder to distinguish one shape from another in the distance. Mary was not eating. Carter asked her if she was OK, asking if she had lost her appetite. She stood up and walked to the car, returning with a bottle of water. She explained that she did suffer with travel sickness every now and again, and the journey had made her feel slightly queasy. She reassured him and said it usually would only last for a few minutes and would then wear off and she would be fine. Carter could not believe that there was no-one out on the loch, he even started to squint his eyes to try and make out any movement on the other side. Then he realised that no-one was on the land either, no movement, no cars driving past, nothing. He mentioned this to Mary and she laughed, suggesting that he was being paranoid. She said that it was better that they were alone. Carter agreed, as it was very peaceful, just having each other for company with no unwanted interruptions. A short time later, Mary came up with an idea. She had packed some towels in the car and shared with him that she had a huge love for swimming. He couldn't believe she was serious. The water must have been very cold, freezing. He pleaded with her not to go in but she was adamant, and urged him to go in with her. He watched as she started to undress, walked out into the water, and dived forwards, the water brushing over her shoulders and cascading down her back. He knew that the idea of him going out to join her was crazy, but he couldn't resist. He felt he would be insane not to join a half naked stunner like that. The absolute spontaneity and absurdity of it was somewhat appealing so he stripped off and joined her. They splashed around together and the water did not feel that cold. It seemed quite warm and pleasant which he found difficult to believe. Mary began to swim a bit further out, heading out towards a floating red buoy about fifty metres from the shoreline. The mist began to get heavy and intense, almost turning to a dense fog. Mary shouted out to Carter, calling for him to follow her and swim further out. He could hear her voice but had now completely lost sight of her in the fog. He swam after her, every now and again stopping, shouting out her name, so he knew in which direction to swim. He could still hear her, albeit faintly, and he realised he was slowing and struggling to keep up. He had to stop for breath.

"Mary . . . . wait! I can't see you. Shout something out so I know where to swim!"

Carter could not hear a response. He shouted after Mary again, and again, but nothing. He was breathing heavily, a misty vapour appearing with every exhale of his breath. It was unlikely that he would've been able to hear a response anyway if not loud enough, as all he could hear was himself gasping for breath. He needed to get closer to her to be able to hear her. He started to feel the cold of the water against his skin, he needed to move. He shouted out one last time. Silence!

Carter ploughed on through the water and he could not see anything in front of him. The fog had now completely engulfed the loch, barely allowing him to see his hands in front of his face. He was freezing cold, even when constantly in motion. His body would just not warm up! Then . . . . the red buoy was there, right in front of his face. By a stroke of pure luck he had swam directly to it. He clasped onto it, using it to keep himself afloat, shivering from the cold; his hands numb. He was worried for Mary. He kept shouting out, making every attempt to get louder and louder each time he called her name. "Mary!" "Mary!" "Mary!"

CHAPTER ELEVEN

Sinking under and gasping for breath, Carter jolted himself upright out of the water and out of his dream. He was in bed, in his hotel room. It took him a moment to familiarise himself with his surroundings after another disturbing nightmare, and again with Mary acting strangely. The sweat was pouring from him, his body shaking. He had been drowning. He was still breathing heavily, trying desperately to regulate it to calm down. He leaned over to the side table and picked up his watch, noticing his hand was shaking. It was 6.45am.

"What is it with all these nightmares . . . . shit!" said Carter.

He believed that this particular dream came from his previous night's insecurities as to whether or not to take a chance on Mary. It made sense. In the dream Mary was leading him somewhere, somewhere where he could not see so didn't know what lay in wait in front of him. This represented a journey; a future; a new path; a new life.

His initial hesitation followed by his decision to follow her, would be his first step into taking that gamble, to take a chance and venture out together into the unknown. He assumed the fog represented either his clouded judgement or obstacles that might arise along the way. Then ultimately when he reached that point, the buoy in the lake, she had gone, leaving him there alone facing his final demise, dying. This part possibly stemmed from Old Man Ragg's personal story the previous night, of losing his wife and spending his final days alone.

Carter stood in the shower, embracing the feel of the hot water, as opposed to his earlier contrasting sensation from his dream. Even though the nightmare was playing on his mind, it wasn't at all a bother to him. He was no longer worried. He was going to have his shower, get ready, get the car, and have a great day with a beautiful woman. He couldn't have any complaints, and he used Jocky's reassuring, positive attitude from the night before to give him strength. As he stepped out from the shower and dried himself, he looked up at his reflection in the mirror, and had to do a double take of his face, he noticed that he was smiling! Usually when confronted by his reflection all he would see was emptiness and sorrow, an embedded sadness looking back at him, but not this day. Instead he saw a face that looked happy; enthusiastic; excited, and open to opportunity. He was once again feeling confident and ready for the day ahead. Before leaving the bathroom to dress he did however say one thing to his mirrored reflection, "If she asks to go for a swim, I'm walking!"

Laughing, he went back into the bedroom.

* * * *

The clutch in the car was a little sticky but nothing of any real issue. He would have liked a car with electric windows instead of the winding ones. The car that Carter had initially been allocated had not been returned to the office in time, and being that there were no other cars available to enable him to be offered an upgrade, he was given another car at a discounted rate. He had no choice. As he pulled out of the parking lot he said "Oh come on, look on the bright side, you have paid less money for this car . . . . even if it is a hunk of shit!"

He pulled down the sun visor and turned on the cool air, desperately trying to cool down the microwave effect that the car was creating. It was another hot day with clear blue skies. People were out in abundance and for midweek it seemed pretty hectic. However, it was rush hour. He sat at a set of traffic lights, quickly running through in his mind, double checking that he had remembered to bring everything.

"Let's see . . . . wallet, phone, water, earrings . . . . shit! Earrings!"

The traffic lights changed to green so Carter immediately spun the car around and headed back to the hotel to retrieve the forgotten gift. He was doing OK for time, even with the cock-up at the car rental company and with his sudden bout of amnesia, he worked out that at worse he should only be a maximum of five minutes late.

As he pulled up in front of the Herald he saw no spaces to park. He continued slowly and still he could find no gaps to accommodate his small car. Then he suddenly spotted one—200 metres from the hotel and on the opposite side of the road. He stopped, indicating to the traffic behind that he was going for it. He looked ahead and there were three oncoming cars that he had to wait to pass before he could glide over and into the space. The first car went passed, then the second. Carter had a strong notion that the third car would pull in there but it didn't. It went straight past.

"Result!" he said turning the steering wheel and heading for the spot. He walked quickly, partly jogging, back to the hotel and up to his room. He noticed a parking space had now become vacant right outside the main entrance.

"Typical!" he said as he jumped up the three steps leading into the main door.

The earrings were right where he had left them—on the table next to the door in his room. How he had overlooked these when leaving earlier was beyond him. He was rushed and returned quickly back down the stairs and back out onto the street. He lightly jogged back up to the car, and spotted a man, a traffic warden, standing close by.

"Oh no, excuse me. Excuse me." said Carter as he reached the car and saw that the man was already printing a penalty notice. "Sir, why am I being given a ticket?"

"Sorry but this is a residents parking area only. There is a sign just up the road there!"

"I'm sorry I didn't see it. I was in a rush and I have only been gone for five minutes!"

"Sorry Sir, but I am only doing my job." said the man handing over the notice, waiting for Carter to take it.

"Please, look. Can you not just let me off this time? I'm genuinely sorry. I was away for literally just a few minutes."

"I cannot do that Sir. I have already registered the penalty on the machine."

"Fuck the machine!" said Carter in anger.

"I will not stand here being spoken to like that. If you have got a problem then call the number on the notice. It isn't down to me." said the man as he turned and walked on.

"This is bullshit. And how did you get here so fast anyway? Do you guys just pop up from nowhere whenever you feel like pissing on someone's day?" said Carter to the back of his head.

The man ignored him and continued walking, not even looking back once. The warden must have been dealing with reactions like that for ages, and as Carter got back into the car he felt a bit guilty that he had sworn at him. After all it was a residents parking area only and the man had carried out his duty. Carter put the notice in the front pouch of his rucksack and switched on the ignition, stalled at his first attempt of pulling out onto the road, prompting a frustrated driver to beep from behind. This wasn't helping and Carter was now feeling more than rushed. He did however manage to compose himself well, and concentrate on getting to Mary's as quickly as possible, and preferably without getting any more tickets. Speeding or jumping a red light the most likely at that point. Exactly as he had predicted, he was five minutes late as he turned into the street where Mary lived. There she was. She was standing wearing a huge smile by the front gate and holding a picnic basket. She wore a striking red dress, and looked a true vision.

"Hey." said Carter as he pulled the car to a halt.

"Oh no, the car is the same colour as my dress!" said Mary as she walked over.

Carter stepped out of the car and opened the boot, took the basket from Mary and placed it inside. He laughed at how Mary was worried about the colour situation and how she felt somewhat camouflaged in with the paintwork. It would have probably been less of an issue if it had been a red Ferrari sitting outside. Mary joked and said it wasn't really a big deal. They both got into the car and fastened their seatbelts.

"Was this the car you ordered?" asked Mary.

"Absolutely not, no way!" "What do you take me for a masochist?" he laughed.

They pulled away. Mary took the road atlas book from the door pocket and flicked through to the page displaying the layout of Edinburgh.

"OK, first destination was?" asked Mary for confirmation.

"Well I thought we could head to Stirling. That's if it is OK with you. Would you like to go there first?"

"Of course sounds great, never made it to Stirling before. It's only about an hour's drive I think." she answered while trying to work out the best route to take.

"OK, we need to get to South Bridge first; then the A700 road onto the B700; the A8; and then finally the motorway, the M9 into Stirling. Sounds easy enough huh?"

"Huh!" said Carter unsure and unconvinced he would remember all of the letters and numbers that Mary had just voiced into the air.

The drive was relaxing, the two of them commenting on the changing scenery upon leaving the city limits. "This place can be truly infectious" said Mary at one point, prompting Carter to instantly agree. There was a moment where their conversation was heading toward the awkward topic of what would happen when he returned to London, but they equally carefully avoided this. It was too deep a discussion to have when they were out trying to just enjoy the time they had together. But both kept reminding themselves that it would be a conversation that they would find hard, and did not know exactly how it would work out. They would cross that bridge when they came to it.

They were on the M9 hurtling towards Stirling. Mary was talking more about her work and about the different characters with whom she worked. Some, she said, were quite weird, some extremely eccentric, and others could be annoyingly obnoxious.

"I know those people." said Carter, as he offered some stories of similar characters with annoying tendencies that he knew at the mobile phone company back in London. Mary wanted to know. She asked him to share some stories with her.

"Yeah OK sure. We have a guy called Derek the Ferret!"

"Oh my God, this sounds funny already!" said Mary already beginning to laugh.

"Yes, this guy is always into everybody's business. You know the sort, a busybody, constantly nosing around looking over people's shoulders at their computer screens to see what they are looking at. And he always thinks he knows best, stands there telling people how to do there job better, pontificating!"

"Yep, I know that guy. Have dealt with soooo many in the past!"

"Another one is a woman called Sally Shitto . . . ." Carter pausing as Mary let out a hysterical laugh.

"No way Carter, you're not serious. That isn't her name?"

"It is, honestly. Yes." confirmed Carter smiling.

"No way!"

"Afraid so, but that isn't even where this person's story ends. When she gets animated her voice takes on this sort of high pitch sound, so annoying. She has become known as the screech owl of the office."

Carter glanced over to Mary laughing, obviously finding these descriptions deeply entertaining, so he continued.

"There is also Christian the Convict, which I know sounds a bit like a contradiction in terms, but this guy has a previous history with theft and dealing, when he was younger. The boss took a big chance when employing him I can tell you. I don't think he is involved in anything illegal now though, but every time anything goes missing from the office, whether it is a pencil, a ruler, or a banana from the staff room fridge, everyone immediately thinks to themselves, Christian the Convict did it!"

"Poor guy!" said Mary trying to contain her laughter and to a more manageable state. Carter wasn't finished yet.

"Wait a minute, there is also Germ Man Craig. This guy constantly seems to be suffering with a cough, a cold or something. Never anything serious enough for him to be off work though. But once, he unintentionally sneezed in Derek the Ferret's face, causing a major argument. It was so funny as everyone in the office started arguing, some shouting at Germ Man Craig saying that he was spreading his germs all over the office, others having a go at Derek the Ferret saying it wouldn't of happened if he wasn't in people's faces all the time."

"Did anyone get in trouble with the boss?" asked Mary, still laughing, but not as excitedly.

"No, it sort of fizzled out before the boss came in."

"Wow, sounds like your office never has a dull moment."

"Oh believe me it does, it has many!"

"See in my office I have to put up with all the usual business jargon and the latest 'buzz words'. If I had a dollar for every time I heard the words ring-fencing, or blue sky thinking, I would be a very rich woman!"

"Luckily I don't get to hear business talk where I work. More repetition of annoying sales pitches, bull-shit basically! Here is another character for you. Our latest recruit, a youngster just out of college called Rupert. He keeps repeating the saying 'go figure' at various points throughout the day, both on the phone and in person. But he uses it in places where it just doesn't make any sense. Like, for example, a few weeks ago Belinda, one of our accountants, came into the office and simply said good morning to Rupert, and he responded with 'go figure', strange boy!"

"We need to come off at the next exit." said Mary noting the next turning off was the Stirling exit.

"OK thanks." replied Carter, to which Mary quickly responded with a slight grin, "Go figure!"

"Very funny."

They both continued to chuckle but were soon distracted by trying to find somewhere to park in Stirling. After about ten minutes they parked just off of Port Street. They walked down to the main high street and started having a look in some of the shops there. They were not planning on staying to visit anything in particular as they wanted to go on to the lake later for their picnic. There would be no time for them to be able to visit any of Stirling's major attractions, even though Stirling Castle would have been of significant interest to Carter, because of his love of history and historic buildings. They looked in a wide range of shops, not just shoe shops much to Carter's delight, and generally enjoyed spending time in each other's company yet again, just looking out of interest and for nothing in particular.

"Oh my God, I have got to go in there!" said Carter as he spotted a shop across the street.

Mary noticed his eyes light up as if he had just won the lottery, and she eagerly looked across the street for the shop that had caught his eye. It was a shop selling replicas of medieval weaponry. Mary followed as Carter moved in haste towards the shop.

She too was impressed as they stepped into the shop, the multitude of swords of all types and representing all ages were hung, trailing around, and covering the inner dark panelled walls. The lighting was dim, and artificial candles were strategically placed, adding character, and lighting the way, revealing different weapon types throughout the ground floor. They stood still for a second in awe of the place. This was heaven for him. A variety of axes, swords, daggers, shields, helmets, samurai swords and armour from all eras were present. One caught his eye. He walked straight over to it so he could see its intricate detail. It was a Roman dagger, for sale at forty-five pounds. Mary joined him having noticed how intently he had been drawn to it.

"Well, what are you saying Mr Jakeman? Or should I say Gladiator Jakeman? Are you thinking of buying it?"

"No, although I am very tempted! I just love these things, I mean the full swords are great but the daggers, especially of Roman origin, are especially fascinating to me. They seem to be ideal pieces of art that symbolise the Roman persona."

"My God, why don't you work in here?"

"Believe me—I would if I could." he replied continuing to explain the dagger in more detail to Mary.

"You see, these are a classic representation of Roman times, the daggers being dramatic illustrations of a meaningful and crucial era in history."

"I love Roman history, although I have not read the full history in any real depth though. But it is so romantic."

"Romantic, huh? I wouldn't say that too loudly around here." Carter said as a joke, highlighting the onslaught of the Roman Empire, and its siege on Scotland all those years ago. Mary laughed while giving Carter a gentle nudge, making him aware that he had made her feel slightly guilty.

"Just kidding around," he said. "Also Mary, look at the detail of the designs. Roman daggers are historically important as they display authentic things of the times, such as the scabbard, the blade and the pommel etc. I hope I don't sound too boring!"

They leaned in closer to look, spending a moment to look in more detail.

"Not at all! I think it's amazing that you know so much about it."

"Yeah well I am a bit of a history buff I must say."

Carter turned to Mary and suggested they leave the shop before he fell victim yet again to his inner urges to buy something. She agreed. They looked in a few more shops, clothes shops and tourist type shops mainly, before deciding to find somewhere to have a coffee and a croissant. They found a little coffee shop not too far from the street that leads up to Stirling Castle. They wished they had more time to spend in Stirling, as it held so much interest, but they wanted to continue on to the place that had meant so much to Marcus.

Walking back to the car he told Mary that he felt quite nervous about going, worried that he might bump into Claire and the girls. He suggested that he may buy a hat, or a balaclava to keep him hidden from public view. Mary laughed at his joking around.

"Why didn't you just tell Claire that you may be visiting the place, but that you would not disturb them?" asked Mary.

"Well it did cross my mind, but, if Claire knew I would be up there, she would've wanted me to go around there, and I didn't want that. I didn't think that would be fair on them. They need time alone to heal. I didn't want to get in the way of that."

"I understand. You did the right thing."

"Thanks." said Carter, appreciating Mary's support.

* * * *

They pulled up and parked in a little village just a couple of miles away from the cabins. The village virtually consisted of one main high street, comprising of shops that provided all the usual local necessities that come with little quaint country villages. There was a butcher's, a mini supermarket, a baker's, a fish and chip shop, an antiques shop and a visitor centre. Right in the middle was the local police station, and there was a petrol garage at the far end off the street. Behind the main street, where they had parked, was the big Scottish Wool Centre. It was busy and obviously very popular. They couldn't help but make it their first place to go. Just outside the main entrance there was a wooden hut with tourists congregated around it. Some of them were having their pictures taken. As they walked closer they could see that the wooden hut was a wooden shelter housing birds of prey, and photographs were available at a price with the lucky tourist holding the bird of their choice. Immediately Mary was sure she wanted to hold one. She looked at each of them, commenting on how sweet they all looked, trying to decide on which one to choose.

"What about the eagle?" suggested Carter sarcastically, as the eagle was huge!

"No, although it is our national symbol . . . . I think I would like to go for the owl."

"Are you sure?"

"Yes the owl definitely."

Carter got the bird handler's attention and kindly asked if Mary could have her photograph taken with the owl. It was a tawny owl and was of a stocky size, brown and white feathers and about forty centimetres in length. Although it was cute, Carter could not help but doubt its robustness, and its unsettling piercing eyes. As Carter got ready to take a picture of his own on his mobile phone, Mary insisted that he join her and the owl in the photo. He slipped his phone back in his pocket and stood next to her. Mary extended her arm and the man slowly moved the bird toward her, the tawny skipping gently from his arm to hers. The owl was surprisingly light and seemed very calm. Carter was surprised as to just how soft the feathers felt.

"OK look at the camera, smile . . . ."

The man took the photograph and after a minute or so gently took the owl from Mary, swivelling around and propping it onto an arm of a patiently waiting child, who was standing to the side eager to feel the Tawny owl. The man informed them that the photograph would be ready in only a couple of minutes. It cost three pounds for the privilege and Carter was only too happy to pay it for as it had made Mary so happy. Carter pressed his fingers on to his temples, trying to relieve the pain of yet another headache, although this one was only mild. Mary realised and asked if he needed some painkillers and reached into her handbag. He thanked her and knocked back two, one briefly catching in his throat before he managed to swallow again and force it down, avoiding the potential embarrassment of choking and coughing it back up right in Mary's face. Upon receiving their photograph, they walked in the Wool Centre. It was a very big, open area, with a range of clothes, tartan kilts, souvenirs and a small canteen area. They looked around, only briefly, parting ways when looking at the male and female sections of the clothes area. The quality of the fabric was of the finest quality and the price reflected just that. Carter tried on some trilby hats, standing at different angles in front of the mirror to see if any suited him. However, he had no intention of buying one. He then picked up a tweed jacket from the rack, but lost grip of it and it ended up a bundle on the floor. His first reaction was to have a quick look to see if anyone had noticed that he had dropped it. Of course someone did. This was the world of Carter Jakeman. An elderly man stood looking at him. No expression, but just stared until Carter picked it up and returned it to the rack. The elderly man didn't work there but was just the nosey type, the type that had an absolute inability to mind their own business.

Mary and Carter rejoined in the middle of the centre, right next to where some golf accessories were on show from a table display. There were miniature bottles of

Scottish whisky, bottled in the shape of golf balls with the world famous St Andrew's Golf Course logo printed on the side. There were also other items displaying the same logo; leather wallets, thimbles, placemats and hats. They decided to head over to the canteen at the far end and get a cold drink, an orange juice or a Coke—anything cold. They sat down at a pine wooden table over by the window, which looked out over a small grassy area, where a couple of goats were standing. Just beyond the grassy area a little stream ran along tricking until it disappeared beneath a small arched bridge. Outside on the small green children fed more goats and one child actually held one of the kids, smiling with the excitement that small children have when experiencing something new. The place had been well designed for all visitors, tending to everyone's needs of enjoyment and refreshment.

"How is your head now?" asked Mary, hoping that his headache had eased, or preferably gone.

"It's still kind of there, at the back. Not as bad as earlier though. It'll go in a bit."

"Do you get them often?"

"Often enough! I just think it is down to the whole thing with losing Marcus, and other bits and pieces, but there you go. It's OK." said Carter, not only trying to ease concern and worry from Mary, but also, from himself.

* * * *

They walked past The Forth Inn which was a bar, hotel and restaurant. It provided a short cut through to the main street. Carter commented on the Inn as it did look wholly inviting. "If I ever come back here that is where I'll be staying. I don't even have to see the inside. The place is class!"

"Agreed, very charming." added Mary. The exterior appearance of the Inn was indeed captivating.

They entered the local visitor centre, partly interested in the history of where they would be heading next, and also just for a general look to see if anywhere else close by was worth visiting. Almost straight away Mary spotted a leaflet stating that there was a waterfall nearby. She turned to Carter to see if he was interested and explained how much she loved waterfalls. Carter was happy to go there. It was only about one mile from the village anyway. Before heading back to the car he picked up a few more leaflets, one on trek routes across the Menteith Hills, one on the area of Port of Menteith, and another explaining which local activities were currently on in the area and neighbouring villages.

Driving back through the village they then turned right and started to climb a hill which led out of the village and up to where the lodge was located. It wasn't long before they could see the turn off. To their surprise the place was buzzing with people, where Carter had hoped it would be quiet and peaceful allowing them to walk through the forest and find the waterfall. However, as got out of the car and approached the lodge they noticed something else, something that immediately explained why the place was heaving. It was a zip wire, a zip wire that turned out to be the longest zip wire in Britain. Carter looked at Mary who happened to already be smiling already, knowing what he was about to ask her.

"Did you know this was here? It must have been in that same leaflet?" he said realising that she had in fact spotted it before.

"Oh come on Carter it will be fun. Have you been on one before?"

"No!"

"Well first time for everything then. Look let's have a go at this, and then walk to the waterfall. What do you say?"

"Christ!" said Carter knowing he couldn't say no. "OK yeah, let's give it a go!"

"Thank you Carter—you'll love it I promise. And I'm paying."

"Hey no way, I'll pay, Mary please?"

"No! You keep paying for things. It is my turn, and it is the least I can do for making you go on it."

Carter knew he was fighting a losing battle and stood back while Mary went to pay. He could hear the screams from people as they took that initial step forward and off of the platform, the point of no return. Then he could hear the buzzing noise coming from the friction being created on the wire, slowly fading into the distance the further away the person travelled down the line. He walked over to the starting point to watch the next person try it. He looked at the wire.

"It goes on for bloody miles. And it's high up. Oh dear, come on, man up. You can't bail out now! Just close your eyes and go for it"

"Everything OK?" said Mary returning with the tickets and at the same time startling him.

"Yes sure, let's fly!"

"You won't regret it. Trust me, you'll love it!" said Mary just before a loud scream belted out from the lungs of the next person in line who had just set off down the wire. Carter replied "Yeah I'm sure I will. That guy certainly sounds like he's enjoying it!"

Harnessed and attached to the wire, Carter stood staring ahead and down through the trees in front of him. He wanted Mary to go first but she thought it better that he did, in case he tried to change his mind at the last minute. He clasped the safety straps with both hands and readied himself to push forward.

"OK you ready? Off you go!"

Carter did not stop to answer and was eager to get on with it. He took one last look around at Mary and pushed himself forward and was off.

"Oh my God, oh shit this is high . . . . Jeez!"

The ground fell away in front of him and the closest thing to his feet soon became the tops of the trees. He could see people wandering about way down below, some stopping to look up as they had heard the wire buzzing. He felt nervous for only a few seconds and then he felt elated. He was travelling so fast and the views were sensational, he was flying, free like a bird. It was his first time on a zip wire and by the time he reached the finishing platform on the other side he knew it wouldn't be his last. He turned to watch as Mary was the next person in line to come down the wire. As she approached he was hit with the sudden realisation that due to her he had just done something that he would never have done before meeting her. He looked at her smiling as she came flying in, and was conscious of the fact that she was already bringing the best out in him. It felt wonderful and he was on the verge to taking another step, a commitment and determination to try and do anything he could to keep her. He was falling for her more and more by the second.

They walked back to the lodge and the starting point of the zip wire.

"Do you want to get a quick coffee or a soft drink before we take the walk down to the waterfall?" suggested Mary, becoming aware that the lodge had a terrace at the side where other visitors were being served snacks.

"Yes sure, I do feel a bit dry. Probably being windswept on the wire!" he said jokingly.

Having already ordered their drinks at the counter they sat outside. The seating area offered spectacular panoramic views. They could see for miles above and below the magnificent mountain tops.

"So you enjoyed the wire, huh?" asked Mary.

"Yes, shockingly I did. I've never really been into to stuff like that before."

"So no chance of you ever going bungee jumping then I suppose?"

"No way! That is just insanity. I couldn't do anything like that, parachuting, hand-gliding. No afraid not. Not even if I was drunk!"

"I can understand that, but I have to admit, parachuting is amazing."

"Really, you've done a jump before?" asked Carter genuinely interested.

"Yes, once. I enjoyed it. They try and teach you how to land and everything, but believe me, my landing was terrible. I just ended up as a heap on the floor!"

"I can understand parachuting but bungee jumping is ridiculous. Why would anyone want to do that?"

"I know, but it is supposed to be one hell of an adrenaline rush!"

They enjoyed their glasses of ice cold lemonade, before choosing to set off on their walk to find the waterfall. It was only about a fifteen minute stroll from the lodge, and they found they could walk there from a choice of three different routes. The routes were colour coded according to walk duration and defining how strenuous each path was. Carter and Mary chose the easy option as they were just interested in a nice calm plod along. The more difficult paths were more favourable with children especially, running off in excitement, leaving their poor parents with no choice but to follow them. The path they chose, the easy route, started with a very slight descent, the path winding around the trees heading further and deeper into the forest. It was mostly silent, with only the sounds of birds singing, the faint sounds of children's voices in the distance, and the occasional buzzing coming from the zip wire above. The light became darker as they became swallowed up by the dense forest, the deeper they walked the darker it became. Further along the trail they began to hear water falling, crashing onto the rocks below. They had nearly reached the waterfall.

Sitting on a bench, they sat quietly, watching the fabulous falling water land on the rocks below, before filtering into the rippling stream. There were a few other visitors around, some stepping across the rocks that were breaking the surface level in the water, just a short distance from the waterfall. Some more adventurous types were attempting to climb the high rocks to the side of the waterfall, hoping to touch the water, before eventually reaching the top.

"Don't even think about it!" said Carter, as he had noticed Mary looking at the climbers with extra interest.

Their intention had never been to stay there that long, so they decided to get underway and head towards the lake for their picnic.

* * * *

A crooked looking white signpost leaning slightly into the country road came into view. Port of Menteith was written on it, and was the next turn off. Mary spotted the sign first and alerted Carter. They slowed and turned right, proceeding on to a long straight road, surrounded on each side by green fields. Just up ahead a church appeared on the right hand side and was set just back from the road. Next to it was a hotel that looked quite large, as if it could accommodate many, and was situated at the foot of the lake. Further on, just before the road headed left and around a sharp bend, appeared another signpost. Priory Ferry was written on it and was the next turn off.

"Shall we try that?" asked Carter.

"Yes, we could take the picnic across to wherever the boat visits if you like."

"OK, I think it may go out and across to the island that has ruins of a Priory on it. Claire mentioned it before. But there is another one. Another island is also out there, an island that you can only get to by rowing up to it. It isn't a tourist attraction like this one though. Shall we see if we can hire out a rowing boat, maybe from here? We can try and find our way across to the other smaller island if you like?"

"Sounds adventurous, I'm up for it!" replied Mary sounding especially intrigued and excited.

They took the turn off and parked up by the lake. There were a few cars already parked, and people were standing further up on the jetty waiting to board the small ferry. A little ticket kiosk was situated just to the left, where prices were on show and maps could be purchased for a small amount.

"Good afternoon Sir, just for one for the ferry is it?" asked the man through the little glass window.

"No, we actually wanted to see if it was possible to take a rowing boat out on the lake?"

"You can hire a rowing boat Sir, yes. We do an hour at six pounds, two hours at nine pounds, or a three hour at twelve pounds."

"Well we were hoping to go to the small island of Inch Talla? So maybe the three hour would make sense."

"You want to go over to Inch Talla?" asked the man curiously.

"Yes, my sister-in-law comes up here every year and she told me about the ruin over there, and that it is not a tourist spot unlike the Priory one, so . . . we thought . . . ."

Carter paused speaking as he noticed the man looked very suspicious all of a sudden.

"Why is there a problem?" asked Carter.

"No, not at all, my apologies. It is just that we don't usually get people asking to go there. It is kind of hidden away from the tourists. It is very uneven there, and no levels of safety have ever been put in place. It is a total ruin. There is barely room to tie off on the shore there. Do you know that?"

"Yes, I'm sure we'll find somewhere."

"OK. Well row around the right side of the Priory, and Inch Talla is the next island just set off to the left."

"Thank you."

Carter handed over twelve pounds, before the man directed him to where the oars were kept, and wished him luck out on the water. Carter walked over to the boot and took out the picnic basket. He signalled inside the car to Mary if she would mind locking up and pointed to where he was going. She was making a quick phone call to the office reminding a fellow worker of a deadline that she had forgotten to mention. She nodded, and carried on with her telephone conversation. The oars stood under a little shelter just along the shoreline and there were two, old, haggard looking rowing boats pulled up and tied off at the foot of a tree trunk. As Carter stood there, deliberating over which boat was the least likely to sink, Mary joined him, and looked equally cautious as to the boats' appearance and capability. One boat was dark green and the other sky blue.

"Well your guess is as good as mine!" said Carter looking at her, unconvinced of the structure of both vessels.

"Let's go for the sky blue one, as then rescue teams can identify us more easily from a distance, when it falls apart and starts to sink!"

Carter laughed and agreed. He took Mary's hand and helped her into the boat, before passing her the picnic basket. He turned and picked out the sturdiest, most robust looking pair of oars from the selection, sliding one of them into boat, slotting it into the fixing on one side. He gently pushed the boat forward, ensuring at least a quarter of the back was in the water, before quickly stepping on board. He twisted the remaining oar upright and used it to push them away from the shore and fully into the water. He slotted in the second oar and took his seat, facing Mary, who sat at the other end of the boat. Carter started to row, feeling his arms tighten at every pull, feeling his muscles strengthen. The current was quite strong but he didn't mind, it wasn't uncomfortable and he was enjoying rowing. Mary was looking out to the right hand side and the breeze was catching her hair, blowing it delicately in the wind. She had a face that couldn't lie, a smile that was never faked and a heart that was unquestionably golden and pure. She was quite a vision and with every pull of the oars he felt himself growing stronger, braver and vibrant. Mary would occasionally look at Carter, share a smile, and offer to share the rowing. He did however resist her best intentions and was OK to continue, for a while at least.

Carter rested the oars down and let them lay in the water, in order to catch a breather and have a rest, letting the boat softly drift with the breeze. They were just to the side of the island where the Priory ruins were. The ferry had already returned to the pick up point by the time they had rowed there. There was a gap through the trees and they caught a glimpse of the Priory. It was bigger than they had first thought. It stood proud and prominent in amongst the woodland. The area was a haven for wildlife. Carter drew Mary's attention up above the tree line, showing her two ospreys flying across the sky, circulating and sweeping the lake, searching out the trout, choosing the right moment to execute their diving attack. Mary tried taking a photo but they were too far away, and it was unlikely they would fly closer to the boat. Carter picked up the oars, taking the decision to continue on to the island that held a more personal significance, where little Eve's Princess lived in the secret castle. It took approximately fifteen minutes to row around to the other island. As they breached the corner they caught their first glimpse of Inch Talla. It looked numinous, and at the same time subtly haunting, sending a chill down Carter's spine, and also causing Mary to shudder.

As they got closer they began to look for an opening at the shore, somewhere to moor up, but most of it was overgrown and inaccessible. They headed anticlockwise around the island and it wasn't until they got nearly three-quarters of the way round that they spotted a gap, an opening in the shrubbery that offered promise. Carter pulled harder on the right, redirecting the boat so it was facing toward the opening. Mary let him know when he was lined up and he pulled his left arm with equal strength to align the boat.

"OK now both together!" she said, and Carter again began rowing, but carefully and slowly.

There was a mass of ducks in the water just offshore, and seemingly reluctant to move out of the way, as if defending the island from a siege. Carter, with Mary's useful directing, managed to navigate around them and ensure that he did not hurt them in any way. With one last final pull on the oars, Carter then let the boat drift in through the gap, allowing it to glide in slowly. He looked over the side, anticipating that he would be able to see the bottom through the water at any moment. As soon as he did he pulled on the oars with force, giving one final surge to their speed allowing them to bank. He grabbed hold of the rope and jumped from the boat onto the shore, pulling the boat in further and more securely up onto the ground. There was a sturdy enough branch sticking out within easy reach so he used that as his tie off point. He took the picnic basket from Mary, and then helped her safely out of the boat. The island's circumference was quite small to scale and they knew where they needed to head for to find the ruins, the secret castle. The walk was somewhat treacherous. With everything overgrown and tangled, it was hard to get their bearings and determine a route through at times. Carter led the way, holding back branches and twigs so Mary could walk through unscathed. They started to feel disorientated and claustrophobic as they reached the middle of the island, where the plant life seemed at its worst. They stopped for a moment and rested.

"Mary, look! What's that up ahead? Look up there! I can see something through the trees. That must be it."

"Oh yes I got it, I can see." said Mary pushing a spider's web from her face.

They could see the stone exterior of a ruin, an outer wall of some kind. They were unable to determine any more detail than that, as their view was still mostly restricted. They walked on, struggling through the obstacles ahead, knowing it wouldn't be too much longer before they were there.

Crumbled stone and gaping cracks were all that remained of the structure, and despite its poor condition they could make out the general shape and layout of Eve's secret Castle. The overhanging arches of what looked like a little chapel were still intact, but were overcome by ever increasing plant life. The ruin sat solemn amongst the trees and undergrowth and had an eerie feel to it, giving a sense of total isolation. The deteriorating building was right at the tip of the island of Inch Talla, and they could see the water's edge, just about, through the trees at the back.

Mary took a picnic blanket and rolled it out at the centre of the ruin of the little chapel. Carter explored the rest of the remains, clambering over uneven rocks around the back of the outer wall, nearly slipping and falling a few times. He walked in through what was left of a stone doorway and saw Mary preparing the picnic. He paused for a moment, before she was aware that he was there, and smiled. He felt a sense of fulfilment. He was so pleased, even if it was to be temporary, that he had come this far. He had brought a woman that was fast becoming the love of his life to a place that had meant so much to his brother, where he had been and enjoyed so much, and many happy memories were created there. He felt very fortunate and could only hope that Marcus would be proud of how far he had come, in such a short amount of time too, in confronting his demons. Carter stepped forward into Mary's line of sight prompting her to smile at him. He walked over and helped her prepare the final bits and pieces of the picnic.

"Wow, this is amazing. Thank you for preparing the picnic. It looks great." said Carter recognising that she had obviously made a lot of effort to make the picnic a success.

"Hey, I love picnicking. Back in the States when I was younger, we would picnic all the time. It was such a family thing to do, and there were plenty of places to go. It was an opportunity where the family could get away from the distractions at home such as the TV, the telephone, or the radio, and go out together and enjoy each other's company. It gave everyone the opportunity to talk, to share things as a family."

Together, enjoying their picnic, they talked more about Mary's childhood and upbringing, her childhood memories and high-school friends. Both had forgotten plastic cups or glasses for the trip, so the red wine had to be drank and shared from the bottle. Every now and again they swore they could hear footsteps from the other side of the wall, sometimes so distinct that Carter went to investigate to see if anyone else was there. There was no-one and they were completely alone. Initially they paid no real thought or attention to it, assuming it was small animals scurrying around, ducks from the water's edge running across and then back before being seen. They carried on and did not pay anymore attention to the sounds after that, and relaxed and enjoyed their picnic. Mary had prepared a variety of sandwiches, also bringing breadsticks, olives, crusted rolls, a few different types of cheeses, some crackers and some grapes. Carter lay back, leaning on his elbow, picking the odd grape with his right hand, alternating between grapes and wine. Mary, noticing how relaxed he looked redirected the conversation onto him, and his own childhood. He started by talking about his parents and how loving they were to both Marcus and himself. He said that he missed them greatly, and now with Marcus gone, it had given him an all time low and he felt like he had been kind of abandoned. The more he opened up to Mary, the more she saw just how sweet the real Carter was, and how he sometimes felt that it should've been him that had died, and not his brother. Mary quickly discarded that thought as absurd, saying that everything happens for a reason, and that it was his fate. Sorrow ridden he felt that he had disappointed Mary with his last statement, but on the contrary, she thought that his heart was in the right place, and felt sorry for his losses. She also knew that the experiences of losing people so close would contribute to his depression dramatically, and having to deal with all of that in his life so far had left him damaged and weaker. She quickly came to realise in those brief moments, listening to him open up, that some people just couldn't handle loss, finding it very, almost impossible, to heal. She listened to him further. Unprompted he had now started speaking about school, and how hollow he used to feel in the mornings, panicking about the day, and what was going to happen there. His school was rough and he was the brunt of the bullies on most occasions. He carried on speaking, not making eye contact with Mary, but zoning out and as if in a trance, a trance that enabled him to speak freely. Mary's feelings started to grow stronger, with every word he spoke, and how delicately he used his words, and how determined he was not to sound rude about things in his life or come across disheartened. She was so engrossed in what he was saying she did not even notice the sensation of a lone tear run down her cheek. For a split second he glanced at Mary, slowly his sentence dwindling to nothing. He stopped talking as he saw her tear.

"I'm sorry. I didn't mean to . . . ." said Carter feeling disappointed in himself, that he hadn't been more caring, now reducing someone so special to tears.

Mary leaned into him, placing her index finger on his lips, stopping him from saying anything further.

"Don't apologise. It's OK. Listening to you then brought warmth to my heart. I know how hard it is, and has been for you to share your emotions. But please, don't stop. I want to hear it all, everything!"

Carter stayed completely still, overwhelmed by the words he had just witnessed from Mary's lips. Everything suddenly stopped for him as Mary leaned in further to kiss him. Carter sensed that a magical moment was about to happen, their first kiss.

But sadly, before their lips managed to make contact some more footsteps could be heard, louder this time and more distinct than before, startling them both.

"Hello!" shouted Carter, as he pushed himself up and onto his feet. He slowly walked toward the doorway in the stone wall. "Hello!" he shouted once more, glancing back at Mary and holding his hand out signalling for her to stay where she was. The sound stopped, and everything was very unsettlingly silent. With caution he slowly stepped forward and through the doorway. There was no-one there. He wasn't so sure. He walked around to the back of the ruin, checking every last little place where it was possible for someone to be. Suddenly, he heard a whisper come from behind him, a whisper that sent a chill down his spine, his body frozen still.

"Carter?"

He spun around in one frantic motion, in desperation to see who it was. It was Mary peering through a crack in the wall, checking to see if he was OK, and if he had spotted anything.

"Christ!" he said, starting to laugh once he had seen that it was Mary who called his name.

His heart was beating fast, and he couldn't talk, so he just waved at her, giving her a thumb's up. He faced forward once again, and feeling his heart beginning to slow to a normal pace he proceeded further around to check the last remaining areas of the ruin. There was nothing. It was clear that no-one else was there. He walked back through the doorway to find that Mary had already started packing away the picnic.

"Are you OK?" asked Carter in a gentle tone.

"Yeah, sorry I'm just a bit freaked out. That was definitely footsteps of something big."

"I agree, but I couldn't see anything. I've checked the whole area outside and nothing! I cannot explain it."

"Well this place is creepy. There is something here!"

"Maybe we should go!" Carter offered, seeing that she had become concerned and worried.

Mary happily agreed and packed away the rest of their things before starting to head back to their boat.

"I bet we get back and the boat is gone!" said Mary adding suspense to the situation.

"Yeah or we don't even make it back." followed up Carter.

Mary took the lead, partly as she felt that whatever had made those sounds back at the ruin would come from that direction. Carter reminded her, a couple of times, to try and stay calm as he noticed her gaining in speed from time to time and starting to panic. He would look behind every five or six steps just to check, reassuring himself that there was nothing there, nothing following them.

"I can see it! Carter I can see the boat, just up ahead on the left!" said a relieved Mary.

The boat was only a matter of seconds away and they quickened their step to get to it, choosing not to waste any more time than was absolutely necessary. Carter helped her back into the boat and loosened the rope before he too stepped back on. He grabbed the oar and quickly spiked it into the water, pushing the boat away from the shore and back into free water. He looked up, making sure one last time that there was nothing approaching as they drifted away. He looked at Mary and they both shared a nervous, but relieved, laugh.

"Well you certainly know how to show a girl a good time." she said watching him lock the second oar into place before sitting down readying to row.

He laughed and followed up with, "Tell me about it, you nearly gave me a heart attack when you whispered to me. I thought I was just about to be the next addition to the local missing persons list!"

They gradually made some distance from the island and were back out into open water. They chose not to go directly back to the ferry point, but row around the other side of the Priory Island, and maybe seeing the cabins where Claire and girls were staying. Mary was just happy to be off the creepy island and didn't really mind where to go next, as long as it was in the opposite direction. The boat gained in speed, as Carter pulled and pulled, until they were at a safe distance. Mary could see something on the far shore. Carter let the oars rest in the water, and he swivelled around to see. There, in the distance was a row of small brown cabins, and to the right the big old greyish coloured house that had been described by Claire.

"That's it. That is the place" he said, pleased that they had located it.

He did however not want to row too close for two reasons. One, he did not want to be seen by Claire, Starlet or Eve as it would look strange, and two, because he felt knackered from rowing already, and still had to turn around and make it back over to the ferry point. As they sat there, embracing the tranquillity of the surroundings, they gave each other a look, a look and a smile that was obviously referring back to what nearly happened on Inch Talla, before being disturbed. The kiss . . . .

Carter thought what better time than now to give Mary the gift that he had got for her. He reached into his jacket pocket and removed the box. He suddenly realised that the little box looked like it could also hold an engagement ring and briefly panicked, wondering how she would react if assuming the same. She didn't bat an eyelid and took the box from Carter with an adoring smile. She gently opened it and was delighted at seeing the beautiful earrings; it was such a romantic gesture. She told him that she absolutely adored them, which was music to his ears, and thanked him. He sat back, watching an obviously happy Mary look at them in more detail.

She was obviously genuinely touched. He looked around, and started to think of Marcus, spotting a fishing boat over by the cabins, two men on board readying their rods for fly fishing. As he concentrated on the boat and looked more intently, one of the men turned and looked his way, raised his hand and waved at Carter. Carter leaned forward concentrating more firmly on the man. It was Marcus's face that he could see.

"Are you OK?" asked Mary, as she had noticed him daydreaming.

"Yeah, sorry! Just drifted off there for a moment!"

He looked back at the men in the fishing boat, before asking Mary if she was ready to return to shore.

"If you are ready Carter, then I am." responded Mary making the point that she knew that being in this place was in some ways closure for him, and letting Marcus go.

"I am ready." he said confidently knowing that Mary was referring to such.

He took hold of the oars and pulled, making haste back toward the ferry point.

* * * *

Carter pulled out and onto the main road, heading away from the lake and back toward the village they had visited earlier in the day. They passed a golf course that was set to the right of the winding, hilly road, and he saw some golfers walking along, bag in tow. Another was searching around in the bushes by the roadside, looking for a wayward ball. Soon after, he noticed that Mary was sleeping. He was so happy that she was with him. At a set of traffic lights, he looked around at her, watching her sleep, before quietly saying "Thank you". He pulled away and headed back towards the motorway, which would lead them back to Edinburgh.

Mary woke as they pulled into the street where she lived.

"I've slept all the way back. I'm sorry."

"No don't be, it's fine."

Carter pulled into an available space and turned off the ignition.

"So . . . . I have really enjoyed today Mary. It has been great."

"The feeling is very much mutual. And thank you for the gift. I love them."

"Look, I was thinking. If you are not too tired, do you fancy doing anything tonight? Dinner or a movie, or something?"

"I would love too. A movie sounds great. I haven't been to the cinema for a while. I'm not sure what is out at the moment, but there should be something worth watching!"

"Hopefully yeah, well, great! Shall I come back and meet you about 7.30pm?"

"Perfect" said Mary as she stepped from the car.

Carter got out and opened the boot. He picked up the picnic basket and walked her to her house. She told him that she was so pleased that he had told her about his parents and of some of his childhood memories, and urged him to embrace those feelings and confront them, not hide from them. He stood watching her, proud of her, feeling blessed that she had come into his life. He thanked her too for listening, and upon feeling specks of rain starting to fall, they each retreated before it fell any heavier. He got back into the car, waving at Mary before driving away, returning the car to the hire company en route back to the hotel.

*   *   *   *

"Now are you sure you don't mind seeing this one?" said Mary, as Carter had agreed to watch a chick flick with her.

"Of course I don't. I have a varied interest in all genres. Although I admit, I wouldn't see it if I was alone!"

"Thanks Carter, you're so sweet. I really want to see this one. I didn't even know that it was out yet."

Next in the popcorn line Carter stepped forward to the counter.

"Could I get one large mixed popcorn and two diet Cokes please?"

"Sure. Any nachos for you?"

"No thanks" said Carter, wishing the person would just get on with the order, as the film was already showing trailers of upcoming movies, so they didn't have much time.

"No Nachos?" repeated the man to Carter's surprise, as if repeating it would make him change his mind into actually buying.

"No Nachos!" said Carter, ensuring the man was now clear on the decision.

"OK, and it was a mixed popcorn wasn't it?"

Mary laughed as she noticed the blank shocked expression on Carters face. The fact that the man had spent so much time trying to sell him something he didn't want, he now had to reconfirm what he did really want. Mary answered for him.

"And two?" said the man pointing to the soft drinks dispenser.

"Diet Cokes!" said both Mary and Carter at the same time, the man becoming aware that they were getting frustrated.

He quickly scooped half from the salted and half from the sweet, hurrying as he knew that these two customers were not his number one fans. He put lids on the drinks and passed them from the dispenser to the counter before charging them. Carter gave the man a twenty pound note, and did not see much change. They thanked the man, as he did manage to get their order sorted in the end with some speed.

"Lucky I didn't go for nachos as well, otherwise I would've been broke!" thought Carter sarcastically as he picked up the items, while Mary grabbed two straws and some napkins from the side.

Settled in their seats in front of the big cinema screen Carter felt like he was in Heaven. He was there enjoying the two loves of his life, the cinema and Mary. The film played and was about half way through when it came to a romantic scene, a scene where the two main characters were about to kiss. Carter looked out of the corner of his eye at Mary, who was obviously into the movie, and captivated by the scene. Coincidently the kiss in the movie was disturbed as his and Mary's had been earlier in the day. He noticed Mary look at him and smile, before holding his hand tightly in hers. She held his hand for the rest of the movie. By the end of it he felt so enthralled he could feel the connection between them growing stronger.

They arrived back at her house just before 11pm. It had been a long day. She said that she would not be finishing work until late the following day, but would be able to see him again the day after, the Friday. They hugged each other and for the first time managed to kiss. It was so passionately tender, divine, and a moment that he wished would last forever. He wanted to let her know exactly how he felt, that he had fallen in love with her, that, dare he say it, wanted to spend the rest of his life with her. However, he decided not to at that point. They hugged one last time and planned to meet each other by the duck pond that Friday afternoon, where he planned to tell her exactly how he felt, that he was in love with her and wanted her permanently in his life.

CHAPTER TWELVE

Thursday was to be a day of tourist attractions. It was a fine day, weather wise, and Carter was determined to make the most of it. He wanted to get an early start and was in the shower by 7.30am. Still buzzing from the night before, and reliving the special moment when he and Mary had kissed, he was suffering a fresh bout of confidence. There was a spring in his step and the he embraced the morning with a new found love in his heart and a wave of expectation in his mind. He was King, if only for a day.

Breakfast tasted better than ever as he sat reading the morning paper in the hotel breakfast room, reading of things that he never usually bothered to read, but all of a sudden he was reading them with a genuine interest and enthusiasm. He had already made conversation with the waitress when ordering breakfast, and he didn't feel uncomfortable in any way; nor did he suspect that the lady had walked away from him thinking he was a weirdo.

This was all new ground to him, and he was relishing it. He felt so extremely different that it was as if he had become someone else, not in body, but in soul, something that had lived within him, and had now been let loose and was free. He finished the paper as well as the last of his breakfast, which had turned from the usual fry up, to cereal and a fruit salad. He momentarily took a double take at himself as if noticing yet another change in Carter Jakeman. The waitress returned with a smile, checking if he would like any more coffee, and again engaged him in conversation. He politely declined another coffee but sat speaking to her for a couple of minutes. Even though Carter had gone to breakfast early, when the room was usually at its busiest, it was quite the opposite that particular morning. He told the waitress of places he had in mind to visit, and she gave him some useful advice as to the best times to visit certain places. One example was the castle's one o-clock gun fire. To Carter's surprise, she even asked how long he was staying, and casually asked as to whether he was in a relationship at the moment. He paused for a second, as not only had he been quizzed about his relationship status once or maybe twice before, but more strangely, he was now in a position to say 'yes', he was seeing someone.

"Lucky girl!" said the waitress.

Carter thanked her. She wished him a good stay for the rest of his time in the city and left. Carter noticed a gentleman sitting at the next table with a smirk on his face.

"You're honest aren't ya?" said the stranger noting that Carter had just turned down an opportunity with a very pretty waitress.

Carter simply replied "Best policy!"

With that he stood up, put on his jacket, picked up his various local attraction leaflets and made his way out of the hotel.

The first place on his mammoth journey to visit was going to be the castle, but after taking the waitress's advice, he decided to go to the vaults instead. He knew that there was a tour on the hour, so he made his way to the Royal Mile to get there by 10am, which would be the first tour of the day. The streets were glistened with the sunlight as he strolled pleasantly along; spotting the little Italian place that he had gone to earlier in the week. For the rest of his walk to the Royal Mile his thoughts were firmly fixated on Mary, and not just the kiss either, but everything about her and the glorious almost life altering situation in which he now found himself. He knew that tomorrow would be the day, the day that he told her he wanted them to be together. But how would he say it; what would he say? He wanted it to be heartfelt, honest and a little poetic. He thought that he might write something down later in the day, perhaps when stopping for lunch, or maybe that evening. He wasn't sure what to do that evening but half expected to feel tired after all the places he was going to see, so thought he would probably have a couple in the bar, maybe bump into Jocky and chat for a while, then bed!

* * * *

Carter, and a few fellow tourists, stood patiently awaiting the tour guide's arrival to take them down to the famous underground vaults of Edinburgh. There was some anticipation amongst the waiting crowd, as the vaults were said to be very dark, closed in, and rumoured to be haunted. Up stepped a man in period attire, who introduced himself as the guide for the morning's tour. He started by explaining a brief history of the area, the people, and the myths and legends of the past. He mentioned Burke and Hare, which Carter had already heard about in detail from Jocky. Following his introduction, he directed the small crowd to follow him, and they were led into a small alleyway. The man shouted "Halt!" causing some tourists to jump, which of course was his intention, adding to the effect and experience of the tour. Carter listened intently as the man delved further into the grim history of the city, notably about what the locals would do with their waste, or more to the point, their excrement. He told of how the balconies, that could still be seen above, were constantly monitored by passers-by on the streets below, as the residents would empty their buckets from above, occasionally hitting the odd person here and there.

"Without warning?" questioned a fellow tourist.

The tour guide, expecting the interruption probably from years actively conducting the tour, abruptly answered: "No Sir! There was in fact a warning. However that warning would not help the drunkards below, who failed to respond, or the people who were too slow in getting out of the way. You see, when someone from above was about to offload their mess down onto the street below they would shout out, wait a second then throw it. If any below had not moved out of the way it was there own fault. They had been warned!"

Everyone laughed at the jovial aspect to this story, even though crude, it was comical. The guide wasted no more time before directing the group onwards and towards the main entrance to the vaults. Carter couldn't wait.

The actual entrance itself was off street level slightly, just a few steps leading down to a dark green door. It felt like you were going into a basement bedsit at first. As the guide unlocked the door and pushed it open, there unveiled a steep staircase, leading down into darkness.

"Mind your step, and follow me into the mysterious world of the Edinburgh vaults, where at every turn there is a story to tell." instructed the guide as he led the way.

He flicked a switch which lit up a string of mock wall candle lights that led you down into the depths. He also carried a sturdy looking torch which he had for back-up and added light in certain places.

"Follow me . . . . if you dare!"

People followed him down cautiously, and his intended act of unsettling people was working on some of the group at least, the girls mainly. Carter was unfazed and positioned himself at the very back. He preferred being at the back of a group when on a tour, as it allowed him to take it more to his own pace, with no pressure, he could stop and look at something in more detail if he wished. Also he would sometimes stray at the back, just for a moment, to soak up the atmosphere of a place, take in the smells, visualise how it would've looked like its heyday.

They reached the bottom of the steep stoned staircase and were lured into a little room to the left. There was barely any light there but the guide shone the torch towards the floor, enabling the group to see where they stepped. The guide started talking about the history of that particular area, how it could've accommodated any number of people at any one time, even though the space was very small and tight. This room acted as a kind of gateway, a starting point that led further down into the vaults, and within a minute they were heading there. They walked through a number of caverns stopping in one large open area, an arched ceiling was high above them, and the smell was more rancid than it had been on their approach through the other adjoining areas. The guide began to explain the history of this area. In fact, it had been a pub. A few members of the group giggled as they, and Carter, found it hard to believe. He went on to say that all sorts of characters would be found down here at one point or another. Not only the poor, but even people of high status would frequent the pub, have their wicked ways with the local prostitutes, before returning to their wealthy world above. He said, however, that the conditions were less than satisfactory to say the least, and the food was mostly rotten. The guide explained that they ate oysters by the handful but it never made them sick. He went on to explain that the reason for this was because with every oyster they ate they would also take a slug of very strong alcohol, generally gin, which would kill off the bacteria in their stomachs. Some of the girls in the group winced at that point. The guide indicated that they had a couple of minutes for photos before they would continue the tour. Carter took his phone from his pocket, activated the flash, and started snapping away. He couldn't help but place his hand on one of the walls, just to feel the site where so much history had taken place. The wall was cold and moist to his touch; damp and slippery. These walls had seen so much, witnessed so much, and as Carter stood there visualising it as a pub, he wished more than ever that at that moment time travel was possible. And not just to see the pub, but for so many significant times and places in history that sadly were never able to be recorded, times that are now gone and lost forever.

"Wouldn't have tried the oysters though!" he said to himself as the guide sprung into view attempting to unsettle the group by sharply raising his voice. It worked. There were a couple of screams at that point, and not just from the women. The group gathered and followed him, with Carter lurking and waiting so he could join the back. Then into the next area which used to be a shoe shop. Shoes that had either been lost or thrown out in the streets up above, would end up here, and be sold for cut down prices.

The experience had been everything that Carter had hoped for, suspense, history and atmosphere. The last stop on the tour was a museum, comprising of various tools and items from the 18th century right through to modern day. It was a small display, only taking the space of one room, but was interesting all the same.

Carter blocked the sun from his eyes as he stepped back out of the vault entrance next to Southbridge, waiting for them to adjust to the sudden change in intensity. He headed back to the Royal Mile and planned to make his next port of call the Obscura Tower. As he neared the tower he just caught the back of a woman walking into a shop on the other side of the street. He was certain it was Mary. He couldn't help but go and check. He crossed the road and went in. It was a clothes shop set on two levels. It was quite easy to see the whole of the shop space from where he stood, but he could not see her there. He presumed therefore that she had gone upstairs, so he walked over to the escalator and stepped on. He looked around the upper floor, but could not see her, or a woman who looked very much like her. He was confused. He walked away from the escalator, determined to locate the look-a-like Mary. At the back was a small shoe section and as he turned into that aisle there she was sitting on a black leather seat and with her back towards him. He walked over, certain it was her.

“Hey!” he said, as the woman turned her head. Carter got a look at the side of the person’s face and realised he had made a mistake, it wasn’t Mary. In fact it wasn’t even a woman.

“Yeah?” said the man in a deep, remorseless voice, while at the same time trying on a pair of high heels.

Carter, not sure what to say, and not wanting to offend the man in any way, simply and calmly said “I think they look great on you!”

“Thanks.” replied the man, in a much softer voice, before turning to try on the other shoe.

Carter made his exit a swift one, choosing not to look back, not even once, not before he was out of the shop completely.

“Oh man, I bet he thought I was hitting on him. I thought it was Mary, holy shhh . . . . I’ll have to tell her. That was funny. Maybe not actually, on second thoughts, don’t think that’s a good idea. Oh yeah by the way Mary I was certain I saw you yesterday, but it turned out to be a man!” he thought as he walked on up to the tower, and hoping that he wouldn’t bump into the guy again.

As he neared the main entrance he could see that the front doors were shut. Sadly it was closed due to building works and would not be open to the public again for another two weeks.

“Damn!” said Carter upon reading the notice.

He deliberated as to where to visit next in place of the tower. He knew that the gun was going to go off at 1pm at the castle, so he needed to build in travelling time for that. He didn’t want to do the whisky experience until the late afternoon, even though it was just on the opposite side of the street and he could be there in seconds. He made up his mind. He was going to pay a visit to the official residence of the Queen and the Royal Family, Holyroodhouse Palace. Carter made his way over to the bus stop and checked out the timetable. The next bus that would be going in the direction of the palace was five minutes away. As he waited for the bus he reflected on his previous day with Mary, and how it was a day that he wished he could relive over and over again. An absolutely perfect day, filled with excitement, adventure, promise, and love. He couldn't wait until he saw her again. He looked down the street and saw the bus approaching, so he fished out some loose change from his back pocket, ready to pay.

* * * *

Carter didn't have much time to spend at the palace before having to head back to the castle in time for the 1pm gun. There were two admission prices on offer, an admission to the palace itself, or a joint visit of the palace and the Queen's Gallery. There was a five pounds difference in price if choosing the latter, which he would've happily paid, but due to time constraints he opted for the palace only. It was made clear upon entry that no photography or filming was permitted, and mobile phones were to be turned off when inside. The building itself was beautiful and the baroque style was especially appealing to him. He did not know much about the palace or its history. As he wandered around he was amazed by its grandeur. He stopped in a room which had a grand fireplace at the back and a stunning painting above it. His natural response was to reach for his phone to take a picture but quickly reminded himself of the etiquette. There was an information point just to his left and he started to read. It stated that Mary, Queen of Scots had been married at Holyroodhouse and witnessed the violent murder of her secretary, Rizzio, by Lord Darnley in her private apartments. Darnley was her second husband and her first cousin. It is understood that it was an unhappy marriage and that his eventual death by apparent strangulation in 1567 was thought to be at the hands of Mary's third husband, James Hepburn, 4th Earl of Bothwell.

Moving on and reading further information points, he began to realise that maybe it had been a stroke of luck that the tower had been closed, resulting in him going to the palace. Standing over to his right was a curator who was informing a small group of tourists that the palace had also briefly served as the headquarters of Bonnie Prince Charlie during the 1745 uprising. He stopped there to listen for a while, but kept note of the time as he still needed to get back to the castle.

* * * *

Carter decided to skip lunch and head straight to the castle. He had spent longer than expected at the palace and was now in a rush to make the 1pm gun. He took the bus back, which in fairness didn't take long at all.

He walked through the big parade ground outside the castle walls, where seating areas were in the midst of being assembled, no doubt for an upcoming event of some kind. He walked in through the main doors and felt instantly at home. There was a warm, safe sensation that came to him whenever he was inside a castle or a fort of any kind. It was a strange feeling that he could never fully understand, but assumed that it may be something to do with a protective aspect, that castles were originally built with the sole intention of staying secure, fending off enemies, keeping evil away. He obtained his admission ticket and with only minutes to spare rushed to the place where the gun was due to fire. There were many people already awaiting the shot, so he had to find a good place to stand, one that had a good enough view. There were a few stone steps to the right which he stepped upon, allowing him to see over people and get a clear view. He quickly powered up his phone and activated his camera. He overheard two men standing behind him, discussing the history of the gunshot. One man said that the gun had been fired almost everyday for many years, all the way back from the year 1861. He went on to say that it was traditionally used as a time signal for ships.

A man in uniform readied the gun to fire, and without fail on the stroke of 1pm it sounded, a distinct and powerful shot echoing out across the city streets below. Carter took a couple of photos which were mainly close ups, trying to capture the smoke coming from the gun. People who had made the firing of the gun part of their itinerary quickly dispersed.

He felt quite hungry and decided he would try and get a bite to eat before doing the full tour. However it was 1pm and most visitors were flooding into the Redcoat Café, conveniently located only yards away from the gun. He headed over and walked in. There were plenty of tables so he fancied his chances of being able to sit and eat. There were a variety of hot and cold meals on offer in the self-service café. It was very simple in design, mostly pine furniture adding a light and spacious feel, and boasted magnificent views. Carter ordered a tomato and basil Panini and a diet coke, and managed to find a seat, sadly one without a view but he didn't really mind. He took his pen from his jacket and started jotting down some lines on the napkins in front of him. He wanted to write down ideas of what he wanted to say to Mary, a bit of preparation. But nothing appropriate came to mind. He took a bite from his Panini, the hot tomato from inside slightly burning the tip of his tongue. He took a gulp of his cold drink to try and balance out the burn, but was left with an annoying tingling sensation on the tip of his tongue. He looked back at the napkin and brought the pen close to it, as if the words were about to flow, but his mind was blank. He didn't panic at that point, and choosing to stop, he decided he would try again once he had had a drink later that evening.

Shortly afterwards he left the café and headed out and across the forecourt and on up towards The Regimental Museum of the Royal Scots Dragoon Guards. He spent about twenty minutes inside here, looking around at the different displays of weaponry and medals, information regarding Scotland's only cavalry regiment. It was there to illustrate both the English and the Scottish antecedents, which dated back all the way to the year 1678. Carter walked back outside onto the uneven cobbled stones, following the crowd up a slight incline deeper into the heart of the castle. At the top of the incline and just to the left was St Margaret's Chapel which immediately became of interest to him once he had read the description. It was the oldest building in Edinburgh, and had been built around the year of 1130. This was an obvious highlight and he entered immediately. It was very small inside, the alter itself situated in a cordoned off area at the back underneath an attractive and charming looking stone arch. There were a couple of religious types in there, Carter noticed them when walking in, sitting at the sides on the wooden benches supplied, and were in prayer. He felt an overwhelming emotion in this particular chapel, maybe because of its history, and he could have easily just sat in there, quietly, for an hour. There was so much respect shown by the visitors inside, all remaining quiet, with only the odd sound of a child's voice or a baby's cry breaking the silence.

Just along from the chapel he noticed a sign directing the way to something called Mons Meg. Curious as to what it was he headed that way. In only a few seconds he was able to see what it was, a massive medieval siege gun.

"Wow!" said Carter, not realising he had said it aloud.

A fellow visitor heard him and added, "That is one hell of a gun huh? That thing there can fire one of those gun stones nearly two miles!"

"Two miles?" Carter answered in disbelief.

"That's right, and it is one of the worlds oldest!" offered the man before moving on.

Carter approached the gun, placing his hand on the one of the wheels, in a way paying tribute to its power and its presence.

Carter carried on and went onto the next highlight en route within the castle walls, The Scottish National War Memorial. He then went onto the Castle Vaults, then The Royal Palace and finally The Great Hall. When finished he felt quite tired, it was a lot of information to take in. As he was about to make his way back down towards the main gate, he noticed something that he had missed, the Stone of Destiny.

Carter took about ten photographs of the stone, trying to get each and every angle he could, the enigmatic piece had been taken from Scotland to England by Edward I in 1296, and was finally returned as recently as 1996, seven hundred years later. The stone, traditionally the coronation stone of Scottish Kings and Queens was stolen by Edward I but still remains a powerful symbol of Scottish independence.

*   *   *   *

It was nearly 3.30pm by the time Carter was outside and back to the main street. He was really pleased with what he had seen so far, and he had so many interesting things to tell Mary. There was no doubt in his mind as to where he was going to visit next, the whisky experience. It wasn't far from the castle entrance, just over on the right hand side, so was not at all far to walk. He could feel the muscles in his legs start to tighten, and the concoction of the various outdoor activities that he had undertaken so far on his time there—were becoming more noticeable. At least he could sit down in the whisky experience tour he thought.

He was excited and keen to get inside. Upon paying, an assistant tour guide told him to wait as the next barrel ride was about to arrive. He waited, impatiently, before he saw the barrel come around the corner and into place, stopping right before him. "Enjoy your ride Sir." said the assistant, as Carter stepped in and sat down on the seat. Luckily enough the only other people waiting were a small group of people who knew each other. They decided to wait for the next barrel so they could all go on together, resulting in Carter having a barrel all to himself. Then the barrel was in motion travelling away from the waiting area and into the replica distillery. Going through, there were many stories told about the whisky making process, throughout history and up to modern day. The replica distillery was very impressive with a collection of waxworks of workers representing different stages through the years, offering their own insights and stories.

The barrel stopped next to a platform, and Carter was greeted by another assistant who guided him into a waiting area. The waiting area was for people who were going in to try whisky tasting, and Carter was certainly one of them. As the next barrel pulled up alongside the platform and the group of people got off, the doors opened and the guide led them into the adjoining room. It was quite a big room with a semi-circular table in the middle. There was a small podium to the right facing the table, where a lady was standing ready to speak about the tasting aspect of the tour. Everyone took their seats before she started to talk about the history of whisky and full whisky making process. She was extremely knowledgeable and Carter was intrigued and wanted to listen and learn, as opposed to some of the others in attendance who just wanted to drink some whisky.

A short while later and the time had come. Out came the glass tumblers along with a varied selection of single malts and blends, and accompanying water. The water was there just to cleanse the palate between tastes. The tasting began and the lady spoke of the history relating to each one as it went along. The variety that was on offer was sublime, and Carter enjoyed every second. The lady also explained how to look out for different signs and characters relating to the whisky's age and body, and encouraged the group to concentrate and try to identify as many different flavours as they could for each and every one. This was close to becoming the absolute highlight of his day, moving from one drop to the next, being exposed to such a fantastic mix of aromas, feeling relaxed and thoroughly enjoying himself. He assumed that the experience would end there, but to his surprise, there was one last room to visit, the whisky room itself. The whole group were instantly amazed by the room; every wall had a glass cabinet, floor to ceiling in height, lined up with bottles of whisky. Everywhere people looked all they could see was a range of varying ambers, closing in on them and caressing them in their splendour. There were also a couple of barrels turned on end in the middle of the room, with some final tasters on top. There were little paper shot sized cups, no more than half a dozen on each, and were filled with a tiny farewell drop. It was a *wee dram* to send people on their way, or more importantly via the gift shop where they could purchase a bottle or two.

Carter walked out into the open air, and feeling the warm sun upon his face, he tilted his head turning his face skywards and closed his eyes. He drew in a deep breath and upon exhaling he felt his shoulders drop, muscles relax, and it felt great. He was, however, feeling a little bit tipsy, which surprised him as he had really only had some tasters, OK maybe more than his fair share he concluded. Underneath his right arm he carried his latest purchase, of course another bottle of whisky, but not for himself this time, it was for Jocky 'old man' Ragg. He hoped that he would see him one last time before he returned to London so that he could give it to him in person. If not he would entrust it to the barman at the hotel as he seemed like a nice guy, the genuine article, so would leave it with him to hand over to Jocky when he next saw him. He got this for Jocky not only as a friendly gesture, but also as a thank you for all his kind words and stories, which little did Jocky know, had helped Carter in a huge way, in helping to build his confidence, restore his belief in himself when doubting about going for it with Mary, and keeping focus on what's important. Carter hoped for another opportunity to tell him this in person.

* * * *

Arriving back at the hotel somewhat tired and dishevelled, he freshened up. He wanted to get a bite to eat downstairs before going and settling down in the bar, partly on the off chance to see Jocky, also to give Will a call and report into HQ, but mainly to try and write down some pointers, some words, ideas of how he was going to tell Mary how he truly felt about her, and for their future, come the following day.

* * * *

Carter arrived downstairs at 7.30pm sharp, and was shown to a table. Strangely it was the same table that he had dined at his first night, and tended to by the same waiter. This brought back some worrying memories for Carter, as it was the waiter who had messed up the order before. He was concerned that the waiter might seek revenge following his debacle last time.

"He may want payback and spit in my meal!" An old adage which Carter had heard in London which he quickly dismissed as paranoia—he was hungry and needed to eat! He would be extra tolerant and polite! The waiter approached.

"Good evening Sir, would you like to see the wine list this evening?"

"Yes please."

"OK Sir I'll be back in a moment, thank you. Any water for the table?"

"No thanks." said Carter with a smile.

Carter placed Jocky's bottle of Glenmorangie single malt whisky on the table, so he didn't have to have it on the floor down by his feet. He then thought the chair next to him was more suitable and was about to move it when he was interrupted by the returning waiter.

"Sorry, excuse me Sir you cannot bring your own bottles in here to drink!"

"I know! It is a gift for someone. I was just about to put it on the chair. Look, the bottle is sealed OK!"

Upon hearing the waiter, a couple dining at the adjacent table took notice, putting Carter in an awkward position. The waiter heard what Carter had said but chose to annoyingly reconfirm all the same, creating an embarrassing moment and putting him on the spot in front of other diners.

"I know Sir but just so you know. It isn't allowed."

"I wasn't . . . ." said a frustrated Carter quickly composing himself and lowering his voice.

He took the wine list from the waiter and started to read through the selection. He peered over the top of the menu and noticed that his fellow diners had returned to eating their meals. But to his dismay the waiter hadn't gone.

"Yes, can I help you?" enquired Carter confused.

"Are you ready to order?" said the waiter stood poised ready to write.

"Order?" "You have only just handed me the list?"

"No Sir, have you chosen what you would like to eat?"

"Well no, funnily enough, because I came in and you showed me to the table. You then asked me if I was having wine, to which I said yes. Then it took you all of ten seconds to walk from here to there, grab a wine list and return it to me just in time to deliver your bring-a-bottle policy. So thus me having no time to look at a dinner menu."

"Well, do you want me to come back then?"

Carter placed his hands over his face in total disbelief, before smiling and choosing to see the funny side of it, saying "Yes please, that would be great."

Carter quickly perused the menu and the wine list, as he knew that the little whippet of a waiter was sure to be back soon. He closed both and placed them on the table, and then reached into his pocket for his phone. There was a text from Will, sent to him only minutes ago. It read "Hey bud. How's it going up there in sunny Scotland! How are things going with the girl? Call me!"

"OK Sir, are you now ready to order?" said the returning waiter with a hint of sarcasm.

"Yes I am thank you." "I would like a half bottle of the Merlot, and for food, could I get . . . ."

"One second Sir." interrupted the waiter, as he was still writing down the letters that made up the one word, Merlot! He nodded to Carter to continue.

"For a starter could I have the crab and for the main the salmon . . . . please?"

"Of course Sir, you can!"

They shared a passing glance of hatred for each other before the waiter retreated. Carter quickly dismissed the waiter's attitude and called Will. There was no answer. He tried again but nothing. He sent a text instead, then at least Will would find out sooner or later that he was OK.

"Hey Will. Yeah cool up here. Went for a drive out with Mary and it was quality. Meeting her again tomorrow. How r u doing?"

He left the text at that, but really wanted to speak to him. He wanted Will's advice on his plans for the following day, and more importantly, an opinion on what to say to Mary. He would try him again later.

* * * *

Carter slowly worked his way through his main course noticing just how delicious the salmon was. On occasion he would look up through the glass window of the restaurant door to see if he could see Jocky walking in, but not yet. He checked his phone for texts, but nothing. The restaurant was now almost full with customers and Carter was pleased to see the waiter rushed off his feet, struggling to keep up with the influx of orders. He was running from here to there, dropping the odd glass on the floor mid mayhem, and a manager eventually came over to assist him and help him recover his chaotic waiting skills, if he indeed had any in the first place. Carter questioned himself as to whether he was being too overly harsh on the waiter, but swiftly decided he wasn't, and concluded that the waiter was nothing more than just an irritating little shit. The time had come for the waiter to return to Carter's table. He was sweating and was trying unsuccessfully to hide his breathlessness, and obviously enraged at the fact that Carter was sitting there enjoying watching him suffer. But to the waiter's credit he tried his absolute hardest not to give Carter the satisfaction, which he admired, and forced himself to speak in the friendliest, most polite voice he could fathom.

"Would you like any dessert Sir?"

"I'll have a look at the menu." replied Carter with a slight grin.

Carter saw the waiter's body tense. However, he turned to get the dessert menu, returning red faced and being bombarded by customers trying to get his attention along the way. He then slapped the menu down on the table. He went back to a table of four to take their order, before rushing to get some drinks from the bar for another table. Then it was Carter's turn.

The waiter walked over, "Well, anything?"

"No I'm fine thank you!" said Carter as he handed the menu back to the waiter.

Obviously frustrated, which in fact had been Carter's intention; he turned and walked away in a strop. Carter found that more recently he was getting to the stage where he wasn't prepared to be the punch bag anymore, and it was time to speak up and say what he knew was right. He had never been like that before. He wondered where this new found bluntness came from, but to be honest with all the emotional changes that he had experienced recently, he wasn't entirely sure what was happening to himself at all. He figured that maybe it had something to do with Marcus, but more likely Mary, and that he now he had something he wanted to protect. He felt that this was making him more defensive as a human being. He decided it was time to go the bar and start thinking about what he was going to say to Mary. He picked up Jocky's scotch and left the restaurant.

* * * *

The ideas for what he wanted to say and how he wanted to say them escaped his mind. Sitting at the same table where he and Jocky had sat the last time, he racked his brain desperately trying to get something written down. He started to panic and did not want to freeze the following day when the moment arrived, and have nothing to say. Various napkins and bar receipts lay crumpled by him on the table, containing a variety of scribbled ideas, mostly nonsensical and containing utter gibberish. He was disappointed as usually he was very good at delivering lines; knitting words together; producing poetry and half written screenplays. But this was different. These were words that would be heard, words that would need to be right, words that opened up his heart and released his imprisoned emotions, recording evidence that would be a clear dedication of his future to Mary. Becoming frustrated he chose to take a break, placed his pen onto the table and slouched back in his chair, taking a sip from his glass of wine.

There was no sign of Jocky. Carter had hoped he would have made an appearance by now, but the time was getting on and it was unlikely that he would see him that particular evening. Carter picked up his mobile and tried Will again. This time there was an answer.

"Stranger, how are you?"

"Hey Will, how are you doing?"

"Don't worry about how I'm doing. I wanna know how Mr Lover man is doing?"

"Ha ha, very funny! Yeah not bad actually. Mary and I have been spending quite a lot of time together."

"Yeah and . . . . ?" Quizzed Will, trying to find out how far Carter had got sexually.

"Well she wants to take things slow. But we did have our first kiss last night."

"Yeah go on . . . . kiss and tell!"

"No that was it. We had a great day, enjoyed each other's company, saw a movie last night and that was it!"

"Oh OK. Where are you by the way? Are you in a pub?"

"I'm in the hotel bar. Will?" Carter said, readying himself to tell Will of his plans to share his feelings with Mary.

"Yeah?"

"I love her."

"What?" replied Will while laughing a little.

"I'm serious. I want to spend the rest of my life with her."

"Wow, hold on there buddy! You have known her for how long?"

"I know, I cannot believe it either, but she is just absolutely amazing."

"Does she feel the same way? Does she know that you feel this way about her?"

"Not this strongly no, and does she feel the same way about me, as in long term, I don't know either. But I'm gonna find out. I'm meeting her tomorrow after she finishes work. I'm going to tell her then . . . . I'm going to tell her that I want to spend the rest of my life with her."

"Hold on!" said a concerned Will. "You are going to tell her that tomorrow! Don't you think that you may be jumping the gun a bit? Don't you think you should wait a while, see how things pan out. She has already said she wants to take things slow, and you're getting out the wedding bells already. Be patient mate. You could end up ruining what you have. Listen to me."

Carter, interrupting, his words becoming more emotional and passionate, "I've been running from things my whole life, and all it has brought me is pain and sadness. I can't do it anymore. I know I can do nothing to stop my depression, but by God I'm gonna put up one hell of a fight."

"Carter" said Will, pausing for a moment, trying to figure out what to say. Carter sounded much stronger in himself and he did not want to sound unsupportive.

"I understand that mate, but just think of the negatives that could result from your actions. Jesus, call me a pessimist but you've got to consider this. Also, how is the relationship going to work? You in London and her up there? A long distance relationship? Come on, they are lame! Are you gonna go up there every other weekend? I don't know the girl but I'm pretty sure she won't leave her job and move down here! Have you thought of any of this?"

"Yes." said Carter with utmost sincerity. "I would be prepared to move up here on a permanent basis."

"What?"

"I'm sorry Will, and I know it sounds crazy, but I love her, and if tomorrow I found out that that feeling is reciprocated then my bags are as good as packed."

There were a few moments silence before Will decided to break it. He didn't want to lecture his friend so decided on a bit of light humour.

"You move up there? Are you breaking up with me Carter?"

Carter laughed, relieved that Will seemed to be coming around and understand his position. As the conversation went on Will became more interested to hear as to how Carter was going to break the news to Mary. Will advised him not to come across as weird or too over dramatic, and to take it easy. Carter appreciated Will's understanding and friendship even though his advice was not as helpful as he had hoped. Will wished him luck and told him to let him know the outcome, either way, and to not be too disheartened if he didn't get the answer he was looking for. They ended the call and Carter took another sip from his glass. He was happy that he had told Will, even if it was initially met with some resistance and doubt, but at least he knew, and that meant a great deal to Carter. He, in a way, felt empowered that he had opened up and was honest with his best friend. He returned to thinking of what he was going to say to Mary, and found himself bearing in mind that it needed to be something that definitely didn't come across as weird or over dramatic, as per Will's in depth instructions!

* * * *

Another hour and another glass of red wine later, Carter was still unaware of what he was going to say. The surface of the table was nearly completely covered with screwed up pieces of paper and tissue, some stained with red wine as Carter had become clumsy as the night drew on, and the alcohol taking effect. He no longer had his pen and didn't know, or care anymore where it was. He had dropped it earlier and it struck his foot, darting off in some direction which he failed to see, and could not be bothered looking for it anyway. He focused his thoughts on Mary, and Mary alone. He concentrated his mind on her smile, her beauty, her elegance. This brought him some comfort. However deep down he had become stressed, ruing his inability to be able to come up with anything to say to her. He was disappointed that he hadn't seen Jocky, as there was a man, in Carter's mind, who could have helped him with his wisdom, such poetry of words and inspiration for love. But it was not meant to be. Carter, suddenly aware that his wine had vanished, stood up and headed to the bar to acquire another. He noticed there had been a change in shift in barmen, and it was now the one who had told him about Jocky's life. Carter stepped up to the bar and ordered another glass of red wine. The barman recognised him.

"Good evening Sir. How are you?" he said as he refilled Carter's glass.

"Good evening, yes feel quite good actually. Yourself?" said Carter with a merry smile on his face.

"So so! Charge to the room, Sir?"

"Oh yes please, thanks. I was hoping to bump into Jocky in here tonight, thought he may have came in for a couple!"

The barman slowly looked up to Carter as he placed his glass down in front of him.

"I'm afraid that he is no longer with us. He passed away yesterday afternoon Sir!"

The walls around Carter seemed to close in with such velocity it made him feel off balance and light headed.

He swayed, took a step back, stunned at what he had just heard. His initial reaction was to clarify and confirm that he had heard the barman correctly.

"Jocky Ragg? He died?"

"Afraid so, Sir. His next door neighbour was hanging out her washing and she saw him sitting in his garden on the bench where he and his wife used to sit in the mornings and watch the birds eat on the feeder there. When she said hello and didn't get a response it made her wonder. She thought he was sleeping at first. But then she realised he had gone . . . . in peace at last. I heard from my aunt first thing this morning. She lives on the same street. I'm devastated. I had some good chats with him in here. They don't make 'em like that anymore."

"No . . . . that they don't." mumbled Carter, shocked and pale.

"Are you OK Sir?"

"Yeah . . . ." said Carter, taking his glass and turning away from the bar, heading back to his seat. "I just can't believe it!"

He sat down, not wanting to accept what he had heard. He suddenly felt cold and with a deep sadness weighing heavily in his heart. He sat there, motionless, staring into oblivion, hardly drinking any more of his wine. It was only due to the sound of the last orders bell being rung that he realised it was time to go. He picked up the bottle of scotch, intended for Jocky, and walked toward the exit.

"Excuse me?" said the barman, catching Carter's attention before he left the bar.

"Yeah?" Carter replied looking drained of all spirit and energy.

"You seem to be quite upset?"

"Well, in the short time that I knew him, I grew very fond of him. He was such a nice guy. It's a shame."

"Look on the bright side pal. He is reunited with his wife, his soul-mate. They are together again as one. That's the way I look at it."

"You're right. Thanks. Goodnight." said Carter, the barman's words reminding him that Jocky was now at peace and back with his one true love.

Leaving the bar and crossing the lobby toward the staircase, he stopped, and looked round at the front door where he had witnessed Jocky talking in the alcove that night. Before going to bed he decided to go and stand there himself, and say a few words as his own personal farewell.

Quietly, almost in a whisper Carter spoke "I just want to say a special thanks to you. You have helped me grow much stronger as a person, and you've had quite an impact on me. Sadly, now you'll never know . . . . I got you this bottle of Scotch here . . . . not gonna need that now . . . . I'll raise a glass to you my friend. You were the kindest man I've ever met, and may you find in Heaven what was taken from you on earth. God bless you Jocky."

As Carter stepped from the alcove and made his way upstairs he made himself a promise. No more panicking about what to write, and thinking too deeply into things, no more stressing about what to say to Mary and how to say it. He knew it would be difficult but was going to do it off the cuff. If his words came out wrong or he made a fool of himself then so be it. Jocky's memory had inspired him to make this his decision, to take life by the scruff of the neck and give it a shot. He wanted to be happy, in a lifetime spent with someone, someone so special, so unique, the one!

* * * *

Carter tossed and turned for about an hour, before accepting that sleep was not likely to be in his immediate future. His mind was now a cocktail of differing trains of thought, each plucking at a different chord of his emotions. He was off kilter, mind unbalanced and confused. He had a storm of colliding emotions; apprehension about his feelings, his love for Mary, the low hollowness of first losing dear Marcus, and now, Old Man Ragg. He tried to balance it but it was no good. After all, extreme opposites in moods were not unfamiliar to him, but with the two extremes acting together in such close quarters and almost synchronised, he could do nothing but ride this storm which began to grow stronger and more unnerving. He tried to keep focus on one thing, Mary, to regain some sort of normality and plateau, but it wasn't working. He needed something. He just wanted to sleep. He began searching his clothes, one at a time, checking his pockets and his rucksack, hunting around to find some Cipralex pills, or any painkillers that were left, anything that would give him some relief. He found the bottle of antidepressants and there were two tablets left. He, recklessly and stupidly, unscrewed Jocky's bottle and knocked them back. The bottle was already a quarter empty following his further drinking when returning to his room earlier that night, drowning his sorrows.

A cracking headache, almost instantaneous overcame him, splintering behind his eyes and bringing him to his knees. He was almost paralysed by the pain. He frantically rubbed at his temples, rotating his fingers desperately trying to relieve any pain at all. For another fifteen minutes he was in severe torment and pain, eventually collapsing to the floor and passing out, falling into a deep sleep.

* * * *

Carter's eyes slowly opened. He was fully covered and dripping with sweat, his body cold and shivering. The sun had begun to rise outside, providing a dim orange glow through the netted curtains at the window. He looked directly up at the ceiling, not wanting to attempt standing, but instead reached out and pulled the duvet from the bed down upon him. He began to recollect the previous night's events, finishing at the point he got back to the room. The rest of what happened was a blank. He didn't know how he had ended up on the floor. Had he fallen out of bed? The headache had gone, and even though he had drunk a lot of alcohol the night before he didn't really feel hung-over. He slowly turned his head, as if to seek out some sort of evidence as to how he ended up there. He saw the empty bottle of Cipralex lying next to him on the ground, and though it did not bring back memories of the full story of what happened, bits and pieces slowly started to filter back to him. As he lay there, alternating his thoughts between the day ahead and the night before, he started to regain strength at last, taking longer to return than usual. After laying there for about an hour, he managed to stand up in stages. The first stage being thinking about standing up, the second, thinking again about standing up, the third being sitting up, the forth being thinking about standing up, the fifth being thinking about the effort to stand, the sixth being applying the effort to stand up, and finally the seventh, actually standing up. He expected his head to spin or have a decrease in blood pressure, but nothing. He was reluctant to believe it but he felt as right as rain. He screwed the bottle top back onto the whisky bottle on the side table, picked up the duvet from the floor and slung it onto the bed. He heard a knock at the door, and knowing it was the cleaner, just said, "No!" He heard the footsteps grow quieter outside as she went on to clean the next room along. He stretched out his arms above his head, before going to the window to have a look outside. It was another bright looking day, and he hoped it remained that way long enough for him to talk to Mary. He wanted to meet her at the duck pond, the special place where they formed a friendship, a relationship and that special connection. He thought it fitting that he should tell her there. He could waste no more time, he picked up his mobile, also from the floor, and sent a text to Mary.

"Hey, what time you finishing work today?"

He turned on the TV to bide the time waiting for a response. He had by now missed the hotel breakfast, so once he had a response from Mary he would then get ready and go out for something to eat. He felt very hungry, so hungry that it was making feel sick. Not even a minute passed before his phone beeped alerting him to an incoming text. He picked up his phone.

"Going to finish at 4.30pm, or maybe a little bit after! Still wanna meet up?"

Carter responded instantly and texted back the message "Duck pond 5pm. I'll bring the bread . . . . !"

* * * *

Carter could not decide what to do to fill up the day before meeting Mary. He wanted to give her flowers, so he would have to pay a visit to the florist on his way to meet her later in the afternoon. He left his hotel room at around 11.50am and made his way straight out to the street, seeking out the first place where he could get a cup of strong coffee and something to eat. It wasn't long before he found a place, a greasy café serving up anything from burgers to pizzas. It would have to do. He couldn't wait any longer.

Sitting drinking his hot coffee, he watched as customers normally do, others flowing in, mostly builder types, ordering large quantities of grease on a plate. Carter's stomach turned as he sat and watched the food flying around the café, the smells making him feel nauseous. But he was willing to stick it out. Before too long up came his toasted sausage sandwich. He looked at it for a minute, building up courage to eat it. It wasn't the fact that it was fried food, as he didn't mind eating fried foods, but he realised that the absence of a hangover earlier was merely the calm before the storm. He blamed the smell of the food. The promise of escaping a hangover was over. However, he fought on, picking up one half and taking a big bite. The more he ate the better he felt, and before too long the severity of the hangover he was expecting started to diminish and fade, and was not that bad at all. He sat there thinking of how he would spend the day. On finishing his coffee, he left the cafe. The majority of the day was his own and he decided to just take a walk around, and see what he found.

CHAPTER THIRTEEN

For the first time in his life Carter began to question his drinking. This was not only due to his numerous experiences of arriving home legless in the early hours, but more recently due to his head injury, his sudden angry outbursts and his constant stream of headaches. He had also begun to attribute his nightmares to the drinking as well, believing that his strange, intimidating dreams were somehow being triggered by it. He dreaded these times, where he was at conflict with himself. Many times in the past he would have to go through this delirium, he would torment and belittle himself so much that it didn't only hurt, it made him even more miserable and enraged with his life. He would poke fun at himself, call himself names in his mind, reminding him of how disappointing and useless he was, how insignificant he was. This was in no way searching for any sympathy at all, as he was not offloading these feelings onto anyone. He became trapped in a cyclic scenario where at certain points in time, when and where provoked by specific things in his life his mind would travel off into these dark unhealthy places and turn on him. It was like having an alter ego to some extent, but without actually leading a double life. He also knew he was doing it. He thought it was similar to something like a mild psychosis, where he would momentarily suffer from conscious lapses, where he would lose contact with reality.

As he wandered the streets he felt more and more vulnerable with every stride, becoming more entwined in self reflection. He was confused. He was reeling from the news of Jocky's death, and the more he thought about it, the angrier it made him. He felt provoked, and felt as if sometimes he was an experiment, a guinea pig used for research to discover just how much emotional torment could be suffered by one human being before they couldn't take anymore, an undercover science project. He quickly dismissed these harebrained thoughts, hating himself more for sounding so pitiful. He knew that it was not only the hangover that morning that was making him so self loathing, but it was the day, the big day, where he was going to commit his feelings to Mary. Everything in him, except his heart, told him to call it off and not meet her. His mind took over and with every step he took a new negative assumption flushed through his brain, striking the pessimism in him ablaze. "Why don't you just go and rot in a bar somewhere? After all, that is all you have ever been good for anyway. Ask yourself something Carter, why would a beautiful girl like her want to spend her whole life with a useless article like you. I have no choice in the matter, I'm stuck with you; she isn't. She can still make that choice. Do her a favour and stay away from her. Don't wreck her life. She is too good for you. God, you make me so sick. Fucking useless! She probably feels sorry for you." Carter suddenly stopped in his tracks at his final thought, realising that he may have stumbled upon an idea that was plausible. "Does she feel sorry for me? Does she take pity on me?"

He sounded delirious, hammering away at himself, his senses doing everything they could to prevent him from taking that plunge into the unknown.

* * * *

Carter arrived at college early that morning, eager to catch Will and Jennifer before class to discuss their latest assignment. It was a three thousand word essay to be written on a character of particular significance in the public eye. Today was deadline day.

As Carter took his usual route through the alley way, crossing the small playing field into the college entrance, he could not help but keep replaying in his mind what he had written in his essay. He had been up most of the night before, working exhaustively to ensure his work was thorough, and did nothing but absolute justice to the man that it was written about. Carter's choice was a person for whom he had a tremendous amount of respect, an American artist who drove the visual art movement known as pop art. Of course, it was Andy Warhol, who fair to say is probably more universally known by his famous Campbell's Soup cans, a piece of art produced by him in 1962.

Carter was originally going to write about another artist, painter and abstract impressionist Jackson Pollock, but upon overhearing Jennifer speaking to a friend about her adoration for Warhol, he changed his mind. That was why he had been up the previous night trying to get it done. He hoped she would be impressed!

Will, Jennifer and Carter had been very close in those last few months of college, spending a lot of time together on and off campus. The three of them connected very well and would always have something to talk about.

Jennifer Shier was very energetic and passionate about the interests in her life. She had strong political views, heartfelt beliefs and a lust for dark psychedelic music, virtually always dressed in black clothes, black boots and had dyed red hair. She was a 'Goth'. Carter, day by day, became more infatuated with her, amazed by her strength and inspired by her motivation. She was the epitome of cool and Carter was desperate to be with her. The longer time went on the more nervous he became telling her about his feelings.

*   *   *   *

The tables and chairs of the bar were heaving that evening. It was quiz night.

Will made his way back from the bar just about managing to keep control of their drinks, not one of them spilling in the slightest. As he navigated through the many bodies en route back to his seat, he recognised a girl over by the fruit machine. It was Zoe Morgan, a girl who he had been meaning to ask out for some time. She was in one of his classes with him, but he had never got around to really talking to her.

Will placed the drinks down onto the table where Carter and Jennifer were sitting, deep in conversation.

"Hey you two. I need to go and talk to someone OK. I won't be long . . . Hello!" said Will noticing his words seemed to be falling on deaf ears.

"Oh sorry what?" said Carter noticing Will standing there awkwardly.

"I just need to go and talk to somebody from one of my classes. You two carry on. I'll be back in a bit OK?" said Will.

"Yeah sure no problem, we'll be here!" confirmed Jennifer, outlining the fact that neither of them had anywhere else to be, or anyone else to be with.

"OK, what were you two talking about anyway?" asked Will, readying to leave the table.

"We were, are, talking about Andy Warhol. I didn't know Carter had such an interest in his work!" said Jennifer, looking both shocked and impressed.

"Andy Warhol? Right, OK, bye!" said Will while straightening up his shirt and walking away, not before throwing a cheeky wink to Carter letting him know he was on to him.

The hour that Will had been away for seemed like minutes to Carter. Jennifer and he were so engulfed in conversation, discussing a variety of subjects and both enjoying such interesting conversation. As the night drew on and the drinks were flowing, Carter saw that Will was still talking to Zoe Morgan, and could see that they were both definitely into each other. He knew it was only a matter of time before they would leave together. Jennifer commented that Will and Zoe did indeed look very cosy, and seemed somewhat concerned at the fact. Maybe she knew a history of Zoe's that Will did not?

Carter was caught in the moment, an urge of excitement rushed through his bones, another whisky shot rushed through his body, and against his better judgement he chose to come on to Jennifer. He had lusted after her for some time, and he couldn't wait any longer. He leant in to kiss her but she immediately drew back, leaving a significant distance between them, looking deeply confused and anxious. Carter instantly retreated into his shell, apologising and feeling utterly embarrassed by his antics. He feared it was because of the way he looked, or his depression, and believed that she was in no way going to start a relationship with a man carrying his own limited qualities. He felt empty and worthless and the silence that followed was overwhelmingly awkward. Luckily for him, Jennifer chose to break the silence.

"Carter, please don't feel bad. Believe me it is not you. I think you are an amazing guy, interesting and so kind hearted. But I have my heart set on someone else. I am sorry."

"Oh well, thanks for being honest anyway. At first I thought it was just that I was repulsive or something, ha ha." He joked trying to put on a brave face and lighten the atmosphere.

Jennifer laughed and felt more at ease after Carter's words. Carter however, deep inside, felt nothing but humiliation and disappointment and knew that once again he was going to have to end up second best. Even though his face carried a smile, his heart carried a scar. He was eager to find out who it was that Jennifer was interested in, and thought it would do no harm in asking her.

"So who is the lucky guy?"

"Well . . . . it's kind of awkward, but it's someone who I have been sitting here watching chat to someone else, and it is driving me crazy that it is not me!" she replied, giving no actual indication as to who it was.

"Really?" "In here? Do I know this person?" probed Carter.

"It is Will." said Jennifer, almost hesitantly, realising the negative effect it could have on their friendship.

"Will, of course. Who else, right? God I should have known!"

At that moment Will approached the table, dropping them off two more drinks. Before returning to Zoe, he realised that something had been said between them, so he asked.

"You two OK? Sorry if I've been a while but Zoe is great, we are really connecting over there. Well that's what she told me anyway!" offered Will, hoping it would make one of them laugh, or something! Nothing! Jennifer and Carter sat, blank faced and awkward, before Jennifer spoke.

"Will, can I talk to you in private for a moment?"

Carter knew that this was the moment when Jennifer was going to confront her feelings for Will head on, and despite his own disappointment, he knew there was nothing further he could do, other than let nature run its course. Will agreed and stood back, leaving Jennifer room to shuffle along the cushioned seat and stand up. Jennifer walked ahead of Will as if leading the way. Will looked back at Carter and noticed that he looked like he was in despair, helpless and dejected. He wasn't entirely sure at that exact moment why, but he was sure to find out the reason in the minutes that followed.

* * * *

There was a tap on the door later that evening. It was Carter's bedroom door. Then another tap, this time followed by a voice, Will's voice, "Carter, are you in there mate?"

Carter stayed sitting in his chair next to his desk, staying as still and silent as possible. Then Will knocked again, and then spoke again.

"Carter, if you are in there, then trust me, I know why you are upset. I had no idea until tonight that Jennifer . . . . well you know . . . . and I didn't know that you . . . . felt . . . . about her like that until tonight OK. I just want you to know that nothing happened between us. Nothing . . . ."

Silence continued, Carter feeling even more distressed and downhearted now knowing that he had prevented a potential relationship from blossoming between his two best friends. He knew that Will was still standing outside his door, waiting to hear a movement or any sign revealing that Carter was inside. He couldn't ignore Will forever. He walked over and opened the door.

"Hey. Look I didn't know she liked me in that way mate. I'm sorry. But so you know I would never let a girl come between us, never." said Will, hoping his words would go some way in repairing Carter's broken feelings.

"I know Will. But it is selfish of me to stand in your way, and hers. I'll get over it. Its fine." responded Carter, confirming that he was aware that it was just one of those things, and that they would have his full blessing if they decided to get together.

"Wait, no you don't understand. I don't like her in that way." Will clarified.

With that a girl's voice came from further down the hallway, through Will's slightly ajar bedroom door.

"Are you coming to bed or what?"

Carter momentarily thought it was Jennifer, but his paranoia quickly settled as he looked up the hallway and could see that it was no other than Zoe Morgan's face peering through at them. Will and Carter looked back at each other and laughed, before Carter asked about Jennifer.

"How did Jennifer take it?"

"Badly, but she'll be fine I'm sure. The three of us had an awkward cab journey back here. She has gone to bed now. She'll be cool come tomorrow morning. I'll have to get Zoe out of here quick then ay?"

"Yep, you better!" said Carter with a smile.

With that Will made his way back down the hallway, and disappeared into his bedroom with the stunning, although not so bright, Zoe Morgan.

Carter sat on his bed, unscrewed his bottle of whisky, and took a sip. He was concerned that Jennifer's reaction towards him in the bar was more then just that she cared for someone else. He started to convince himself that even if it hadn't been the case, she would have still shunned him. A tear fell to his cheek. The little confidence that he had left, for either talking to or approaching girls, was near to becoming extinct. He knew that from that moment on this experience would haunt him, and would most likely prevent him from ever having a relationship again. Why would he put himself through that again?

*   *   *   *

He carried on walking, before quickly becoming aware that he was lost. He had been paying no attention to where he was going, however his rant at himself had now worn thin, and he was back to normal, hangover symptoms all but cleared. Starting to think more realistically about his life and the world around him, he understood deep down that a fraction of his unhappiness was self inflicted. He had always relied on drinking as more of a companionship than anything else, something that was always there, and there to stay, relieve some of the pain and comfort him through the days. It was also useful as a means to forget, to hide, to saturate his mind in disillusionment, rather than go on living with the facts of a boring existence. It also acted as his medication to some extent, as nothing else prescribed had made any difference to him, other than Cipralex, but only if it was mixed with alcohol.

Feeling tired, he couldn't be bothered walking anymore and wanted to rest. After all, he didn't even know if the direction he was now headed was the right way anyway! He looked around, searching for any signs or directions that would indicate where he was, but nothing helped. He was in a residential area that much he did know, by the flats surrounding him. There was a small green beside them and he decided to sit on a wooden bench to rest his feet. He was now absolutely sure that he was going to go ahead and meet Mary, and that come 5pm that afternoon he was going to take the biggest gamble of his life. He would follow his heart and try. His chest felt tight and his stomach unsettled, so he stretched out his arms and shifted position to try and ease the discomfort. His heart suddenly turned and he questioned that if he felt this nervous now, how nervous was he going to be at 5pm?

Walking in the direction of no idea! He couldn't believe that there seemed to be no signs telling him where the hell he had ended up, or in which direction he was walking. There was no-one around to ask, the streets were empty and desolate. Only passing vehicles held any sign that other human beings were still in existence. At last he found a bus stop. He had somehow managed to roam south-east of the city, out and beyond an area called Fountainbridge. He stood alone waiting for a bus for what seemed an eternity, before it came trundling along merrily, with a driver whose face looked as if it hadn't a care in the world. The bus was almost empty with only an elderly couple sitting right at the front. Carter went to the back and sat in the corner seat next to the window. He was curious to see just how far he had come, and was still a bit dumbfounded as to how he hadn't even noticed. He tilted his head to the left and rested it on the window, watching different things pass by as the bus carried him back to familiarity.

* * * *

"Up we get Sir, excuse me! This is the last stop!"

Carter opened his eyes and saw the bus driver stooped over him.

"Oh thanks!" muttered Carter, still half asleep. He stood up and walked wearily to the automatic doors, before stepping off onto the pavement. He recognised where he was straight away, and was only a short distance away from Edinburgh Castle. He yawned, rubbing his eyes clear of any sleep, as he heard the bus pull away from behind him.

"Coffee time!" he said as he looked around for the nearest dwelling.

* * * *

It was 3.20pm, and Carter was in a little café on Carrubber's Close, on his second cup of coffee. His nerves were still bubbling away inside as the time to meet Mary was fast approaching. He stared out of the window and watched as the world passed by, the different characters each with their own stories to tell. He started believing that there could be an opportunity, a chance for him yet. A chance to become something significant and have a life that deep within him he yearned for. He began to visualise the future and what it might hold for him, even though only hypothetically. He saw himself married to Mary, working in a job that was fulfilling and rewarding, and hearing the pattering of tiny feet in the distance. He saw them visiting San Francisco and meeting her parents for the first time. He saw them attending their children's weddings, becoming Grandparents themselves and growing old together in each other's arms. These thoughts were helping Carter believe whilst at the same time steadying his nerves, giving himself an insight into possibility. He sipped at his coffee, closed his eyes and smiled. He knew that the time was almost upon him. There was no turning back now.

He took strength from Jocky and would try and use that go and get attitude from then on. The old man had been quite an inspiration to Carter. He began to wonder whether or not he should attend Jocky's funeral. As he had no family left, the funeral may only be a small turnout, neighbours and the odd friend still knocking about. He decided to ask the barman later that night if he knew when the funeral would be as he would like to attend. It was the least he could do. Even though he hadn't known him long, the little time that he had was very important to him. As Carter wiped the small moist molecules of coffee away from his stubble covering his chin, he said to himself "Two funerals in a week! Shit!"

* * * *

On his way back to the hotel he saw a minimarket which reminded him he needed to get some bread, so he crossed the street and walked in. The lucky people, who had managed to skip off work early that Friday afternoon, were already in there getting their shopping in for the weekend. Baskets and trolleys filled with wine, beers and frozen comfort food were whizzing around the aisles, anxiously and impatiently jostling with others to be the first out the door. Carter picked up a thick sliced granary loaf that he would take with him to feed the ducks and headed for the checkout to pay. As he walked back past the fruit and vegetable section he noticed bunches of flowers for sale. He wanted to get some flowers to take with him for Mary, why not! He was very conscious of the time, and it was getting on; now 3.40pm. He looked at the arrangements and it didn't take him long to make up his mind on which ones to choose, the red roses. He picked up the ones that looked most likely to survive the longest and paced over to the self checkout. He knew, even though slightly pushed for time, he would make it to the duck pond by 5pm definitely, as long as there were no hiccups along the way!

"Please work you little bastard!" said a growingly frustrated Carter as the self checkout failed to read and scan the bread. He looked around for an assistant, but no-one was available to help. He tried scanning it again, moving the bar code backwards and forwards in front of it, pleading with it to beep and scan the item in—nothing.

"Come on, for Christ sake, just do the one thing you are here for. Make it easy for me. Please? Bollocks!" Giving up, he walked over to join the back of a long queue to be served there instead.

"Is that the only two items you have Sir?" said a voice from behind him.

"Yes." replied Carter, hoping that it was a fellow customer pointing him towards a shorter queue. It wasn't, it was the self checkout shop assistant that he had in fact needed moments earlier.

"You can do those through the self checkout if you wish?" she said.

"No!" said Carter bluntly, turning back to face forward.

"It will save you waiting!" said the assistant as she started to walk back over to the self checkout area.

Carter let off a sharp, instinctive loud sarcastic burst of laughter. The laughing sound he made was a mix of mania and insanity! Other customers looked straight at him, the old lady immediately in front jumped out of her skin, dropping her brussel sprouts all over the floor.

"Oh I'm sorry." said Carter, as he rushed to her aid, trying to grab as many of the bouncing brussel balls as possible before they disappeared off in every direction. He looked more like a juggler on crack!

* * * *

Despite Carter's minimarket mayhem, he managed to arrive back at his hotel just shy of 4.15pm, leaving him enough time to shower and get ready to go. He walked into the bathroom, pulling off his shirt as he walked in, tossing it to one side. He turned on the hot tap of the sink, desperate to squeeze in a quick shave. Before applying the razor to his cheek he reminded himself to take it slow and steady, as the last thing he wanted was to do was turn up looking like a pitbull terrier had been set loose on his face for the last hour!

Finished shaving, successfully without cutting himself, he went straight into the shower. Barely waiting for the temperature to reach a comfortable point, he opened up his shampoo bottle and squeezed out a big gloop onto his head. The water was not hot, lukewarm at best, but he didn't care. He started to feel rushed, but was still positive he would get there on time.

It was 4.40pm, twenty minutes to go. He straightened his shirt in the mirror, before sitting on the bed to put on his shoes. In the midst of his manic rush to get there on time he accidently knocked his jacket onto the floor and heard something drop out of one of the pockets. He looked down and saw the small box which held the ring from Marcus. Suddenly, the sight of that brought so many things into perspective for Carter. It reminded him again as to why he had given it to his brother all those years before, and that in some kind of way he contemplated the notion of whether this was a sign from Marcus. Was it his brother returning the favour and now presenting the ring to Carter to support him in his own time of need? The ring signified so much, strength, belief, hope, support and undying love. Carter reached out and collected the ring and put it on his little finger. He smiled and felt an overwhelming sense of calm. It was as if he had his brother by his side. He would keep the ring on for his date with Mary.

Carter was as ready as he would ever be, and the time had come for him to try and make a change to his life. The balance of nerves outweighed the feeling of excitement, but only slightly. A wave of emotion surged through his body like a bull to a cape. He soon would find out whether or not it could his life could change on an astronomical scale. Before opening the door to leave, he stood perfectly still for a moment and said "Oh well, this is it! Wish me luck Marcus . . . . Jocky . . . . here we go!"

Carter walked through the foyer of the hotel, stopping momentarily debating whether or not to pop into the bar and have a quick shot of something, a bit of last minute Dutch courage. But as quickly as the thought entered his mind it was gone. He was determined not to have to rely on alcohol for this occasion, for it was far too important. This was the beginning, a fresh start. He walked out of the hotel, carrying the bunch of vibrant red roses in one hand and the granary bread for the ducks swinging from the other. Feeling upbeat but in no way at all ready, he convinced himself as best he could that it was going to be OK. As he caught first sight of the park he felt another headache coming on. He only hoped it would remain a mild one, or better yet disappear quickly. The stress was already building within him, his legs felt wobbly and he had to try hard to keep his breathing regulated. He walked in through the gate and headed straight for the duck pond. The setting was perfect, the sun was shining and birds were singing. There were many people in the park that afternoon, mainly lazing around on the grass in the sunshine, some were playing ball games, and others jogging.

* * * *

Arriving at the duck pond he noticed that Mary was already sitting there waiting. He looked at his watch and it was exactly 5pm. He was not late. The moment of truth had come. He stopped behind a tree trunk for a second, out of sight from Mary, taking in one last deep breath, before stepping forward and into the unknown.

As he stepped into Mary's line of sight her face lit up with a smile at him romantically carrying a bunch of roses.

"I hope they're for me!" she said reaching out her hands.

"They were, but I gotta tell ya, I've just spotted a duck over there that looks pretty tasty!" said Carter joking around, before handing them to her.

"Wow! They are beautiful, thank you Carter." she said while leaning in and giving him a kiss on the cheek.

"No problem, beautiful flowers for a beautiful woman." said Carter, with a slight nervousness to his voice, which she noticed.

"You OK?" she asked.

"Yes, fine."

Carter coughed trying to clear his throat, while also trying to disguise his nerves by opening the bread bag. It wasn't working as his hands were noticeably shaking. He handed Mary a couple of slices to feed the fast approaching ducks. He could feel the sharp pains in his head worsening as he desperately tried to keep focused on building up his courage to confront Mary with his feelings. It was a distinct stabbing pain, as if about to pierce through his skull, and he thought it so typical that it would pick this precise moment to torment him. They sat there quietly for a moment, each tearing off pieces of bread and launching them 'duck-wards'!

Mary was aware that he seemed very uneasy, and had a feeling that he was hiding something, or something was bothering him. She debated in her mind as to whether to probe but didn't want to seem pushy, as he had however told her minutes before that he was fine. She decided to use a different tack and ask him about his day, and what he had been up to that morning. Carter explained that he had got lost which she obviously found amusing. He began to settle slightly and seemed more relaxed as they talked about what he had been up to that day and the day before. He told her about the vaults and how cool they were, and the castle especially. He told her that when he left the castle, as he was approaching the gate he could hear the sound of Scottish pipe music playing. He couldn't figure out where it was coming from, and as there was no-one around he did a little jig as he walked to the exit, just fooling around. But as he stepped out of the gate, he looked in through an open door to the left where the castle security officers were. Two guards looked up at him and were in hysterics as they had seen him on the security camera.

Mary laughed, and was also impressed that he had shared such a story with her, a funny but embarrassing story where the joke was on him. It showed her another side of him. Shortly after, there was another period of silence.

The wait was over and it was time. He turned to her and they both spoke at the same time. Carter apologised and insisted she carry on with what she was going to say, but she immediately put the emphasis back on him urging him to get whatever it was off his chest. He looked deep into her eyes and began.

"Well Mary. The thing is . . . . Well . . . . Christ this more difficult than I thought!"

"It's OK. Take your time. What's up Carter?" said Mary, in a soft comforting voice that tendered Carter's apprehension. He continued.

"OK. Here goes. Mary, we have been seeing a lot of each other in the small amount of time I have been up here, and I have absolutely loved every second of it. It has been the best time of my life, meeting you . . . . and I don't want it to end."

"Go on Carter." urged Mary.

"You are so perfect in everyway, and I just don't want to go back to London without telling you that. I . . . I . . . . I'm sorry, I hope this is not making you uncomfortable?"

"Not at all, please say what you have to say."

Carter felt a drop of sweat on his brow, but refused to wipe it away, embarrassed that he might actually draw her attention to it. He started to doubt himself once again, his mind drawing a blank, unsure of himself, struggling to keep it together. He kept trying to reassure himself, telling himself to go for it. His headache was now severe and showing no sign of alleviating, stabbing away viciously with no remorse. He looked away from Mary and at the duck pond, trying to ignore the pain, and desperately trying to get back on track with what he wanted to say. Then, something happened, as if everything around them stopped in time, a final snap of confidence came to his rescue. He looked back at her and with one last epic effort said.

"You are the chapter of my life that I would want to read over and over again, memorising every sentence, every word, every emotion regardless of consequence . . . . endlessly and effortlessly."

"Carter that is so beautiful." said Mary, a tear appearing on her cheek, as she reached out to hold his hand. He smiled and continued.

"I didn't want to leave without you knowing how much you mean to me. I have never felt this way before, and I do not want to spend the rest of my life regretting if I hadn't. A fire now burns within me and I don't want it to go out. Please forgive me as I know this seems a bit sudden, but I needed to say this, it's been driving me crazy. You mean everything to me . . . . you are enchanting. I want us to be together . . . . I love you Mary Lee."

Carter stopped there, knowing that he had said enough, and eagerly awaited a response. Mary looked back at him with a smile, a smile that he found hard to distinguish as to whether or not it was a happy or a sad one. She knew how much of a big deal that was for him and she was so proud that he had managed to say the things he did. She looked into Carter's eyes as he waited to hear if she felt the same. This was the moment.

CHAPTER FOURTEEN

The soft drizzling morning rain fell gracefully onto the grass outside, creating a glistening blanket of diamond like sparkle. The dark grey clouds above were trying desperately to secrete the sunlight. Only a few rays were successful, managing at times to find gaps between the dreary and monotonous mass. The trees were swaying awkwardly backwards and forwards as sudden infrequent bursts of fierce winds treacherously burst through. Birds stayed close to their nests, as if cowering away from any temptation of venturing out into the uninviting bleakness. Foxes and squirrels were hidden, and no scurrying or disturbance of any wild life was visible in the foliage. It was as if the wildlife had come to a standstill, as if they were expecting the arrival of something threatening and sinister, something resembling a predator.

The Saturday morning full of sunshine that everyone in Edinburgh yearned for had not come. Instead it was the exact opposite; a dreary day of lazy slumber indoors was the most pressing thing now on everyone's agenda. It was dark and the hospital corridors of Edinburgh's Western General Hospital looked as though they were closing in at every turn, as a number of doctors and medics carrying patient medical notes were walking along, heading to their next patient destination. Odd members of the public were walking more slowly, looking lost amongst the maze like layout of the building, desperately trying to speak to someone who could tell them where they needed to go. Some were seen walking aimlessly and in tears after either finding out bad news about themselves, or their loved ones who had either died or who were in suffering. Porters, with no time to spare, would appear here and there, some pushing patients on wheelchairs from ward to ward, others on their radio being instructed as to where to go next for the next job coming in.

*   *   *   *

Mr Crispin Walsh, a brain surgeon, walked out of the elevator on the second floor and through the double doors leading into Prendle Ward. He was present the night before after being called in to perform an urgent surgical removal on the head of a man who had been rushed in. The man was unconscious. Following an urgent MRI scan, a brain tumour had been diagnosed that needed to be operated on and removed immediately.

As he walked into the ward, a nurse quickly approached and informed him that his patient had just woken up. Mr Walsh had not had the opportunity to speak with his patient yet as by the time he arrived in theatre the gentleman had again lost consciousness. The patient had only managed a few sentences to the nurse before his scan, describing his symptoms and the way he felt. Before he lost consciousness he kept repeating the name Mary, asking where she was. Mr Walsh asked the nurse whether or not the patient had been informed of the full extent of what had happened. She said that he had only been informed that he came into the hospital the previous night due to a fall and that his assigned surgeon would be in shortly to talk to him. Mr Walsh, accompanied by the nurse, walked into one of the private rooms located to the side of the ward. There was the patient, head bandaged, and laying slightly upright on the hospital bed. He looked anxious and slightly disorientated, but was fully awake.

"Mr Jakeman, how are you feeling?" asked Mr Walsh.

"Never been better thanks, and you are?" responded a sarcastic and frustrated Carter.

"I am your surgeon. My name is Mr Crispin Walsh."

"Sorry, but did someone fire a staple gun at my head?" said Carter waiting for a good reason as to why his head was bandaged up and in pain.

"We did have to carry out a procedure late last night."

"Well it really hurts!"

"We can get something to help with the pain Mr Jakeman." said Mr Walsh while signalling to the nurse to go and ready some pain relief.

"I'm here to talk to you about why you came in here last night and why we have had to perform an urgent surgical procedure on you." the surgeon said while pulling up a chair and sitting down next to Carter.

"OK!" replied Carter eagerly but also hesitantly, awaiting the reason.

"Mr Jakeman. You were found, unconscious, lying on the ground next to a park bench late yesterday afternoon. A cyclist saw you and called for an ambulance. You were brought in here and we took some blood tests and carried out an MRI scan."

"M R what?" asked Carter trying to keep up, finding it difficult to process the information.

"Sorry MRI. A head MRI stands for magnetic resonance imaging and is a scan of the head, an imaging test that uses radio waves and magnets to create pictures of the brain and surrounding nerve tissues."

"And what is this on my hand?" asked Carter noticing some slight bruising.

"Some exams require a special type of dye. The dye was given before the test through the vein in your hand. The dye helps the radiologist to see certain areas more clearly. The team were only able to bring you around to talk briefly, where you told us you had been suffering from severe migraines. It was clear that you had a wound already sustained to your head so we started there. We tried to determine who you were, where you lived and if you had a next of kin, someone we could contact. We managed to talk to a Will Harrison, who I believe is your flat mate in London. He informed us of your accident and that you had been treated only a week ago at the Whittington Hospital in London. He is on the first train up this morning so should arrive here a bit later. Upon seeing the result of your MRI scan it was clear to us that you had a brain tumour Mr Jakeman."

"What?" interrupted a shocked Carter, his mouth suddenly feeling dry, and unable to believe what he was hearing?

"I was then called to come in and carry out the emergency removal of the tumour. I was the on-call surgeon last night."

"And, did it work?" asked Carter impatiently.

"We removed the tumour Mr Jakeman, but I'm afraid that does not necessarily mean that due to the surgery and nature of the tumour that certain things may not reoccur. That is why we are going to keep you in under observation for the time being . . . ."

"Wait! What things?"

"Well, we need to be prepared for things such as an intracranial haemorrhage, which means a bleeding could occur, and depending on the exact severity of the tumour there is a possibility that it could reappear. Your specific tumour was a benign, non-cancerous type. It is a mass of cells that grow slowly in the brain. It usually stays in one place and does not spread."

"Usually, what is the likeliness of this coming back?" asked Carter beginning to come to terms with the seriousness of what has happened. Mr Walsh responded trying to sound more positive.

"Generally, tumours of the brain are graded on a basis of one to four. This is in accordance to their behaviour, such as how fast they grow and how likely they are to spread. Grade one tumours for example are the least aggressive and grade four the most cancerous and harmful."

"Which grade was mine?"

"Grade one. We do need to carry out further tests and then reach a diagnosis. However grades one and two tend to be slow growing and unlikely to spread, so are usually classed as benign."

"Well let's just hope that's the case! Well that definitely explains the headaches then, huh?"

"The symptoms of a low-grade, or benign tumour, is dependent on where it is in the brain and the size of it. Some may not cause any symptoms at first. Eventually, it can put pressure on the brain and may cause seizures, or in your case Mr Jakeman, headaches. It can also prevent an area of the brain from functioning properly. This could be things like loss of vision in some cases if the tumour has grown in the occipital lobe at the back of the brain."

"How long have I had this thing? Why wasn't anything picked up at the hospital in London?"

"Copies of your medical notes arrived here this morning, and I need to review them in more detail. There is no telling as to the exact duration of your tumour. Brain tumours can affect people of all ages. There are about 4,500 new cases of primary brain tumours in the UK each year."

"What now, I mean after more tests and all that?"

"Mr Jakeman, benign brain tumours can be serious if they are not diagnosed and treated early enough. In your case this has been achieved, we have managed to remove it at an early stage. Many don't return once removed, causing no future problems. I'll be back to see you later. In the meantime just try and relax, sleep if you can."

Mr Walsh stood and moved his chair back and away from the bed. Carter laid back down resting his head softly onto the pillow, wincing at the point of contact and turning to face away from Mr Walsh, who then excused himself and walked to the door. The nurse returned to the room. Mr Walsh looked back at Carter and said "Mr Jakeman, it is a good thing that this was found and treated now. Have you eaten?"

"No!" replied Carter abruptly.

"Would you like . . . ?"

"No!" said Carter even more sombre in tone.

Mr Walsh smiled, compassionately understanding Carter's bluntness, and was more than used to this attitude of patients who had been through similar ordeals. It would take time to come to terms with it. He turned to leave the room when Carter spoke.

"Mr Walsh?"

"Yes."

". . . . Thanks!" said Carter wanting him to know how appreciative he actually was inside, even though his manner was cold and incensed.

* * * *

Carter opened his eyes. Time must have passed. Had he slept? He could hear only flutters of sound from outside his private room on the ward, but he could not distinguish any of the sounds. He hadn't moved position since Mr Walsh had visited him, still laying on his side and facing the wall. All he wanted to do was sleep, hoping that the next time he awoke he would find that it had all been just another one of his nightmares. He needed to see Mary. Where was she? How was she?

"Nurse!" shouted Carter. "Nurse!" again and louder. She walked into his room and pointed to the button on the wall behind him, the one to push if he needed help or assistance, rather than shout. He acknowledged her point somewhat graciously and quickly moved onto his more pressing issue.

"Nurse did anyone accompany me here last night, a woman?"

"No. You were brought in on your own."

"Has anyone called for me? Where is my mobile phone?" asked Carter glancing around the room for his personal belongings.

"No, no-one has called for you. But your friend will be here soon. He is travelling up . . . ."

"From London I know. Can I have my mobile please?" asked Carter impatiently.

"Mr Jakeman, doctor's orders are that you get some rest. If you would like us to call someone then we are more than happy to do it on your behalf. Your belongings are in a safe place."

"Why can't I have it? I just want to make a quick call. It was a lady who was with me in the park yesterday. I need to find out if she is OK. She might be worried." said Carter becoming more animated.

"OK Mr Jakeman, just take it easy. Do you know the lady's telephone number? If so I can write it down and go and call her for you?"

"Not off by heart! It is stored on my phone."

"Do you mind if I search through the address book on your phone and locate the number for you?"

"No problem. Her name is Mary Lee."

"OK I will go and call her now. Just try and rest." said the nurse trying to be helpful and keep him calm.

Carter waited and wondered if Mary had got cold feet and left him in the park after he told her that he was in love with her. But he couldn't remember her leaving. He assumed that the operation was the reason for this. He racked his brain trying to jog his memory for the slightest piece of useful information that would tell him what had happened. Nothing came. Maybe there were some blanks that would come back to him at a later point he thought.

He rolled over and onto his back so he could just about see out through the window in the door toward the front desk. He saw the nurse pick up the phone, while scrolling through his mobile contacts in the other. He couldn't strain his eyes any longer so closed them and waited for the nurse to return. He concentrated on the sounds in the distance, trying hard to hear if the nurse was speaking. He began to focus on how lucky he was to have been treated at that moment, and briefly contemplated what might have been if he hadn't. He stopped thinking, it was no use. Going around in circles is not something he was interested in. He was just grateful that he was in safe hands. He heard the handle on the door open and he opened his eyes. The nurse walked in.

"I tried her number Mr Jakeman but there was no answer."

"Damn. Did you leave her a message?"

"I did. I left my name and telephone number, so hopefully she will give us a call back soon."

"OK, well thanks for trying."

"No problem." said the nurse as she pulled the door closed, leaving Carter alone again. He shifted around on the bed, trying to find a more comfortable way in which to lay, and before he knew it he was back on his side staring at the wall. He had absolutely no appetite, and to be honest wasn't in any mood to eat following the news he had received. He just prayed he would be OK. Closing his eyes he pictured Mary's face in his mind. He was desperate to see and speak to her. He remembered the look on her face immediately after he told her he loved her, and that she seemed to look uncertain as what to say or do. Maybe he was just over exaggerating. He felt tired and couldn't stay awake any longer, moments later he was asleep.

* * * *

Later that afternoon Carter was awoken by a bang. He was briefly disorientated but it didn't take him long to remember where he was and why he was there. He was alone in the room. He turned onto his back again, trying to see out of the window into the reception area outside. He could just about make out someone picking up plates from the floor, which accounted for the crashing sound that had startled and woke him. Somehow they had been dropped. Carter knew it was only a matter of time before Will would turn up, and he couldn't wait. He needed him there. He wondered if Mary had called back yet, and as he was about to shout out for the nurse, he remembered the button rule. He stretched his arm back behind him, feeling around for the call for help button and pushed it. The response time was very impressive and the nurse was already in the room by the time he had rested his arm back onto the bed at his side.

"She hasn't called yet! Or is there something else?" said the nurse reckoning that was the reason for his call.

"Could you try her again please?"

"Yes sure. I'm just about to serve supper then I'll call her for you."

"OK thanks."

"Oh by the way, Mr Walsh will be dropping into to see you shortly before he finishes his shift."

"Looking forward to it!" said Carter smiling.

Becoming more disappointed at the fact that they hadn't managed to contact her, he also wondered why she was not picking up the phone. He hoped there was nothing wrong and that it was nothing he had done that resulted in her not wanting to answer her phone. He felt so helpless, his inner frustration growing as every movement he made caused him pain. He knew the pain would wear off with time, but it was becoming very exasperating. He felt tears in his eyes as the feeling of doom started to rise up within him. He couldn't stop thinking of how close he had come to finding true love, and then almost instantaneously, how close he had come to death. More tears followed as his crying became uncontrollable. He didn't try to fight it. He let the tears roll, releasing those bound up jumble of emotions.

The door swung open as a very tired looking Mr Walsh entered the room.

"You look wrecked!" said Carter noticing the bags under the surgeon's eyes.

"Thanks. Trust me I feel wrecked. Busy one! How are you feeling?"

"Shit. Sorry! Not good, in fact every time I move my head hurts!"

"It will for a while. We can give you some more relief. Has anyone been in to check on you?"

"Well I called a nurse in earlier. I am trying to contact a woman that I was with yesterday, in the park. I have not heard from her, and the nurse has tried calling her but no response. She said she would try her again. Do you think you could chase that up? I am worried about her."

"Of course I will. Have you eaten anything?"

"No not hungry."

"You'll need to eat something Mr Jakeman!"

"OK, Will, my friend should be here soon. Hopefully he'll bring me some grapes or something. I cannot bring myself to eat hospital food at the moment!"

"I'm going to be going off shift now. I'll be back in tomorrow. I will be visiting you in the morning, by which time I want you to have had total rest and have eaten something substantial. Understand?"

"Yes. I'll do my best."

"Thank you. You'll feel better for it."

"Oh, please could you chase the nurse about whether or not she managed to contact my friend?"

"Yes sure. I'll see you tomorrow OK."

As he watched Mr Walsh walked out Will walked in.

"My God mate! You're gonna give me a heart attack one of these days!" said Will, instantly trying to lighten the mood.

"Thanks for coming mate. I've missed you."

"Yeah, well I missed you too. Here I bought you some grapes."

"Good man. Knew you would. So I take it you know everything already."

"Yep, lucky they got it when they did mate!"

"I know!"

"So where is this Mary? I want to meet her!"

"Tell me about it. I've not seen her since before . . . . you know. I've been trying to get them to call her from here but no answer. My surgeon is going to ask the nurse now if she had any luck getting through."

"Well I'm here now. What's her number, I'll try?"

"I haven't memorised it. It is on my mobile which I'm not aloud to have and is with the nurse out there!"

"Leave it to me."

Will walked out to the desk. Carter strained to hear the conversation but couldn't make out any words at all. He opened up his bag of grapes, picking a couple off and eating them. The freshness of the grapes was just what he needed, and he ate some more before Will returned to the room.

"No luck buddy! Still no answer." said Will as he sat down on a chair by the bed.

"Shit, I'm concerned. I need to know that she is OK!"

"Well the nurse said she has now left two messages, so hopefully not too much longer and she'll call." said Will trying to remain positive and optimistic.

"I hope so!" said a worried Carter.

"So can't you remember anything from the park yesterday afternoon? Had Mary already left by the time . . . . you know?" enquired Will.

"Well I can't remember if she did or not, no. The last thing I remember was that I told her that I loved her. Then I woke up here!"

Will understood how frustrated Carter was and this added stress wasn't doing him any good, so he offered to help some more. Visiting hours were nearly over so he would have to come back and see him the following day. He started to ask if Carter had anymore information that would improve their chances of locating Mary.

"What about her work number? Actually it's Saturday today, she may not be there. Does she work weekends?"

"Sometimes yes, but no I don't have the number." replied Carter, sounding somewhat defeated.

"Well what about her home address and her work address?"

"Don't know her work address, but yes her home address. I don't know the number but I know the street name and where on the street it is. It's about half way down and has a red door."

"Well that's good enough. Write down the street and what her place looks like and I'll go and knock there on my way to the B&B."

"Really, that's great. Knew I could count on you Will. You are a true friend. But no trying to hit on her you hear me!" said Carter half joking.

"Promise, this one's yours."

"How long are you staying here?"

"As long as it takes, until I know you are OK."

"Thanks Will. Sorry for the hassle."

"Carter, you had a brain tumour. I don't really think that counts as a hassle!"

Will took down the street name and house description and slipped the details into his back jean pocket. Moments later the nurse popped her head in and informed Will that visiting time was over. Carter asked Will if he would be able to call the reception desk later and ask the nurse to let him know if he managed to speak to Mary. Will shook Carter's hand and said that he would be back in the following morning. He asked if Carter would like him to bring anything especially, to which Carter promptly replied "Mary!" before asking for some more fruit and a newspaper. Will smiled and left.

Desperately trying to find a position where he felt most comfortable Carter started to reflect on the past few days. How things only a day ago felt so far away from him now, and whatever he had grasped in his hands had now dissolved as though gone forever. It was so easy to be pessimistic when lying on a hospital bed and he did try his best to resist and stay positive, but as the minutes passed, silence his only companion, he was alone with his thoughts, thoughts that were beginning to come from the dark side of his mind. "I wish the surgeon had cut the depressive demons from my fucking head as well. Oh no, these are here to stay. Tormenting little gremlins corrupting my head my whole shitty life, and look at me now, fucked!"

He cried himself to sleep not too long after; tears penetrated his pillow, sweat seeped into his bed sheets, as lay with one arm hanging out from the side of the bed.

* * * *

Will turned into the street that Carter had told him earlier, the street where Mary lived. He double checked the name on the piece of paper to the street sign, making sure he had the right one. About half way up the road he saw a house with a red door. He looked slightly further up and on the opposite side of the street and could see no other doors of the same colour. It had to be the one. He was eager to see Mary, as he presumed she must be something of wonder to have Carter so wrapped up in love like he was. He opened the gate, strolled up the small path leading to the door and knocked with a rat tat. In anticipation and wanting to make a good first impression he quickly ran his fingers through his hair, and tried to check his appearance in the reflection of the frosted glass door window. He could see the silhouette of someone approaching from the other side. This was it. It must be Mary. The door opened.

"Wow, oh. My . . . . ?" said Will as he found himself looking at the total opposite of what he had expected to see.

"Yes can I help you?" replied the woman, looking Will up and down, obviously impressed at his good looks.

"Wait, you're not American are you?" he said noticing her deep strong Scottish accent.

"Excuse me?" she said somewhat confused.

"Sorry. Forgive me. I'm looking for an American lady."

"Well sorry to disappoint you pal but only Scottish women live here."

"Sorry to have bothered you."

"Wait, I can assure you there is nothing an American girl could do that a Scottish lass couldn't!" said the women with an inviting smile, which exposed her two front missing teeth.

"I'm sure there isn't." said Will already retreating up the path.

"Wait. Don't rush off!" the woman said eager for him to stay.

"I'm sorry to have bothered you, I have to go!"

The woman slammed the door closed in disappointment, as her wish for a Prince Charming arriving at her door and sweeping her off her feet had come and gone in a flash. As Will walked off back up the street, he said to himself "Thank God! I swear Carter, if that would have turned out to be Mary I would have slapped you!"

The woman who had answered the door was of middle age, although she looked much older. She was haggard, hair greasy and matted. Her shirt, sweat stained and too tight to fit her overweight body, exposed a roll of fat hanging out from beneath it. She looked quite manly and for a brief second Will had to do a double take to make sure. Will was so relieved that she didn't turn out to be Carter's dream girl.

* * * *

Loud screams brought the immediate attention of the ward nurse, who lazily sat at the front desk. It came from the private room, Carter's room. She ran to the room and burst in. Carter was frantically moving around in the bed, as though possessed, and still not awake from what she assumed was a nightmare. She rushed over to his side and tried to wake him, while also trying to avoid being struck by his flailing arms.

"Mr Jakeman! Mr Jakeman, it's OK." shouted the nurse, as Carter's eyes opened.

He looked around the room trying to ascertain his location, before the pain of his wound reminded him instantly. The nurse informed him that he was shouting. He could remember the dream, and even though he was now fully awake it was still disturbing.

"I'm sorry, that was . . . . could I get some water please?" he asked.

"Certainly." said the nurse.

She quickly poured him a glass from the water jug on the bedside table. He drank it straight down. He asked her the time and it was just after midnight.

"Perfect, just after the witching hour. How fitting!" he said trying to reassure the nurse he was back to his normal self with some light humour.

Inside, however, he wasn't alright. The terror he had experienced in his nightmare was still rattling around in him, playing havoc with his nerves. As the nurse was about to return to her station, Carter asked if they had received any calls or messages for him. She said that she hadn't personally but she would go and check the log book just in case someone did before she came on shift. He asked if she could possibly check his mobile phone for any messages or missed calls. He prayed for one from Mary. The nurse was gone only a matter of minutes but it seemed like hours. Also being cooped up, in that small, stuffy room was having adverse effects on him. When she returned she informed him that one message had been left earlier from Will, which was "No luck finding Mary. See you tomorrow."

Carter thanked her for checking before slouching back on the bed. The nurse couldn't help but see how disappointed Carter was, and she wished there was something she could do. He couldn't understand why she hadn't called or why she hadn't texted him, or anything. He was starting to become concerned for her wellbeing.

The night went on and Carter stayed awake for at least an hour worrying about Mary, before building up the courage to return to sleep and the possibility of another nightmare.

4am and Carter woke up on the floor after falling out of bed. The nurse was too late to stop him. He had experienced a reoccurrence of the same dream from earlier but woke before it had time to go too deep and too frightening.

"Mr Jakeman are you OK?" said the nurse holding his arm trying to help him back into bed.

"Yes fine. Must have just turned in my sleep too far and . . . . !"

Carter assured the nurse that he felt OK and she left him alone. As soon as she closed the door behind her, he started to cry, holding his head in his hands, frightened at what was happening to him. He couldn't bear it. It was too much. He wasn't sure how much more he could take. He had no control and was becoming more and more erratic.

"Mary!" he shouted out, screaming at the top of his voice. "Mary, please!" he shouted again, before the nurse rushed back to the room. Other patients were awoken by his outburst.

"Mr Jakeman calm down!" said the nurse rushing to his bedside.

There was no giving in and he shouted again, maniacally crying out Mary's name, sorrow ridden and shaking. "Where is she?" "Find Mary!" He repeated again, screeching out the words. The nurse could do nothing to calm him. Another nurse joined her on the other side of the bed, pleading with him to quieten down. He became more and more infuriated, and they feared he would try to escape.

"I need to call someone." said the nurse, already making haste for the phone on the reception desk.

Other patients had already started getting out off their beds and walking round to see what was happening.

"I can't hold him much longer!" screamed out the other nurse, while desperately trying to keep him still.

Another patient, a man in his mid-forties, stepped in to help, helping the nurse to try and keep Carter in one place. The man was very toned and obviously worked out so was able without too much stress to keep Carter's arms down until someone else came in. The nurse kept repeating "We will find her Carter, we will find Mary."

Carter began to tire and settle down as an on call doctor and a night security guard entered the room. The nurse gave a rushed description of what had happened as the doctor sat at his side and began asking Carter what had happened. Carter began to regain some composure and realised he had got out of control. However to cause such a fuss was not his intention. It was more venting frustration than anything else. He needed Mary.

"Mr Jakeman do you feel OK. Do you know why you got upset? Was it another dream?" asked the doctor.

"I need to see Mary. They won't even let me have my mobile phone for Christ sake. I feel like I'm in prison in here."

"Mr Jakeman you are recovering from an operation. You need rest. It is normal to feel stressed and apprehensive but you need time to properly heal."

"I'm not talking about recovery time. I want to speak to Mary!" he said again, with growing frustration in his voice.

The doctor looked around at the nurse for an explanation on who Mary was. She informed him that Carter was with a lady named Mary the day he fell unconscious in the park, and hadn't seen or heard from her since, and he was worried about her. She said that nurses on duty had tried calling her and they had been checking his mobile telephone at regular intervals for any incoming calls or text messages. The security guard stepped forward cautiously as he noticed Carter shift on the bed abruptly, looking as if he was going to get out.

"Why can't I have my mobile phone?" asked Carter, relaxing down, realising that any chance of getting out of there at that point was impossible.

"Can we give him his phone please nurse?" instructed the doctor.

"It was Mr Walsh that has made the decision for him not to have his phone for a period of 24 hours." replied the nurse.

"Why is that?" questioned both the doctor and Carter simultaneously.

The doctor did not wait for an answer but assumed that Mr Walsh's reason for this was a just one, and he wasn't prepared to question that decision further. He turned to Carter and asked if he would be kind enough to wait to speak to Mr Walsh later that morning about the phone. Carter was too tired to argue anymore and agreed, before stressing a sincere apology to everyone for the scene he had caused. The doctor told the nurse, in front of Carter, that later that morning she would phone Mary for him, and keep him constantly informed of progress. Carter was happy with this as an interim solution and understood that they were trying their best to put his wellbeing first, but that didn't help his predicament, and it was only a matter of time before it was likely to flare up again. The security guard left and the helpful patient was accompanied back to his bed by the nurse, leaving only the on call doctor and Carter in the room.

"Mr Jakeman, I know how hard this is. I have seen many cases in the past where patients have worries outside of these walls, and it seems that they are kept from them, and that no-one is willing to help. But I can assure you that this team here will do everything in their power to make your stay here as comfortable and as stress free as humanly possible."

"Thank you Doctor. I'm again very sorry." Carter offered sincerely, relaxing his posture and lying back down onto the mattress.

"No problem."

The doctor stood and walked to the door, briefly glancing back and wishing Carter well, and hinting that he may bump into him again soon, but not screaming in the night. Carter laughed, and before the doctor closed the door, Carter said "Wait!"

"Yes?" said the doctor, pushing the door back open and looking in.

"I had a really bad dream. I mean, I've had bad dreams before but this was . . . . Is that normal?"

"Carter your body has gone through a traumatic time. You are worried about your condition and getting better. You are in a different environment. It is normal to feel anxiety, and yes it is more than likely that all of this could feed nightmares. Give it time Carter. I'm sure everything will be fine."

"Thanks again." said Carter turning onto his more comfortable position on his side.

The doctor left as the sound of his bleeper went off, alerting him to urgently call someone else who was in need.

* * * *

"This scan will not take long Mr Jakeman. Just try to relax and stay as still as possible." said a radiographer as Carter began moving into the 1.5 metre long tunnel of the MRI scanner.

He had a receiving device around his head which would detect the tiny radio signals emitted from his body.

He had been reminded again and again to stay as still as possible, otherwise the scan could be blurred. He knew it was likely to take anywhere between thirty minutes to an hour for the scan to be complete, so he was only happy to have some quiet time to just relax. It had been one hell of a traumatic night for him, and even though he felt slightly better, he was still tired and still very worried about Mary. He comforted himself with the thought that Mr Walsh would be in to see him a little later, and that he would get his phone back at least. He also knew that by the time he was taken back to the ward the nurse would have tried calling Mary and may have had more luck in getting through to her. One of his biggest questions was going to be for Will later on during visiting hours. He wanted to know if he had tried the house again, maybe he had now met Mary? Maybe Mary and Will would arrive together that morning to see him, and everything would be alright?

"Everything OK in there for you Mr Jakeman?" asked the radiographer through the intercom. Carter did have earphones in as the scanner was very noisy but he did feel quite at ease.

"Yes fine thanks."

The radiographer sat in the control room next to the scanner, observing through a window. Thirty-five minutes later and the scan had been completed, meaning Carter could return to his bed on the ward.

* * * *

Carter attempted eating his hospital breakfast, porridge, and to his disbelief it didn't taste half as bad as he had expected. The tea was pretty good as well, but tea is tea he thought, not even hospital catering could mess that one up surely. The same nurse from the early hours was just about to finish and go off shift, but stopped off in Carter's room before leaving.

"Good morning Mr Jakeman, how are you feeling this morning?" she asked optimistically.

"Yes much better thanks. Sorry again for my behaviour last night."

"That's OK, it happens. You do look brighter this morning, and eating as well I see."

"Yes, quite nice it is too. Did you manage to call Mary?"

"Yes I have, twice, but I'm afraid it went to an automated voicemail."

"Did you leave a message?"

"Not this time. She has already received a couple of calls from us where we have left messages for her. I'm sure she'll pick them up soon."

"I hope so." said Carter disappointed again.

"Maybe she has just been too busy to answer, or misplaced her phone or something. Remember it's not even been a couple of days yet!"

"Yeah, you could be right. Maybe because it comes up as an unknown number she may choose not to answer it. But that doesn't explain her not returning the call after listening to the voice messages."

The nurse said goodbye and left for the day, as the next shift were already hovering around outside, answering calls and speaking to patients on the ward. Carter finished his breakfast and felt better for it. He spent the best part of the next half an hour staring at the wall, waiting for someone to arrive. He wanted to have a wash and kept deliberating over when to get up and do it, or maybe he would call the nurse to bring a bowl of water in and he could do it within the confines of his room. He wrote a message down on a piece of tissue which read *Will—Herald*, which was a reminder for him to give Will his hotel key so he could go and get some belongings later and bring them in for him, basic stuff like a couple of shirts, a toothbrush and so on. He spent the following minutes again racking his brain, attempting to remember what had happened to Mary in the park. He kept replaying the last moment in his mind, hoping it would continue and play out the rest, but nothing. The last picture of her imprinted on his brain was her looking in contemplation after he disclosed his love for her.

His concentration was broken by a knock on the door. It opened and Mr Walsh walked in.

"Good morning Mr Jakeman, how are you feeling this morning? I understand you had a bit of an eventful night last night?"

"Good morning, and yes afraid so. I had some really disturbing dreams, one that I don't even want to think about. I guess I just lost it. I am still worried about Mary, she still hasn't made contact. But my friend Will has arrived now, and I gave him details of her address so hopefully he has managed to find her. He went there last night but I received a message saying no luck, but finger's crossed he'll have more luck this morning."

"This girl really means the world to you doesn't she?"

"Absolutely, everything." said Carter.

"I take it you blacked out before you got an answer?"

"That's right. Well I think so. Either that or I've got amnesia! You know what? Maybe she doesn't want to talk to me. Maybe I scared her off when I told her that I was in love with her."

"Maybe, or maybe not. Tell you what I'll call her now, I might get lucky. Give me a moment."

He walked out to reception, picked up the phone and dialled the number. He stood there, wishing that she would answer, hoping, but it went to voicemail once again. "The person you are calling is not available. Please leave your message after the bleep. When you have finished your message, please select hash for more options or hang up to send your message." Mr Walsh waited patiently for the automated message to end so he could try and leave a message that should hopefully push Mary to call back.

"Hi, this is a message for Mary. My name is Crispin Walsh and I am a surgeon at Western General Hospital. I am calling in regard to one of our patients, Mr Carter Jakeman whom I believe you know well. He is doing OK and there is nothing to worry about. My colleagues have been trying to contact you but no response. It is becoming imperative that you call, as Mr Jakeman is worried about you. This is causing Mr Jakeman stress and is having a negative effect on his recovery, which concerns me. Look I'll give you my personal bleep number, in case you have tried calling and was not able to get through to the ward for some reason. Just call up and ask if they could bleep 06197. Thanks. Hope to hear from you soon."

Mr Walsh returned to the room and informed Carter that he had left a message stressing the urgency for her to call. Carter held hope that she would, and that maybe Will would arrive soon with news that he had managed to speak to her.

"And what about these dreams. Do you want to talk about them?" asked Mr Walsh, hoping to change the dialogue to a more related subject.

"Will it help?" asked Carter unconvinced.

"Maybe, it is worth a try. Most dreams, well nightmares, can be representations of things in our everyday lives, or can be indirectly related to experiences in our lives. Talking about them can allow us to maybe understand them better, or find a way of improving these things in our lives that are being reflected in our dreams."

"OK I'll make you a deal. Give me back my mobile phone and I'll tell you my dream."

"Deal."

Carter sat up into a more comfortable position, and at the same eye level as Mr Walsh. Carter drew a deep breath to compose himself before unveiling the details of his nightmare.

"I don't know where to start." said Carter.

"Take your time." replied Mr Walsh.

"I was in theatre. And at first I was hovering above looking down at myself being operated on. But it wasn't you Mr Walsh. I couldn't see their whole face but I knew that it was someone else, someone I didn't recognise. Then, I started to feel my body being pulled down toward my body. Then I was in my body and awake looking up at the surgeon. The surgeon was me. I was cutting into myself, and it was becoming more and more ferocious. I could feel the pain, the cold steel of the instrument, the scalpel, against my skin. I could feel the stinging sensation as it cut further and deeper into my brain. In the other hand were forceps, readying too to enter my open head. Then something was pulled out of my head and held in front of my face. It was a sickly looking blob covered in blood, a pulsating mass of cancer on a part of the brain. I was screaming for help but no words came out. I looked around to try and escape, and when I looked back it was no longer the cancerous tumour but Mary standing there and covered in blood, as if it was her that had been removed from my head, my mind."

Carter apologised as he started to get emotional reflecting on his horrific dream. Mr Walsh was immediately supportive, saying it was understandable that Mary was in his dream, as he was obviously worried about her and desperate to see her. Also, due to his recent operation his imagination could be heightened by the experience and his growing frustration at not being able to speak to Mary would have contributed even more to this. Carter understood and opted to believe with Mr Walsh and focus on his logical analysis. Mr Walsh cheered Carter up further by retrieving his mobile phone. Carter looked straight away but there were no messages and no missed calls. Crispin Walsh carried on with his check-up, perusing his medical notes from the sleeve at the end of the hospital bed, checking his pulse and discussing how his wound felt and asking what he had managed to eat. Shortly after Mr Walsh had to carry on with his ward round but assured Carter that he would pop back in the afternoon to check how he was doing.

Crispin Walsh left the room and walked back out into the main corridor on his way to the next ward. He was becoming more concerned at how the effects of not being able to speak to Mary were affecting Carter mentally. As he walked into the next ward he checked his bleeper, making sure it was on and in perfect working order. He hoped that his message would do the trick and that Mary would call him back soon.

* * * *

"So, Will, did you go to the right house, explain it to me again."

"Carter I told you. It was the house about half way down with the red door. I checked the other houses in close proximity as well, and no red door."

"And you are sure it wasn't Mary?"

"Trust me, that wasn't Mary. Not unless Mary strikes an uncanny resemblance to Shrek. And yes I mean Shrek, the male ogre, not Princess Fiona!"

"And you checked again this morning?" pressed Carter, sounding confused.

"Yes, although I didn't go too close to the door in case she saw me and thought I was stalking her or something!"

Carter sat totally confused as he was sure that it was the house with red door. "OK you are going to have to go back and check the doors either side again, in case I'm mistaken."

"Oh God! Have you tried calling her again?"

"Yep, I've tried like a hundred times in the past hour!"

Carter gave Will his hotel key and asked him if he could go and pick up some of his stuff from the hotel later in the afternoon. He also asked if he would let the front desk know what had happened in case they had noticed he wasn't there.

Visiting hours seemed to go so quickly. The nurse poked her head into the room with a reminder that it was time for Will to go. In the brief time that Will had been there they had been talking about the city, about Marcus, and what Carter had seen so far. They chatted about where Will could go that day to kill some time as he was going to come back and visit Carter again that evening, but in the meantime would try and locate Mary's house. Carter was less than optimistic but was thankful to Will for trying again.

"I'll definitely give it a go Carter," said Will, as he left the room.

Carter was again alone, confronted with what he felt like was going to be an infinity of silence. He was desperate for the evening visiting hours to begin so Will would be back. The time ticked so slowly when no-one was there. He hated this, being alone with no company but himself. He didn't like his own company, in fact he despised it. He looked around at the boring white clinical walls that surrounded him, and as the longer the time went by without news of Mary, he became more and more irritated by menial things. He was trapped, he had no power to go and search for Mary himself. All he had now was his mobile, which was of no use as Mary was not replying to either his calls or his messages. He threw it to the side in disgust, as if making a protest that modern technology was nothing but a farce. He wanted to leave, but knew he was in no fit shape or form to do so. It was a waiting game, a test of patience, a call for him to be calm in the face of tension and indecision. Something he wasn't used to. He never liked being the centre of attention, having people crowding around him, as if on show. He was far too shy and nervous around people to ever be able to come across than anything other than a shivering wreck. His heart was bleeding within him, aching at times at not being able to conquer anything that would counteract these problems. His mind was ravenous for some kind of release, an answer, or a breakthrough.

His whole life had been a constant battle against himself, a civil war of emotions within him that never seized.

He rested his head back on the pillow gently and stared up at the ceiling, as if looking to God for an answer. He briefly contemplated praying for Mary's safety, for him to see her again, a hope that a future for them both was still possible. However, he could not muster the confidence to do such a thing, refusing to ask help from someone whom he felt had offered him nothing so far in his life. He became even more enraged within, thinking of Mary over and over again. His skin began to feel quite tingly and itchy. He started scratching at his arms, reducing them to red, nearly drawing blood. He could feel sweat dripping from his forehead as his anger grew, his temperature rose as his rage swelled and intensified. He wanted to see Mary. He was desperate to see her. His patience at waiting was almost at an end, and he felt at that moment capable of attacking anyone who stood in his way.

He recognised, in a moment of unclouded fury, that he was a mess. He looked at himself, and anger was quickly replaced with fear. He started to doubt his sanity. A lonesome tear joined the moist layer of sweat on his cheek. His temperature seemed to plummet dramatically, leaving him feeling cold and clammy. Shivering under the bedclothes, unable to stabilise, he began speaking to himself, trying to calm himself with reassuring words.

"It's OK Carter. It's all going to turn out OK. You will be out of here before you know it. The scan will come back and will be good news. Mary will be fine and you will see her again. You will see her again. You will see her again!"

* * * *

"Mr Walsh, have you just come from the ITU, as Melissa was looking for you?" asked a passing consultant as he was heading to the staff canteen for a quick bite of lunch.

"No. Did it sound important?" asked Mr Walsh, trying to determine if it was necessary to go there immediately, or if it could wait until after he had eaten.

"No not urgent. She just wanted to ask you about some dictations. She said it could wait!"

"OK, thanks for letting me know. I'll see her later."

Mr Walsh turned and headed downstairs to the lower ground floor toward the canteen. As his foot was about to touch down on the last step his bleeper sounded. He had to answer it so he sourced the nearest telephone to call the switchboard back. He stepped into the post room, picked up the receiver from the handset on the wall and dialled the switchboard.

"Hello switchboard, how can I help?"

"Hi, this is Mr Crispin Walsh. I just got bleeped!"

"Oh yes Mr Walsh, just one moment please. I have a lady on the line who said that you have been trying to reach her?"

"Oh yes, great! Yes sure, put her through to me please." said the surgeon, sounding relieved, as it could only be one person, Mary Lee.

He waited a second for the call to be connected and then he heard the voice of a woman on the other end of the phone.

"Hello, Mr Walsh. You have been leaving messages on my phone about one of your patients, a Carter Jakeman?"

"Yes. Thank you so much for returning my call. He has been very worried about you. I understand you were with him the other day, in the park. He has . . . ."

"Sorry, excuse me! I think there has been some kind of mistake." said the lady, cutting the surgeon's sentence short.

"Mistake?" enquired Mr Walsh, slightly confused.

"Yes. I do not know a Carter Jakeman!"

"This is Mary Lee isn't it?"

"No, my name is Laura Miller."

"Laura Miller. Right OK. I must have dialled the wrong number when I left the message. I am sorry for any inconvenience. Thank you for calling me back all the same." said Mr Walsh, quickly coming the most logical conclusion that he must have misdialled. He replaced the receiver and walked out of the post room, adamant that he had made sure that he had dialled the number correctly earlier. He was sure he had.

Sitting down at a table in the canteen with his ham salad, bread roll and fruit juice lunch, Crispin Walsh began to wonder whether he had in fact actually punched in a wrong number when dialling before. He hoped that Carter or the ward had heard from Mary by now. He would see him later that afternoon anyway, so would find out then. He started to feel slight concern as to why, if Mary and Carter were getting on so well, why she hadn't returned the calls. He now, more than ever before, felt the need to contact her, as it began to alarm him that it did seem strange that she hadn't. He started running through the possibilities in his mind. He thought that maybe she was busy and hadn't had a chance to pick up her phone, maybe she had misplaced or lost her phone, maybe she didn't want to know Carter anymore and wanted out of the relationship, or maybe she was in distress of some kind.

"Hey you, how is your day going?" said one of the senior nurses, pulling out a chair to sit down and join him for lunch.

Mr Walsh, momentarily distracted from his thoughts of Mary, replied "Hi Rhonda. You know, same stuff, different day! How are you doing? Are you still planning on doing your voluntary care abroad?"

"Yes, got about another six months to go. Then I'm off."

"Think it is wonderful that you are doing it. How long are you intending to go there for?"

"Probably for a year initially and then see what happens after that!"

"Come back and work here?"

"Maybe, although not likely."

"Well you'll certainly be missed."

"Thank you Crispin. I will miss this place."

They had worked together off and on for a few years and had got to know each other fairly well in that time. Well enough for Rhonda to know and be able to tell when something was on Mr Walsh's mind.

"Are you OK Crispin. You look like something is up?"

"No nothing, just, well nothing really."

"Doesn't look that way. You looked deep in thought when I came over to the table. Sorry, maybe I'm just being nosey. It's none of my business."

"No it's OK Rhonda. You are right. There is something playing on my mind. I have a patient who came in the other day with a brain tumour. It was been removed and he is currently recovering on the ward. However, there is this girl, a girl he had been seeing, who was with him in fact on the same day he was admitted. We haven't been able to get in contact with her and it is really becoming an issue for the patient. He is distressed. We have tried calling her, leaving numerous messages but nothing."

"Maybe, she doesn't want to know him anymore?"

"That had crossed my mind. He does seem to have somewhat of a complex personality."

"Really? Is she registered as his next of kin?"

"No. I had a call from someone just now who I expected to be her, but it was someone else. I called and left a message myself but must have dialled the wrong number."

"Are you due to visit him this afternoon?"

"Yes."

"Confirm the number you dialled with him then."

"Yes I will. Well I hope she has contacted him by now or vice versa. The sooner we locate this girl the better he will be!"

Rhonda and Crispin Walsh carried on with their lunch, conversation turning more toward work related issues, restructure, upcoming lectures and so on.

* * * *

A beeping sounded which stirred Carter from his sleep. It was two distinct beeping noises. It was his mobile phone receiving a text message. Carter quickly realised and lunged for it, paying no consideration to his injury or his instruction to rest. He picked up his phone and, at arms length, for a split second thought it said Mary. Wishful thinking was, however, all that it turned out to be. When he brought the phone closer it was a text from Will. "Sorry mate, no luck on that street. Knocked on some other houses and no-one knows who she is. See you a bit later."

Carter instantly became infuriated and shouted to the nurse to call the police and find out what has happened to Mary. The nurse ran in pleading with Carter again to calm down. He won't relent, not this time. He just shouted for her to call the police, over and over. She was at a loss and concerned as to what to do. She rushed out to the phone and bleeped Mr Walsh and called security. She looked back to the room and he was already sitting upright in his bed, readying himself to stand up.

"Are you phoning the police out there? Tell them that her name is Mary Lee and she is missing. Do you hear me?" he shouted, sounding more maniacal with every word. "Do you hear me?" he repeated before struggling to his feet.

"Mr Jakeman, sit down!" said the nurse before slamming the receiver down.

She returned to the room and stood in front of him, determined to do whatever she could to prevent him from walking out before security and Mr Walsh arrived.

"Don't you dare leave Mr Jakeman. Sit down. You are supposed to be recovering! Sit down. Think of the other patients on this ward. Do you think it is fair to them? They are trying to rest!" said she nurse becoming increasingly uncomfortable and apprehensive.

"Get out of my way!" said Carter in a much quieter voice, looking deep into her eyes to ensure that his point was made, and that he was prepared to go.

"I will not. You need to stay here!" she repeated, taking one step back with her left foot, to increase her stance and balance, giving her a little more strength to be able to stop him if he suddenly surged forward.

He noticed that she was looking worried, and he did feel guilty inside, but Mary's safety was of far more importance. He needed to get out of there and find her. He needed to break free from this prison and rescue her. He moved left and right, trying to get out around the other side. But the nurse was ready and quickly matched his movements. It was cat and mouse for a few more seconds, before to the nurse's utter relief she heard a supporting and familiar sounding voice come from behind her. It was one of the security guards, one of the bigger set guards.

"Sir, sit down now! I won't ask a second time." said the voice.

It was one of those commanding voices that just resonated around the room, sending vibrations through the bones. Carter wasn't stupid and knew it was in his best interests to sit down at that point. Coming from behind the guard was a very concerned and angry looking Mr Walsh, red faced and looking disappointed.

"Mr Jakeman this has to stop right now! Do you understand?" said Mr Walsh, his tone spoken with absolute unquestionable importance.

Carter's emotions and frustrations hit a low once again at that moment, and upon looking at the nurse's face and how frightened he had made her, he could not believe in the man that he was becoming. He looked at her and could only say sorry. Mr Walsh demanded an explanation, to which Carter immediately said that he wanted to know if Mary was alright, and that was all. He wanted the police to be contacted to locate her and check that she was safe.

"Carter, I will personally do everything in my power to find Mary for you. You have my word. I promise. But you have to do me one thing. Do you understand me Carter?"

"OK." replied Carter willing to strike a deal.

"You stay in bed and you rest, you do not shout, you don't abuse any members of our staff, and you remain calm and do what I say. Can you do that for me Carter?"

"OK. I'm sorry but you must understand my frustration. I mean, where is she? My friend has tried finding her. I told him to go to her house, and nothing. I'm worried for her!"

Crispin Walsh did sincerely understand, and although Carter's health and safety was his number one concern, he was becoming extremely disturbed at the impact this was having on Carter. He was also becoming quite concerned for Mary as well. He began to try and find out some more information that may help track her down.

"OK Carter. What about her work number?" he asked, taking a pen from his shirt pocket, and readying to take down some vital details.

"I don't have her work number. We only ever spoke using mobiles!"

"What about where she works? The company name? Anything where we know we can find her?"

Carter stopped for a moment, realising that he didn't know. How didn't he know those things? He looked up at Mr Walsh, and with almost embarrassment replied "I don't know!"

"You don't know who she worked for or where she worked?" asked Mr Walsh finding that very hard to believe.

"Well no. I knew it was for a magazine publication but I don't think I ever asked her what the name of the company was. And I never met her at work, so?"

"Great. So your friend has already tried her home address? Is that right?"

"Yes. He must have knocked at the wrong house or something!"

"The wrong house?" he said becoming slightly frustrated.

"Yes, well I know the street, and I know that it was about half way down the street, the house with the red door. I just never got the door number!"

"Carter you know how difficult you are making this for me. I have no information to go on. Even the number I dialled before . . . . was . . . wait, give me your phone."

"Why?" said Carter, looking intrigued.

"I want to make sure the number I called earlier was the right one that I have written down."

"Why, hold on have I missed something?" asked Carter, sounding confused.

"Well the message that I left before, for who I thought was Mary, was not Mary. It was someone else. I must have dialled the wrong number."

Carter handed Mr Walsh his phone. As he walked toward the desk to double check the number on Carter's phone to the number written down, Carter said "Wait, wait Mr Walsh. My sister-in-law, Claire Jakeman. She knows Mary from when Mary used to work at my brother's company. She should have the contact details of where she works."

Mr Walsh walked back in and asked for her number.

"Wait! She is at the cabin at the Port of Menteith for a getaway. I don't know the number of the place."

"Don't worry. I can get the number. Lets me go and do a search on the internet. What is the name of the place they are staying?"

"I think it is called Lochie Chalets. I am sure I saw the sign for it when Mary and I were driving around up there."

"Well that's something. Let me find out the number."

"Mr Walsh. Could you talk to her for me? She has just lost her husband, my brother in a tragic car accident, and I don't feel I have the strength to talk to her about my situation. I'm sorry. Will you do that for me?"

"OK, I'll talk to her. And I'm sorry to hear about your brother." he said and left the room to go to the internet to run a search for Lochie Chalets.

"I need to use the computer. Can you make Mr Jakeman a cup of tea or something please?" he asked as the nurse quickly excused herself from the computer. He ran the search for Lochie Chalets and it appeared straight away. It was in Port of Menteith like Carter had said. Without any hesitation he picked up the phone and dialled the number. It rang for only a few seconds before it was answered.

"Hello, Lochie Chalets, Archie speaking."

"Hi there. I wonder if you can help me. My name is Mr Crispin Walsh and I'm calling from Edinburgh's Western General Hospital. Do you have a Claire Jakeman staying with you at the moment?"

"We do indeed, yes. Is there something wrong?"

"No. I just need to ask her something in regard to some contact details on behalf of a patient of mine. Could you possibly put me through to her, or pass on a message?"

"Certainly Mr Walsh. Could I have your contact details and I'll ask her to call you right away."

Crispin Walsh thanked him and gave him his contact details, before hanging up the phone and returning to Carter's room.

"Please tell me it is good news!" said Carter.

"I have left a message with a guy there who is going to get Claire to call me asap. In the meantime you have to keep your end of the bargain, and get some rest."

"I will, and thanks again for trying. I'll keep trying her as well from my phone."

"OK. Now you rest up. And I'll let you know as soon as I hear something."

"Ok thanks."

Crispin Walsh turned to leave the room just as Will came in for the afternoon visiting hours.

"Ah, Mr Walsh I'd like you to meet my best friend Will Harrison, Will, Mr Walsh."

"Nice to meet you Will." he said offering his hand to shake Will's. Will returned the gesture.

"So you are taking good care of my mate are you? When do you think it is likely he can leave here?" asked Will openly.

"Well. We need to review his MRI scan, do some more tests before making any determination on a discharge date. For the time being he needs rest!" said Mr Walsh, looking back at Carter, giving him a judgemental look. Carter smiled and acknowledged that he got the message loud and clear, before Mr Walsh said goodbye and left the room.

"So, did you get my text Carter, about the houses I tried?" asked Will.

"Yes, it woke me up. I thought it was Mary!"

"Oh well sorry to disappoint you mate but I did say I'd let you know as soon as I could."

"I know. Thanks Will. I'm sorry, I've just managed to cause another scene here earlier. Security came, again. I'm just worried about Mary, Will. I feel so useless in here, and it seems that no-one is even trying to look for her!"

"I know. Look I'm not going to say I know how you feel because I don't, alright? But what I do know is that you're not going to do yourself any favours by keep getting worked up. Just stay calm and concentrate on recovering. Otherwise you'll end up being kept in here even longer. And if you keep flipping out, they'll end up putting you in a mental home, and I'm not coming to visit you in one of those places!" he said jokingly.

"I know. But look, why isn't she calling me back? Don't you find that a bit strange? What happened today? Whose house did you knock at?" asked Carter.

"I knocked at a few. They didn't know who I was talking about."

"Maybe you should go to the police and report a missing person?"

"No way Carter, come on, a missing person? Why don't you call, your mobile is right there?"

Carter had no answer, and as quickly as Will had fired this question, Carter chose to dodge it.

"Well Mr Walsh is taking it into his own hands now. He is waiting for a call from Claire. She'll know how to find her. Mary used to work at my brother's company, and she was at his funeral."

"Well let's hope she calls him back soon. I want to see you happy mate, and also of course, I want to meet her!"

"Oh I bet you do!" said Carter, before they started laughing together.

The nurse walked in carrying Carter's tea, pointing out how nice it was to see him smiling and laughing for a change. She jokingly offered Will to stay the night, to keep him laughing rather than ranting. Will took the tea from her, keeping it for himself before saying "Well I've always had a thing for nurses. You see this Carter, I've only just met her and already she is making me tea and asking me to stay the night."

The nurse blushed and smiled at Will before saying "I'll make another cup of tea for you".

Will and Carter laughed more as the nurse walked out to make another cup. Will was just so happy to see him laughing. He couldn't remember the last time that he had laughed so much. The nurse gathered that Will's main intention was to make Carter laugh, but she did have her doubts as he did come across as a bit of a lady's man.

* * * *

"Mr Walsh there is a call for you. Shall I take a message?"

"Who is it?" he asked his secretary discretely, ensuring the caller did not hear.

"A Claire Jakeman." she replied.

"I'll take it!" he said without a second's hesitation.

* * * *

The long winding corridors of the hospital were becoming more spacious as the evening approached. Cleaners were sweeping areas of the floors following the day's accumulation of dust, cleaning the toilets and mopping the marble floors. Most of the administration staff and visitors to the hospital were leaving and making their way to the exits, Will being one of them.

"Mr Harrison. Please could I have a moment?" came a voice calling from the top of the stairwell. It was Crispin Walsh.

"Hi, Mr Walsh right?" said Will hoping he had remembered his name correctly.

"Yes. Look I was wondering if I could have a moment of your time to discuss some things about Carter?"

"Yes sure, absolutely, if it will help."

"I hope it will."

Mr Walsh led Will back up to his office, the two not really engaging in any real conversation until they were inside the office itself and the door closed.

"Please take a seat Mr Harrison." he said pointing to the chair opposite his own, a mahogany desk in between them.

"How can I help? Wait is this something serious about Carter that he doesn't know about yet? Is he going to be alright?" asked Will, beginning to worry that he was about to receive bad news.

"No Mr Harrison. Well kind of. The fact that he has yet to make contact with this Mary character is not helping in his recovery. He is becoming stressed, animated, angry, and are not the things that I want to see from a post op patient."

"What are you saying? Do you want me to have a word with him?"

"Don't take this the wrong way, but I don't think that you talking to him will help."

"OK, then what do you suggest?" said Will not entirely sure where the conversation was headed at that point.

"Well I understand that you went and knocked on the door of the exact house that Carter had described, on the exact street that he specified, and what did you find?"

"I knocked at the doors of a few properties actually. I asked them if they knew a Mary Lee. They all looked at me with a blank look on their face. It was as if she didn't exist!"

Mr Walsh held his expression, but gave a slight smile indicating to Will that he may be onto something, the same thing that had crossed his mind that very afternoon. It took Will a few moments, but he quickly worked out that what he had just told him was in fact exactly what he was waiting to hear.

"Wait a minute. No. What are you implying? That she isn't real?" said Will, not wanting to accept anything of the kind. He stood up, speaking more loudly, as if protecting the dignity of his closest friend. He continued "No not Carter. He couldn't . . . . No way. We just haven't found her yet that's all. Bit quick to be jumping to that as a conclusion isn't it? Christ, where did you graduate anyway, fairyland? Thinking up imaginary friends, come on, you're not serious. Are you?" said Will, his tone lowering to a more fragile and susceptible tone.

"Mr Harrison, I understand your feelings on this. And trust me up until this afternoon I would have considered the notion ludicrous myself. But I received a call a little earlier from Claire, Carter's sister-in-law."

"Yes, I know who Claire is, go on!" said Will eager to hear an outcome.

"Well for a start she has no recollection of meeting or knowing anyone by the name of Mary Lee, or even knowing anyone named Mary in fact."

"Well she may have forgotten."

"No. Carter told me that she was at the funeral of his brother."

"So?"

"Well Claire doesn't remember seeing Carter speaking with anyone that day. She said most of time he sat in the lounge alone!"

"No, I'm still not buying this!" said Will trying his hardest to reason with what he was hearing. Mr Walsh continued further.

"I know Mr Harrison. Maybe it was just a coincidence, or the trauma she had suffered that day, that may have blurred Claire's memories of who he had, or had not been talking too! I was prepared to give him the benefit of the doubt, so I asked Claire which company Marcus used to work at. I asked this because Carter told me that Mary used to work there with Marcus. I called the company and spoke to a very nice lady called Deborah, who had worked at the company for fourteen years no less. She knew Marcus very well, and missed him very much. She also informed me that she had no recollection of meeting anyone called Mary Lee. She double checked the books for me, and no-one of that name had ever worked at that company."

Will sat back down on his chair, slowly accepting the possibility but still unconvinced of its actual truth.

"But . . . . he has spent all this time with her. He has described her to me in such detail. He has her number on her phone. Who the hell has he been texting or calling if not her?" asked Will, searching his mind for anything that could substantiate a claim for Carter.

"Oh yes I forgot, the telephone number. I meant to call it from his phone earlier, but he distracted me by talking about something else."

"Let me go and call her from it!" said Will.

"No, he has had an eventful day as it is. And visiting times are over. I need to think about this further and get some advice if this turns out to be true. By all means come back tomorrow but please keep this discreet, if not for me, for Carter?"

"Yes of course." said Will, knowing that Carter's health and sanity could be threatened if this wasn't played out correctly.

Mr Walsh told Will he would try and contact a colleague that he knew very well the following morning, to try and get some more information into this area of expertise. Will agreed, and asked to be present when and if news was broken to Carter about the existence of Mary Lee. Mr Walsh gave him his word as he knew that Carter could only take the news badly, and he would need all the help and support of those around him to ease the reality of what he may be told the following day. Will walked out of the office in total shock, head lowered, shoulders dropped, gutted for his best friend. Mr Walsh too, had a slight hope that he could be wrong. The possibility of luck looked like it had been snatched from Carter's grasp once again, this time his mind going to extremes in order to protect himself. Will kept a minute bit of belief back, hoping that this was not the case, and that Mary was real. He prayed that Crispin Walsh had been misinformed, as he knew that if it was true, it could be unpredictable as to how much damage the truth could do to such a fragile human being like Carter Jakeman, his best friend.

* * * *

Mr Walsh walked slowly into the ward area. It was just before 10pm. He approached Carter's window, being extra careful not to be seen. He opened the door, managing to remain silent. Carter was asleep. He could see Carter's phone on the side tray next to his bed, and tiptoed over to get it. Successfully obtaining it, and without making the slightest sound, he retreated back and out of the room. He pulled the door closed and walked back out into the main corridor. He scrolled the names of the address book, rushing to get to L in alphabet, and there it was, Mary Lee. He pressed the button to call. It rang and rang, which seemed like a lifetime, before it was answered. He couldn't believe it, as he heard the voice of a lady at the other end.

"Hello, who is this?" he asked, standing impatiently awaiting her name. Then it came, the voice responded disclosing her identity, and once heard he could do nothing but stand there in complete shock.

"This is Laura Miller."

CHAPTER FIFTEEN

The morning greeted Mr Walsh with the inevitable reality that he would have to confront Carter with last night's discovery. His mind was thrown back and forth as he tried to ascertain a mental structure of how these events had panned out. Was Carter even aware that she wasn't real! He wondered. Maybe Carter had never even physically called the number that he had logged as Mary Lee on his phone? Maybe he just imagined that he did? Maybe he didn't ever talk out loud when out in public view with Mary, maybe it was all just being played out in his head? Mr Walsh was slightly fascinated by this story, but was also deeply distressed by it, and concerned as to how this would affect Carter long term, not only his physical health, but now his mental health as well. He had never witnessed anything of that nature before, and he knew he would need assistance from the right person, a leader in the field of Psychiatry of which, in Mr Walsh's mind, there was only one. She was a close friend of his and had been for years, Professor Annie Lewis, a consultant in Neuropsychiatry. One thing that he was absolutely sure of was that Carter had to be told right away. This was imperative, the longer the truth was kept from him the worse his health could become, the possibility that Mary was still out there somewhere was real to him, he would continue to suffer. This had to end.

Into the kitchen came toddling his eighteen month year old daughter, Chloe, and she headed straight to him, arms reached out seeking his comfort. He picked her up, placing her on his knee before giving her a big hug. She was wearing the white, pink dotted scarf that his late mother had knitted for her not too long ago, not too long before his wife had been taken ill. He knew only too well how it felt to lose someone so close and that had meant so much to you. He felt for Carter, and knew within him, beyond any doubt, that Mary in fact didn't exist. Well at that point it was a 99.9% certainty. He knew the wallowing sadness and emptiness that lay in wait for him. He couldn't get the bipolar disorder thing out of his head. He knew that brain tumours had adverse effects on the nervous system and the likely cause for Carter's hallucinations, but he also debated whether or not somehow his disorder had helped with these manifestations, a sort of defence mechanism that had been triggered somewhere within his brain. Mr Walsh's sister, Lorna, arrived—as punctual as ever, ready to babysit Chloe as per usual. She was currently unemployed so Mr Walsh was paying her to babysit, and providing her with a helpful interim income before she could find another job, a sort of win-win situation. She was twenty-eight and not married. She had been in and out of many jobs since leaving school, not really committing to any, or gaining any fathomable or substantial experience to progress higher elsewhere in a career. She was much happier to float around, taking a job here and there when she felt like it, keeping herself tied over. But one thing she was good at was baby sitting. She loved Chloe to pieces and would do anything for her. Her brother on many occasions had tried to encourage her to take up something job wise that was more child focused, teaching or child minding. Sadly she steered clear of anything of the sort, doubting her ability to be able to give anything of the kind the justice it deserved, but mainly because she was afraid to commit to anything like that. She had never handled pressure well within a working environment. She would become flustered and stressed quite quickly, clamming up and would freeze.

Mr Walsh closed his briefcase, pressing down the latches ensuring it was locked. He picked up his tinfoil wrapped cheese sandwich, banana and yogurt and put them inside a carrier bag before reaching over and kissing Chloe on her cheek saying goodbye.

"I may take her out to the park today Crispin. If you call, call my mobile, not the landline just in case."

"OK. Well you two have a great day together. Chloe, you take care of Auntie Lorna OK?"

Mr Walsh walked outside, unlocked his car, and slid into the driver's seat. He revved up the engine, as if preparing for a long fast race ahead of him. He waved goodbye once more to Chloe and Lorna, who he could see looking through the window smiling at him as he readied to drive away.

That drive to work was one of the hardest journeys of his career so far. Inside he was fluttering with nerves, apprehensive as to how Carter would react. He hoped that Professor Lewis was in work that day and not off on annual leave or too busy to spare a few moments. He knew that she would always be willing to help him out when called upon. He pressed the button for the automatic window, allowing some fresh air to circulate around the stuffy car interior. He loosened his tie around his neck, unbuttoned the top button to give himself some relief; he was becoming uncomfortably hot. The tension was already building within his shoulders. He would also find out the results of the second MRI scan later that day, and he just hoped that that would not produce any further bad news for Carter. As he pulled into the staff car park he pulled into his usual spot, a spot that had become like a superstitious omen for him. He had always managed to acquire that exact car parking space solidly for the last couple of months, and usually on days that he was unsuccessful in getting that space something bad tended to happen. A few incidents rattled his mind before he turned off the ignition. One time he went in to find a patient whom he knew quite well personally had passed away overnight; another was when he came down with food poisoning, and the other, that was spiked in the forefront of his mind every time he entered the car park and sought out his space, was the day he found out that his wife had died. She suffered a brain haemorrhage while sitting at her desk. Her colleagues thought she had drifted off to sleep, so did not want to disturb her. It happened shortly after she gave birth to Chloe, so her work colleagues, who were also mothers themselves, understood the effects of sleepless nights when having a new born baby and was only to happy for her to get some rest. It was a whole hour before someone decided to give her a nudge, and then found out what had really happened. Mr Walsh now thought of this space as his good luck space. Even though it was superstitious and that past events occur on selected days were only coincidental, it brought him comfort if he was parked in that space. It made him feel that nothing bad would happen that day.

* * * *

"Good morning Mr Walsh. How are you this morning?" asked his secretary as he breezed into his office.

"Fine, thank you. And you?" he said with a slight nervousness in his voice.

"Are you sure?" she repeated, noticing a slight difference to his usual upbeat and confident manner.

"Yes, just got a big day ahead."

"So it's admin time this morning is it? Just catching up, any dictations you wanna throw my way?"

"Yes and no. I need to go and speak to one of my patients this morning, which is what I am dreading to be honest. It is a complex case to say the least, but I need to get a hold of Prof Lewis first. I need her advice and attendance when I speak to him," he said taking off his jacket and hanging it up by the door.

"Do you want me to get Annie on the phone for you Crispin?" offered his secretary kindly.

"No it's fine thanks. I'll make the call in a moment."

He walked into his adjoining office, turned on his computer and quickly checked his emails. Thankfully for him there was nothing pressing or needing his absolute urgent attention. He quickly fired off an email to the radiographer requesting Carter's MRI scan to be reported as soon as possible. He leant over and picked up the phone, about to call Professor Lewis, but hesitated, then returned the handset. He slouched back in his chair, taking a moment to think of what to say to Annie. The whole situation needed to be dealt with delicately and professionally. He wanted to make sure that everything was clear in his own mind before making that call. Briefly thinking back to the day before, he made sure that he had covered all bases so far, in respect to whether or not Mary Lee existed, and upon further reflection he was convinced. He picked up the phone and dialled Professor Lewis's extension.

"Good morning Professor Lewis's office, can I help you?" answered Annie's secretary.

"Hi Jackie, Crispin here. Please tell me that Annie is in today?" he said.

"Hi Crispin. Yes she is. She has just popped over to Haematology. Should be back shortly."

"Thank God! How is her schedule today?"

"Busy as usual, she has a full morning clinic. Actually there is a gap in the middle as two patients have called in and cancelled this morning."

"I need to speak with her urgently. Could you ask her to call me as soon as she comes back into the office? And provisionally block those middle slots as I would like her to see one of my patient's with me."

"Of course, I will make a note. Do you want me to ask her to call you on your mobile or extension number?"

"Thanks Jackie, my mobile please in case I'm called away."

"No problem, bye."

Mr Walsh hung up the phone, making sure it was firmly placed on the hook, and sat eagerly awaiting her call. His secretary brought him his usual cup of green tea and placed it onto the coaster next to his computer. She closed the door behind her as she walked out, respecting his privacy as usual. He sat tapping the table with his fingers, and couldn't stay still for a second. He looked out of his window, which offered a view of a side entrance into the management offices adjacent to his building. He started to pace up and down in his office. His secretary could see him through the window, and felt concerned about his behaviour. She chose to pay no further attention and put on her headphones and started to type her dictation. Crispin Walsh's patience was being tested greater and greater with every minute that passed. He debated whether to call her again, and started to wonder whether Jackie had told her yet. He knew how competent Jackie was as a secretary but these things happen, maybe it had gone completely out of her mind. He couldn't wait anymore, he reached over for the phone and as he was about to lift it up it rang.

"Crispin Walsh speaking." he said, managing to answer the phone before it had completed its first full ring.

"Wow, that was fast Crispin, do you have that phone stapled to your head or what?"

"Annie. Thank God it's you. I need to talk to you about something urgently. Are you OK to talk now?"

"Well yes. My clinic starts in fifteen minutes but go on."

"OK I'll tell you quickly. I've got a patient who came in a couple of days ago. He had a brain tumour that needed immediate excision. This was done and he is now recovering on the ward. However, since coming round he has kept on about a lady, a lady who is someone he has been seeing, and who he is obviously deeply in love with."

"OK Crispin. And . . . . what do you need me for?"

"This lady . . . . she . . . . she doesn't exist!"

"What?" asked Annie sounding curiously intrigued by the revelation.

"Trust me, I have tried everything except going to the authorities and I believe this lady does not exist. It is all in his head. He suffers from bipolar disorder, recently suffered the loss of his brother, and I feel that this and his developing tumour somehow created this being. Does that sound plausible? Also I haven't confronted him with this yet. I am worried that he will take it very badly, and could almost definitely need a psychiatrist's input. I need you Annie. Will you help me with this?"

"Are you sure you have explored all avenues? Are you certain?"

"I am!" he answered with no doubt in his mind.

"Well, Jackie has told me that you have already pencilled yourself into my mid morning cancellation slots, so happy to come over then. I'm only too happy to help Crispin, and on such an interesting case as well, wow! I'm sure your patient will be referred on to me formally from you afterwards anyway, so at least I have a chance to try and get to know him now."

"Great, thanks Annie. I'll be in my office this morning so when you are free come and meet me here."

"OK, will do. Should be about 11ish if I'm running to time. Will only be able to be with you for about forty minutes max though before my next patient is due."

"Great, just as visiting hours start. Oh, I need to inform a friend of the patient about this first, as he is partly aware of my analysis and doubt over the lady's existence. Think it will be good to have him in the room when we tell the patient."

"OK no problem, see you a bit later, got to run!"

"Thanks Annie. And you as always are a star."

"I know I am! Oh by the way what is his name?"

"Carter Jakeman."

Mr Walsh replaced the handset with an added sigh of relief. All of a sudden the morning no longer looked as daunting as it had done earlier. Professor Annie Lewis was well respected in her field, known throughout the UK as being one of the top, most experienced and skilled neuropsychiatrist's around. She gave lectures internationally, as well as nationally, focusing specifically on areas such as the disorders of the brain and the mind, the life adjustment caused by brain and mind disability, among others. The surgeon was convinced that if Carter had any chance of a quick and speedy recovery mentally, then Annie Lewis was the one to do it. He sat back, picked up his cup of green tea taking a sip. He contemplated the next conundrum that faced him . . . . telling Will Harrison. He paid particular attention to how Will had become very protective of Carter when he had first made mention of the phantom relationship the day before. Although it would be perfectly natural for someone to protect the integrity of a dear friend, he found that Will and Carter had a stronger bond than that, more like a brotherly bond. Mr Walsh assumed and expected that there would be some resistance to believe from Will initially, but thought he would quickly come around to accepting it. It was so fortunate that Carter had a friend who was as close and as supportive as Will. Someone he could trust and rely on, someone to fall back on.

* * * *

"There you go Mr Jakeman, some cereal for you." said the nurse, propping up Carter's pillows behind his head, making him more comfortable.

"Great!" he said unconvinced by the appearance of that particular cereal. He quickly averted his thoughts to more important issues. "Has anyone received any calls for me here this morning?"

"No Mr Jakeman, but as I told you before, if we do we will let you know straight away." said the nurse aware of his anxiety.

"Where is Mr Walsh?" he asked as if dismissing her capabilities to help.

"He will be along to see you later this morning I'm sure." said the nurse already half way through the door.

Carter picked up his spoon and started on the mysterious looking cereal. He couldn't tell exactly what it was, but it looked very similar to wood shavings he thought. It must have been bran of some kind he guessed. It wasn't too long after that his taste buds just gave in, and accepted that he had no chance of avoiding the taste of shit for the foreseeable future. He checked his mobile, nothing again. He couldn't help but wonder that maybe he had scared Mary off after all. Maybe she wasn't interested in a serious long term commitment. He understood this if it was the case, but why wouldn't she tell him? Or maybe she was afraid that letting him know would hurt his feelings? Maybe she was just as confused as he was? He glanced up at the clock and knew he still had a while to wait before Will would arrive, so he turned on the small portable TV by his bedside to pass the time. He had not had the urge to watch the TV up until then. He just needed something to take his mind off things for a while, a burst of escapism.

* * * *

The automatic doors of the hospital's main entrance opened and Will strolled in. He was wearing his brown suede jacket, blue denim jeans and a pair of sunglasses. He had not stayed at his own hotel the night before, but instead went out, ending up in a nightclub. He ultimately found himself back at the house of a beauty therapist not too far from the Royal Mile.

He swaggered down the corridor, still buzzing from the night's activities, and headed for the elevator. His primary intention the previous evening was not to go out and party, but was to go out and have a quiet drink and think about what the surgeon had discussed with him. But with Will, once the combination of alcohol and beautiful women become one, he turned into, Wild Will. This was a nickname that Carter had given him many moons ago. He walked into the lift, pushed the button and leaned up against the inside panel of the elevator. He took off his.sunglasses and rubbed his eyes, and aware that if Mr Walsh was right in his predictions then today would be the day that Carter would have to face up to this as a reality. Will, dreaded this. The doors to the elevator opened and Will stepped out into the corridor, turning left to head to Carter's ward, when he heard his name being called from behind him.

"Mr Harrison . . . . Mr Harrison." called Mr Walsh, almost jogging down the corridor towards him, eager to speak to him before he made it into Carter's room.

"Mr Harrison," said Mr Walsh, as he came to an abrupt halt in front of Will, gathering his breath. "Could I have a quick word with you in my office please?"

Will realised that was it. He knew at that moment that the surgeon had found the evidence he was after to prove that Mary didn't exist.

"Yes sure." said Will already preparing himself for what he was about to hear.

As they entered the office Will dropped down into a chair, massaging his eyes, relieving some strain. He looked up at Mr Walsh who was just about to speak, when Will pre-empted "I guess you found what you were looking for huh?"

"Afraid so." he replied with a regretful tone.

"She doesn't exist does she?" said Will seeking final confirmation.

"No!" replied Mr Walsh.

They paused for a second and stayed silent, when a tap on the office door broke their attention. It was Professor Lewis. As she walked in Crispin Walsh immediately introduced her to Will explaining that she was here to help Carter deal with whatever the potential outcome was going to be. If there were to be any post-traumatic stress or psychiatric indications then Professor Lewis would be ideal to give Carter the best care available. Crispin Walsh handed Professor Lewis Carter's medical notes which she quickly read through. Will was grateful that she was on board, but was at the same time feeling empty and horrified by the reality of what was about to happen. Crispin Walsh explained to them both.

"I have explored further this morning, just to be totally sure. I have been on to other authorities trying to track Mary down, eliminating every possibility, every avenue ensuring that my assumptions are correct. There is no Mary Lee. I am totally sure. Trust me!"

"Shit!" said Will.

"Well I haven't got very long so I think we should go and speak to Mr Jakeman about this now!" said Annie Lewis, already standing, not expecting the other two to disagree. It was time.

"Who are you calling?" asked Will, noticing Mr Walsh rush to the phone before leaving.

"Security . . . . Just a precaution." he replied.

"Really?" said Will, not believing that Carter would necessarily need to be restrained or become violent.

* * * *

Professor Lewis, Crispin Walsh and Will stood in anticipation just outside of the ward area, awaiting the arrival of a security guard. The nursing staff on the ward had been made aware by Mr Walsh earlier that Carter was going to be receiving some bad news. This enabled the nurses to be as prepared as possible for any commotion.

"Good morning Mr Walsh." said the security guard, as he turned the corner and into view.

"Good morning Lloyd. We are about to deliver some very disturbing news to a patient here, and his actions as a result of this are unpredictable. If you could stand outside of the room, just in case, that would be great. If he does take a turn for the worse when we break the news to him, I'll call you in."

"No problem at all." replied Lloyd, sounding as if his vast experience of similar incidents meant that this was just another day in the office for him.

They walked toward Carter's room. Crispin Walsh tentatively opened the door, before the three of them walked in. Lloyd stepped in front of the door as it was closed, ready, and preventing anyone else from entering the room and disturbing them.

Carter lay silent on the bed, turned on his side and watching the TV. The three had been so silent when entering the room that he hadn't even noticed that they were there.

"Hey man!" said Will, breaking the silence.

Carter turned to see them all there, and sat up in bed, somewhat wary of why all three of them had all appeared at the same time. Carter immediately sensed that something was wrong.

"Hey. Good morning. What is this, a party?" said Carter, looking for a laugh, or a smile at least in response. There was nothing, just three glum looking faces looking back at him. He tried again. "Anybody told you that three's a crowd!" Still nothing. Will looked to Mr Walsh, expecting him to start speaking, but he didn't. He looked uncomfortable, as if struggling to find the right words to say, not wanting to be the one who had to break Carter's heart. Professor Lewis realised and quickly stepped forward to the front.

"Mr Jakeman, nice to meet you. I am Professor Annie Lewis, a neuropsychiatrist here at the hospital."

"A neuropsychiatrist huh? Christ! Am I that bad?" That was his last attempt at trying to be humorous. He knew inside that something was wrong and was now ready to be serious and hear what they had to say.

"Does this have something to do with Mary? Or my scan? Mr Walsh? Will? Does this have something to do with Mary? Is she OK?" said Carter starting to become distressed, before Will shouted out, bringing the truth bluntly to the ears of his best friend, the only way to say it.

"She doesn't exist, Carter!"

There was immediate silence. Will looked uncomfortable; shifting in position, saddened that it was him that had been the one to shatter Carter's dreams.

"What?" said Carter slowly sinking back onto his bed, deflated and desperately trying to process the words he had just heard. He looked up, scanning the three of their faces, hoping that it was some kind of prank, but knew of course it wasn't. "Is this some kind of fucking joke?"

"Carter . . . ." Said Mr Walsh, finally ready to disclose what he had uncovered and try and make Carter understand.

"No!" Carter shouted abruptly, causing Lloyd to become poised at the door, ready to pounce at any moment. Mr Walsh turned and indicated to Lloyd to stay outside. Carter noticed and realised what was going on.

"Oh shit. Who is that out there, Rambo? What did you expect me to do, go on a rampage? Hey you, wait outside. Do you understand me, don't come in here!" shouted Carter, before Will quickly seized an opportunity to come forward and try and calm Carter down to listen.

"Carter, wait a minute. Listen to me. I am your best friend, and I would not let anything happen to you unless it was for your own good. OK?"

"OK." said Carter, agreeing to hear him out.

"This girl you have been seeing, this Mary Lee, she does not exist. You have created her in your mind. I know it sounds ridiculous OK, but it is true."

"Yeah OK. Do you expect me to really believe in this bullshit? How do explain all the places we went to together, the phone calls, people would have seen her with me. She used to work with my brother for Christ sake! Talk to Claire, she knows Mary."

"I have Carter. I have spoken to Claire. She has no idea who Mary Lee is." said Crispin Walsh softly.

"But she was at the funeral reception. We were talking right in front of Claire!" insisted Carter.

"Claire told me that most of that afternoon you were sitting on the sofa . . . . alone!"

Carter shook his head in frustration, disagreeing with what he was being told.

"Let me get this straight. OK. So what you are really trying to tell me here is that my head is fucked? Am I right? Well sorry to disappoint you all, but I've known that my . . . . whole . . . . life!" screamed Carter, becoming flustered, emotional and unable to control his breathing.

"OK Carter you must try to calm down." suggested Professor Lewis.

"And I certainly don't need a shrink thank you very much, so you can leave!" said Carter, arms folded, looking away from them in disgust.

"I'm sorry Carter. I know how much she meant to you." offered Mr Walsh hoping to see if Carter was willing to start to listen to an explanation.

Annie Lewis stepped back and let Crispin and Will stay closest to him, relieving some of that tension of Carter feeling cornered. Carter looked back at them, not convinced and in no way prepared to accept defeat.

"OK how do I know that you three are real?" "Well?" asked Carter, condescendingly.

"Carter, this isn't going to help?" said Crispin Walsh.

"Answer me. If my mind is so creative, then how can I be sure? Maybe Mary is real and you three and made up. Huh? Yeah, let's run with that shall we?"

"Come on Carter, how long have we known each other?" said Will.

"Well I don't know anymore Will. All of a sudden I can't remember. Maybe that was stored in the part of my brain that he ripped out of my fucking head!" said Carter pointing his finger at Mr Walsh.

"Maybe Mary was that part, that is now gone?" said Will abruptly.

Carter went to continue ranting but stopped, reflecting momentarily on what Will had just said. Mr Walsh and Professor Lewis noticed a similar breakthrough, as if those words had touched upon something within Carter, something that made sense to him. However, Carter continued, but less forcefully.

"Come on Mr Walsh, how do I know that Will exists?"

"Carter, look, Will is your friend, and has been for years. He is the real deal!"

Carter couldn't help but notice the unintentional but equally comical use of words chosen by Mr Walsh, and how they rhymed.

"Real deal Will. That's funny! Real deal Will, what is this, a comedy show?"

"Carter, come on let's get back on track here. He is trying to help you." said Will interjecting.

"No. I wanna know. I mean what exactly is going on here, the fucking Truman Show?"

No-one answered but instead let Carter dwell and reflect for a few seconds more. Will spoke just as Carter was about to continue ranting, beating him to it.

"Carter, shouting is not going to bring her back. I'm sorry, but she is gone. It is a fact!" said Will, raising his voice, drowning out Carter's in a desperate attempt to finally get through to him.

Carter jumped, choosing not to challenge Will's outburst. Instead he became quite calm, as if about to express his feelings. Professor Lewis attempted to shed more light on things, providing some reasons as to why his mind had created Mary. She explained that Mary had been created by Carter as a kind of defensive reaction, possibly starting with the trauma of his brother's death, alcohol effects, a need for a companion and love, and a fear of abandonment. She mainly attributed events to the wound sustained to his head back in London.

"Do you know how ludicrous this sounds? I hope you all understand and appreciate why I am finding it hard to come to terms with." Carter said, before turning to Will and speaking to him directly.

"All my life . . . . I have accepted that I am weaker than most, and also, that I would probably end up alone because of it. OK? I accept that, I got it! Big deal! Then I meet someone; right out of the blue, on the same day of my dear brother's funeral, and everything in my life changes, so dramatically, so uniquely. I meet the girl of my dreams, and unbelievably she likes me too."

Tears became visible, running down Carter's cheek. He wiped one away before continuing. The other three stood captivated, listening intently "That is it. Have I really created the girl of dreams in reality? My deepest thoughts must have known how incapable I was in being able to find someone and be happy, that it created an illusion for me. My God . . . . I finally found a girl, love, and the possibility of a life worth living and before I know it, it is gone!"

Inconsolable, Carter broke down. Will rushed forward to embrace and comfort his friend. Will held him as he cried uncontrollably. Will signalled to Mr Walsh and Professor Lewis to leave.

"It's going to be OK mate, trust me. Everything is going to be OK!" said Will, doing all that he could to sound positive.

"Why is this happening to me Will?"

"You have suffered a hell of a lot recently, and things have just taken their toll on you. But you are going to have to deal with this situation Carter. There is no other way!"

Carter leant back and looked at Will, nodding, agreeing that Will was right.

"I want to be alone!" "I want to be alone!" said Carter.

"You gonna be OK?" asked Will.

"No! Well not yet anyway. I just want to sleep."

"OK, but remember these people are here to help you Carter. Listen to them. I'll come back for the pm visiting hours to see you OK?"

"OK." said Carter, already lying down on his side and closing his eyes.

Will stepped out of the room, closing the door gently behind him. He noticed that Professor Lewis and Lloyd had already gone, leaving just Crispin Walsh standing there. As soon as Will looked at the surgeon's face he knew something was wrong.

"Mr Walsh, what is it? Everything OK? I thought it didn't go too bad in there. He is resting at the moment." said Will, confused at the reaction.

"Mr Harrison. I'm afraid we may have some bad news." said Mr Walsh putting a hand on Will's shoulder to comfort him.

"More bad news?" said Will.

"I have just had a call from the radiographer who has now had a chance to review Carter's latest MRI scan. I still need to see it myself, but there is a fear that there might be a slight bleed on the brain. This has yet to be confirmed, but this could be a massive concern. I will let you know for sure once I have reviewed the scan myself."

"Is Carter going to die?" asked Will.

"Mr Harrison, bleeds can be very serious. Let's not jump to any conclusions until I have had a chance to review the scan myself."

Will looked down at the floor, finding it hard to believe, not wanting to believe it. Mr Walsh said goodbye and that he would catch up with him in the afternoon to confirm either way. Will stood there for a moment in shock. He slowly walked over to the window, looking into Carter's room, watching him as he lay there, peaceful and still. After a few seconds he turned and walked away, not looking back.

* * * *

"It is this area here that caught my eye Mr Walsh." said the radiographer pointing to the area in question on the scan.

"OK let me have a closer look at this." said Mr Walsh leaning in to see in more detail.

He and the radiographer examined the image further, before finally coming to agreement on the result of the scan.

Will walked out of the main entrance and through the hospital car park, no destination in mind, just away from that place. He was in shock. He had never had to endure anything on that scale before, anything so horrendously real. He stood looking out across an empty green field. There were two crows fighting over a piece of food about twenty metres out and on his left. This gave Will something to concentrate on as he tried to process his thoughts, especially the most recent piece of bad news whereby now Carter's life hung in the balance. Will realised just how much Carter meant to him, and in fact how, in many ways, he looked up to Carter. His sense of humour and his intelligence were two that immediately sprang to mind. Will leant forward onto a wooden fence separating the field from the car park, and interlocked his fingers as if preparing to pray.

* * * *

Carter could feel the plastic from the bag containing the loaf of bread clasped in his hand, swinging in motion and rhythm with his body as he walked briskly toward the park to meet Mary. In the other were a beautiful bunch of rich red roses, illuminated with beauty as the rays from the sun caught their tips. He had no headache whatsoever, and his thoughts had never been so clear. He couldn't remember the last time he had felt so invincible, maybe childhood. His feelings were very balanced and grounded. All of his insecurities had gone, he felt confident in himself and in all he witnessed around him.

There was a hunger within him, an assurance that no matter what he did he could do no wrong. He felt as if anything was possible, he could be anything he wanted, get whatever he wanted, and go wherever he wanted. As he approached the duck pond, the love of his life stood there waiting, surrounded by overexcited ducks that had seen him approach, treat in hand. They sat down on the bench together, feeding the ducks and talking about their day. It felt like heaven. Then everything changed. His headache returned, and he was sweating and overcome with nerves. All of his insecurities had resurfaced, charging down the doorways of his emotional blockade. He could hear nothing but the sound of his heart pounding, each beat becoming louder and dull in tone, and slow in sound. He was back at the point of disclosing his love for Mary and awaiting her response. This was the moment where he had blacked out before. He waited for the answer. Mary had that concerned look on her face, as Carter desperately tried to avoid missing her response for a second time. She looked at him, as if looking deep into his soul, into his most private and almost impenetrable inhibitions. With her next words she unlocked everything inside of him, all which had been so unhealthy, entwined and rotting away for so long, releasing belief. These were not to be the three words that he yearned for, but instead she parted her lips and whispered.

"I don't exist!"

Carter awoke from his dream, calmly, with no concern or confusion where he was. He felt fresh from his sleep. He thought that a break in alcohol whilst being in hospital was allowing him to regain some sense of normality, and memory for that matter. He smiled, reflecting on his dream. He was surprised at his reaction, as he thought that the loss of Mary in any way would be catastrophic for him to conceive. But he felt composed. He felt honoured to have known her at all, even if it was just his imagination. He was fascinated by how his mind had created her in the first place, and noted how different he felt after waking up, following the three words she had whispered to him in his dream. He remembered something else. He reached for his mobile phone, quickly activating his photo album, and scanning through looking for the one where Mary and he had their photo taken with the owl. There it was. Mary was not there after all. The photo was of Carter standing there, alone, with the owl happily perched on his arm. That was the clincher for him. He pulled himself up into an upright position, placing his phone back down onto the table. He noticed the ring on his little finger. The ring that represented protection and support, his brother's ring. Carter smiled again. He was distracted by a tap on the door. In walked Crispin Walsh.

"Hi Carter. How are you feeling?" said Mr Walsh optimistic of improvement.

"OK, I think. Well as far as I know. I feel much fresher than before that is for sure."

"Well that is good. And how do you feel about the other thing we discussed earlier? Mary?"

"Well I am getting used to the idea. I know that . . . . well that . . . . she does not . . . . well you know?"

"I know." said Mr Walsh sharing a supportive smile.

"Carter. We are going to have to carry out another MRI scan on you."

"What was wrong with the other one?"

"It has come back inconclusive. We need to do another just to be sure . . . ."

"Sure of what?" said Carter, concerned.

"Just to be sure that everything is healing nicely."

"With all due respect Mr Walsh I think I have been through enough. Please be honest with me, as you have done so far. Please, I need to know. Is there anything else I should be aware of?"

Crispin Walsh hung his head slightly, knowing that Carter was right and deserved to know. He had a right. He felt sorry for him, and the least he could do was to be up front and honest. He looked at Carter and began.

"Carter, we think there might be a bleed on your brain. It was hard to determine from the latest scan, so we need to do another one before we go any further. I am sorry."

Carter did not respond. There were no words that would come close to describing how he felt at that moment. His mind was a whitewash of disbelief, a canvas of fear with splattering marks of uncertainty and panic. Mr Walsh gave him a moment, before Carter, without making eye contact and still looking as though in a trance like state, said "I may not live through this right?"

"Carter, you are in the best possible hands here. And none of us can determine anything. But we do need to do that scan!"

"OK. Thanks for your honesty. I appreciate it. And sorry for before, but . . . . well . . . . I'm sure you understand?"

"Carter you do not need to apologise. Look, we'll try and get your scan done before afternoon visiting hours begin, so you can be here when Mr Harrison arrives."

"OK then. Thanks . . . . for everything."

Crispin Walsh smiled and left the room. Once the door was closed and he was out of Carter's view, he brought his hand up to his face, covering his eyes, as if shielding from the events unfolding.

Carter sat alone, distancing himself from getting too drawn into any possibilities other than that of the scan proving to be fine. He watched the second hand of the clock above the door ticking, and ticking. Time was the utmost enemy of all. He watched, comparing the second hand to that of a lifetime, and that when the batteries ran out, that was your body stopping, shutting down, and dying. He wondered how much longer he had left. Was his own body clock nearly out of power? When would the second hand play its final stroke on the life of Carter Jakeman?

It was only forty-five minutes later when they came to collect Carter, wheeling him down to the MRI department to carry out his scan. All the way through he held Marcus's ring tightly in his right hand. After the scan they wheeled him outside for some fresh air. It was the first time he had been outside since first being admitted. Everything looked so much more colourful. The birds seemed to be tweeting louder and more people seemed to be smiling. Maybe he was more susceptible to his surroundings now he was aware that his life may be in danger he thought. The porter who had wheeled him outside asked if Carter minded if he had a quick smoke before going back in. Carter didn't mind, and was only too happy to get some more minutes outside in the sun. He looked at the tree tops and the skyline beyond.

"So where are you from in England?" asked the porter.

"London. North London." said Carter looking up just as a stream of cigarette smoke passed his way.

"Sorry, I'll stand on the other side of you." said the porter trying to wave the smoke away from Carter's direction.

"It's OK don't worry." said Carter, this now being the last thing on his mind.

"So North London?" said the porter in an attempt to relight the conversation.

"That's right. You ever been to London?" asked Carter, doing his best to sound interested.

"No, never been. Furthest I've been south is Newcastle."

"Oh right." said Carter, not really sure what to say next.

"You ever been to Newcastle?" said the porter.

"Only passing through on occasion." Carter replied, now paying more attention to the cigarette, trying to calculate how many more seconds it had left before the porter would finish it. He worked out that each pull so far was taking between two to three millimetres off of it, and the remaining length of the cigarette at that point was about two centimetres. He was taking a drag every ten seconds or so, so that would mean that the remaining two centimetres, or twenty millimetres, taking off three millimetres on an average of every ten seconds give or take, meant that it would take about another one minute and ten seconds before he would finish and they could go back inside.

"Sir? Sir, did you hear me?" asked the porter, looking slightly concerned.

"Sorry, mind is wandering. What?" said Carter, noting him take his expected drag removing three millimetres and staying on course.

"I asked if you liked it in London?"

"Well, no not really. It is OK. It has its ups and downs, as does any city really."

"How long have you lived there for?" the porter asked.

"Too long!" said Carter noticing the cigarette was being ready to be flicked from the porter's hand. To Carter's surprise, the porter reached into his pocket and took out another cigarette, planning to smoke a second.

"Do you mind if I have another? You get some more fresh air that way?"

"Well, actually . . . . no. I think I'd like to go back in now."

"You sure?"

"Yes!" said Carter.

The porter returned the cigarette to the almost empty pack from which it came, before walking around to the back of Carters wheelchair, and pushing him back inside. Carter sensed that the porter had realised that he didn't want to engage in conversation, so didn't say another word. It was more that Carter had enough going on his own mind as it was, and in no way was he in any mood for conversation with a complete stranger. He found that hard to muster most of the time as it was, so definitely wasn't prepared to do it when he had his own mortality playing heavily on his mind. Carter got back into bed and was given a nice hot steaming cup of tea. The supper that he had preselected from the options earlier would be delivered soon. He had chosen sausages with mash potato and green beans. It wasn't too long before the afternoon visiting hours were due to start either and he was eager to see Will.

* * * *

"Crispin, it's Annie." heard Mr Walsh as he answered his phone.

"Hey Annie. You OK?"

"Yes I just wondered how Mr Jakeman was doing since receiving the news this morning."

"Surprisingly well considering. Well that's how it seems. I saw him earlier and he looks to be coming to terms with it. However there is something else!"

"What?"

"I reviewed his second MRI and it looks like there may be a bleed on the brain."

"Oh no! You say may have a bleed?"

"Yes, but I have arranged for him to have another just to be sure either way. I have informed him of the possibility."

"My word, he has had one hell of a day today!"

"I think most of his life has been a living hell to some extent! Look I think it is a good idea for him to sit down with someone, hopefully you, to go over the things that have occurred and why have they occurred. If you could explain to him how it was possible for his mind to have created this person then that would be, I think, beneficial."

"Well the best I could do would be able to give some insight into the possible reasons of how this has happened."

"That is what I would like. How busy are you?"

"Well I have got two hours tomorrow that I was going to take as leave, but would be more than happy to commit some of that time to Mr Jakeman."

"Yes, that would be great. If you don't mind that is?"

"No it would be my pleasure, such an interesting case."

"An interesting man as well."

"OK, I could see him at 12pm, my room."

"Clinic Room B is that . . . ?"

"Yes that's right. See that shows just how much you come to see me. Oh, would you have given him the MRI results by then do you think?"

"Yes hope so. I am actually waiting for the radiographer to call me."

"Please let me know as soon as you find out?"

"Will do, Annie. I'll also talk to him about meeting you tomorrow. And thanks."

"OK Crispin, speak later."

At the same time as Mr Walsh hung up the phone, it rang again.

"Good afternoon, Crispin Walsh speaking."

"Good afternoon Mr Walsh, I'm calling from MRI. Patient Carter Jakeman's recent scan is ready for review. Do you want to come down?"

"Thanks for getting back to me so quickly, on my way!" said Mr Walsh, standing and already pulling his jacket from the back of his chair before hanging up the phone.

* * * *

Will walked into the room just as Carter was finishing off his supper. One look at Will and Carter could tell that he knew something; something was on his mind and troubling him. Will placed a bag of grapes down onto the side table. He pulled up a chair and sat down, looking pale faced and fretful. Carter noticing something was wrong did not want to let on that he could tell, so pretended that he hadn't noticed.

"Well . . . . Hi!" said Carter indicating that Will had come in and sat down without saying a thing.

"Sorry mate. How are you doing?" said Will, looking about as confident as a cat in a room full of rocking chairs.

"I'm OK. Food is really growing on me." said Carter trying to force a smile from Will.

"Has Mr Walsh been by to see you?"

"Yes he has Will. Look I may as well tell you now. But I must admit you look like you already know something!"

"No, sorry. Go ahead Carter. What did he say?"

"He said that I needed to have another brain scan. That they had seen something on the original that looked like a bleed of some kind, but weren't a hundred per cent sure." said Carter while trying to play it cool, putting the last fork full of mash into his mouth.

"Well when do you find out?" said Will impatiently.

"Don't care!" said Carter dismissively, annoying Will.

"Yeah well you should!"

"Yeah well it's not you who could be lying on his fucking death bed here is it?" shouted Carter, in such a rage, that it was clear that all of that built up fear came out at once.

"I'm sorry Carter. I didn't mean to lose my temper. I'm just worried." said Will, trying to calm him down.

Carter dropped his knife and fork on his plate, before saying "You can add indigestion to the list as well now!"

Will sat back in his chair, not knowing what to say, as an awkward silence filled the room. Two minutes passed before Carter chose to end the uneasiness.

"Look Will. I know you care. And Christ am I glad you are here! I just don't know what . . . . I'm frightened Will. This is so hard for me to try to deal with, on top of everything else that has happened. At some points today I thought I may just die. I feel so fucking alone, and hurt, and lost. I just don't know how much more I can take! Will, I'm not sure things are going to be OK." said Carter, wiping fresh tears from his eyes.

"Neither do I, but we can only hope Carter. That's all we've got, all any of us have got. A belief that everything is going to be OK."

"I know." said Carter, taking Will's statement on board. He knew that hope would be a soul companion through the darker moments in a person's life. However Carter believed more in luck. It was a game of chance. Some live, some die, it's that simple. As Carter strongly believed that there was an afterlife, he felt some comfort in that he may be seeing his lost loved ones sooner than he thought. Up until he met Mary the thought of death did not really bother him that much, however he had since acquired a certain willingness and desire to try, to improve, to live.

The door to Carter's room opened, seconds before visiting hours were due to end. It was Crispin Walsh. Carter and Will looked at him, waiting for any sign or expression that would give away the result.

"Hi. Will, would you mind giving us a moment please?" asked Mr Walsh.

"It's OK. I'd like him to stay here." said Carter.

"OK you have told him?" confirmed Mr Walsh.

"Yes. I'm ready, go on."

"Carter I have just reviewed your recent MRI scan."

"It is clear." said Mr Walsh.

Carter in no way expected to hear those words. Deep inside he thought it was the end. His whole life so far seemed to be on a road to no luck. Suddenly something had changed, derailed, for the better.

"What?" said Will, taking a few more seconds to process those three words.

"It is clear. I'm sure. The initial scare turned out to be nothing. It is clear Mr Jakeman," said Crispin Walsh, with a big smile beaming across his face.

"Yes!" shouted Will, as if celebrating a goal in a cup final. The nurse walked into the room after hearing the yell, only to find an overjoyed Will, who turned, and kissed her with joy.

"Stop shouting!" she said but with less conviction, as she momentarily reflected on the fact she had just been kissed by a very handsome gentleman.

"It's OK. Mr Jakeman has just received some very good news. This is his friend, who is obviously relieved!" said Mr Walsh, as Will calmed down but still unable to remain still.

"Mr Walsh, I can't believe it. I thought that . . . . I just can't believe it. Let's just hope this is real and not something my mind is making me believe." said Carter, but tongue in cheek, causing the surgeon to see the funny side and share in the joke.

"Carter, I cannot begin to explain just how personally relieved and happy I am for you. You have obviously had a very rough time of things. I hope things will start to get better for you now."

"Thanks." said Carter, still reeling from the news.

"OK. Tomorrow I have arranged for you to go and see Professor Lewis."

"Oh, the lady who was here before?"

"Yes. She is great at her job and a very dear friend of mine. I would appreciate it if you would spend some time talking to her. She may be able to offer you insight into certain things. Will you do that for me Carter?"

"Absolutely. I think I do need to speak to someone, mainly about Mary. I still find it hard to completely come to terms with how she . . . . came to be!"

"That's great news. Well I've got to go. I'll see you tomorrow. And congratulations once again!"

Carter smiled but before he could say thanks and goodbye himself, an overexcited Will spoke instead, "Yes thanks Mr Walsh, you are my hero. I swear anything you need, its there. Girls . . . ."

"OK Will, that's great." interrupted Carter, stopping Will in his tracks. Crispin Walsh took one last look back at Carter, giving a raise of his hand as a goodbye, and Carter did the same.

Will turned back to Carter, briefly looking up as if to the heavens.

"Oh my God! Thank you, man I am so, so, so happy for you."

Carter's face turned from utter surprise to a fragile wreck of emotion.

"Oh man. Carter, are you alright?" said Will stepping closer to Carter.

The realisation of just how different things could have been just hit Carter like a freight train.

"Holy shit!" he said as his brave facade wilted away, his face now carrying an expression more like that of a terrified child.

* * * *

That following morning felt completely different to that of any other he could remember. His body felt as light as a feather, the clarity of his thoughts second to none, and his emotions were, unnaturally to him, balanced. As he arrived for his morning appointment with Professor Lewis he was greeted first by her secretary, who proceeded in showing him straight through, with not a single moment's delay. Carter first noted how professional looking it was in that particular office, and that everything seemed so efficient. He assumed that Professor Lewis had somehow managed to fit him into an already busy and hectic schedule. He felt somewhat rejuvenated, feeling that his care was being treated very seriously and appropriately. The secretary gave a tap-tap on a door, waited for a voice before opening it. The name on the door read, Professor Annie Lewis—Professor in Neuropsychiatry—Clinic Room B.

"Yes? Come in!" said a voice from inside, prompting the secretary to push the door open and enter.

"Mr Jakeman, Professor Lewis." said the secretary before disappearing back outside and closing the door gently behind her.

"Mr Jakeman, nice to see you again." said Annie Lewis, walking around her desk toward him and shaking his hand.

"Nice to see you again. And please just call me Carter."

"OK, Carter. I had a call from Mr Walsh informing of the good news in regard to your scan?"

"Yes, very good news." said Carter with an expression of relief on his face, ensuring she gathered just how grateful he was.

"Please take a seat."

"Professor Lewis, before we continue, can I just say sorry for the way I acted the last time we met, I . . . . well I just lost it!"

"Mr Jakeman, sorry Carter, if it was me who had found out what you had I'm sure I would have reacted in the same way. I too am sorry, sorry that you have suffered so."

"Thank you." said Carter immediately reassured that there were no hard feelings, ensuring the mood within the room was now completely relaxed.

Carter took a quick look around the clinic room, and was firstly aware of her many accolades. He could also make out her graduation photograph behind her on the windowsill. Her awards and certificates varied from all sorts of places and institutions, one of which was an honorary membership from The British Neuropsychiatry Association. The room itself was very bright but not overbearing, simple and everything very neatly placed.

"Carter, the reason for this meeting is mainly to give us both the opportunity to discuss and hopefully provide you with some clarity in regard to your recent experiences. I have worked many years in the field and have witnessed many things. The brain can act very sporadically if it wants to, even creating hallucinations such as yours. I'm sure that you can appreciate that us discussing these issues or anxieties that you may have, will do nothing but benefit you when you return to your life outside."

"OK, I understand that sure. To be completely honest I need to talk to someone, someone like you. I don't quite have it all figured out in my head just yet." he said preparing himself for her take on events.

"OK, good, then let's begin. The place I would like to start with is this lady Mary Lee."

"Yes of course." said Carter expectedly.

"The first question I want to ask, that I have to ask, is are you now convinced and accept that Mary Lee was a figment of your imagination, and does not actually exist as a human being?"

"Yes I do."

"OK here is how I would like this session to go, if it is OK with you. I will start talking, based on what I know about you so far, what I have read about your medical history, and also your recent experiences. I'm not going to force you to speak, but if at any time you would like to expand on something I say, or question something I say, please do. Are you happy with this?"

"I am, go ahead." said Carter happy to listen, hoping to learn something or at least get some aid into his convoluted troubles.

"Mary was a reaction, a defence mechanism created by your mind, assisted by the tumour. She was an imaginary friend that you conjured up to deal with a very traumatic time in your life, a time of need, to combat an emotional rollercoaster that was speeding out of control. Having her around, flattering you, a distraction gave you the opportunity to feel love for someone and also use as kind of a self healer. Maybe at the point when your feelings were at their most vulnerable, when you poured your heart out to her and told her you loved her may have been the trigger to shut down, effectively resulting in your blackout."

"Because deep inside my mind it knew that there was no possibility for this to go any further?" offered Carter.

"Could have been, yes. See so far, your mind had protected Mary from the world around you. When you were out with her, at dinner, in the countryside, you weren't actually speaking aloud to an empty space, but were instead playing out conversations and scenes in your mind. When you were at your brother's funeral reception for example, the first time you encountered Mary, Mr Walsh was told by your sister-in-law that you spent most of the afternoon just sitting alone, talking to no-one. The same would have been at a restaurant, out loud you would have ordered a meal for yourself, but in you're mind you ordered two, one for Mary and one for you. And as time went on and you fell deeper and deeper in love with her, your emotions were so heightened, almost at boiling point. The tumour, along with all of these added stresses in your life, not even taking into account your history with suffering with depression and your alcohol intake . . . . forgive me for saying?"

"No that's fine, and true. Will must have said right?"

"Yes, Mr Harrison had informed Mr Walsh, for your own benefit."

"OK." said Carter, understandingly. Professor Lewis continued.

"Well, it was just too much happening all at once, and your body and mind must have gone into overdrive and shut down. It seems to me that somehow you created a self therapy as a last resort!"

"What now? Is the fact that now my tumour has been successfully removed, then these visions of Mary have been removed with it?"

"Most likely so yes. Well you haven't seen her since. And now that that pressure has been released your body, and mind, should be in a state of recovery, not decline."

"OK. I can't believe it, well I can, more now, well I guess it just shows just how complicated the human body is, and it's capabilities. Amazing really."

"I agree. It is. I must say Carter I am very impressed with how quickly you have come to terms with this."

"I have no other choice."

"That's right, you don't," confirmed Professor Lewis. "Also Carter one other thing I would like to say, and this information was also offered by your friend, who obviously is someone who cares a hell of a lot for you, that this medication that you are on . . . ."

"Cipralex!" said Carter, noticing Professor Lewis referring to her notes to find the right name.

"Yes Cipralex. You take this with alcohol?"

"Well yeah, it only then has an impact. If I just take it on it's own it does nothing for me!"

"You should not be taking your medication with alcohol! What I would advise is stop one or the other!"

"I understand." said Carter sincerely.

"OK, Carter I would like to ask how you feel in yourself about what has happened in your life. Are you happy to discuss this with me?"

"What, other than Mary? Like what, the tumour? My brother?"

"Well all seem to be interrelated so anything you feel like talking to me about. For example do you think that any of these experiences have changed you for the better, had an impact on you that you would grow stronger from? I have seen many cases in the past where people who have had major trauma in their life, have come out the other side with a different perspective. Try to be as positive as possible. You've had to endure a lot in recent days, but you have come out of it stronger. I also respect that you suffer from bipolar disorder, and that will make things extra hard to cope with. It's kind of like the long and the short of it in a way."

"Yeah, and I got the short of it! Look, if we discount me being bipolar, as I know that I will have to deal with this irrespectively, then yes in some ways I think I will be more positive when back out in reality, more confident maybe?"

"Well what I would say to you Carter is these experiences may be a blessing in disguise. Your time spent with Mary, for example, has opened up your boundaries and seen your confidence grow. Inside your mind, unknown to you, your brain knew that by enabling this to happen it made it easier for you to follow your dreams, whether that be a relationship, marriage, career-related, or just generally."

Carter looked up at Annie Lewis and smiled, and realised that she had a point, even though it did sound completely radical to him. He nodded as if in agreement before speaking.

"I see. These events have proved something. Since meeting Mary I felt more and more confident with each day that passed, and could talk with confidence. I have felt happiness and love, feelings that I had forgotten long ago. It has given me a taste of possibility, that there is still a glimmer of light at the end of a long dark tunnel,"

As Carter continued speaking those words he started to become more confident, and Professor Lewis noticed his manner change. As he spoke, it was like he was unearthing new discoveries, finding the real Carter within him, the Carter that had been dormant for so long. This was a start thought Annie Lewis. A positive attitude oozed from Carter, a side of him that she did not expect to witness so soon. He continued.

"I feel like I have been handed another chance to make a go of things, and in a strange way a kind of parting gift from my brother. I know I may not achieve everything I want from life, but I am sure as hell going to try. I'm not going to let him down again." Carter concluded.

"Carter I am so pleased that this is your attitude. I wish you all the very best and hope that if you don't live all of your dreams, you certainly find happiness."

"Thank you Professor."

"Well I will have no issue in discharging you. As long as Mr Walsh has not got anything further to add or discuss with you, then it shouldn't be that long and you will be OK to go."

"I hope so. No offence, but I'll be glad to get out of here."

Carter stood to his feet, as Professor Lewis walked around the table before escorting him to the door to say goodbye. He shook her hand and thanked her from the bottom of his heart for everything that she had done for him, and wished her every success for her future. She too wished him well, and that there was nothing but good things lying in wait for him for his future. Before she closed the door she gave him a few last words of advice, words that became embedded in Carter's memory from that day forth.

"You have been given a second chance. Not everyone has that luxury. Make the most of it"

As Carter walked away from her office he reflected on their session and the information shared. He finally understood and accepted what had happened, or as much as he would ever be able to understand anyway. Those final words from Professor Lewis were rattling around in his mind, and were considerably significant for him. He felt stronger, more assertive and assured of himself. He walked down the long corridor leading back to his ward, a smile growing wider on his face with every step that he took, before he was almost laughing. There was a spring in his step, an eagerness to make up for lost time when outside, as if chasing something that he had let go, something that now he had to rescue, and save himself.

* * * *

Crispin Walsh sat down at his computer, and saw that amongst his long list of emails in his inbox there was one from Annie Lewis. It read.

> "Dear Crispin
>
> Thought I would drop you a quick email as I am sure you are anxious to know the outcome from Mr Carter Jakeman's appointment with me this morning. I have to say, it has given me great joy in being able to be involved with this patient's care and recovery. I thank you for including me on this and I feel a great sense of accomplishment and pride following the appointment. I saw

> a sparkle in his eyes Crispin, like that of a child, a man reborn, well I hope! He grew stronger and stronger in the appointment and by the end I was more than convinced, and more than happy that these experiences have in fact had a positive effect, and that his life going forward will improve, given he retains the same standard of enthusiasm that I witnessed first hand this morning. I will provide a proper discharge outcome letter from my care for your perusal in due course, but thought I would bring you up to speed now to save your concern.
>
> Ax
>
> P.S I have to say I shed a tear for him after he left. And I am not usually the type to cry or show emotion, so don't you tell anyone!!!!"

The surgeon slouched back in his chair, letting his muscles relax for a moment. He smiled, before standing up and walking to the window. It was particularly significant and heart warming for him, especially, that Carter had seemed to deal with and recover so well from his ordeal. Mr Walsh took a brief moment to think about his wife, how proud she would have been of him in saving Carter. He returned to his desk and carried on trawling through the rest of his emails.

* * * *

The graveyard seemed extraordinarily peaceful that day, the hovering morning mist rose, adding an overwhelming sense of calm and serenity to the appearance. Carter and Will walked along the path, slowly, heading towards Marcus' grave. Carter was explaining to Will about how Mary came to be, and what had been discussed with Professor Lewis at the hospital, as Will wanted to know everything. Carter explained how Mary had become like an addiction in many respects, a medication of sorts that his inner self had created to delude him from dealing with the reality of his fragile emotions. Before Will could ask anything else they stopped, as they had reached Marcus' gravesite. Fresh flowers had been laid, and the haziness of the sun caressed their colour, making them look even more picturesque and impressive. Will offered to leave Carter alone for a moment, to which Carter replied.

"I am done talking. I believe my brother deserves actions from me now. I will come back here, when I have something to say, something that would make him proud."

"OK." said Will, smiling and happy to hear that from him.

As they walked on, Carter caught a passing glimpse of a name he recognised on a gravestone, not far from the exit gate of the cemetery. He stopped in his tracks to get a more steady view. He couldn't believe his eyes. It was the grave of Jocky 'old man' Ragg.

"You OK?" asked Will, not entirely sure of what Carter was looking at.

Carter smiled, noting the coincidence, but also that it seemed as if it was meant to be. It was as if it was a chance to say one last goodbye to the man himself, a man whom Carter had come to admire since knowing him, a man who had in some ways inadvertently played his own role in Carter's story.

"Can you give me a minute Will?" said Carter, eyes still firmly fixed on the gravestone.

"Sure. I'll be . . . . here!" said Will choosing to slowly wander over to the wall and sit down.

Carter was already walking over to Jocky's grave. As Carter stood over, casting a shadow over the stone, it allowed him to read the rest of the engraving more clearly, the main sentence particularly standing out and prominent to him. The engraving, describing Jocky, read simply as, "A cherished man who was the heartbeat of the city. May you once again rejoice with those you held most dear."

A lonesome tear fell from Carter's cheek as he felt moved by that sentence, and was so pleased that someone had made the effort to have it written. If anyone deserved such attention and respect it was Old Man Ragg. Carter thanked him one last time, finishing by saying,

"Hopefully one day our paths will cross again."

Carter turned and walked back over to Will.

"You OK buddy?" asked Will.

"Yes fine."

"Who was that?" said Will pointing back to Jocky's grave.

"A great man. I'll tell you all about him on the train home!"

As they reached the main gate and about to leave the cemetery, they stopped and took one last look back over the graveyard.

"Are you gonna be alright?" asked Will.

"Yes, as long as I don't find anymore imaginary friends!" replied Carter, laughing, seeing the funny side of things. Will briefly joined in with the laughter.

"Man she was gorgeous though!" said Carter, causing Will to laugh some more, but at the same time also making the point that he was dealing with it. Will placed his hand on Carter's shoulder, before saying,

"There are plenty more Mary's out there, trust me. You already sound better to me, and you said that you feel better. I think you are going to be all right!"

Carter glanced past Will, as if looking ahead at his future, and the new life that lay in wait for him. Before walking away, he simply said,

"Sometimes I guess it takes that one special person to come along and teach you how to feel."

Always being creative in both music and the arts, **Matt Brown**, from London, chose to finally turn his full focus to writing novels. Years of unfinished scripts and random thoughts and ideas going to waste are now behind him. He has found what gives him the most satisfaction, to write.

Follow me on Twitter - @MLegend3